The Gangs of Royalty

AARON S. HAGER

DEDICATION

In loving memory of Irene J. Golinski, child of God and friend to the world.

CONTENTS

ACKNOWLEDGMENTS

There are far too many people for me to thank for helping me get this novel published. That, in and of itself, would take an entire book, still I would like to name a few. First, I would like to thank God, who has given me a passion for telling stories, followed by Christine, my wife, who encouraged me to finish writing this book, and my mother, Debbie, who raised me well and did the best a single mother could to raise a once-rowdy young man. Thanks to my aunt Mary, who initially encouraged me to write this novel, and to Sally, my grandmother, for passing on some of her writing genes to me. Thank you Mike for asking "How's that book coming along?" every time you saw me, which motivated me to hunker down and get this thing finished. Finally, thank you to all of my close friends and family who supported me along the way. Thank you Adam, Alec, Mark, Justin, Nicole, Mr. Forgione, Mr. McShane, all of the Golden Embers, and everyone else for showing any amount of support, however small, which has ultimately led to the production of this novel.

The Gangs of Royalty series is a work of fiction. Names, characters, places, and incidents are the product of the author's imagination. Any similarity to actual events, locations, or persons, living or dead, is entirely coincidental.

PROLOGUE

"C'mon, Ash! What's takin' so long?" shouted Judge, sergeant-at-arms of the Cut-Throats motorcycle gang. He was short in stature but as mean as a pit bull and as intimidating as a grizzly bear. He wore ripped jeans and a leather jacket that displayed the Cut-Throats insignia—a Longhorn skull with two bloody daggers under the neck. Covering his eyes was a pair of round-lensed sunglasses that looked like welder's goggles, and his face was framed with long dirty blond hair and a giant, well-groomed beard.

Ash buckled his backpack across his chest, tucked his shiny chrome pistol into his back waistband, and stumbled out of the front doorway of the Wild West. "Take it easy! I told ya I'd be a minute!" he shouted back at Judge as he joined the rest of his gang, who had already mounted their motorcycles, every engine purring but his own. Ash was in his early twenties, but had been around the Cut-Throats more than half of his life. Like a lot of the members of the various gangs in Royalty, he was a runaway orphan. As an infant, he was left with the Royal Priests of

St. Titus Orphanage, but only stayed until the age of 11. A few years prior to that, he was enamored by the idea of becoming a Cut-Throat after he saw a group of them blazing down Rooke Avenue, right past the orphanage. It was the longing for freedom that made Ash want to join their ranks at such a early age. He wanted to feel the wind on his face as he rode down every street in the city, without a single care in the world. Just him, his motorcycle and the road in front of him. This was his idea of "making it" in Royalty. After leaving the orphanage, the boy showed up at the entrance of the Wild West bar and after little convincing, was taken in by the gang's president, Brutus, who raised Ash like a son and when he turned 16, began his prospective period and two years later was fully patched into the gang.

Judge scowled at Ash, then scoffed.

"Aw'right, fellas! We got work to do. Let's get a move on!" Brutus, president of the Cut-Throats, announced. Brutus was a mountain of a man with giant burly arms and a barrel chest. He had long blond hair that he kept tied in a ponytail and a long, thick handlebar mustache.

Ash mounted his bike and flipped the kickstand up before starting the engine and revving it up a little. Brutus signaled with a single hand gesture, and his gang followed behind him down the main road. "So, what's the plan anyway?" Ash shouted to Terrace over the roar of the engines.

"Some sort of weapons shipment! Should make for a good haul to the Jackets!" Terrace shouted back as they rode off into the pale moonlight.

The tall pine trees that bordered the highway between Royalty and Freetown swayed in the autumn breeze. This had been Ash's favorite season for as long as he could remember. The light chill in the air. The smell of burning wood from people's fireplaces. The warm sensation of a swig of alcohol. It was calming. Blissful.

The convoy approached a large box truck with the name *Vallario* printed on either side. Brutus gave a pleased look to Riggs, his vice president, who smirked with satisfaction as they sped up, came to the front of the truck, and began breaking to slow the large vehicle down. At first, the driver leaned on his horn in frustration and considered just plowing into the crazy bikers he knew were attempting to hijack his truck. But a tap on his window from the barrel of Judge's shotgun made him reconsider. The driver pulled over, but this didn't stop him from reaching for his cell phone.

"Out!" Judge motioned with his shotgun once the driver had brought the vehicle to a complete stop and turned off the engine.

The driver slowly opened the door and stepped out.

Judge grabbed the driver by his shirt collar and threw him to the ground. "Stay put, unless I say otherwise!" he barked as he rested the barrel against the back of the man's head.

Brutus approached the driver and knelt down in front of him. "Whatcha got here, partner?" he said, grinning.

The driver tightened his lips and looked down.

In frustration, Judge poked the back of the man's head with the barrel of the gun. "He asked you a question!"

"Woah, easy there, brother!" Brutus chuckled and held out his hand to abate Judge's aggression. "That's fine if you don't wanna talk. We're taking your shipment anyway.

Ash! Go and check the cab!"

"On it!" Ash replied as he parked and removed the chrome pistol from his waistband and peered into the cab, making sure it was clear before he climbed up into the driver's side. It smelled of greasy fast food and cigarettes. He pulled the keys from the ignition and began rummaging through a stack of paperwork on the passenger's seat. "Hmm?" Ash raised an eyebrow as he spotted a delivery schedule for the next few weeks. While studying it, a small buzzing sound caught his attention. He turned his head to see the driver's cell phone with the name *Vallario* blinking on the screen. There was a message on the phone: *we're sending a squad to you now*. Ash scrambled out of the truck and approached his president. "We got a problem, boss!"

Brutus raised an eyebrow. "What's going on?"

"Looks like we're about to have some company." Ash bit his lip and looked down the highway as a white SUV with its high-beams on approached from the distance.

"Everybody take cover!" Brutus commanded, and he and the rest of his men readied their weapons and took defensive positions.

Judge grabbed the driver once more, threw him behind the truck, and motioned for Wolf, a prospective member, to guard the man so that he could join in the action.

A hail of bullets peppered the shipping truck right after Ash took cover behind it and readied his pistol. Gunfire erupted from all around as the Cut-Throats blasted back from their positions. Ash swallowed hard before peeking out from the front of the truck and watching a group of well-armed men donned in body armor exit the white SUVs that had now come to a full stop. The men moved in on the rest of his gang as they exchanged fire. The young Cut-Throat raised his pistol and fired off a few shots toward what looked like their leader. Two of the bullets caught the man in the back of his head, and he went down face first onto the pavement, which caused the rest of his men to spread out.

"Savino's down!" one of the unidentified men emptied an entire magazine toward the truck, while the rest of the men took cover.

Ash quickly crouched back down behind the front tire as bullets whizzed past him.

Brutus and the other Cut-Throats laid down heavy cover fire for their young comrade. "Come on, kid! We gotta get the hell out of here!"

Motorcycle engines could be heard approaching from behind their assailants, which caused Brutus to grin. "Doesn't hurt to keep some backup nearby!"

"You're a brilliant man!" Riggs heartily patted his leader on the back. "Now let's get moving!" he called out and looked to the rest of the Cut-Throats before tumbling forward and hitting the ground.

"He's hit! Get him out of here!" Brutus cried out as their reinforcements began opening fire on the armed men.

Ash and Terrace grabbed Riggs and helped him up onto the back of Judge's motorcycle. Everyone else got onto their own bikes and sped off back toward the clubhouse, leaving the weapons shipment and the mysterious armed men behind. Everyone made it back safely that night, except for Riggs, who died shortly after they got back to the Wild West. As soon as the Cut-Throats' vice president was laid to rest, it was back to business for

Brutus and the rest of the crew.

"For our first order of business, I want to nominate Judge for the position of VP. Does anyone disagree?" Brutus looked around the table that was used for the Cut-Throats official meetings.

The room remained silent.

Brutus smiled warmly at Judge as he placed the 'Vice President' patch on the table in front of the seat next to him. They both stood and gave each other a tight hug before Judge took his seat next to Brutus.

"What about sergeant-at-arms?" Judge took the patch between his finger and thumb, staring at it with pride.

"I had someone in mind, but did you have any suggestions?"

Judge looked over at Terrace and gave him a nod. "What do you think about Ter?"

Terrace's eyes widened as he glanced at Ash and then at Judge. "Me? For real?"

"I'd say the kid's proven that he's worth his salt. All in favor?" Brutus looked proudly at the younger member. The room erupted into applause as Brutus beckoned the him over, embraced him, and then pointed to Judge. "Now, you might have to fight him to get that patch from his vest, but he's gotta make room for his VP patch anyway." He chuckled, and Terrace took his new seat across from Judge. "Well then, it's settled. Judge is your new VP, and Terrace, your sergeant-at-arms. You all know the drill: make sure to inform the prospects you're sponsoring."

Brutus's demeanor became more sober as he cleared his throat and waited for the applause to cease. "I know we are all still grieving over Riggs—God rest his soul—but knowing him as well as I did, I know that he would want us to carry on with business as usual." The president paused as everyone nodded silently. "Even though we weren't able to snag the Vallario weapons shipment, we still have some guns in reserve that we can sell to the Yellow Jackets. What my main concern now is how are we gonna make up for our lost wages since we're coming up short for that deal? Things may have to be a little tight around here, Brutus started to say but stopped as he noticed Ash holding up a folded piece of paper. "Did you have something for us, Ash?"

Ash smirked and passed the paper down the table toward Brutus, who unfolded it and studied it with furrowed eyebrows. "I think this might solve our problem."

Brutus's face lit up as he continued to look it over briefly and then set the paper down.

"What is it?" a quizzical look playing Judge's face.

"This here is the weapon shipment schedule and route for the next month." Brutus grinned and then slowly looked at each member around the table, stopping at Ash. "Son, if they still stick to this plan, then this gives us a fair shot at getting a hold of one of those weapon caches and will keep our bellies full for some time."

"It was sitting on the dash when I was checking the cab. I figured it might be good to know for future interests."

"That's assuming they haven't realized it's gone and switched everything around," Terrace interjected.

"You make a fair point," Brutus looked at Judge. "I'm gonna put you in charge of reconnaissance. I want you to make a copy of this schedule and see if they're still sticking to it. We do *not* want another run-in with their security force."

"No problem, Boss," Judge picked up the document and studied the information within.

Brutus turned to Terrace. "In the meantime, I want you, Ash, and a couple of the prospects to take what you can over to the Jackets and just hint to them that we may be coming across a much broader selection for their next delivery. That oughta appease them for the time being."

"We'll take care of it," Terrace then paused and cleared his throat. "About the Vallarios . . ."

Brutus tightened his lips and nodded. "Listen, I would love to avenge Riggs just as much as any of you would. I hate that he's gone, and I hate that he was taken from us the way that he was, but this is the life, gentlemen. Nobody forced us to rob that shipment. We knew the risk. Every time we do a hit or a grab, there are certain risks we take. This life is not for the faint of heart. Riggs knew that better than any of us. He was a highwayman. We're all highwaymen. The last thing I want is for this to turn into some kinda blood feud, like what's brewing between the White Crows and the Shadows. We fight if we have to, but I don't want none of you going out looking for revenge."

Though conflicted, Terrace nodded slowly and accepted Brutus's judgment. The newly appointed sergeant-at-arms stood and beckoned for Ash to follow him. "We'll go and round up what we have and head over to the Hive now."

"One more thing," Brutus held up a large, ring-cladded hand. "Some kid from a gang called the Arch Angels came by earlier inviting us to some kind of secret meeting next month—something about the Lyone family. He said they're still getting a few of the other leaders on board and asked us if they could count on us being there.

What do you all think?"

Terrace cocked his head. "The Lyone family? What's going on with them?"

The others looked at one another and shrugged.

"Not sure. The Arch Angels kid said something about a growing threat or something. I'm gonna be honest with ya—I wasn't really paying too much attention, but maybe it's worth checking out just so we're in the loop if anything goes down."

"Yeah, probably not a bad idea," Judge touched his beard. "Why don't me and Terrace check it out and report back to everyone. The kid leave a contact number or anything?"

Brutus shook his head. "Nah, just said he'd be in touch."

"Whatever. We'll cross that bridge when we get there." Judge shrugged.

"Very good. Meeting adjourned!" Brutus shouted before slamming down the gavel, and everyone went their separate ways.

Terrace and Ash led one of their smaller delivery trucks through the front gates of the Hive after the guard at the gate permitted them to enter to the mercenary compound. One of the prospects drove the truck, while another was in the cargo with the guns. Terrace and Ash brought the truck in front of a large warehouse, where they were greeted by two identically dressed figures wearing black hooded jackets with yellow stripes—their iconic gas masks poking out from under their hoods. They were both armed with submachine guns, which hung at their sides. The Cut-Throats brought their vehicles to a stop. As Terrace and

Ash dismounted, the Yellow Jackets greeted them.

"Welcome, Cut-Throats. What do you have for us today?"

Ash glanced at Terrace before answering, "Not a whole lot today, honestly. We ran into some complications during our last haul." Not wanting to disclose too much of his gang's business to the mercenaries, "These are some leftovers from our last deal with you. We're going to sell 'em all for half price."

Terrace shot a subtle questioning look at Ash but remained silent.

"Half price?" a voice emitted from one of the Yellow Jackets.

"That's a good deal!" said the other. "What's the catch?"

"No catch, fellas. But just so you know, our next shipment is going to be three times the size of this—possibly bigger. You buy us all up when we bring that to your doorstep, and I think that'll make this a fair trade."

The two Yellow Jackets glanced at each other and then back to the Cut-Throats, while the prospects started to unload the cargo. "We'll talk to Ginzo before we give you a solid answer."

"Sounds good to me. Whatcha think, Ter?"

Terrace nodded. "Just give us a buzz when you've got an answer."

"Very well." The Yellow Jacket reached into his jacket, removed a small rolled-up wad of crown bills held together by a rubber band, and tossed it to Ash.

After quickly inspecting the wad, "This is a lot more than half price for these guns."

"Your willingness to sell these at half price shows

your good faith."

A warm smile broke out across Ash's face. "You guys are all right, you know that?"

The Yellow Jacket laughed. "Just keep bringing us more weapons. Ammo too."

"I think we will do just that," Ash assured them.

Terrace eyed the prospects, who were still unloading the guns. "Let's get a move on, prospects! We ain't got all day!" he barked, after which the two new recruits quickened their pace.

"We'll be in touch," said one of the Yellow Jackets, and they turned and walked back toward the warehouse.

Terrace and Ash mounted their bikes and started their engines. "Man, they are weird!" Terrace commented.

Ash shrugged. "I don't know. I kinda like 'em."

"Like 'em? You can't even see their faces!" Terrace chuckled.

"Yeah, but that's just the thing. They seem genuine enough."

"Psh, whatever." Terrace shook his head. "What're you getting into tonight, anyway?"

"I was thinking about hitting up the Shamrocke. I heard McDroogin's Home Brew is pretty good. Wanna come?" Ash asked as they each lit up a cigarette.

"Not particularly," Terrace said, his expression changing. "You really think it's a good idea to be hanging out at the McDroogin family's headquarters?"

"Why not? We've never had any beef with them."

"Just watch your back, alright?"

"Of course, brother. I'll catch ya later," Ash flashed his companion a grin.

There was already a commotion at the Shamrocke when Ash passed through the small iron gate that led to the front porch area of the Kaelish pub. A haze of smoke permeated the air as he entered the building and made his way towards the main bar area. As he approached, he noticed a crowd that was circled around a young man who looked to be close to his own age.

"—and his wife goes: 'O'Brien, what happened? I thought you went to go ask Murphy what a sample was?' and he replies, 'Aye, I did! He told me to piss in a jar, so I told him to shit in a hat, and the fight was on!'" the young McDroogin took a bow as the crowd surrounding him howled in laughter.

Ash found himself joining right in on the laughter. He missed most of the joke but got the gist of it. "Great joke, man," he offered a hand to him.

The McDroogin looked at Ash's hand and then at his leather vest, examining the patches on it. "Yer a Cut-Throat, are ya?" his face revealed no emotion. The crowd around him fell silent.

Ash cleared his throat as his smile left his face. "I am. Is that gonna be a problem?" He was friendly, but he also knew what kind of world he lived in and had acquired a tough side for the appropriate situations.

The young McDroogin stepped forward. "It all depends . . ." he began, his eyes locked with Ash's. "Whattaya drinkin'?" the present crowd could be heard snickering when this question was asked.

"A pint of the famous Home Brew, of course." Ash said with a smirk forming on his face.

"Aye! Get this man a pint of Padraeg's finest!" The McDroogin and everyone else around him laughed. He took

Ash's hand and gave it a firm shake. "Name's O'Connor!"

"Ash. Pleased to meet you." He relaxed a bit.

"You shoulda seen yer face! 'Is that gonna be a problem?'—bahahaha! Come now, let's have a seat and a pint!" he led Ash over to the bar.

Two pitchers later and the two were carrying on as if they had known each other for a life time.

"Y'know, I gotta say that this is the longest amount of time I ever really spent hangin' out with someone from a different gang," O'Connor admitted, taking a small sip from his glass.

"Really?' Ash raised an eyebrow, taking a sip from his own. "I've got a few friends from different gangs."

"*Friends*? Are yer mates okay with that?"

Ash thought of his best friend Terrace. "Well, I suppose it does make them a little uncomfortable."

"So, why?"

"Why *what*?" Ash squinted and then realized what he was being asked. "Why go out of my way to make friends with outsiders?"

O'Connor smirked and raised his eyebrows as he took a puff from a cigarette that he had taken from Ash's half-empty pack that rested on the surface of the bar top.

"Well . . ." Ash took a long sip from his beer, then a drag from his smoke, and exhaled through his nostrils. "I think it's good, y'know? Not just for me but for the city— maybe the world."

"Whaddya mean?" O'Connor's eyes widened.

"Think about it. What good does everyone being separated do for anyone? You've got all these gangs, which are all like private societies or even armies. They stick to themselves and their territories, and they shun anyone who's not like them. But imagine if things weren't that way. Imagine what kind of society we could have if everyone looked out for one another. What if everyone cared for each other the way the gangs care for their own?"

O'Connor let the idea stew in his mind for a while before noticing the ashes building up at the end of his cigarette and flicking them into the ashtray. "You mean, like a society where everyone contributes equally for a greater cause?"

Ash played with the idea for a moment before shaking his head. "Nah. More like a society where people are valued equally and everyone has the choice to contribute to it as a whole. My gang, the Cut-Throats, are relatively cool with me branching out and making contacts with other gangs, but not every gang is like that. I don't think the Bishops or the Golden Dragons would ever allow one of their members to have friends from other gangs or backgrounds. Sure, they've got alliances or deals with other gangs, but that doesn't make them friends . . . more like business partners."

"I see." O'Connor chuckled and finished his cigarette. "And just how would you bring about this utopian society that you're imagining?"

"Well, it's not something just one person can do. It's a decision that everyone has to make for themselves." Ash grinned and took another sip after snubbing out his cigarette. "What you and me are doing right now—that's me doing my part. This is how we make Royalty and maybe even Rathe a better place."

"I'll drink to that!" O'Connor returned the smile and gave Ash a firm pat on the back before raising his glass to him, and they polished off their drinks.

Ash glanced at his watch. "Oh man, the guys are gonna worry about me if I don't get back soon."

"Aww, an' I was just startin' to like ya." O'Connor laughed. "Nah, get outta here! Come back and we'll continue where we left off some time this weekend, aye?"

"Sounds good, man," Ash shook hands with the McDroogin.

At that moment, the most beautiful girl that Ash had ever laid eyes on came by to collect his empty glass. She had long light-brown hair that was braided and hung over her left shoulder. Her eyes were bright blue, and she had a remarkably cheerful smile. She was dressed modestly, especially for a girl her age. She wore a blouse with long frilly sleeves that came down just below her neck and a skirt that came down to her knees. "Hope you enjoyed your brew, gentlemen!" she said, her voice rich with life as her eyes met Ash's for the first time.

"Thanks, Rayn!" O'Connor called after her as she turned and began washing the dirty glasses.

"Rayn . . ." Ash repeated, his eyes not leaving her.

"Aye. Rayn McDroogin. The boss's daughter. Pretty little thing, ain't she?" a sly smirk started to play on his face as he nudged Ash.

"Pretty . . . yes . . ." Ash spaced out as he continued to stare.

"Whelp! Night's over. See ya later, boyo!" O'Connor stood up and gave him a final pat on the back.

"Oh! Right! Gotta get home! It was good to meet you! See ya soon," Ash snapped out of his stupor, stood up, and headed toward the door.

As he left the Shamrocke to get on his motorcycle and head back to the Cut-Throats' clubhouse, he suddenly felt the presence of someone behind him. He turned around and noticed a group of four men a little older than himself surrounding him. He reached for the pistol tucked in the back waistband of his pants and looked at who he thought was their leader in the eyes. "Can I help you?"

The four were dressed in fairly nice clothes. They wore dress shirts with what looked like Kevlar vests. Each of them had a silver lion's head emblem on the left side of their chest armor. The one with whom Ash locked eyes had dark-brown hair that was slicked back and a small patch of hair on his chin. He smirked and sized Ash up. "Cut-Throats, eh?" he pointed to Ash's vest.

"Yeah, what of it?" Ash subtly gripped the handle of his pistol.

The leader chuckled as two of his goons stepped forward. "It seems like you all have been busy lately, hmm?"

Ash stepped back "I don't know what you mean."

"Your little attempted heist almost cost my family some precious resources."

"I don't know what you're talking about," Ash studied the lion's head emblem and trying to remember where he had seen it before. "What family are you with anyway?"

"The Lyone family," the young man's lips curled into a smile.

Ash remembered what Brutus mentioned at the last meeting about the Lyone family and them being a growing threat. He knew that the Lyone family was heavily involved in construction and had just been at a war with the Vallario and Mazzarelli families within the past year. *Were they planning on robbing that truck?* Ash wondered. "Like I said"—the Cut-Throat slowly brandished his pistol, causing the two approaching Lyones to halt—"I don't know what you're talking about. You probably have me confused with someone else. I suggest you take my word for it and back off."

The young Lyone grinned and chuckled once more. "Now, now. No harm, no foul. Just consider this a warning. The Vallario family is off limits."

"Yeah, sure, whatever. See ya later." Ash dismissed the Lyone emissary before stepping over to his motorcycle and mounting it.

"Pass that along to your superiors," the Lyone said.

Ash started the engine and revved it up a few times. "Don't have any!" He shrugged and pulled out onto the road, speeding back toward the Wild West.

When Ash returned to the Cut-Throats' headquarters, he informed Brutus and Judge of his encounter with the Lyones. They were both just as perplexed as Ash was, as they had never really had any interactions with any of the organized families before and didn't expect the Lyones to be so concerned about the Vallarios' affairs. They all agreed not to let this interfere with their next operation, however, and that they would simply need to exercise more caution next time to avoid any detection or, God forbid, casualties. Judge told Ash that the meeting with the Arch Angels and other gang leaders had been called off because their leader had been killed.

For the next few months, Ash frequented the Shamrocke to meet with O'Connor. He quickly became a regular and earned the respect of most of the McDroogin family. When they had time alone, Ash and O'Connor would share ideas that they had for the future of Royalty.

They bounced ideas off one another, such as the gangs becoming functioning parts of society rather than small armies that fought over trade and territory. They talked about building a government and having laws to protect people from future gang violence and perhaps even having a police force. The more they talked about it, the more they could see their dream becoming a reality. In turn, the more Ash met with O'Connor at the Shamrocke, the more he saw Rayn McDroogin, and after some encouragement from O'Connor, he finally decided to talk to her.

"Was everything good t'night, Ash?" Rayn collected his and O'Connor's empty pitcher.

"Aye—I mean, uh, yes! Thank you!" Ash fumbled with his words, and his face turned bright red.

"*Aye?* Yer startin' to sound Kaelish. You must be hangin' around here too much!" she joked and nudged Ash on the arm a little.

"Haha, yeah! Probably . . ." Ash replied and grew quiet for a moment before receiving a hard kick to the shin from O'Connor from under the table. "*Ow!*"

Rayn's eyes shifted from Ash to O'Connor and then back to Ash. "What are you two up to?" She smirked.

"Oh, my boy, Ash here just had somethin' that he wanted to say to ya is all," O'Connor winked at her.

Rayn giggled and then turned to Ash. "*Well?*" she gave the Cut-Throat another playful smirk.

"Well, I . . . uh . . ." Ash swallowed and attempted to gain some composure. "Would you . . . like to go out with me sometime?"

Rayn's face flushed completely as her eyes widened. Now it was her turn to clear her throat. "Are you asking me out?"

Ash looked away sheepishly and nodded. "Yes," he said quietly.

"Hmm," Rayn hummed, pretending to think for a moment. "Okay, sure!"

"Wait, really?" Ash turned back to face her.

"Of course! But only if ya give me a ride on that motorcycle of yours," she said with a giggle.

"Deal!" Ash thought for a moment. "So, dinner? Coffee?"

"I prefer tea, but I think Malone's serves both," Rayn suggested. Her expression changed as she looked at O'Connor. "What do you think?"

O'Connor looked around, spotting Rayn's father, his boss, behind the bar with a couple of his generals. "Well, they don't seem to have a problem with Ash as it is. Maybe I'll try t'smooth things over with them for ya."

"Why don't I just ask him myself?" Ash volunteered, secretly dreading the thought of having to interact with his crush's father.

"Uh, I don't know—"

"You know what? That's a brilliant idea!" O'Connor grinned as he stood up and nearly pulled Ash off his barstool.

"Wait a minute!"

"O'Connor, I really think—" Rayn called after O'Connor, but he was already pulling Ash toward Padraeg and his generals, who all stared at the sight with amusement.

"He'll be fine!" O'Connor chuckled as he led Ash right up the bar between Padraeg's most trusted men, who all looked at Ash perplexed.

Padraeg was a large, burly man and taller than most, with a barrel chest, a pot belly, and arms like tree trunks. He wore a green golf cap on his head and had a dark-brown goatee. The McDroogin leader raised an eyebrow at the two young men and leaned forward slightly. "How can I help ya, boys?"

Ash looked at O'Connor, then let out a sigh. "I was hoping that, uh, you might give me permission to take Rayn out for coffee sometime." The Cut-Throat's voice was shaky.

"You want to take my daughter out for coffee?" Padraeg's eyebrows dropped as he looked at his generals, a couple of whispers in the old Kaelish language escaping their lips. "That's a very big problem, laddy."

"I-it is?" Ash swallowed as he felt a bead of sweat running down the side of his face and looked back at O'Connor, who shrugged.

"Of course it is!" Padraeg roared, causing everyone in the pub to fall silent. The only sound that could be heard at this point was the folk music coming from the jukebox at the back of the bar. Everyone stood frozen still before a smirk appeared on the McDroogin leader's face. "She doesn't like coffee."

Chuckling and laughter filled the Shamrocke as everyone quickly resumed their conversations.

Ash let out another sigh, this time of relief. "So, I can take her then?" his eyes met with the McDroogin's.

"Aye, you can take her." Padraeg smiled and then lifted his chin in his daughter's direction. "My Rayn is a smart girl. Strong too. She doesn't need me to decide for her who she should or shouldn't see. I raised her that way. Nonetheless, I respect you for askin' me in advance," he offered his enormous hand.

Ash took his hand and squeezed it as firmly as he

could despite his struggle to get a proper grip. "Thank you, sir. She will be in the best of care!"

"Aye, she had better be, or I'll send McGregor here after ye." He chuckled and nodded to McGregor, who scowled menacingly at Ash.

Ash swallowed once more and nodded. "Duly noted," he turned to O'Connor, who gave him an approving nod and walked his friend toward the Shamrocke's main entrance, where Rayn was waiting for them.

"I'm guessing it went well?" Rayn was still flustered, especially after hearing her father shout.

"I'll see you Friday night." Ash winked to the pretty McDroogin maiden, who blushed and smiled at the young Cut-Throat as he left to head back home.

Ash and Rayn hit it off naturally from the start. Although she was relatively tame compared to Ash, she still found him charming. She knew he wasn't like most of the other members of gangs that she had heard about, and he reminded her more of one of her own than anything. Ash also learned that she shared his ideals about the city becoming more unified, and as they continued to date and fall in love, they even worked out what steps they could take to make their dream a reality. A year went by fast for the young couple, and in between gang business, Ash took every opportunity that he could to be with his beloved Rayn.

The Cut-Throats carried on business as usual and during that year were able to more covertly take over shipments from the Vallarios and sell them to the Yellow Jackets, which yielded them more profit than ever before. The Cut-Throats were thriving and decided to take a break from robbing the Vallarios for a short time to catch them off guard in the future. Brutus and Judge had ordered Ash to get hold of another one of the Vallarios' shipment schedules so that they would be prepared for their future heist, but until then, he was permitted to take some time off. This delay in business was like a short vacation for him, and he spent most of his time with Rayn.

One night, while the two were together, the question of marriage came up. Rayn was nervous about the prospect because intermarriage between gangs was typically taboo in Royalty. She knew that her father liked Ash well enough but was afraid that he wouldn't accept the idea of her marrying an outsider. Ash had a feeling that Brutus and the others would mostly hold the same view, and thus, the two decided to marry in secret and consummate their love for one another. The McDroogins had a relatively religious background, being followers of the Old Way, but mostly in profession rather than practice. Rayn, on the other hand, had taken a more practical approach and considered herself an active follower of The Way, which was much more uncommon in those days. Marriage was a much bigger deal to her, as any type of sexual relations outside of marriage was considered sinful according to the teachings of The Way, and she couldn't deny the growing physical attraction that she felt toward Ash.

The two made secret arrangements with a member of the Royal Priests named Welch, who performed the wedding ceremony in the Lotus Garden with O'Connor present as their witness. The documents were signed, the vows read, and the young couple was deemed to be one flesh as they sealed their love with a kiss. The only problem was that it wasn't long before the two longed to be together more often. Although they were married, they still felt so far apart. It didn't feel right that Rayn had to spend her nights in her bedroom alone and that Ash had to return to the Cut-Throats' clubhouse. They knew that they couldn't continue to be apart from each other, and this became an even greater concern when Rayn's pregnancy test came back positive after only a month of being married.

"This will be a no-brainer. We'll set up a party. Food. Plenty of drinks. The works. Once everyone is there, I'll tell 'em that I have an announcement t'make. That's when you two come up, and we'll announce the good news," O'Connor plotted.

Ash and Rayn held hands as they listened and happily agreed. "My father is going to be so mad at me!"

"I'm sure he will be a little hurt that he didn't get to attend his own daughter's wedding, but I don't doubt everyone will want to throw you two another once they find out. How could they resist?" O'Connor laughed.

"Well," Rayn began, but then looked down. "There is more to it than that."

Ash smirked and looked away as O'Connor furrowed his eyebrows and leaned forward.

Rayn put a hand on her belly and flushed red even more. "I'm pregnant."

O'Connor's face lit up. "Yer gonna be a *dad*?!" He gave Ash a playful shove. "And you didn't tell me?"

Ash nearly fell over as he chuckled and smiled at Rayn. "We wanted to wait a few moynths first to make sure before we told anyone."

"This is the icing on the cake! Padraeg's a sucker for children!"

"Okay…" Ash paused to light up a fresh cigarette.

"So, why don't we give it some more time. I'll talk to Brutus and Judge and see if they'd be willing to bring over some of our next shipment to Padraeg as a gift, which should help begin a new relationship between our respective gangs. We'll have them thinking that the meeting is more or less a business deal until we make our little announcement."

"That's great! In the meantime, I'll talk things over with him and let him know that you're setting something up with your people. He may not be too happy that I've set this up behind his back, but if your people can bring the guns, I don't see how that won't turn him around."

They all agreed to the plan. Ash waited for the right opportunity to bring the proposition to Brutus and Judge, although he knew that it was only a matter of time before Rayn would start showing as she approaching the end of her first trimester.. At first, Judge was outright against the idea of giving away anything that they had earned. But Brutus thought about it more diplomatically, considering all the benefits that a potential alliance with the McDroogins could bring. Judge was eventually swayed, and Ash assured them that once they got close to the next shipment heist, he would get a concrete time for them to meet with the McDroogins.

O'Connor was right about Padraeg, who was furious that one of his lower-ranking captains had set up such a deal without even so much as running it by one of the generals. The young McDroogin pleaded for forgiveness but assured Padraeg that the only reason that he did not reveal this to the McDroogin leadership up front was because it was supposed to be a surprise for him. At the mention of free guns, Padraeg softened up to the idea and gave O'Connor permission to coordinate with the Cut-

Throats and set up a meeting. He also assured O'Connor that he was to be fully responsible if anything went wrong. The young McDroogin was confident that once the announcement about the marriage and the baby was made, everyone's hearts would soften and it would bring the two gangs together.

Ash and Terrace managed to break into one of the Vallarios' storage facilities and gain access to their latest shipment schedule. They brought it to the Cut-Throats' meeting table, and the gang decided that they would hit the next large shipment, which was due to happen in three weeks. Ash told Brutus and Judge that he would set up a date for their meeting with the McDroogins soon after receiving the weapons. They agreed, and Ash met with O'Connor to give him as many details as he could. Finally, a day and time was set, not only to announce the union of the two lovers, but also to bring harmony between two of the toughest gangs in the city of Royalty.

The night before the announcement, Ash and Rayn were sitting on a small stone bench that was placed next to a little duck pond. The Cut-Throats successfully managed to rob the Vallario shipment with ease the night before. They sat there in silence at first, holding one another closely as they watched the white-feathered ducks swim in formation from one side of the pond to the other. Winter was approaching, and there was a light chill in the air, but the shared warmth of their bodies kept them from getting too cold.

"I'm so glad you're okay," Rayn's pale blue eyes looked up into Ash's.

Ash chuckled and caressed her shoulder with his

thumb. "This was probably the easiest hit we've ever done, honestly."

"Will you ever stop?" her expression becoming somber.

"*Stop?*" Ash had not considered this. He had been with the Cut-Throats almost his entire life, and stealing shipments from other gangs or companies had always been a way of life for him. "I-I don't know what else I'd do."

Rayn reached up and touched her husband's cheek. "There's a lot you can do. Look at my dad. Sure, his hands aren't the cleanest, but running the Shamrocke is good, honest work."

Ash rubbed his chin while pondering this. "I don't think I'm much of a businessman."

"Says who? Look what you and O'Connor have set up. Think about the connections you've made. Maybe you're not a businessman, but perhaps a diplomat? A liaison? You're a *leader*, Ash!"

"A leader?" Ash focused his attention back on the ducks, and let out a sigh.

"I'm sorry to stress you out before our big day. I'm nervous too."

"I promise that I will be the best husband that I can be to you"—he placed his hand on her belly—"and the best father to our child."

"I know you will." She let out a sigh and then straightened up. "You've gotta get going soon, don'tcha?"

"Yeah, sorry. I told Ram I'd stop by TNT's tonight before heading back home. I should go while it's still early."

"Aye," she cooed and leaned over to plant a gentle kiss against his lips.

The day of the announcement had come. Ash started his day with a cup of coffee, and what would be his last cigarette. He had been a smoker since he was a boy and had ingrained the habit into much of his daily life. As he took the last drag from his cigarette, he held the smoke in his lungs to cherish his final puff before exhaling a long trail from his nostrils. Part of leading his family would involve changing his habits. He finished his cup of coffee and suited up, preparing for his delivery across town before the celebration at the Shamrocke.

"Hey!" Terrace called out to him.

Ash turned around. "Yeah? What's up, Ter?" he continued securing some new models of pistols in his saddlebags.

"So, what's the deal with this thing tonight? You sure we're not being set up?" Terrace tended to be more cautious than most, as his role within the gang was to ensure that they were well protected.

Ash laughed. "Positive. This is mostly *my* plan," he assured him. "This is a good opportunity for us to begin to build a relationship with another gang. They're a lot of fun, and they're genuine guys. I think you might be pleasantly surprised."

Terrace nodded and smirked. "Alright, fine. You want me to send some prospects with you for the delivery?"

"Nah, I got Wolf coming with me. Shouldn't need anyone else. You just stick with Brutus and enjoy your time with the McDroogins until I arrive."

"You make it sound like it's a party," a confused look formed on his face.

Ash shrugged and started up his bike. "I mean, who says it's not?"

"Just be safe!" Terrace shouted over the rumbling engine. "I'll catch you tonight!"

When Ash arrived at the Hive, he noticed that all the Yellow Jackets were outside, loading up their vehicles as if they were preparing for something big.

Two of them approached him once he pulled into their parking lot, with Wolf driving the cargo truck as they shut the gate behind them. He greeted them both with a smile as he shut off his bike. "Hey, got your delivery!"

Wolf got out of the driver's seat of the truck and opened the back hatch as a few of the Yellow Jackets came over to help him unload the weapons.

The other two Yellow Jackets looked at one another, and then one tossed a roll of crowns to Ash.

Ash looked around as the other Yellow Jackets quickly moved around their compound. "What's going on anyway? A war break out or somethin'?"

"A lot is going on. Those Lyones are making moves. Forcing people to join them. Killing those who won't."

"*Forcing?* How could they force people to join them? What's the deal with these guys anyway?" He then remembered his encounter with them over a year ago, when they had warned him to not hit any more Vallario shipments.

"Scare tactics. Making examples out of people—out of **entire** gangs. Their leader Lucien Lyone comes from a wealthy family. His father just died recently, and he's taken over the family enterprise. He's young but ambitious, and our sources tell us that he's allied with the Mazzarellis *and* the Vallarios, among a few other gangs. It seems that if you aren't with them, you're against them. That's why we're stocking up. I doubt that they'll try to attack the Hive, but we're not taking any chances."

"I think I may have had a run-in with some of those guys a while ago. You said they were killing people who won't join them?"

"YES!!" the Yellow Jacket's voice in a mild panic could be perceived through the chamber of the gas mask that covered his face. "We didn't know what to believe until just last week. They completely wiped out the Jackals! All of them except their leader!"

Ash's mouth hung open. Tears formed in his eyes. "How did I not hear about this? Ram . . ." he blinked twice. He began to wonder if he was dreaming. He had just spent time with Ram and the Jackals the previous night at TNT's. "They killed all of them except for Ram?"

The Yellow Jacket nodded gravely. "You watch yourself out there, Ash."

Ash called Wolf over just as he was finishing unloading the truck.

"What's up, boss?" Wolf wiped the sweat from his brow.

"We've got an emergency. Head back to the Wild West and prepare our weapons for a full assault."

"Oh shoot, what's going on?"

"I don't know too much right now. Just do what I said, and I'll be in touch as soon as possible."

Rayn was in the middle of wiping down the countertop of the bar when the door opened. All the McDroogins seemed to turn around at once as O'Connor came in through the back door of the Shamrocke and walked straight up to Padraeg and his officers. "They're here!"

Padraeg and his officers all stood up and walked over toward the door, where the Cut-Throats stood, expressionless. Standing behind Brutus and his officers were two of the prospects carrying a large wooden crate. "That what I think it is?" the McDroogin leader smirked.

"Sure is," Brutus turned to his prospects and gave them a single nod as they stepped forward and lifted the lid off the crate, revealing five semiautomatic rifles all lined up in a row. "And I've got four more boxes with your name on them."

Padraeg extended his large hand toward Brutus, who stood similarly in size to the McDroogin leader. Padraeg was a bit pudgier than Brutus but still presented himself as a large, powerhouse of a man. They almost looked like they could have been brothers.

Brutus took Padraeg's hand in his and gave it a firm shake with a smile as he looked around the pub. "This is a nice place you got here. Can't believe I haven't been before!" his eyes scanned the interior of the renowned pub and admired the finish of the dark wooden floors and matching tables. The Shamrocke gave off a warm vibe to all her guests.

"Welcome!" Padraeg grinned and guided Brutus forward, patting him on the back.

The two of them laughed as they walked to the bar, with everyone following behind. It was not long before drinks were served, and both gangs began to make conversation with one another. Rayn and O'Connor couldn't stop glancing at one another and smiling as they saw that their mission was already being accomplished. It took little effort on their part for the two gangs to get along. They only needed a few good souls to help set things in motion.

The front doors to the Shamrocke opened once more. Rayn and O'Connor both looked over immediately, their hearts pounding with anticipation for Ash to arrive. Was this finally the time to make their big announcement?

Both were disappointed when they could not recognize the man who had stepped through the door. He was not dressed like a McDroogin or a Cut-Throat. He was well dressed, wearing black dress shoes, black slacks, and a silvery-gray dress shirt tucked into his pants. Over the dress shirt was a bulletproof vest. He had dark-brown hair that was slicked back and a thin goatee. With him were four other men who were dressed similarly. Each of them had a pistol strapped to their thighs.

Padraeg stood up, approached the younger man, "Another gang to join the party?"

The young man returned the smile. "No, no. I wouldn't dare crash your party. I'm here on business. It seemed like now would be a good time since I have both of you here with *my* stolen guns," he motioned over to Brutus's prospects, who had just finished bringing in the last crate, which had the name *Vallario* stamped on the side.

The wind whipped Ash's hair straight back as he pushed his motorcycle to its limits to get to the Shamrocke. The announcement could wait. While both gangs were together, this would be a good time to talk about a possible alliance to prevent the Lyones from doing any more harm. He could handle brawls between gangs; that was commonplace. However, he refused to tolerate genocide. To Ash, this was unacceptable.

This could be good, though, he thought to himself.

Perhaps it would be better to have the gangs allied before breaking the news about the marriage and pregnancy to them. It could give them a chance to form a bond, and then they would probably be a lot more comfortable with the news.

The Cut-Throats became tense as they looked at one another. Brutus stepped forward. "You with the Vallario family?"

The young man chuckled and shook his head. "Not quite. If anything, the Vallario family is with *me*," he clarified. "They are, however, a business interest of mine and are under the Lyone family's umbrella of protection. Because a profit from those guns goes to me, I'll count them as my property. In fact, you can have your prospects start loading them up in our vehicles out front."

Brutus smirked and took another step forward with Judge and Terrace on either side of him. "Listen kid, I get that we rattled your cage a little bit by hijacking those trucks, but we brought these guns as a gift for these guys right here"—he motioned toward Padraeg—"so, here is what I will offer ya: what if we started working with you? Maybe we could provide protection for the trucks for a percentage that you make from the guns?"

"You're making *me* an offer?" the young man attempted to stifle his laughter. "I would have been more than happy to listen to this proposal before you decided to make a routine out of robbing my associates. I'm going to make *you* an offer now. Twenty-five percent of all your income now goes directly to me. If you want to lower it to twenty percent, then you will provide that protection for our trucks for each shipment. Consider this your tax to your new government."

"*Government?* We ain't got one. And we ain't payin' you squat."

"Oh, yes you do. From this day forward, you will recognize me, Lucien Lyone, as the mayor of this city. My family, along with the Vallario and Mazzarelli families, will be providing public safety to all who pay their taxes, and together, we will bring this city up from the ruined state that it has been in for too long into a place its citizens might be proud to call *home*."

"Sounds like extortion," Padraeg reached underneath the bar and produced a black combat-style shotgun and racked the pump.

Lucien shook his head. "You and your crews will fall in line. If not, we will make an example of you. That's not the road either of us wants to go down." His demeanor changed from jovial to a chilling calm.

His threat caused members from both the Cut-Throats and the McDroogin family to scoff and shout profanity at him and the men accompanying him.

"I suggest you leave," Padraeg lifted the barrel and aimed the large shotgun at Lucien Lyone's chest.

"We're going to step outside. You boys enjoy your barbecue," a sinister smirk spread across Lucien's face as he and his associates exited the building.

"*Barbecue?*" Brutus raised an eyebrow at Padraeg.

"There's no barbecue . . ." Padraeg looked around at his men, who shook their heads.

"They're gonna smoke us out!" Terrace shouted.

"We gotta get the hell out of here!" Judge cried out as everyone inside the pub evacuated the building.

Each of the members from both gangs stopped in

their tracks as they soon realized that they had been baited into coming out and were now surrounded by a superior force of armed men from the Lyone, Vallario, and Mazzarelli families.

"Now that I've got your attention, why don't we try having this conversation again," Lucien folded his arms over his chest.

Some of the McDroogins advanced on Lucien and his men. A young man with L'Orandan features who was with Lucien in the bar swiftly drew his pistol and shot one of them in the head at point blank range. The others instantly froze. Everyone else, including the Cut-Throats, drew their weapons.

"This is your chance to comply. If you do not agree to a monthly twenty-five percent of your income, then I will make an example out of your leaders until we can find someone competent enough to handle business with us." His eyes glided over each individual member of the two gangs.

"Business?! How dare you demand our hard-earned money!" Padraeg's face burned bright red.

"Oh, but it *is* business. Allow me to reiterate." Lucien cleared his throat. "We will keep this city safe. You see, Royalty, for so long—*too* long—has been a haven of chaos. No order. No law. No boundaries. Only territory and silly wars. It's time that we start to become a civilized society. As your newly appointed mayor, I intend to see to the reformation of this city. But that comes at a price. As long as everybody contributes, we can make our dreams come true."

"Mayor?! More like dictator!" Brutus spat and stepped forward.

Another gunshot went off. This time, it was a Cut-Throat that fell to the ground dead. Both the Cut-Throats and McDroogins stepped back in terror. They knew that they could easily be wiped out. There was nowhere to run, and they didn't have enough men to fight. Both Padraeg and Brutus looked at each other once more as the Cut-Throat leader gritted his teeth and shook his head.

"We're not paying you anything!" Padraeg shouted, followed by many others shouting in agreement.

"Fine," a few of his men stepped forward, guns pointed in the faces of those who surrounded their leaders, and forcefully grabbed Padraeg and Brutus, dragging them in front of Lucien and pushing them to their knees. He then removed his own pistol, which was holstered on his thigh. The chrome flashed in the waning light of the sun as he put the barrel of the gun to Padraeg's forehead.

"Nooo!!" came the cry of Rayn, who ran straight toward her father and Lucien.

"Rayn! Get back!" O'Connor shouted as a single gunshot rang out.

Rayn fell at her father's side and took his hand in hers.

"Rayn . . . My precious daughter . . ." Padraeg stroking her hair with a shaky hand.

A pool of blood quickly formed around her as she lay there in the middle of the street, a bleeding hole in her chest. "I couldn't let him hurt you, Daddy . . ."

Lucien took a step back and again aimed the smoking barrel of his pistol at Padraeg. "Her blood is on your hands!" he shouted, his men stepping forward with guns aimed at both gangs once more.

Padraeg's will to fight left him. "Call the Priests!

Please, call the Priests!" tears streamed down his face.

Lucien nodded to the L'Orandan man, who got on his phone and began calling the Royal Priests for an ambulance. As he spoke with them, the faint sound of a motorcycle could be heard in the distance.

"You're a monster," Brutus growled as he scowled at Lucien. The sound grew louder.

"You truly believe that this is my fault? You started this when you decided to steal from our business partners!" Lucien spat as he aimed the barrel of his pistol toward Brutus.

VRRRRRRRRRRRMMMMMMMMMMMMMM MMMM!

Ash's motorcycle crashed into Lucien Lyone, running directly into his right knee. A loud crack could be heard as the machine slammed into it. Ash rolled off the bike right before it crashed into Lucien and slid across the asphalt. His leather jacket seemed to help a bit with the fall, but he was still unable to move once his body came to a halt.

The Lyones rushed to Lucien's side to make sure he was okay. He groaned in pain as he gripped his mangled right leg. "He broke my leg!" he shouted. The other Lyones kept their guns pointed to keep the two gangs at bay while the others helped him up.

After about ten minutes the Royal Priests arrived on the scene in one of their white and gold ambulances. Some of the Royal Priests who were armed rushed in front of Rayn, creating a human barrier in case anyone attempted to stop them from doing their duty. The others quickly got Rayn onto a stretcher while Padraeg cried, "Please just save her! Please save my baby!"

O'Connor looked over to where Ash was lying,

then at Rayn. "I'll go with her!" he climbed in the back of the ambulance as they were getting her fastened in. Once the doors were shut, they got inside and sped off, the sirens blaring as they headed back to St. Titus Memorial Hospital.

Both Cut-Throats and McDroogins stood frozen. Brutus made it over to Ash's side to make sure he was okay. Aside from a large scrape down the left side of his face and a broken arm, he seemed to be alright.

Lucien's men helped him limp over toward Ash and Brutus and asked for one of his men's pistols.

Brutus looked up at him. "Wait! We'll pay, okay? We'll pay whatever you want!" he raised his right hand.

"Yes, you'll pay!" one of Lucien's men kicked Brutus in the face, sending him flat on his back. Lucien then aimed the pistol at Ash's chest and unloaded into him, continuously pulling the trigger, even after the slide locked into place when all of the ammunition was spent.

The L'Orandan man gently lowered Lucien's arm and said under his breath, "Alright, boss. I think you got him."

"Of course, I got him!" Lucien winced as a surge of pain shot up through his leg. "I'm never going to walk normal again because of that stupid kid!"

"What do you want to do, boss?" the L'Orandan raised his eyebrows.

Lucien turned around after loading a fresh magazine into the pistol. He then pointed it in the direction of the gangs. "I'll be sending one of my men to collect our payment next week. *Thirty percent.*" A stylish gray sedan pulled up, and one of Lucien's men opened the back door for him as they helped him into the car and slowly all of the Lyones left.

One by one, the gangs of Royalty submitted to the Lyone family. Almost every gang paid taxes to them. Some paid more and some less. Those who were most loyal to the Lyones received the most benefits. As for the others, they were left to fend for themselves. The only thing that changed about the city of Royalty was that a tyrant ruled it by force under the guise of protection. The new generation that followed knew no better. They never questioned why things were the way they were. Most of the gangs were content to pay the Lyones as long as no more blood was shed. This was just the way things were. This was the world in which they lived. This was Royalty.

CHAPTER ONE

"Alright, folks, tonight we have something special for you!" announced Blitz, a member of the Immortals, the gang that ran the fight club at the Asylum every Friday night. On the outside, the building looked like a normal storefront attached to a strip mall that spanned the entire block. The interior was dark and lit only by strips of bright red LED lights that ran along the ceiling. In the center of the establishment was a large fighting ring encircled by an aluminum fence with two gates on opposite sides. A bar took up the length of the east side of the building, where every seat was occupied by patrons holding out crown bills, hoping to gain the attention of a bartender before the fight started. "On one side, we have Lance, a prized yet humble fighter representing St. Titus Orphanage!" The crowd cheered loudly. "On the other, we have our very own Shade, cofounder and champion of the Immortals! Heavy will be around to collect your bets before the fight begins!"

Heavy made his way over to Seraph, who was cheering on his best friend, Lance. Seraph was almost eighteen years old, two years younger than Lance. He wore a lightweight brown jacket and a pair of ratty blue jeans. His hair was on the longer side and hung just a little above his eyes. In contrast, Heavy was a large, dark-skinned Amakoran man and one of the founding members of the Immortals. He wore a black leather jacket and always seemed to be puffing on a cigar. "Whatchu throwin' down tonight, big man?"

Seraph dug around in his pocket before pulling up a wad of folded crown bills. "Give me a hundred on Lance." He smirked with confidence.

Heavy's eyes widened before responding with a smokey chuckle. "Big balla tonight, huh? You n' Lance been friends a long time, huh?" He quickly counted the crowns before adding them to a much larger stack and securing them in his front pocket.

"That's right! I practically owe him my life. Back at St. Titus, when I was eleven, these older boys were sweatin' me in the restroom. I tried to stand up for myself but instead tasted yellow death."

Heavy cringed. "A *swirly*?"

"About halfway through my little dunking session, this kid comes in, tells them to back off, and threatens to give him the same treatment as me if he don't beat it. Let's just say they got a *taste* of their own medicine," Seraph lifted his chin in Lance's direction.

"That was Lance, huh? He's a tough kid. Haven't seen him lose too many brawls. This one oughta be interestin'." Heavy took a large puff of his cigar and knocked the ashes off.

"You're tellin' me. Shade's a tough dude. I have to admit, I'm a little nervous. You guys have been through quite a lot, haven't you?" Seraph watched the smoke from the cigar stream upward toward the black painted ceiling of the building.

"Oh, yeah! Shade, Damien, 'n me all grew up together on this street. Been friends for as long as I remember. We formed the Immortals out of necessity after Damien got jumped one night by the Soldiers. They was much bigga than us back then, but we held our own. We took our beatings when we had to, as well. Luckily, it ended in a truce, 'cause the Arch Angels intervened. They was a different group entirely back then."

"Yeah? All I know is those guys run La Noche. I try to avoid that place. Not really my scene, ya know?"

"Ha, f'sho, young brotha. Anyway, I gotta collect more dough. Good luck to you and your boy!" Heavy grinned before tucking the cigar between his teeth and bumping fists with the young orphan.

"Likewise, Heavy!" Seraph called out as the large man continued to make his rounds to the other betters.

Once all the bets were collected, Blitz began shouting again. "All bets are in, and we are ready to begin the fight! But don't worry, folks, if you forgot to bet for one of these two killers, there will be another fight right after! In the meantime, let's get this show on the road!" Lance and Shade touched fists and Blitz yelled, "Fight!"

Both men had their guards up as the gap between them closed. Shade confidently threw a few punches at Lance, who weaved them with ease. Lance was not the most aggressive fighter. He preferred to hold a strong defense and wait for his opponent to attack while he looked for an opening.

"You even trying?" Lance attempted to provoke

Shade.

Shade furrowed his eyebrows and rushed him. Lance threw a hard left toward Shade's face, but he was quicker than Lance had expected. Shade went low, grabbed hold of Lance's left leg, lifted him up, and then planted him firmly on the floor of the ring.

Seraph winced as he saw his buddy go down hard on the mat. "Come on, Lance! Don't let him dog you, man!"

Shade mounted Lance and threw a few punches, his fist scraping against Lance's face without making full contact. Lance wedged his knee between their bodies, extended his leg to pry Shade off him, and quickly slipped out from beneath him before scrambling to his feet.

By now, both fighters were beginning to lose their breath, so they took a moment to gather themselves before going at it again. In the meantime, Blitz seized the opportunity to comment on what had just occurred between the two.

"That was close! It looked like Shade almost had him, but Lance was able to escape! Maybe he won't be so lucky next time!" everyone cheered.

Three young men who appeared to be Seraph's age approached him, while Lance and Shade started going at it again. One of the three was dressed particularly grungy, wearing ripped baggy jeans, a plain dark-gray shirt, and a dark unzipped hooded jacket. He wore gloves with the fingers cut off and a black bandana folded so that his dark-brown ponytail could hang over it. He also sported a small patch of hair on his chin. The other two were dressed similarly but had significantly shorter hair.

"That your boy?" he pulled out an electronic cigarette and took a deep drag from it before exhaling the smoke through his nostrils.

Seraph nodded. "Yeah, why?" his eyes narrowed involuntarily.

"He's pretty good, man," the young man's two counterparts nodded in agreement as they watched Lance throw a hard uppercut into Shade. "Which set do you guys rep? I heard Blitz say something about St. Titus Orphanage? I didn't know the Royal Priests took part in fight clubs."

Seraph laughed and shook his head. "Nah, man, we're not reppin' the Priests per se. No affiliations, either. Just two guys surviving."

"Woah, for real? He's a pretty good fighter for someone who has no affiliations. Where'd he learn to fight like that?"

"Well . . ." Seraph had a feeling of what direction the conversation was headed in as he started to answer but hesitated as the fight intensified. Shade jabbed twice at Lance, both punches connecting with the side of his face. He attempted to follow up with a heavy right hook, but Lance anticipated it and rushed him, wrapping his arms around Shade's torso and lifting him off the ground. Shade kicked furiously at Lance, which caused him to set Shade back down, and the gap between them widened. Lance was now crouched over. Shade ran up to throw a knee at his face, but Lance swiftly countered him with a right punch to the middle of his chin. Shade's body became rigid for a moment before he fell straight back. It seemed as though Lance slid on top of him in full mount as he began to ground pound him before a couple of the Immortals rushed over and ripped him off Shade and held him still until he calmed down. "Yes!" Seraph cheered for his friend. "Way to go, brother!" he then redirected his attention to the young man he had been talking to and continued, "out of necessity, I guess."

Blitz brought Lance a cold bottled water and raised his right arm up in victory. "We have a winner! Everyone give it up for Lance!" Blitz placed a wad of crowns into his hand as the crowd cheered. Once Shade regained consciousness, he was helped to his feet and led over to Lance. The two clasped hands and hugged. "You see that, folks? What sportsmanship! All in good fun!"

"Necessity?" the young man raised his eyebrows, taking another puff from his e-cig. "Well, anyway, I'll let you guys celebrate your victory. I'm Lazarus, by the way—or Laz, for short—leader of the Switchblades." He offered his hand to Seraph.

Seraph bore a knowing smirk. "Nice to meet you." He took Lazarus's hand and gave it a firm shake. "I'm Seraph."

At that moment, Lance joined them. He had just begun to catch his breath as he held the bottle of water to the side of his face. Seraph congratulated him, and the two clasped hands and embraced.

"Great job out there, man!" Seraph grinned.

"Thanks, bro! It wasn't an easy win," Lance admitted with a winded chuckle and opened the bottle of water before taking a long sip. He then lifted his chin toward Lazarus and company. "Make some friends?"

"Uh, well—" Seraph started before Lazarus stepped forward and offered his hand to Lance.

"Lazarus. Nice to meet you." Seraph narrowed his eyes at him.

Heavy approached the group and handed Seraph a wad of crown bills and congratulated Lance with a pat on the back. "Not bad, brotha," and moved on to the next bettor.

"How much did we score?" Lance began counting the money that Blitz had handed him.

Seraph followed suit and added up the money. His eyes lit up, "Six hundred, bro!"

Lance let out a satisfied sigh. "Won't be long, man. Maybe a couple more weeks and we can finally get out on our own."

"We still gotta decide what the heck we're gonna do. An apartment is a given, but what about profit? Are you still settled on the bar idea?"

"I mean—with the right connections, maybe we could make it work." Lance suddenly became distracted by an approaching group of well-dressed young men.

"You're quite the fighter," said the one who appeared to be in charge. He had blonde hair that he wore short, similar to Lance's haircut. He wore an indigo suit and a formfitting trench coat with fancy embroidery on the cuffs and a lion's head on each shoulder, the emblem of the Lyone family.

"Thank you," a bashful look displayed on the young victor's face before he pointed to the lion emblem. "You're a Lyone?"

The well-dressed man nodded. "I'm Vincent," he said, cocking an eyebrow. "*Lance*, was it?"

"Oh! Yes! Nice to meet you, um, sir!" Lance blinked as he straightened his posture.

"No need for the *sir* stuff. Just because Lucien Lyone is my dad doesn't mean you have to treat me a certain way."

"Sorry!" Lance grinned.

Seraph noticed that Lazarus and the other two Switchblades looked uneasy and remained silent during the interaction.

"Listen—I'll cut to the chase. I'm actually here looking for someone who can hold their own. I want to offer you a once-in-a-lifetime opportunity to join the Lyone family—if you think you can handle it."

Lance's eyes grew wide as he looked at Seraph, who had a similar expression on his face. "You want *me* to join the Lyones? Like, actually patrol the city and protect people and stuff? Like . . . a full-time job with benefits and all?"

"The whole nine yards. I will personally sponsor you if this is something you want to do. You would have to come live at the Lion's Den while you're in training. That's free room and board on top of your salary."

Lance stared quietly at Seraph, searching for guidance.

Seraph nodded at Lance. "Dude, do it! There is no way you can pass this up! Don't worry about me, brother. I can manage on my own. It's not like we won't still be friends or anything, ya know?"

"I'll tell you what—join us. Learn the ropes. Get nice and acclimated. When it comes time to recruit again, I'll put your friend first on my list," Vincent winked at Seraph.

"See, man? Who would have thought that the Lyone family would ever want anything to do with us?"

Lance loosened up a bit. "You got a point, bro," he said and then directed his attention back to Vincent. "Okay. Alright. I'm in!"

"Great!" Vincent shook Lance's hand before looking at Seraph. "What was your name?"

The young orphan regained composure and cleared his throat. "Seraph," he felt his face becoming warm.

"Seraph. Good. It won't be long before we get in touch with you," Vincent assured him, then turned to Lance. "In the meantime, I understand that you are currently staying at St. Titus? Why don't we swing by there; you can grab your things, and then I'll take you back to the Lion's Den with us tonight." He then looked at Seraph. "You can catch a ride with us, too, if you want."

They both agreed and followed Vincent and the other Lyone's through the backdoor of the Asylum. Vincent's driver pulled up his car as soon as they stepped outside. It was an expensive-looking white sedan with a large chrome grill and rims that seemed to sparkle, even in the darkness of night. The young Lyone opened one of the back doors of the car, and he and Lance climbed in.

Seraph was about to get into the passenger seat when Lazarus called out to him from the back door of the Asylum. "Wait up!"

"What's up?" Seraph turned around.

"You know where TNT's is at?"

"Right near Kings and Queens, right?"

"Yeah! You seem pretty cool, man. Me and the guys are gonna be there tomorrow night. Look for us in the back."

"Well . . ." Seraph searched for an excuse so that he could politely decline but was interrupted by Lance:

"What's the holdup?"

Seraph nodded to Lazarus. "Okay, see you then."

Vincent and the other Lyones waited out front of the orphanage while Seraph and Lance headed up to their room to pack up Lance's things.

"It probably won't be so long, bro! I mean, I dunno how long it takes for their recruiting process to start again, but I'm sure the faster you move through training and get yourself established, the sooner I'll be hearing from them for me to start my training," Seraph encouraged him.

Lance nodded. "Yeah, you're right, man. I'm gonna give it my best. Who knows. Maybe I'll even get promoted by that time. I wonder if we could be in the same squad."

"Well, I'll tell you one thing: it seems like Vincent really likes you. If you stick close to him and do what he says, I don't see why he wouldn't be willing." Seraph picked up a framed photograph of the two of them from when they were only eight years old during a holiday feast in the food hall. "Hey," Seraph handed the picture to Lance, "you should take this." Lance took the picture and studied it.

"We were just little kids," Lance smirked. "Man, I thought you were never going to hit your growth spurt! You squeaked like a rusty hinge until you were fourteen!" Seraph lunged at him and got him into a headlock. Lance gritted his teeth and forced Seraph off him with ease by digging his elbow into his ribs and flipping him onto his bed. "Nice try!"

"If you can call it that." He stood up.

Lance handed him back the photograph. "You keep it. That way you can leave it behind for the Priests to remember us once you join up."

"Good idea. Keep in touch, okay?"

"Yeah, I will. Once I finish training, I'll hit you up, and we'll get a drink together! Try not to get yourself into too much trouble while I'm away." Lance reached into his pocket, pulled out his prize money, and put it into Seraph's hand. "I want you to take this. Use it sparingly until we can get together. I'll help you out as much as I can until you're in."

"Don't worry about me. I can hold my own," Seraph pocketed the crowns. "Maybe I'm not good enough to fight at the Asylum, but that won't stop me from betting."

Lance smirked and grabbed his knapsack and slung it over his shoulder. "See you, brother."

"Sooner than later." Seraph listened to Lance's footsteps fade as he went downstairs and left the orphanage. He thought about going to the window to watch him leave but decided not to.

Seraph lay back down on his bed and looked up at the ceiling, wondering what might become of the rest of his life. Never in a million years would he have dreamed that they would someday work for the Lyone family. The two poor orphans finally had a chance to do something with their lives, and although he knew it would be challenging, it wouldn't be the same kind of struggle as before. *I know Lance will be able to handle it—no doubt about that. But what about me? When it comes down to it, will I be able to prove myself?* Seraph wondered as he closed his eyes and slowly drifted into unconsciousness.

TNT's was not your typical bar. In fact, it looked more like a convenience store than anything else. There was a wooden deck with various chairs, tables, and benches out front of the main bar area, which was where most of the patrons sat. A man sat on one of the benches strumming an acoustic guitar, while a man next to him was freestyle rapping, which sounded like a mixture of folk music and rap. Thick clouds of smoke filled the air as Seraph passed through to meet up with the Switchblades. The door jingled as he passed through the entrance into the main area and headed straight through to the back porch, which was surrounded by a tall wooden fence. He quickly spotted Lazarus and the other two from the previous night along with some additional guys whom Seraph had not yet met.

Lazarus grinned and stood up. "Hey, man! Glad you could make it!" He walked over to Seraph and touched fists with him.

Seraph looked around. The back porch was dimly lit, with citronella candles on each table. Everyone, including the Switchblades, had a bottle of beer and seemed to be smoking which was a habit Seraph had not picked up. "I appreciate you inviting me out. What's the occasion?"

Lazarus's expression became solemn. "Have a seat, my man," he motioned toward the seat across from his. "I'll get you acquainted with everyone and then give you the scoop."

They took a seat, and Lazarus introduced him to everyone present.

"This is Edge," he pointed to a shorter, stalky boy who looked to be in the same age group as Seraph and Lazarus. He then motioned towards the other one who had accompanied him the night before at the Asylum who was taller than both of them, but skinnier as well. "And this is Zero."

"Nice to meet you, guys," Seraph forced a smile.

"These two aren't members of the Switchblades, but close friends and mentors." He pointed to a heavyset man with long chin hair. He wore all black, except a dark-blue denim vest that had various spikes and studs on it. The other man was small and scraggly looking. His clothes were grungier than everyone else's, and he wore a similar vest to the heavyset man's.

"I'm Ram," the large one's voice was like gravel.

"Mongrel, nice t'meet ya." The other one scratched his hairy chin.

"Nice to meet all of you." Seraph smiled and shifted in his seat.

Lazarus looked at Zero and asked him to get a beer for Seraph, "Alright, enough build up. I'm sure you're guessing that there's more to me inviting you out than for us to become friends."

"I had a feeling. I gotta be honest with you guys, though. I don't really have any interest in joining any gangs," Seraph shifted a bit in his seat.

Zero came back and set a bottle of beer in front of Seraph and popped the top for him. Seraph turned and thanked him, before putting the bottle to his lips.

"That's not why I asked you to meet up with us. Well, initially, we were going to ask your buddy Lance if he might be interested in joining us, but now we want to warn you and him both about getting involved with the Lyones."

"Warn us about the Lyones? They protect this city. What do we have to worry about?"

Edge scoffed. "They say that they protect this city . . ."

Seraph furrowed his eyebrows, yet remained silent.

"Let's try this another way…" Lazarus thought for a moment. "Instead of us telling you a bunch of stuff, why don't I just ask you some questions?"

"Go on," Seraph tried hard to not roll his eyes.

"Do you know *how* the Lyones became the *protectors* of this city?"

"Yeah, well, they . . ." Seraph paused and thought.

"They weren't always regarded as the protectors of Royalty. Why do you think that they're so wealthy and powerful? You think they earned that? That everyone one day decided that they were going to start paying taxes to these guys to fund them to protect their neighborhoods and businesses? Do you know that's why the original gangs formed in the first place? If that's the case, then why would they feel the need to pay someone else to do what they had already been doing for centuries?" Lazarus unloaded all of these questions on Seraph and then gave him time to digest and respond.

"Okay, so what are you implying? What is it that makes the Lyone family so awful?" Seraph stifled a sigh.

"Allow me to educate you, my friend," Lazarus motioned to the empty bottle that now sat in front of him. "How 'bout another drink first?" and Seraph nodded. Edge stood up to get another round for everybody. Lazarus then produced an electronic cigarette, brought it to his lips, and took a deep drag before exhaling the water vapor through his nostrils in two thick streams. "Right around the time that I was born, the Lyone family was just a small street gang from Diamond Road. In those days, the Arch Angels were the top gang in the city. They kept the peace on Kings Avenue all the way from Bishop to Sunrise. Nobody realized at that time that the Lyones were recruiting en masse. By the time some of the other gangs *did* notice, it was too late. The Lyones began wiping out some of the small-time gangs to make an example out of them and absorb their surviving members—"

"And my gang was one of them," Ram interjected, running his fingers through his long, greasy hair.

Lazarus patted Ram on his shoulder and nodded sympathetically. "Ram is the only survivor from his old gang, the Jackals. They let him live as an example and to warn others, but also, in a twisted way, to show their *mercy*. It's all a facade."

There was silence for a moment, and then Seraph looked at Ram, "I'm sorry. But why didn't the gangs just fight them? Couldn't they have worked together to get rid of them or stop them from taking over?"

"They probably could have, honestly. There was one man who could have united the gangs in a heartbeat and stopped the Lyones dead in their tracks." Ram inhaled sharply. "But he was killed too."

Seraph's eyes grew wide. "Who?"

"Jin. The original leader and founder of the Arch Angels," Zero chimed in.

"The Lyones had him killed?"

"Who knows? Wasn't a coincidence, though. It was one of his own who killed him," Zero's face expressed utter disgust. "Blackjack."

Seraph was beginning to feel a little lightheaded and decided to cut himself off for the time being as he set the beer down on the table in front of him. "Blackjack?"

"He was the next in line for leader of the Arch Angels. One of Jin's top generals. Most people think Blackjack killed him so he could replace him. No one knows for sure. Armand, who was also a high-ranking member, and a group of loyal Angels captured him and turned him into the Golden Dragons. He's still locked up in the Dragon's Lair," Lazarus motioned behind him toward Rooke Avenue, where the prison was located. The Golden Dragons were a Sengoan gang that operated one of the few private prisons in Royalty. Sengo was an island east of the mainland. They were a lightly tanned people with slanted eyes and dark hair. Sengoans had a reputation for their martial prowess and unique style of art. Although the Golden Dragons kept the prison well-guarded, they did not act as police. The Lyone family was known to make good use of the prison by locking up anyone who didn't pay taxes or who broke their laws. This helped to maintain a good relationship between the two organizations.

"Why didn't they just have him executed?" Seraph wondered aloud.

Lazarus shrugged. "A lot of people want Blackjack dead after what he did. Even as we speak, Jin's twin sister, Rin, and her group of assassins have been raising money to pay the Lyones to hand him over to them. She would give anything to be able to avenge her brother. Personally, I think that's why they never had him killed. They keep him segregated from the other prisoners in solitary confinement just so the other prisoners can't get to him. His life is worth a fortune to certain people. Of course, the Lyones are going to capitalize on that and get as much as they possibly can for his head."

"How do you even know all of this anyway?"

"Let's just say that I have my connections and reasons for keeping certain things under wraps."

Zero nodded. "Trust me, there's stuff that even we're in the dark about."

Edge smirked and patted Lazarus on the back. "Yeah, but we trust him. He's a good dude."

Seraph couldn't help but worry about Lance. He hadn't known all of this when he was encouraging him to join up with the Lyones. *Yes, they have wealth and power and promise the same to whoever joins them, but none of that matters if they're actually corrupt. In that case, what makes them different from all the other gangs?* he thought to himself. "What can I do about Lance?" He fiddled with the empty bottle in front of him, pulling back the label.

"The real question is, how much does success, wealth, and status mean to him? He's just become part of an empire—corrupt or not. You ever hear of anyone quitting the Lyone family?" a sorrowful look formed on Lazarus's face. "If you're going to try and convince him to change his mind, best do it sooner than later—before they brainwash him completely."

Seraph stood up and started to push his chair in. "I'll head over tomorrow afternoon and tell him what's up," he started to turn towards the exit and then stopped. "Thank you." He looked at each of them. "I appreciate you all looking out. I'll let you know how it goes."

"For sure, man," Lazarus's face remained stone-still, "We'll be at the Shamrocke tomorrow night. We'll save you a seat. Be safe!"

CHAPTER TWO

Lance came out from the main gate of the Lion's Den compound, wearing the Lyone family uniform minus the bulletproof vest. He had just finished his daily training with some of the other new members, which consisted of endurance training, weight lifting, and combat. Low-ranking members of the Lyone family carried small black clubs. Officers carried pistols. Because Lance was still in training, he carried neither of these and was expected to earn his right to carry a weapon and wear the vest. The Lyone family made it a point to make sure that their newer members were physically well trained before earning full membership. Lance was already relatively fit and fought well, so he wasn't worried about being in the initiation period for too long.

Lance and Seraph clasped hands and hugged. "Good to see you, bro!" Lance gave him a couple of pats on the back.

"Yeah, man, for sure!" Seraph tried sounding casual. "Hey, you wanna go grab lunch somewhere real quick?"

Lance gave a slight frown and shook his head. "Sorry, bud, no can do. I have to stay at the compound until my training is over. We can go for a walk around the outside, though, if you wanted to talk. I've got about twenty minutes before I have to get back."

"Fair enough. Let's go for a walk."

They started walking down Noble Road, and once they had gotten away from the main gate of the compound, Lance put a hand on Seraph's shoulder, "So, what's up, man? Everything alright? Don't tell me you already spent that six hundred crowns in one night!"

Seraph laughed a little bit and then cleared his throat. "Nah, I still got all of it. It's something else, actually. I was thinking . . . is this something we really wanna do?"

Lance stopped. He had a confused look on his face. "What kinda question is that? I mean, no, it's not our childhood dream, but bro, what an opportunity! And trust me, it's cool. I mean, look at these clothes!" He fanned his arms out to display the uniform for his friend.

"I get it, man. For sure, there are a lot of perks to joining these guys, but how much do we really know about them?" still trying to take the same approach that Lazarus had taken with him.

Lance scoffed. "Come on, man. What's really going on? Vincent told you himself that you would be next on his list for potential recruits. It won't be long."

"No. It's not that, Lance. Look, I met some guys the other night. The ones that I was talking to before Vincent approached you. They were telling me some stuff. About how these guys came to power. About the things they did. The things they *continue* to do. I don't think we should be getting involved with them. I'm sure they will let you leave if you hand everything back over to them and explain that maybe this isn't for you."

"I don't want to leave." Lance's eyes locked with Seraph's. "Look, man, every gang, every organization in this city has dirt. Nobody is perfect. It's what they are doing now that makes a difference. The Lyone family protects this city and taxes the gangs because the *gangs* are the corrupt ones. They don't care about laws or structure. They want chaos. That's how things get out of hand. The Lyone family protects the city from that."

Seraph shook his head. "Their organization is built on a foundation of lies!" he raised his voice. "The Priests taught us better than that!"

They were silent for a moment. "I have been waiting my entire life for an opportunity like this. Seraph, you and I come from nothing. Our parents didn't want us. We have no connections. No hope. This is our only chance to become something! I want you with me, man, but at the same time, I can't let you stand in my way."

Seraph sighed. "Please, just think about what I said, okay?"

Lance nodded. "I gotta get back now. I'll see you around," he turned to head back toward the main gate of the Lion's Den.

Seraph watched his friend disappear around the corner. *Lazarus wasn't kidding,* he thought to himself. *Who in their right mind would abandon such an opportunity? Could it be possible that Lance was right? The gangs certainly don't have a reputation for being the good guys. Maybe the Lyones did what they did to make Royalty more civilized. Even if the outcome was good, that doesn't make what they did to achieve it right.* He decided to meet the Switchblades at the Shamrocke that evening to seek more answers.

The Shamrocke was a little different front TNT's. The people who frequented TNT's were typically grungy type people with ripped, baggy clothing and messy hairstyles with scraggly beards. They often wore colorful bracelets or armguards and lots of spikes on their clothing. Quite the contrast to the crowd at the Shamrocke. Most of the men there dressed well and had short, neat hairstyles. The women dressed casually, and most of them had long braided hair. The Shamrocke was also owned and run by the McDroogin family, which was more of a clan than a gang. They were one of the oldest gangs in Royalty, and their history ran deeper than most. Seraph stepped through the gate of the front porch, where various crowds of people tried to talk to each other over the loud fiddle music that blasted through the speakers.

Seraph entered the building and looked around. The word 'crowded' would have been an understatement. Although he had never been to the Shamrocke before, he knew it had a reputation for being one of the most popular bars in the entire city.

A middle-aged man wearing a ballcap with a fish logo approached and made eye contact with him. "What? Ya just gonna stand there blocking the door?" he raised an eyebrow.

"Sorry! Just looking for my friends," Seraph quickly moved out of the way of the entrance.

"You mean Laz and the other knuckleheads?" the man smirked.

Seraph looked confused for a moment and returned the smile. "Yep. That's them!"

The man nodded. "In the back. Corner table." He turned and pointed. "Over there, by the back door."

"Thanks!" Seraph headed over toward Lazarus and the crew.

Zero stood up as soon as he noticed their new friend, "Hey, Seraph's here!"

Lazarus and Edge followed suit and greeted their new friend.

Once they all sat down, Lazarus grabbed the handle of a large pitcher of dark beer and poured a glass for the new arrival. "Here, drink up!"

"Thanks," Seraph took a sip of the dark brew. "Mmm . . ." came the sound of satisfaction as he licked his lips.

"So, how did it go?" Lazarus broke the silence.

Seraph frowned and shook his head. "Nah . . ."

"I'm sorry, bro."

"What more can I do?" Seraph shrugged and took another sip of beer.

"So, is this your new recruit?" came the voice of the man who pointed Seraph in the direction of Lazarus and the others. He was now holding a glass of beer in his right hand and had another man with him who had blond, slicked-back hair and was wearing a black leather jacket.

Seraph and Lazarus made eye contact; "Not exactly. Er—I mean, not unless he wants to be," Lazarus shifted in his seat.

Seraph sighed. "I don't know what I want anymore."

There was a brief silence before Lazarus broke it. Pointing to the man with the hat, "This is McGregor, by the way,"—he then pointed to the blond man—"and this is

Malone. They're both captains in the McDroogin family."

"Ah, okay. Yeah, everyone knows about the McDroogins. Nice to meet you."

"Yeah, you too, kid," McGregor took a swig of his beer.

Malone nodded at Seraph and smiled.

"What do you guys do anyway?" Seraph directed his attention back to Lazarus.

The two McDroogins continued smirking as Lazarus shifted his eyes back and forth, quickly scanning the faces in the bar. "Here may not be the best place to discuss that," he said quietly.

"Sure, it is! We're all friends here!" McGregor chuckled and came around to Lazarus, playfully slugging him on the arm.

Lazarus narrowed his eyes at McGregor and then looked back toward Seraph. "I'll say it like this. We're looking to bring the balance back to Royalty."

"Balance?" Seraph raised a brow.

"He's thick, this one," McGregor rolled his eyes.

"Regarding what we were talking about before . . .?" Lazarus hinted.

"You mean about the Lyones?"

Lazarus nodded and took a drag from his electronic cigarette.

"It's what everyone wants, but they're afraid to say it. I'm tired of pretending that everything is fine. It's almost been eighteen bloody years, and the feeling is still raw. But what can we do? I'm sure Lucien Lyone would just love the opportunity to make another example out of us," Malone remarked.

"Enough, Malone! You know we ain't supposed to

bring that up," McGregor narrowed his eyes at his fellow captain.

Seraph noticed another man standing behind McGregor and Malone. He was a little younger than the other two. He had long, dirty blond hair and wore rectangular-framed glasses. "It's best that the boys know if they haven't heard already."

The two McDroogins' eyes widened as they turned around. "O'Connor, I don't think—" McGregor started, but O'Connor raised his hand and shook his head.

He looked at the four boys and nodded solemnly before recounting the tale of Ash and Rayn to them, thin tears streaming down his cheeks as he reached the part about the young lovers' deaths.

Lazarus's and Seraph's eyes met once more. "That's why we want to take them down."

Seraph watched as O'Connor stood up and walked away somberly, while Malone guided him toward the back of the pub. He sat quietly for a moment, staring at the surface of the table before nodding slowly. "Alright, I'm in."

Lazarus took a deep drag from his e-cig and exhaled a cloud of vapor. "I can't tell you too much, except that we are currently coordinating with other like-minded groups. Once we have enough people on board, we can start making moves, but in the meantime, we are liaisons working between the gangs to earn their trust and respect."

McGregor nodded slowly. "When the time comes, I'll get the boys on board. Padraeg deserves justice for the crimes of Lucien Lyone. No parent should ever suffer the loss of their child."

"Much appreciated, McGregor," Lazarus raised his glass to him.

McGregor touched glasses with Lazarus, and everyone took a deep sip from their brew.

"What do I have to do to join?" Seraph finished his beer.

The four boys stood in a circle behind TNT's, a fenced off, wooded area. The sun had set, and darkness encompassed the city of Royalty. Edge and Zero each held a lit candle with both hands. Lazarus pulled out a switchblade and pressed the button, causing the blade to flick out. He held it up in front of Seraph. "Now repeat after me…"

"I solemnly swear
To devote my life,
From this point on,
Until I die,
To restore peace to Royalty,
And to eliminate anyone
Who threatens that peace,
Even my own brother—"

Seraph hesitated but repeated the lines.

"I solemnly swear
To protect my fellow Switchblades,
To follow all orders,
And to carry out its objectives,
Even if I am the last member alive;
This, I do solemnly swear."

Lazarus then took Seraph's hand and pricked the

middle of his palm, drawing a small droplet of blood. Edge and Zero both stepped forward, allowed a drop of hot candle wax to drip on top of the wound, and then blew out their candles. Lazarus then closed the knife and embraced Seraph in a hug. "Welcome to the Switchblades, brother," he handed Seraph the knife and a folded black bandana.

"What you have to remember is, out here on the streets, all of the gangs are your enemy," Vincent instructed Lance as they cruised down Rooke Avenue.

"What do you mean, exactly?" Lance cocked his head.

"Well, like, they show respect. They pay their taxes and all that. They might even seem friendly from time to time, but beneath it all, they're parasites. They leech off of this city—off of *us*!" Vincent sneered as they passed a small group of Jade Serpents standing on the corner of Vespula Way. "You get what I'm saying?"

Lance nodded vigorously. "Yeah, I think I understand." Lance had been with the Lyone family for two months now. Unlike the other Lyones who rode with them, Lance and Vincent wore short gray trench coats with the Lyone lion head emblem on the shoulders. Their clothing was fine: designer brand dress clothes with various designs trimmed in black and gold.

Vincent had the driver bring the car to a halt next to the sidewalk closest to the vehicle, and everyone got out. Vincent adjusted his sword, which signified his position as a captain within the Lyone family, and lifted his chin toward the group of Jade Serpents. "Go collect."

Lance started forward, but Vincent pulled him back by his arm and handed him a chrome pistol.

"Take this- Y'know, just in case."

Lance swallowed and took the gun, tucking it into the waistband against his back. He approached the group of Serpents, with Vincent and the other Lyones following behind.

The Jade Serpents were one of the most eccentric gangs in Royalty when it came to fashion sense. They wore a combination of black and lime green colors with various chains and studded wristbands. The riffraff straightened up as the Lyones neared, and one of them lowered the volume on a radio that had been playing some electronic music. A Jade Serpent stepped forward with an envelope in hand and extended it toward Vincent, despite Lance being directly in front of the group.

Vincent angrily slapped the envelope away, causing it to fall to the ground. "What're ya handing it to me for? You see, my man Lance here is right in front of you! Don't you think that's a little rude?"

"It's fine, man—"

"No, Lance. He disrespected you," Vincent pointed to the envelope that was now on the ground. "Now pick it up and hand it to Lance," he commanded the Jade Serpent.

The Jade Serpent blinked and tucked his lips inwardly, his eyes locked with Lance's.

Another Serpent placed his hand on his shoulder. "Just do it, Zyre. It's not worth it."

Zyre, leader of the Jade Serpents, closed his eyes and sighed. He picked up the envelope off the ground and held it out toward Lance this time.

Vincent let out a single "*huh*" in an annoyance, "Slap it out of his hand."

At this, Zyre looked back at his people, then at

Vincent, and finally at Lance, his eyes locking once again, daring Lance to do as Vincent instructed.

"Vince—"

"Lance, do as I said."

Lance cleared his throat and met Zyre's eyes one more time before quickly bringing the back of his hand against the Jade Serpents leader's wrist, sending the envelope to the ground again.

Zyre's eyes widened in rage as he stepped forward, the rest of his gang becoming uneasy.

"Now make him pick it up again, and *this* time have him apologize for disrespecting you."

Rather than argue, Lance resolved to comply, thinking that this would be best for all parties. He pointed at the envelope and said, "Pick it up and apologize."

Zyre licked his front teeth, eyes still ablaze as he bent over once more, retrieved the envelope from the ground, and held it out to Lance. "Sorry for disrespecting you, *Lance*," he said through clenched teeth.

"I forgive you," Lance snatched the envelope from the degraded Jade Serpent and then looking back at Vincent with a smirk of satisfaction.

Vincent took the envelope, opened it, and started to count the crown bills that it contained. "Now hit him."

"Hit him?" Lance gave Vincent an uneasy look.

Vincent sighed. "What, is there an echo around here?"

Lance took a deep breath and turned to face Zyre.

The Jade Serpents shuffled and stepped forward, preparing to fight.

The two other Lyones swiftly pulled out their pistols and pointed them in the direction of the Serpents.

Vincent finished counting the money, placed the envelope in his trench coat, and brandished his own pistol, which had an ornate grip that displayed the Lyone family crest on it. "You all might want to think twice."

The Jade Serpents reluctantly stepped back in defeat while the Lyones advanced, creating distance between them and their leader, who stood helplessly in front of Lance.

Lance's breathing intensified as a bead of sweat dripped down the side of his face. *I've done this a thousand times before*, he coached himself.

Zyre shook his head and frowned, his adrenaline now having worn off. "Just do it."

Lance cocked back his right fist and sent it into Zyre's cheek, leaning into it, which caused the Jade Serpent to stumble backward a few steps.

"Again," Vincent shouted from over his shoulder.

Civilians from all over the neighborhood watched as the Lyones shook down the Jade Serpents. They watched the gang that was responsible for protecting their neighborhood from being publicly humiliated, despite paying their taxes on time.

Zyre was sent crashing to the ground as he caught a hard left hook from Lance. His face split open underneath his eye as a streak of crimson ran down his cheek.

"Good!" Vincent grinned and holstered his pistol nonchalantly as the other two Lyones followed suit and rejoined Lance. "You gotta make an example every once in a while"—he sent his neatly polished dress shoe into Zyre's solar plexus—"keep them in line, y'know?"

"Yeah . . ." Lance swallowed uneasily and nodded.

"Good. Now let's get outta this rat hole." Vincent

led his goons back to the car and everyone got in. The driver started the engine and turned the vehicle around. Vincent rolled down his window just as they were passing the Jade Serpents, who were helping Zyre to his feet. "I'll see ya next month, eh?" He laughed as his driver sped off. Vincent looked at Lance. "You understand now, right?"

"Yes, sir."

"Alright, that's all I needed to know. You see, I got something cooked up here in the near future, and I need you to be ruthless—just like that—when the time comes. They're not people, Lance. The only way this city will thrive is if we get rid of all the gangs one by one."

"Yeah, that makes sense. They don't really contribute anything to society anyway."

"Exactly! That's my father's vision. Always has been. Things've slowed down a little bit since he took over, but no worries: we're about to pick up the pace here very soon."

"What do you mean?"

"Let's just say that I've been working closely with one of my father's generals. We're going to create a little proxy war here and there between some of these slum mongrels."

"Sounds good, boss."

"Not only is this going to get Royalty that much closer to being gang free, but this is gonna get us recognized by my dad and *trust* me—I plan on taking you straight to the top with me."

"Seriously?" Lance beamed, as he felt that his dreams of success were starting to become a reality.

"Would I lie to you? You stick with me and do as I say, and we'll go far together."

CHAPTER THREE

"It's your turn to get the drinks, man!" Edge playfully shoved Zero's arm. He and the rest of the Switchblades sat in the back outside area of TNT's with the sound of live rock music blaring from the speakers.

"No way! I got them last time!" Zero shoved back.

"Here we go . . ." Kendyl, a pretty young girl who sat nestled up close to Lazarus.

Lazarus sighed and shook his head.

"Hey, relax, you two. *I'll* get the beers," Seraph put out his cigarette and stood up.

"Too late!" came Ram's voice from behind him.

"Hey!" Seraph clasped Ram's free hand as he set a case of beer on a nearby table and brought him in for a hug.

"Ram! How ya been, buddy?" Lazarus grinned, standing up and greeting him in a like manner.

"*Pfft!* I should ask you the same question. Me n' Ram ain't seen you guys around here in a hot minute," Mongrel chimed in as he joined the group of friends.

Lazarus smiled sheepishly. "Let's just say we've

been busy."

"You call that busy?" Seraph's eyebrows shot up, "I feel like I'm back at St. Titus all over again, learning church history from Brother Luther. All these history lessons and pop quizzes, sheesh!"

"Yeah, yeah. When *you're* the boss, you can decide how new recruits are taught the ropes," Lazarus chided.

"New recruit? He's been running with you cats for what, three months now?" Ram's own eyebrows ascended.

"Yeah, just about," Lazarus touched his chin.

"Those were the days, huh, Ram?" Mongrel reminisced dolefully.

Ram cleared his throat before unscrewing a bottle cap using his forearm and took a long swig. "Oh man, how rude of me!" Ram looked over toward Kendyl and Mercedes, who was Edge's girlfriend. "I didn't bring drinks for you, ladies. What are you sipping on this afternoon?"

"Just another Crescent," Mercedes swirled around her mostly empty bottle before finishing the last sip.

"I'm good." Kendyl smiled at Ram, who gave an overdramatic bow and left to get the drink for Mercedes.

"Still a sore subject after all these years, huh?" Lazarus frowned.

Mongrel nodded and took a seat near Lazarus.

Mercedes broke the silence. "How's Edge's old room workin' for you, Seraph?"

"Huh?" Seraph blinked. "Oh, yeah. It's been great. Never had my own room before."

"What, really?" Zero squinted.

"Yeah, me and Lance were paired together to share a room when we were about twelve. Before that, I was with nine other kids in the same room."

Ram returned with Mercedes' beer and sat down at the table between Lazarus and Mongrel. "What'd I miss?"

"Nothing." Seraph chuckled. "Just appreciating having my own room for once."

"You know, I thought since Edge moved in with me that I would get to see him more often. Boy, was I wrong." Mercedes smirked and looked at Kendyl, who raised her eyebrows at Lazarus and nodded.

"Well, we've been busy!" Lazarus's face flushed.

"Yeah, and you still won't tell us what you all are up to," Kendyl added.

"I know that's right, girl." Mercedes narrowed her eyes.

Edge stood up and playfully took Mercedes's head in his hands, her dyed red locks interwoven with his fingers. "What we are working on is top-secret Switchblade business, and if we told you, your lives would be in the utmost danger," he wiggled his fingers faux-ominously in her direction.

"*Psh!*" Mercedes pushed Edge's hands away.

"Uh huh . . ." Kendyl gave Lazarus a sidewards glance.

Seraph moved into Lazarus's apartment shortly after joining the Switchblades. Prior to that, Lazarus, Zero, and Edge all shared the same space. Lazarus had the master bedroom, Zero took the futon in the living room, and Seraph took over Edge's room. The Switchblades kept the apartment relatively tidy between the three of them, despite them being young men. Zero in particular was a bit of a neat freak, and Seraph noticed that he usually seemed to be straightening things up around the house in his downtime.

"You and me are lucky to be single, huh?" Zero

nudged Seraph's arm.

"Oh yeah! The single life is just *spectacular*!" Seraph rolled his eyes.

Lazarus's phone vibrated twice from the surface of the table. He picked it up and glanced at it before standing up. "I gotta take this," he gave Kendyl's shoulder an affectionate squeeze and headed back into TNT's.

"Is everything good?" Kendyl furrowed her eyebrows in Edge's direction.

Edge shrugged and took a long sip from his beer. "Far as I know."

"Don't worry, hon," Mercedes placed her hand on Kendyl's leg. "I go through the same thing with Edge and grew up with Ramón doing it too. It's just gang business."

"I always forget that your brother is coleader of the Hustlers now," Ram mentioned.

"Yeah, well, I don't," Edge looked away.

"Aww, the big tough Edge isn't afraid of my big bad brother, is he?" Mercedes teased.

Edge gave his girl a playful push. "Let's just say I'd hate to be on his bad side."

"I'd have your back, bro!" Zero grinned.

"You two are *not* fighting my brother!" Mercedes proclaimed.

"Yo, tighten up!" Lazarus returned. "We got work to do."

"What's going on, Boss?" Seraph looked up.

Lazarus glanced at Kendyl and Mercedes. "Sorry, ladies, we gotta run."

Kendyl gave Lazarus a hug and kissed him on the cheek. "Be safe, babe."

"Let's roll," Lazarus spoke sternly.

"What's up?" Zero asked once they were away from the crowd.

"There's some tension between the Immortals and the Soldiers. This might be a good opportunity to try and get the Immortals on board."

"Tension?" Seraph scratched his head.

"Yeah, well, that was then," Lazarus hastily led his gang down Castle Road across the Queen Street intersection, the atmosphere changing as a group of Amakoran gang-bangers could be seen shooting dice next to a broken-down car parked on the side of the road. "Hold up," he raised a hand. There was a small squad of Lyones ahead that were walking towards the dice players.

Seraph squinted to see if he could spot Lance among them. "It shouldn't be an issue if we just act casually, no?"

"My source tells me the Lyones have been shaking people down a lot more lately. This is exactly what I've been saying. Only a matter of time before they become more and more aggressive. Come on." Lazarus led them down an alley that connected behind Castle Road Spirits.

From Pewter, Lazarus brought the boys to Kings Avenue toward the front entrance of the Asylum. The sun was high in the sky, and Seraph could feel the inside of his jacket sticking to his skin as he perspired. Traffic flowed heavy at this time of day as most gangs and civilians alike scrambled to get lunch, which reminded Seraph that he was hungry, especially after drinking a couple of beers at TNT's.

The Switchblades entered the building and were instantly surrounded by Damien's men at the door. The Asylum was dimly lit with pink neon, except for the small fighting ring in the center of the establishment, which was almost totally dark. The bass from the electronic music surged through the four boys as their heart rates increased in unison.

"Easy fellas, we came to help," Lazarus raised his palms toward the Immortals.

"*Seraph?*" Shade, coleader of the Immortals, ignored Lazarus completely.

"That's me!"

Shade lifted his chin in the direction of the other three. "I've seen you all hanging around during fight night," he focused his attention on Seraph. "What brings you guys here?"

"Like I said, we're here to help," Lazarus lowered his hands. "I heard you all were beefin' with the Soldiers again."

"CR's beefin' with *us!*" Blitz interjected. His left eye was nearly swollen shut.

"What happened?" an uncomfortable look displayed on Seraph's face.

Damien approached and placed a hand on Blitz's shoulder. "One of the Soldiers jumped him last night. When me and Shade went to confront them about it, they outright denied it and then threatened to bust up the Asylum if we didn't leave."

Lazarus stroked his goatee. "What if it wasn't really them though?"

"Not really *them?*" Blitz looked insulted, "I got jumped by three Amakorans *right* across the street from their projects!"

"So, what's the plan, then?" Lazarus challenged.

"I don't know," Damien sighed "but we can't just let this slide."

"What if we went to go talk with them?" Seraph suggested, catching surprised glances from everyone.

"Seraph, Castle Road Projects is no joke. They do *not* like Sartovans around their neighborhood," Lazarus cautioned.

"So, what then? We join the Immortals to start a war against the Soldiers? What would that accomplish?" Seraph tried to reason.

"No, *they* started this!" Damien insisted.

"It doesn't matter," Seraph raised his voice. "What do we gain from fighting them?"

"What's this *we* business?" Blitz didn't hide his skepticism, "What do *you* all gain from helping us anyway?"

"Good question, Blitz." Damien looked at Seraph. "Well?"

Lazarus cleared his throat. "There's something bigger at stake here."

"Well, what is it?" Shade's eyes met Lazarus's.

"We need your help to take down the Lyone family."

Damien looked around at his men, perplexed. "What do you mean?"

"We want to bring an end to the Lyone family's corruption. We're trying to bring as many gangs together as we can to go up against them and change things in Royalty for good."

"Are you serious?" Blitz wondered if Lazarus was joking.

"No disrespect, kid, but you probably weren't even alive when the Lyones took over. Back then, I was about your age. Do they even tax you guys?" Damien's eyebrows rose.

"Well, no, but—"

"Maybe we weren't alive yet, Damien, and maybe they don't tax us," Lazarus spoke, "but what they've done has affected us all in one way one another."

Damien nodded. "There's no doubt about that, but come on, guys—is it really that bad?"

"Considering what the Lyone's have done to come into power, yes and it'll get much worse, trust me.," Lazarus answered. "You can count on it. They've been stepping up their game against the gangs a lot more lately. It's only gonna get worse from here."

Shade shook his head. "Look, I'm sorry, guys, but that's just not something we want to get into. If the Lyones really killed a lot of people to be where they are right now. Just imagine what they would do to keep it that way."

"Well, one thing is for sure: whether it's the Castle Road Soldiers or the Lyone family, there is going to be bloodshed either way," Edge looked gravely at the Immortals.

"Look, at least let us try to talk to the Soldiers as a show of good faith," Seraph volunteered.

"*Seraph*, I got this," Lazarus fumed under his breath.

"If you got the balls to go and try, all the power to you," Damien shrugged, "but no matter what, we are going to need some sort of justice for what they did to Blitz."

"Don't worry. We'll work something out."

Lazarus sighed. "Sure—if we survive long enough."

The Switchblades exited the Asylum through the back door, back onto Castle Road. They stood directly across the street from the entrance of the Castle Road projects and a row of old apartment buildings. They heard loud Amakoran hip-hop music, and the faint smell of scratch permeated the air.

"Lead the way, *boss*," Lazarus held his hand out to invite Seraph to lead the group.

"Isn't this the whole reason why we came here?" Seraph huffed as he stopped and faced Lazarus.

"You could have at least given me a minute or two to think of the best solution to this. I'm the leader here. You can't just-" Lazarus was cut off as a silver sedan screeched to a halt in front of the Switchblades as they started to cross the street, causing them all to leap back.

"What the hell is this?" Edge watched as the doors opened and a squad of Lyones stepped out, led by Vincent Lyone and Lance.

"There you are!" Vincent approached Seraph and the others.

"You've been looking for me?" Seraph's left eyebrow shot up.

"Well, yeah! Honestly, I was about to give up. Lance seemed to think you might not be interested in joining anymore, but I'm a man of my word."

"Oh."

"*Oh?* Was Lance right after all?"

"Well, I—"

"I see. You couldn't wait any longer, so you joined these guys here? What gang do you represent?"

"Uh, we're the Switchblades, man," Lazarus cleared his throat.

"The Switchblades, *man?*" Vincent mocked. "And do the Switchblades pay their taxes, or do they just operate under the radar?"

"We're more like a brotherhood—"

"We're not paying you anything," Seraph stepped forward.

"Is that so?" Vincent smirked and closed his eyes for a brief moment before springing forward and uppercutting Seraph in the gut.

"*Oof!*" Seraph gasped as he stepped back and clutched his midsection.

Lance and Seraph looked at each other. "Don't worry about them, Vince," Lance came to Vincent's side and straightening out his long gray coat.

"I won't. You take care of him."

Lance and Seraph exchanged glances once more. "That's not—"

"Yeah, Lance. Take care of me!" Seraph straightened up and raised his fists.

"Seraph, no!" Lazarus attempted to hold his friend back.

"I got this," Seraph insisted, shaking Lazarus away and stepping toward Lance. "Let's go, tough guy!"

"Fine." Lance sighed, removed his gray coat, and rolled up the sleeves of his blood-red dress shirt.

Seraph lunged forward with a right hook that caught Lance on the cheek.

"*Damn!*" Lance cursed and stepped back, bringing up his guard.

"*Heh.*" Seraph scoffed and threw a few more punches in Lance's direction.

"Come on, Lance!" Vincent shouted.

The Switchblades silently watched in horror.

Lance shook his head and dove at Seraph's legs, dragging him to the pavement. Lance attempted to mount his adversary, but Seraph wedged his knee between them.

Lance broke the gap between them pressed his head against Seraph, grabbed him by the forearms, and lifted his upper half quickly before slamming him down into the road several times.

"*Ah!*" Seraph felt his strength and energy begin to leave him. By this point, a crowd had gathered from the projects across the street. The Immortals were also watching from the back door of the Asylum.

"*Hmph!*" Lance got back to his feet, and dusted himself off. "Next time, watch how you talk to me," he warned and then planted a firm kick into Seraph's side.

"*Urgh!*" Seraph groaned and rolled over.

Vincent handed Lance back his coat.

Lazarus, Edge, and Zero rushed to Seraph's side.

"You better have something for me when I see you next time, understand?" Vincent's eyes narrowed at Lazarus.

"Yeah," Lazarus caught the glance for just a moment before focusing back on his friend.

"Let's go!" The Lyones got into the car and drove off toward Knights Way.

"Damn it, Seraph," Lazarus said through clenched teeth.

"You got some stones, lil' homie," came an unfamiliar voice.

The Switchblades looked up to see a group of Amakoran's led by a tall, slender man. They all wore dark-blue baggy jeans, a white T-shirt, and a green, military-style jacket—the colors of the Castle Road Soldiers.

"Thanks," Seraph propped himself up with his elbow.

"I seen you told that Vincent dude that you wasn't gonna pay him. Honestly, we surprised they ain't killed you f'that," the leader smirked.

"You don't have to pay them either," Seraph brought himself to a sitting position.

The Soldiers' eyes widened. "Whatchu mean?"

"I mean"—Seraph stood up with some help from Lazarus and Zero—"if you quit your beef with the Immortals and work together with us, we can get rid of the Lyones, and no one will have to pay taxes ever again."

"Dang, man. You really are crazy," said one of the Soldiers, which made the others start laughing.

"For one, we don't got no beef with the Immortals. I already done told that to Damien," the leader shrugged.

"Then why the hell did your guys jump Blitz, Deonte?" Damien and the other Immortals approached.

This didn't seem to faze the Castle Road Soldiers, who stood still and stared them down.

"It wasn't us, dawg."

"Hol' up!" one of the Soldiers said. "I seen some cats around here yesterday. They was Amas, but they wasn't no Soldiers."

"Whatchu mean, Jerel?" Deonte looked towards his associate.

"I mean, if it was them, then maybe that's where all da confusion comes from," Jerel rubbed his chin.

"Why didn't you say anything when Damien n' his boy came the otha night then?" Deonte sighed.

"Shoot, I dunno, dawg. I didn't think of it."

"You see, Damien. It was probably them other dudes Jerel talkin' bout," Deonte offered to the leader of the Immortals.

"It's like a conspiracy, man. Maybe someone tryna set us up," Jerel suggested.

"Unbelievable." Damien shook his head. "Do I really look that stupid?"

"Wait . . ." the gears in Lazarus's head began to turn. "Has there been a bigger presence of Lyones in the area lately?"

"Now that you mention it . . ." Deonte looked at his men, who all nodded with surprised looks on their faces.

"What does that have to do with anything?" Damien looked from Deonte to Lazarus.

"This is what we've been trying to tell you!" Lazarus stressed. "This is why we have to work together before it really hits the fan."

"I don't know, man," Deonte looked back at his men.

"We got your back, bro," Damien stepped forward and placed a hand on Lazarus's shoulder.

"Thanks."

"If you all won't join us, can you at least continue the peace treaty with us until all of this Lyone business is over?" Damien locked eyes with Deonte as the two leaders approached one another.

"The treaty was never broken in the first place, homie." Deonte smiled as he and Damien clasped hands and embraced.

"Perfect," Damien looked at Lazarus. "So, what now?"

"We gotta figure out which gang to approach next."

"What about the Bishops? They the biggest Amakoran gang in Royalty," Jerel suggested.

"Bishop is even more dangerous than CRP, but . . ." Lazarus smiled at Deonte and said, "—no offense."

"Don't worry 'bout it."

"But what?" Seraph hadn't learned much about the Bishops from Lazarus yet.

"Laz used to sell scratch for them before he started the Switchblades," Zero blurted out.

"You *sold* scratch?" Seraph narrowed his eyes at Lazarus.

"That was another life," Lazarus gave Zero a sidewards glance.

"You think Turrell might be down to help?" Edge lit up a cigarette.

"I sorta ended our relationship abruptly and Turrell isn't known to forgive debts easily," Lazarus admitted, "but maybe I can try to patch things up."

"I'd offer to write a letter of recommendation if we was on mo' familiar terms with the Bishops," Deonte joked sympathetically.

"Ha, thanks. I'm gonna need some time to figure this one out."

"Well, one thing you oughta know is that unlike us and the Immortals, the Bishops really is beefin' with the Disciples, so if y'all do go to them, expect to get y'alls hands bloody," Deonte admonished.

"This might just be the opportunity we needed," Seraph remained optimistic.

"I'm with Lazarus on this one," Damien didn't hide his pensiveness, "Take some time to think it over."

"Yeah," Shade agreed. "In the meantime, why not hang around with us for a while? I can show you some moves too, Seraph."

Seraph smirked as he clutched his ribs. "I may have to take you up on that."

"Yeah, n' if y'all need some heat, I gotchu," Deonte

proposed.

Seraph and the Switchblades spent the next couple of months around the Immortals. Staying under the radar was a top priority, so during the weekly fight night at the Asylum, the Switchblades went to TNT's and spent time with Ram and company. Blitz took the liberty of recording the fights and in his downtime would watch the highlights with the boys, pointing out techniques and faults, teaching them the science of fighting. Meanwhile, Shade handled the physical aspect, from proper form to defense and grappling. It didn't take long for Edge to prove to be the best fighter of the four.

"No, Seraph, like *this*," Edge instructed as he gripped the back of Zero's thigh just above the knee and lifted his leg.

Zero landed on his back with a soft thud. "Why am I always the test dummy?"

"Because you're the skinniest," Edge teased and helped him up.

Zero brushed himself off. "I'm gonna go hit the head."

"Alright. Seraph and Lazarus. Let's see if you two learned anything," Shade directed.

Lazarus smirked at Seraph as he climbed into the ring between the ropes. They touched fists and squared up before Shade stepped back and shouted, "*Fight!*"

Seraph and Lazarus danced around in a circle, trading unsuccessful jabs. Seraph attempted a right hook, but rather than connecting the punch, he caught Lazarus's left fist on the cheek.

"*Oof!* C'mon, Seraph!" Blitz coached.

Seraph shook away the pain, came back, and feinted a kick to Lazarus's ribs but instead came at him with a left hook. Lazarus sidestepped his attack with ease and landed his left fist into Seraph's cheek a second time.

Seraph's face now contorted in anger as he pretended to come at Lazarus with a right haymaker. Lazarus prepared to weave the oncoming assault as Seraph quickly switched and planted a left uppercut into Lazarus's diaphragm, followed up by grabbing a hold of his thigh like Edge had previously demonstrated and lifted his leg, throwing Lazarus off balance and sending him to his back. Seraph swiftly mounted him and chambered his fist.

"Alright, alright! You got me, man!" Lazarus wheezed.

Seraph got to his feet, then helped Lazarus up. "Good fight, bro."

"Yeah, sure." Lazarus hunched over, catching his breath.

"Not bad at all, Seraph," Shade came over to them and patted Seraph on the back. "You alright, Laz?"

"I'll be okay," Lazarus reached into his pocket, retrieving his e-cig and taking a long drag.

"Oh, yeah. Like that's gonna help!" Seraph rolled his eyes.

"You're one to talk, bro. You smoke like a chimney!"

"Yeah, and who's the one who got me started in the first place?"

"Uh huh." Lazarus put the electronic cigarette back into his pocket. "Last I checked, you were a big boy, capable of making your own decisions."

"Okay, you two, settle down," Shade shook his head

and laughed.

"We're just bustin' chops." Lazarus smirked and punched Seraph on the arm.

"Is it over already?" Zero stepped out of the restroom.

"Alright, fellas! We gotta get this place straightened up for tonight!" came Damien's voice as he stepped out from his office behind the bar. "What do you all got going on tonight?"

Lazarus shrugged and looked at the other Switchblades. "I was just gonna hit up TNT's."

"Same," Seraph looked toward Zero.

"Can't tonight, guys. I told my sister I'd spend some time with her and my aunt this weekend."

"How is Mara doing anyway?" Lazarus met eyes with his associate.

"She's good. Got a job at Marty's recently."

"That means a free cappuccino once in a while, right?" Lazarus bantered.

"Ha, you know Marty's never hassled us before." Zero laughed.

"I'll be in the neighborhood, myself. Got a date with my lady," Edge smiled looking toward the ceiling.

"We should go together, since we're headed in the same direction," suggested Zero.

"That is not a bad idea," Lazarus leaned against the ropes of the ring.

"Definitely. Just cause I'm dating Ramón Torres's sister doesn't give me a free pass. Trust me." Edge sighed and lifted his chin toward Zero. "Let's go while it's still light out."

"Cool," Zero held up the "peace" sign. "Later

dudes!"

Lazarus and Seraph smiled at one another. "Let's go, bro!" Lazarus held the ropes open for Seraph to step out of the ring.

"Huh, no Ram or Mongrel," Seraph observed as he and Lazarus made their way through the back door of TNT's after buying their beers.

"Eh, sometimes they don't show up till later."

Seraph lit up a cigarette. "Looks like it's just us, boss."

Lazarus nodded. They watched the opening band began bringing their sound equipment into the establishment. "Hey, I've been meaning to mention something to you."

"What's up?"

"I should have said something sooner, but we've been so preoccupied, I haven't really had a chance to say that you did a good job with that whole situation between the Immortals and the Soldiers," Lazarus smiled with sincerity.

"I didn't do anything special, man."

"Are you kidding? You totally took the initiative when it came to helping Damien and his crew. Plus, the way you stood up to Vincent Lyone . . . you got stones, man. I'll admit that I wasn't too happy about it at the time, but looking back, that was pretty brave of you, brother." Lazarus raised his bottle to Seraph.

"I dunno what to say, Laz," Seraph was unsure if he had ever received such a heartfelt compliment.

"Just accept it for what it is." Lazarus grinned and briefly gripped Seraph's shoulder. "You're a good guy and you got potential to be a good leader."

Leader? Seraph thought to himself. "Uh, so . . ." he cleared his throat, "any thoughts about the Bishops yet?"

"I hate to throw us into this kinda situation, but we should strike while the iron is hot."

"So, war, huh?"

"Yep. That is, if Turrell will even accept our help."

"Dang, that bad?"

"If there's one thing about Turrell, it's that he's a businessman and does not like his enterprise disrupted."

"What made you stop selling for them anyway?"

"That, my friend, is a story for another time."

"Come on, Ramón, he's a good guy!" Mercedes pleaded with her older brother, coleader of the Hustlers, as he and a small group of his people cornered Edge in a dead-end alley.

"So, you just decided you was gonna move in with my little sister without my permission first?" Ramón and his men advanced upon him.

"She's a big girl," Edge sneered "Didn't think it was necessary."

"*Ramón!*" Mercedes was afraid that this would trigger his rage.

"Yo, get her out of here!" Ramón instructed one of his men, who guided Mercedes away from the alley, as she made a futile attempt to fight back. "I'm gonna make sure you never see her again, punk. Yo, Chicho, crank it up."

The Hustler called Chicho grinned and turned up the music in a nearby lowrider. The repetitive L'Orandan beat drowned out all the sound in the area as Ramón and the other Hustlers closed in on the lone Switchblade.

Edge twisted his face at them and brought up his

fists. "Come on, then!"

Ramón smirked in amusement and drew in a sharp breath as he chambered his fists.

"*Hey*!" a deep, masculine voice shouted. "Back off."

Ramón's expression quickly changed as he and his crew turned around to face a man with a youthful complexion whose hair was dyed white. He wore black dress clothes, with the shirt unbuttoned at the top, and a navy-blue trench coat that had a silver sword with a wings emblem on the left shoulder. "Ghost . . ." Ramón said under his breath.

Ghost looked directly at Edge and motioned with his finger for him to come.

"W-wait!" Ramón's face contorted. "This doesn't concern you!"

Ghost raised his eyebrows, standing statuesque as Edge slinked past Ramón with an arrogant smirk. "It *does* concern me. Consider the kid untouchable. Is that understood?"

Ramón frowned and looked back at his crew, who silently shook their heads.

"Come on," Ghost led Edge safely out of the alley.

Edge looked over his shoulder as he stepped onto the sidewalk of Queen Street. "Wow, man. Thanks a—" he started to say but stopped suddenly, realizing Ghost had vanished. "Thanks a lot."

"So, you mean to tell me that Ghost from the Arch Angels saved you from an ass beating?" Lazarus almost choked on his beer once Edge and Zero rejoined him, Seraph, Ram and Mongrel at TNT's.

"Dude, I know! I couldn't believe it!" Edge

reiterated.

"I thought the Arch Angels were supposed to be pretty sketch, no?" Seraph sought clarification.

"*Psh!* This doesn't prove otherwise," Ram's expression showed apparent antipathy. "There's always an ulterior motive with them."

"Look, alls I know is he saved my skin and then disappeared."

"Like a… *Ghost?*" Lazarus joked as the others joined in the laughter with him.

"Whatever, bro!" Edge huffed. "I just can't figure out when he would care to help me. I never even met the guy."

"So, guys," Lazarus cleared his throat and looked around at his friends. "Seraph and I think it's time we approach Bishop."

Everyone's expressions abruptly became blank as they stared at the leader of the Switchblades.

"You sure, man?" Ram expressed concern.

"Yeah. It's piss or get off the pot at this point."

Ram nodded.

"You kids just be safe out there, huh? If things get crazy, it's okay to bail, you know?" Mongrel frowned.

Lazarus shook his head. "No. We do this, or we don't."

Seraph stood and raised his bottle. "I'll drink to that!" he placed a hand on Lazarus's shoulder.

"Yeah!" Edge stood, also raising his bottle.

Zero cleared his throat and raised his bottle too. "I'm with you till the end, brothers!"

"I guess this's goodbye for now." Lazarus offered Ram a hand.

Ram pushed Lazarus's hand away and embraced him in a bear hug. "It would have been either way."

"Huh?" Lazarus shot Ram a puzzled look as the massive man released him.

"Yeah, me n' Mongrel got a project we're working on."

"Not another band, I hope . . ." Lazarus ridiculed. "I mean, you guys can jam, but—"

"It's not another band, dufus." Ram playfully shoved Lazarus's shoulder.

"Heh," Lazarus chuckled. "Be easy, bro."

"Yeah, you too," Ram replied pensively.

CHAPTER FOUR

The Bishop projects were more populated than Seraph had expected. As they crossed Diamond Road and entered the Bishop Brotherhood's territory, the four Switchblades caught glares from a group of older Amakoran boys standing on the corner who looked to be engaged in a game of dice before they turned their attention to the Switchblades. Lazarus simply smiled and nodded to them as he led his crew toward the apartments where Turrell, leader of the Bishops, was supposed to live.

The atmosphere had now completely changed, as they quickly realized that they were the only ones in the neighborhood who were of Sartovan decent, except for Zero, who was half L'Orandan. Amakoran hip-hop filled their ears as they passed another group gathered around a stylish purple car with large tires and shiny golden rims. Again, they caught unwelcoming looks as uneasiness began to overwhelm them.

"You know where you at, white boys?" came an adolescent voice from the group of boys playing dice.

They turned around, and Lazarus stepped forward. "It's all good, lil' homie. Just comin' to see Turrell."

"Lil' homie? *Maaaaaan*, you best chill out with that," the leader approached Lazarus at an uncomfortably close distance. "And Turrell don't wanna see no beak-nosed Sars anyway, so you can go now."

"Come on, man. We don't want any trouble. I got a business proposal for T."

"Yeah? He expectin' you then?" the boy's face expressed an annoyed look.

"Well, I lost contact with him some time ago."

The boy rolled his eyes and shoved Lazarus so hard that he fell to the ground. "Dawg, get the hell on outta here!"

"Hey!" Seraph stepped in front of Lazarus as Edge and Zero rushed to help their leader to his feet.

"What?" the boy lifted his baggy white T-shirt, revealing the black grip of a pistol tucked into his jeans.

Seraph swallowed and locked eyes with the kid, raising his hands slowly.

"*Seraph* . . ." Lazarus groaned.

"That's what I thought, sucka!" the Amakoran chuckled and lowered his shirt. "Now get!"

Seraph sighed and shook his head as he turned to face his friends. "Now what?"

Lazarus shrugged when a black SUV pulled up next to them, and five adult Amakorans, all wearing a combination of purple and black, got out and surrounded the Switchblades, shoving them into one another as they encircled them.

"What's up, fool? Y'all tryna flex on my lil' nephew?" asked one who had a short afro and a thin goatee.

He wore a tight black sleeveless undershirt and baggy blue jeans, with a purple bandana hanging out of the back pocket.

"Nah, man. We were coming through to see Turrell," Lazarus raised his hands.

"Turrell don't know you!" the group he was with all burst into laughter.

"Wait, ain't that Lazarus?" a different one squinted at the leader of the Switchblades. This man had short hair and a medium-length beard.

"Shoot, I think you right, Ezra," another said.

"*Lazarus?*" the first man got directly in Lazarus's face. "Don't you owe T some crowns?"

"Look, man, I'll pay whatever I owe him, just—"

"Oh, yeah?" Money ain't a problem no mo'?" the Amakoran nodded to his men who all grinned. "Shake 'em down."

The other with him, except for the one named Ezra, began reaching into the four boys' pockets, taking their wallets, keys, money—whatever they had on them. Seraph attempted to resist but caught a hard fist just under his eye.

"Get their shoes too!" the ringleader laughed as he pocketed a wad of crowns that were rolled up and fastened with a rubber band. "Damn, Laz. You ballin' now, ain't you?"

Lazarus exhaled and bit down on his lips, looking away as he noticed a red sedan pulling up slowly.

"DeAndre!" one of the Bishops cried out.

"*Disciples!*" Ezra roared. "Move!"

The Bishops instantly spread out and drew their guns. As the red car cruised by, with all its windows down, a different group of Amakorans clad in blood red opened fire indiscriminately. While the two gangs exchanged bullets, the Switchblades did their best to get out of the line of fire. Seraph ended up taking cover behind the Bishops' SUV as the continuous loud popping cracked off and the smell of gunpowder infiltrated their nostrils.

"*Edge!*" Seraph placed his hand on his friend's shoulders.

Edge groaned and blinked as he checked his side, seeing that a bullet had pierced him.

Seraph started to panic, looking around, trying to figure out how to help his friend. "Help! Edge is hit!"

The Bishop named Ezra dove behind the SUV right next to Edge, reloaded his pistol, swiftly popped up from behind the hood of the vehicle, and unloaded his gun at the Disciples' car as it drove off toward Diamond Road and then knelt back down next to Edge once more. "You a'ight?"

Edge looked up at Ezra and then down at his wound. "I think so."

"Put pressure on it," Ezra told Seraph, who quickly obeyed.

"What do we do?" sweat dripped from Seraph's forehead.

"*We?*" Ezra shook his head and then reached into his pocket, took out his phone and tossed it to Seraph. "Call the Priests, man. They'll get him straight."

Seraph swallowed and nodded, immediately feeling anxious at the mention of the Royal Priests. "Okay," he began dialing Brother Calvin's personal phone.

A cloud of smoke seemed to hover above the shootout site as every one of the Bishops reloaded their weapons and started to check for causalities. A loud yell pierced the air as everyone crowded around one of the fallen Bishops who lay dead in the middle of the street.

"Jon Jon!" DeAndre wailed.

"*Seraph?*" Brother Calvin answered, but Seraph's attention was on the Bishops who were grieving over the death of the young Amakoran who had initially confronted him and his gang. "*Seraph, are you there?*" came Calvin's voice once more.

Seraph snapped out of his daze. "Yeah! Yes, sorry! We need the Priests here at Bishop and"—he looked up at the crooked street sign—"and Stone. There was a drive-by."

"*We'll be right there! Are you okay?*"

"Yeah!" Seraph looked down and scanned his body briefly. "Please hurry!"

"Thanks, bro . . ." Edge groaned in pain as tears ran down his cheeks.

"You're gonna be okay," Seraph continued keeping pressure on the wound.

"He's going to be alright," Brother Calvin told the Switchblades as a couple Priests lifted Edge onto a stretcher and got him in the ambulance.

"Thank you," Seraph met eyes with Calvin.

"Do you have a moment, Seraph?"

Seraph looked at Lazarus. "Go ahead, man. I'm gonna try to talk to the Bishops," Lazarus and Zero walked over to DeAndre and Ezra.

Calvin looked at Seraph and frowned. "What did you get yourself involved in?"

"I . . ." Seraph began, unsure of how much he could say. Calvin was nearly ten years older than him, and he had always seen him as a big brother, so he didn't like that he had disappointed him.

"You're not a bad guy, Seraph, but making choices like this—running with gangs? Why?"

"It's worse than it looks, Calvin. There's bigger things at stake."

"Bigger things?" Brother Calvin's face tightened as he pointed toward the body bag that Jon Jon was being zipped up in. "That could have been you!"

Seraph watched as the Priests carried the young kid away in the body bag and shook his head.

"Seraph, it's not too late to come back home. I heard about Lance joining the Lyone family. It makes sense that you would get mixed up in this, but this doesn't have to be you. You can still come back."

"I can't. You wouldn't understand. Not yet."

"Your friend—Edge, he's gonna be all right. I'll call you when he can go home. He's gonna need at least a month to recover after we get him stitched up."

"Thanks . . ."

"Be safe out there, Seraph." Calvin tightened his lips, then motioned to the other Royal Priests. "Let's go!"

The Royal Priests piled into the ambulance and drove off down the road toward St. Titus.

Seraph approached Lazarus, Zero, and the Bishops.

"—and how you gonna help? Four-no, three of you. No guns. No experience. Whiter than milk. Useless," DeAndre said.

"Just give us a chance! Trust me, man. You won't be sorry," Lazarus said.

"Why not see what Turrell says?" Ezra asked DeAndre.

"Shoot! And risk pissin' him off by bringing these lil' punks to him? They ain't even got nothin'."

At that moment, a black luxury car equipped with chrome rims and elevated on hydraulics, followed by a convoy of four other vehicles pulled up next to them. DeAndre and Ezra abruptly straightened up and fell silent as the back door opened up and out stepped a short man with dreadlocks with blond tips. He wore a black sleeveless undershirt tucked into baggy jeans and a long gold chain that a had a pendant of praying hands hanging from it.

"Laz, is that you, baby?" The man grinned with a pearl-white smile.

Lazarus returned the smile and approached the man. "Yeah, T. How ya been?"

The two clasped hands and embraced. "What happened here?" Turrell asked, lifting his chin toward DeAndre.

"The Disciples came through, man. Shot up Jon Jon," DeAndre replied through clenched teeth.

Turrell's face dropped. "Oh, we gon' get them," he swore and then looked back at Lazarus. "As you can see, we got some pressing matters at hand, so what can I do for you?"

"Let us help you hit them back," Lazarus said.

"What?" Turrell narrowed his eyes at Lazarus. "You go mercenary or somethin'?"

"Not quite. I was thinking maybe you could repay a favor for a favor."

"I'm listenin'."

"We're gonna be going up against the Lyones, and we're gonna need every gang that we can get to help. We already have others down to fight. If we help you take care of the Disciples, in return maybe you could help us"

The Bishops all laughed at Lazarus. Even Turrell chuckled and looked away. "Who you got?"

"I can't say right now, but they're solid."

"Uh huh. Tell ya what, Laz. Since we used to do business together, I'll talk to my generals and see what they say. Y'all ain't got plans tonight, do you?"

"Nah, man."

"Good," Turrell nodded to Ezra. "Yo, Laz and his boys gon' ride with you back to the crib, a'ight?"

"F'sho."

"What about the Disciples?" DeAndre's eyebrows tightened.

"We gon' discuss that too." Turrell got back into his car, which pulled away toward a large apartment building.

The neighborhood seemed to return to normal as the Bishops and Switchblades got in the vehicles and followed Turrell. The street was littered with bullet casings, and the smell of gunpowder lingered as the civilians of Bishop continued on with their day as if nothing had happened.

To the Switchblades' surprise, Turrell's home was much cleaner and organized than the neighborhood it was in. Lazarus had been to Turrell's house plenty of times in the past, but it seemed even more well-kept than before. Turrell and his generals went into one of the back rooms while a few of his lieutenants sat in the living room with Lazarus and his crew. The Bishops stared at the Switchblades with contempt as they sat across from them in silence.

"Did y'all want something to drink?" came a feminine voice from the entranceway of the kitchen.

"No thanks—*Charita*? Hey, girl!" a big smile formed on his face as he recognized Turrell's girlfriend.

"I thought that was you, Lazarus! How you been?" Charita stepped into the living room.

"Been alright, I suppose. Just came here to meet with Turrell"

"You mean my *husband*," Charita grinned.

"Husband? You two got married?"

"Haha, yeah! Right around the time you disappeared."

"Oh . . ."

"Hey, things happen. I get it." She smiled and shook her head.

"Lazarus,"—the door to the back room opened as one of Turrell's men poked his head out—"you and your boys can come back."

They entered the back room, which was dimly lit. The Bishop generals sat around a large round glass table. "Have a seat," Turrell said.

They sat down and looked around the table, anxious to hear what decision they had made.

"A'ight, Laz, here's what's gon' happen," Turrell cleared his throat. "We're taking the Disciples' little hit on Jon Jon as a war declaration, so of course, there needs to be some retaliation."

Lazarus swallowed and looked at Seraph and Zero, who looked equally uneasy.

Turrell smirked. "You boys are gon' go hit 'em back. Because you all are Sartovan, they ain't gon' suspect anything if they see y'all, so we want it done while you can still take 'em by surprise. You do this, and your debt is cleared with the Bishop Brotherhood."

The Bishop generals all smirked, except for Ezra, who remained quiet and stared at the Switchblades, expressionless.

"And what about helping us against the Lyones?"

"That will be determined after you complete the task at hand."

Lazarus shook his head. "We ain't doing anything unless we have your guarantee that you'll join our cause."

"No, Lazarus. You owe us. You lucky I didn't send some boys after you when you just decided to cut ties with us all of a sudden. Now,"—Turrell stood up and retrieved a pistol from his waistband and placed it on the table with the barrel pointed toward Lazarus—"you gonna do this or we gon' find another way to resolve that debt. Understand?"

Lazarus raised his hand. "Yo, relax, man! I get the message. If we hit the Disciples, that's gonna bring a lot of heat to our gang and pull us into this war."

"We know. After you handle that, you can stay with my man here," he pointed to Ezra. "Y'all can't officially be Bishops cause of y'all's complexion, but you'll still roll with Ezra's crew until the beef is over."

"Okay, that's fair. Look, Turrell, we're gonna fight for Bishop and do our best to help against the Disciples, but I want you to highly consider helping us against the Lyones. This affects the whole city—Bishops included. We remove them from the equation, and this recurring stuff with the Disciples will be a thing of the past."

"Not unless we kill every last one of 'em," DeAndre chimed in, and the rest of the Bishops nodded solemnly.

"Duly noted, Laz," Turrell closed his eyes for a brief moment. "Now go on and take care of it. I don't care how you do it as long as they bleed sevenfold for what they did to Jon Jon. Call me when it's done," he wrote his number on a napkin and passed it over.

"Got it."

Turrell picked up the gun from the table and tucked it back into his waistband. "You better not screw this up."

"I'm sorry I got you all involved in this mess." Lazarus sighed before taking a long drag from his electronic cigarette as the three sat on one of the benches at the community park in Bishop.

Zero patted Lazarus on the back. "It had to be done, man."

"Yeah, Laz. Don't beat yourself up. We knew what we were getting into," Seraph sympathized.

"Yeah, I just . . ." Lazarus frowned and shook his head.

"I wish instead of fighting the Disciples that maybe we could make peace between them and the Bishops and have them *both* help us against the Lyone family," Zero deliberated.

"Well, couldn't we try?" Seraph wondered aloud.

Lazarus shot Seraph a sideward glance. "You aren't so familiar with the Disciples, huh?"

"I mean, I know they're pretty violent and stuff, but they can't be any worse than the Bishops, can they?"

"You'd be surprised," Zero frowned.

"Yeah, you know how Turrell let me off, even though I cut ties with him? Letrelle would have killed me for that without a second thought."

"They're ruthless, bro," Zero shook his head.

"They are. I half wonder if they intended to kill

that poor kid earlier," Lazarus suggested.

"So, what's the plan?" Seraph shifted uneasily. "I never killed anyone before."

"Yeah, us neither, and I'm not exactly sure I want to."

"What other way is there?"

"I wonder if we could attack the Disciples without killing them," Lazarus attempted to think outside of the box.

"Like espionage?" Zero rubbed his chin.

"Sorta. Like, what if we found their ammo cache or where they keep their money? Or maybe hit one of their drug labs or something?"

"Or hit *all* of their drug labs," Seraph smirked. "No drug labs, no drug production. No distribution. No compensation."

Lazarus's face lit up. "Seraph, you're a freakin' genius, man! I think this could work. Truth be told, people are still going to get hurt and most likely die, but if we're careful, maybe we don't have to risk any unnecessary casualties."

"You think we should still consider getting some protection? Ya know, just in case things go south?" Zero tried to hide his anxiety.

Lazarus nodded. "Probably not a bad idea."

"The Castle Road Soldiers told us they could hook us up if we need it." Seraph reminded the group.

"Good idea. Let's get a move on before I lose my nerve."

The Castle Road Soldiers treated the Switchblades with respect and sold them three semiautomatic pistols at a discounted rate because of their previous interaction with the gang. Deonte cautioned them about how dangerous it would be going up against the Disciples. Lazarus thanked him for the warning but kept their goal a secret to avoid any information getting leaked to the Disciples.

After purchasing the firearms, Lazarus led Seraph and Zero toward Diamond Road to see if the Diamond Cutters had any information on the Pawn Road Disciples. The boys entered K. Reynolds Jewelers and walked over to the front counter.

A young man in a white business suit looked at the three over the rims of his glasses. "How can I help you?" a hint of mischief displayed across his face.

"We're here to see Dex Wallace," Lazarus looked around the shop. Glass display cases boxed in the young, well-dressed man. The shop was full of all sorts of gold and silver jewelry. The Diamond Cutters had a reputation for making custom jewelry for the different gangs around the city.

"Is he expecting you?" the man squinted at Lazarus.

"Uh, well, not exactly. I was hoping to get some info from him."

"*Info?*" The man smirked. "You know that information from Dex Wallace is no cheap commodity," he studied the boys' attire.

"Money's not an issue," this statement caught Seraph and Zero off guard.

"Hmm, if that's the case . . . then what would you like to know?"

"*You're* Dex Wallace?"

"Am I not what you expected?"

"Well, I guess not."

The Diamond Cutter flashed Lazarus a bright grin but said nothing.

"So, uh, we were hoping you had some information on the Pawn Road Disciples."

"Ah, and what business do you have with *them*? They sell you some bad bola?" Dex chuckled.

"Something like that. We're trying to get their recipe, actually."

Seraph and Zero stayed silent as they subtly glanced at one another.

"I'll be honest with you. Even if I had that sort of information, you wouldn't be able to afford it. The amount of danger someone would have to endure to get that recipe is what you would be paying for, and even if you had the crowns, I would not be willing to risk one of my men to obtain it." He folded his hands together in front of him and frowned, but then his expression changed suddenly. "However, there may be an alternative solution."

"I'm listening."

"Well, I do know where their labs are. I could charge you for one of their locations, and if you've got the stones, then you could try to find out their recipe for yourselves. I'd even give you a discount, considering how slim your chances of survival are."

"Hmm . . ." Lazarus rubbed his chin and looked back at his crew. "We want all the locations."

Dex grinned. "I can give you all of their locations—but it'll cost you."

Lazarus nodded and Dex started jotting down the information on a small yellow pad.

"I'd like t'think that sellin' you boys explosives of

this magnitude would go against my conscience," Malone helped load the satchels of homemade explosives into the trunk of an old tan-colored sedan.

"Conscience? *What* conscience?" McGregor laughed and slapped Malone on the back.

"It's for a good cause," Lazarus covered the bombs with a blanket and closed the trunk. "How much is this gonna run me?"

Malone held up his hands and shook his head. "No payment necessary, y'know, fer the *cause*," he winked.

Lazarus nodded. "Thank you."

"Aye, don't mention it. Just don't go getting' yerselves killed."

"Yeah, and don't tell nobody you got the stuff from us. The car included. You get rid of it as soon as the job's done," McGregor cautioned.

"That's fair," Lazarus opened the driver's side door and gave a quick nod in Seraph and Zero's direction. The three of them got into the car and started north toward Pawn Road.

"That was super generous of the McDroogins to give all this to us," Zero leaned forward between the front seats.

"Well, technically, it wasn't from the McDroogins. This was more of a personal gift from Malone and McGregor."

"I didn't realize you had so much money, man," Seraph could no longer keep it to himself.

"It's from donations. People who are against the Lyones have secretly been funding this operation," he kept his eyes on the road.

"Like who?" Zero prodded.

"Well, it wouldn't be much of a secret if I told you, would it?"

"Even from your own gang?" Seraph's eyes narrowed at his leader.

"I can't say anymore. You'll just have to trust me."

Seraph nodded and looked out the window. The street lamps started to turn on as dusk descended on Royalty. Pawn Road had a reputation for being the worst street in the city. Amakoran hip-hop blared as the sound of distorted bass pulsed. The Switchblades passed a parking lot, where several older Amakoran men stood around a parked car. Lazarus pulled up at a gas station a little further down the road and took out the piece of paper Dex had given him.

"Okay, the first spot is just down the street here. I'll cruise by it, and we'll scope the place out. Discretion will be our best friend; otherwise, the whole neighborhood will come gunning for us."

"When we figure out how exactly we're gonna do this, I'll plant the bomb," Seraph volunteered once again to Lazarus and Zero's surprise.

"You sure, man?" Lazarus bit the inside of his lip.

"Yeah, man. I got this."

"Once the bomb goes off, we won't have too much time to hit the second location, and even worse, after the second, they're gonna know that it ain't a coincidence, and we'll have to get really creative for the last couple locations. We want to avoid getting into a fire fight with these guys."

"People are still gonna get hurt from the explosives though, won't they, Laz?"

"There's no other way, brother. I'm not gonna lie. A lot of people are probably going to lose their lives tonight because of us."

"Oh, man," Zero held his breath.

"Laz . . ." Seraph's face began to lose color. "Are you sure this is worth it? All these lives—is bringing down the Lyone family really worth the cost?"

Lazarus took out and drew on his e-cigarette. "If I thought there was a chance to get the Disciples on board with the plan, I would go to them in a heartbeat. I would vie for peace between them and the Bishops if I thought it were at all possible, but it's not. The Disciples are different from the Bishops and even the Soldiers. And if taking them out secures us an alliance with the Bishops, then for me, it's a no-brainer."

"That makes sense. I mean, they *did* kill that kid Jon Jon earlier," Zero agreed and looked at Seraph.

"You do have a point," Seraph nodded solemnly.

"We just have to stay focused," Lazarus took charge. "This is war and there are casualties in war. It's the result of that war that determines if the casualties were worth it. The war that we fight is for freedom against a tyrant who oppresses the people of this city and rules over them with an iron fist—who came to power through genocide!"

"You're right!" Seraph became resolute. "Gotta stay focused!"

"Let's keep moving while it's still dark out."

The tan car circled around a cul-de-sac lit by a single streetlamp that flickered every so often. All the yards were overgrown with tall grass and weeds. Even the sidewalks were so unkempt that the pavement was barely visible from the large tufts of foliage that grew between the cracks. The target house was the only one on the street that still had lights on. The Switchblades were relieved when they saw that no one was guarding the outside.

"Let's make this quick, Seraph. Plant it out front, run back to the car, and we'll go down the street a little before we detonate it," Lazarus dictated.

Seraph rubbed his palms against his jeans. "Right," he picked up the satchel charge. He took a deep breath before opening the car door and made a mad dash to some bushes underneath one of the front windows of the house. Seraph set the explosive under the bush against the house and turned to start back toward the car.

At that moment, the front door of the house opened, and two Amakoran men stepped onto the front porch, laughing about something.

Seraph quickly ducked down behind the bushes and held his breath as sweat began to accumulate on his forehead.

"Yo, who dis, man?" one of them pointed to the tan car.

"Prolly some Sar-trash tryna get high," the other said as they walked over to Lazarus's car.

Lazarus and Zero glanced at one another briefly before rolling down the passenger's window.

"Whatchu white boys want?"

"Uh, just some scratch, man," Lazarus failed to hide his nervousness.

"*Scratch?* I thought you Sartovan boys like the hardcore stuff? Y'all sure y'all don't want no bola?"

Seraph watched from the bushes, his heart ready to jump out of his chest. *We're so screwed,* he thought as he tried unsuccessfully to hear what the Amakorans were saying.

Lazarus looked from left to right and then scratched his neck fiendishly. "I mean, if you're holdin' . . ."

"Payment first."

"*Product* first," Lazarus insisted.

The drug dealer raised his eyebrows and then looked back at his partner. "How much you want?"

"I'll take a half-o," Lazarus scratched his arm fiendishly.

"A'ight . . . I'll getcho stuff. Sit tight."

The two turned and walked back toward the house. Seraph heard one of them say "Get my piece. We'll take whateva they got," as they walked through the door.

Seraph waited for what seemed like a millennium as he felt his shirt become heavy with sweat. Once he heard the door close, he bolted for the car, swung the back door open, and jumped in as Lazarus peeled off down the street. "Go, go, go!"

"Dude, that was too close!" Zero swallowed.

Seraph took the small detonator from his pocket and stared at it, his palms saturated with sweat as his breathing intensified. He removed a small plastic cap, which revealed a little red button.

"You want me to do it, bro?" Zero offered.

"No," Seraph let his mind settle on the fact that the two Disciples were planning on robbing his friends. "This one's mine," he pressed the button with his thumb.

A loud explosion rocked the neighborhood as the drug house became engulfed in flames. Seraph watched from the rear window as the burning home illuminated the previously dark cul-de-sac. He wanted to feel bad about what he had just done. He knew that the men in that home were drug dealers. He knew that they were responsible in part for killing Jon Jon because of their association as Disciples.

Lance, Seraph thought, *have you killed anyone? I never heard of the Lyones killing anyone before meeting Lazarus. Does that make us the bad guys?* Seraph closed his eyes and rubbed his temples with his fingertips.

"The way I figure, we can hit one more lab before they realize what's up." Lazarus looked back at Seraph, who nodded. "After that, we're either going to have to be less subtle or get creative for the last two."

"It'd be nice if we had more soldiers so that we could attack them all at the same time," Zero sighed.

"What if we called Ezra and let him know what we're up to? If he'd be down, we could coordinate with his crew and do just that," Seraph suggested.

"You two are brilliant!" Lazarus smiled weakly and handed his phone to Zero. "Call Ezra and see what he can do."

CHAPTER FIVE

"I'll ride with you and set off the charge," Seraph told Ezra as he grabbed one of the satchel bombs and handed the other to Zero.

"Sounds good, but you said they got three mo' labs. What do we do about the last one?"

"Here's where things get a little more complicated," Lazarus started. "Once we blow these two labs, there's no more subtlety. We both meet up near the last location and hit it up front, guns blazing."

"Well, they gonna be expectin' somethin' f'sho and I don't think your crew and my crew is gon' be enough to attack them head on like that," Ezra warned.

"I mean, it's war anyway, isn't it? What if we got all the Bishops to come for the final lab and end things then and there?"

"And have a bloodbath in the middle of the streets? That would bring the Lyones down on us hard, and then what? Everyone loses if it comes to that."

Lazarus took a long drag from his cigarette as he

contemplated what their next plan of action should be.

Ezra rubbed his chin, "I think I got an idea. I gotta make a phone call real quick, and then we'll head out. We'll meet up at Grove and Heritage and go from there."

"You sure?"

"Yeah, let's get movin'." Ezra and the other Bishops, along with Seraph, got into his SUV and drove toward Crimson Street.

Ezra's crew pulled up in front of a rundown apartment building that made St. Titus look like a palace in comparison. Seraph realized how many civilians must live there and how many innocent lives would be lost if they set off another one of the deadly explosives.

"What's the holdup?" Ezra turned and faced Seraph.

"I see why they chose this location." Seraph lifted his chin toward a group of young boys who, rather than gang-banging, looked to be playing and laughing.

"Yeah, you right . . . *shoot*!"

Seraph blinked and looked up at Ezra, surprised that the Bishop general felt similarly. "What do we do?"

"We go in shootin'. Take the place quickly. Smash up they gear. Take what we can. You strapped?"

"Strapped?" Seraph raised an eyebrow until he realized what Ezra meant and then lifted up his shirt, revealing the brown grip of a pistol.

Ezra nodded to his men. "Let's get busy."

Lazarus brought the car to a halt across from Amaryllis, nearly four houses down from the drug lab. He and Zero both noticed ten or so Disciple guards that were posted up in front of the location. "They must have been alerted already."

Zero nodded.

"I'm having a hard time trying to figure out how we're gonna pull this off."

"We could drive the car into them."

Lazarus allowed the idea to play out in his mind and then shook his head as he visualized the car going up in flames with them in it as the Disciples rained bullets down on them. "Too risky . . ."

Zero brandished his pistol. "Drive-by?"

"Hmm . . ." Lazarus preferred this plan, although it presented similar risks to the first plan. "What about a distraction?" What if, instead of using the bomb to blow up the lab, we use it to blow up one of these cars? That might distract them enough to give us a chance to get in and wreck the lab."

"But how do we get past all those guys out front? Even if they are distracted, they'll figure out that something is up, and we'll get popped."

"We gotta take them out, bro."

Zero nodded.

Lazarus planted the explosive underneath a nearby sports car. It was dark enough on the street so that he could creep around undetected and prepare the distraction. Zero crouched next to the tan car, waiting for his boss. Hip-hop music emanated from the house while the Disciple guards chattered out front. These sounds were almost completely drowned out by a dull ringing in Zero's ears as his heart pounded and his hands shook.

"Hey! You ready?" Lazarus appeared next to him, causing him to jump a little and grasp his chest.

"Oh, man! I almost crapped myself!" Zero responded hoarsely back to him and then took a deep breath. "Yeah, I'm ready."

The Switchblades drew their pistols and chambered a round. Lazarus pulled out the detonator and removed the cap before gently placing his thumb on the button. He counted backward from three to one but stopped as he noticed one of the Disciples take a phone call, his loud voice echoing down the mostly empty street.

"What? *Ah, shit!* I knew it! Well, whatchu want us to do? A'ight, a'ight," he practically shouted and ended the call. "That was Derae. Jus' like I thought, that explosion over at Reginald wasn't no accident. Bishops is retaliatin'. We gon' hold up here and wait for orders. I want some of y'all to guard the back. The rest of y'all spread out on the front. You see anything, you shoot," he ordered as the group split up.

Lazarus pressed the button, tightly holding it down with his thumb. The eruption from the bomb and the exploding car sounded like the impact of a freight train smashing into a solid block of concrete. Lazarus and Zero winced from the sound and ducked their heads. The explosion seemed ten times louder than before because of how close they were this time. A thick fog of dark gray began flooding the street as it made its way upward toward the clouds. The Disciples all instinctively hit the ground in a panic.

"What the hell was that?" one of them cried out.

"It's the Bishops! Get up and spread out!" the man who was previously on the phone shouted.

The Disciples all got up and drew their guns as they fanned out down the street in the direction of the burning car.

Lazarus and Zero looked at each other. There was enough distance between them and the Disciples in case they needed to escape, but they knew they would need to either act now or run while they still had the opportunity.

"What do we do?" Zero's expression became tense.

Looking around, Lazarus spotted a car close to the drug house and several tall oak trees in Amaryllis Park across the street. "Okay, listen: I'm gonna make a run for that car over there. Give me cover fire until I make it over there. When I start firing, I want you to run into the park and take cover behind the trees. Pick your shots and take out as many as you can. If I don't make it, run through the park, and get out of here. Call Ezra as soon as you're safe."

Zero winced when Lazarus mentioned that he might not make it but stayed focused as he prepared to provide cover for him.

Lazarus started toward the car near the house. Zero rose up from behind the vehicle and began firing shots toward the Disciples, struggling to pick his shots carefully, as his hands now shook violently. The Disciples hardly had a chance to return fire as they took cover behind whatever was closest to them. Zero crouched back down once he had fired all the rounds in his magazine, while bullets whizzed above him. He dropped the fresh magazine while struggling to reload the pistol. Once he got it loaded, he cocked back the hammer.

"Move up! Hurry!" one of the Disciples shouted as they came out from their cover and slowly advanced toward Zero's position.

Lazarus seized the opportunity and aimed his gun at the back of one of the Disciples who was closest to the tan car. He held his breath, steadied his hand, and fired three rounds, catching the Disciple twice in the center of his back. Lazarus winced at the loud bang of the gun, and he felt heartrate skyrocket.

"They all ova', dawg!"

Zero held the pistol over his head and fired a few blind shots in the direction of the Disciple's voice before mustering all of his courage and darting toward the park like Lazarus had instructed.

"'Ey! One's runnin'!" a Disciple began to fire in Zero's direction.

Lazarus popped back up from behind the vehicle and fired, taking out another Disciple and taking cover once more.

"Yo, we gotta get the hell outta here!"

"Ke'on! Call Derae, dawg!"

"I been tryin', man! He ain't pickin' up! We jus' gotta go!"

Both Lazarus and Zero's hearts leaped with relief as they continued firing more shots at the diminishing group of Disciples, who all began running away from the gunfire.

Lazarus suddenly became aware that he was gasping for breath as he produced his last magazine and reloaded the pistol. He heard rapid footsteps approaching his position, and once the gun was ready to fire, he braced himself to take down whoever was approaching.

"Woah, woah, woah! It's *me*!" Zero panted and raised his hands.

Lazarus lowered the pistol and exhaled. "Thank God! Are you okay?"

Zero quickly patted himself all over and nodded. "I'm good. You?" he looked his leader up and down.

"Yeah, thanks to you. Good job, bro!" Lazarus looked past Zero and scanned the street behind him.

"You too," Zero tried to catch his breath.

"We're not done yet. Come on!" Lazarus led Zero to the front door of the drug house. They cocked their guns before Lazarus tried the handle. "Locked," he screwed up his face.

"Damn it! What now?"

Lazarus tucked his pistol in his waistband, picked up a wicker rocking chair, and threw it through a window while Zero positioned himself to fire if necessary.

They stood motionless, listening for any movement inside. After a few seconds, Zero grabbed a baseball bat leaning against the house and knocked out the remaining glass. "Cover me," he said to Lazarus, who pulled his gun from his waist and checked to make sure there was no one waiting for Zero on the other side before he crawled through. Once inside, Zero carefully checked to make sure it was clear. It looked like a normal living room with a full furniture set and television. Lazarus crept through the opening behind Zero, and they made eye contact before Lazarus nodded toward the hallway past the kitchen.

They slowly started toward the hallway, where there were two closed doors adjacent to each other. Together, with guns drawn, they approached the door on the left. Zero tried the handle as Lazarus raised his pistol. He turned the knob and cautiously pushed the door open. He quickly raised his hands, as he was greeted by the long barrel of a shotgun.

"Don't make me do it! We got kids in here!" came a feminine voice from the other end of the shotgun.

Lazarus's eyes widened with fear as he kept his

pistol trained on a pretty, slender Amakoran woman with a red bandana around her forehead. "Easy!"

"We didn't come to hurt any women or children!" Zero affirmed as his eyes met with the woman's.

"*Shut up!* Y'all just killed all them out front. My *man* was out there!" tears rolled down her cheeks.

"We didn't kill anyone out there!" Lazarus lied, unsure of how many of the men that they shot ended up dying.

"Yeah! They all ran after we fired at them," Zero kept eye contact with the young woman.

The woman stepped forward, causing Zero to back up against the wall. "You lyin'!"

"Easy . . ." the sights of Lazarus's pistol aimed at the side of her head. "Just put it down, and you and the kids can leave. We're just here for the drugs."

The woman took a sharp breath and glanced back at the group of children huddled together in the corner of the room. "Please don't hurt my babies!" she lost composure, holding the shotgun out for Zero to take as she started sobbing.

Lazarus exhaled and lowered his gun. "Thank God."

"Shh, it's okay. We won't hurt you," Zero took the shotgun by the barrel and held it at his side.

"Yeah, just tell us where the dope is and get outta here. This place is too dangerous for kids." Lazarus told her as their eyes met.

The woman nodded towards a door across from them and wiped away her tears. "Come on, babies. We gotta go now!" she forced a smile as she beckoned the children.

"Go on, now," Zero watched as she led three small

Amakoran children to the front door. One of the little boys turned and looked him in the eyes before following his mother outside.

"That was too close. We need to make this quick!" Lazarus felt the perspiration that coated his entire body.

Zero approached the door the woman nodded to and turned the knob, raising the shotgun as he pushed the door open. "Here we go!"

There was no one in the room. It smelled heavily of chemicals, with tables covered with large beakers connected by plastic tubing, along with various other chemistry equipment. There were metal containers and other devices that were unfamiliar to them. Despite the fact that Lazarus used to sell these same drugs for the Bishops, he was not well versed in all of the equipment required for manufacturing them. On one of the tables were two packages shaped like bricks full of a white substance. "Flare," Lazarus said as he snatched the two packages and grinned while holding them up. "This will earn us some extra credit, for sure!"

"Not bad at all."

"Okay, let's torch this place and get out of here!" Lazarus nodded toward a folded bedsheet that sat on a chair between two of the tables. "Grab that sheet." He traded the packages of flare to Zero for the sheet before tying it around the leg of one of the tables and stretched the other end of the sheet toward the entrance of the room. "Give me your lighter."

Zero reached in his pants pocket, retrieved a small disposable lighter, and handed it to him.

Lazarus knelt down and ignited the bedsheet. "Let's go!" he tossed the lighter toward the center of the sheet before shutting the door and heading toward the exit of the house.

Lazarus and Zero met up with Seraph and Ezra's crew after they were certain that the lab on Acorn Lane had been destroyed and handed the packages of flare to Ezra. "Managed to snag these on the way out."

Ezra returned the smile and passed the packages to one of his underlings, who stashed them away in his SUV. "Turrell will be happy about this."

"What's the plan now?" Lazarus cleared his throat.

"This is the last lab right here." Ezra nodded toward the rundown apartment building in front of them. "Let's go," he led the Switchblades and his crew to the entrance of the projects with an air of confidence.

"You sure you wanna just walk right up in there?"

"I got this under control," Ezra walked right up to one of the doors and knocked twice.

Lazarus, Zero, and Seraph all looked at each other perplexed as they each prepared themselves for whatever was going to happen next.

"Whatchu want?" came a voice from the other side of the door.

"It's me, sucka. Open up!"

The door opened, and Ezra flashed a grin at Lazarus before leading them all inside, where they found DeAndre and his crew with a handful of Disciples on their knees at gunpoint.

"Letrelle!" Ezra sported a broad grin. "What's going on, homie?"

The Disciple that Ezra had addressed turned his head away from him.

"What? You thought y'all was jus' gonna get away with poppin' my lil' cousin? You thought we was gonna let that slide?" Ezra knelt down and forcefully turned Letrelle's head to face him and placed the barrel of his pistol against his forehead.

"Kill this fool, Ez'!" shouted DeAndre, who was holding a shotgun to the back of another Disciple's head.

"No," came a familiar voice as Turrell entered the apartment with his entourage behind him. "Ease up off the man, Ezra."

Ezra complied, joining Turrell at his side.

"So, what? I smoke a couple of your dealers and you go and start blowin' up all my business?" Letrelle's face twisted in rage.

"Stand up when you speak to me," Turrell ordered the Disciple leader, who defiantly took his time getting to his feet. "Those *dealers* that you had killed were kids, man. Barely teenagers. And one of them was Ezra and DeAndre's lil' cousin."

"Ke'on . . ." Letrelle shook his head. "They weren't supposed to kill no kids. We ain't about that. With that said—if those kids were dealin' for the Bishops and got popped, that sounds more like it's your fault."

"Oh?" Turrell's eyebrows rose. "So, this is my fault, is what you sayin'?"

"Look, dawg, this—"

"First, I ain'tcho *dawg*. Second, I'll tell you how this gon' go down from now on. Y'all can keep this lab. We ain't gon' blow it up like we did the other ones. You still gon' deal, too, but from now on, you gon' pay *us* 10% of all earnings."

"Oh, *hell no* we ain't! Whatchu think, y'all the

Amakoran Lyones? You might as well blow this one up too, 'cause we ain't payin' y'all nothin'!" Letrelle clenched his fists.

Turrell pulled out his gold-plated pistol and pointed it at Letrelle. "Why don't I just kill you then, right now and see if one your boys here is willin' to cooperate with our new business model?"

The Switchblades silently watched as the two gang leaders went back and forth. Lazarus wished he could intervene and reason with them, but he knew that the blood-feud between Bishop and Pawn Road had deep roots and some random Sartovan kid wouldn't be able to broker peace between them.

Seraph hardly paid attention to what was happening around him as he recounted in his mind the carnage that had played out earlier when he raided the lab on Crimson with Ezra's crew. A surreal numbness overtook him as he stood between Lazarus and Zero.

Letrelle looked back at his men, who were still on their knees at gunpoint. "You really gonna take it to that level? Petty ass—"

"Hey, this is your choice!" Turrell stepped forward. "Now choose!"

Letrelle looked down and sighed. "Fine."

"Good," Turrell lowered his pistol. "From now on, once a week, you gon' send one of your boys on foot to Bishop and Pawn. He gon' bring us our cut. Y'all try anything at all, and that's *it*. We finish this for good. What you need to remember is that you allowed to live right now because of me. Don't get caught up in them feelings. Have a little appreciation for what happened here tonight. It's a beautiful thing," he slipped his pistol in his waistband and looked around at all the Bishops there. "Let's bounce!"

Back at Turrell's house, the Switchblades and the Bishops' leadership sat around the living room drinking and discussing the events that had transpired. The light from the breaking dawn outlined the windows as the night of bloodshed finally ended. Seraph noticed that Ezra and DeAndre seemed quieter than the others before recalling the loss of their cousin Jon Jon. Seraph had never lost anyone before. In fact, Lance leaving him to join the Lyone family was the closest thing to loss he had ever experienced, aside from being an orphan.

"Y'all boys did good tonight, Laz," Turrell patted Lazarus on the back. "And I heard about the two bricks of flare you salvaged. Good work, bruh!"

"So we're all squared up then?"

"Oh, for sure! More than enough! As soon as DeAndre told me what y'all had hooked up with Ezra, I knew that this was the Bishops' chance to come out on top once and for all. I anticipated that this retaliation might end in a war, but thanks to y'all boys, we get to enjoy some peace on top of the spoils of war."

"So, just to clarify, you *will* help us against the Lyones, right?"

"I didn't say all that. You cleared your debt with us, for which I'm grateful. If you want an *alliance*, then you gon' need to put in some work for more work for Bishop. It was a good start—that's f'sho. What? Did you think the Disciples were our only problem?"

Lazarus stood up and raised his voice, saying, "So, you want us to solve all of Bishop's problems before you agree to help us?" This caused the Bishops in the room to shift.

"Hey, dawg, y'all solve our problems, n' we solve y'alls. That's how this works. How you expect us to take on y'alls enemies if we got problems of our own? How you expect us to focus?" Turrell smirked before casually taking a sip from his bottle.

"Focus? Turrell, they're your enemies too! They tax you the same as everyone else! You're content having them as your masters?"

"Easy with that *master* shit, dawg. As for the Lyones . . . that's just the way things is. Have been for a long time now. Why not jus' accept things for what they are? Then you wouldn't have to be here doin' my dirty work," Turrell and his men nodded in unison.

"Because I give a damn about this city and the people in it!" Lazarus shouted.

Turrell calmly motioned with his hand for his men to relax.

"Aren't the Bishops one of the first gangs to even exist in Royalty? Don't you care that no one is free anymore? That the Lyone family controls everything and forces everyone to pay them?"

"The Bishops were the *first* gang in Royalty," Turrell corrected him, "and I get what you sayin'. I do. But some things just ain't right. Not everything goes the way it's supposed to."

"The things you can't change, sure. There is a point where some things are just out of our control. I accept those things, but not this. We could make a *difference*!"

"Look, homie, we called a vote earlier, before y'all helped us. Truth is: my generals really ain't keen on gettin' into it with the Lyones. They could easily do to us what we did to the Disciples tonight, except I'm sure they would just kill every one of us."

"Why can't you all just give us time to get some other gangs on board and give us a chance to change the odds?" Lazarus addressed all of the Bishops in Turrell's living room.

The Bishop generals all looked down in silence, choosing not to acknowledge the question.

Turrell frowned for a moment before speaking, "Here's what's gonna happen. Y'all hang out and put in work for Bishop and we'll *consider* what's you're asking us. I can't offer you anything beyond that."

"If that's the case, they could roll with my crew. That's if they willin' to give it mo' time fo' us t'see that they can hold they own," Ezra looked toward Lazarus.

"Was tonight not enough proof of that?" Lazarus scoffed.

"Like I said—it was a good start," Turrell smiled. "That's our final offer. Otherwise, we done here."

Lazarus sighed and looked back at Seraph and Zero.

"What choice do we have?" Zero met eyes with Lazarus.

"We've already gone this far," Seraph added, flashbacks from the devastation still flooding his mind.

Lazarus swallowed and nodded. "Okay, but I want a timeframe."

Turrell nodded, looking toward his generals again. "You got six months. That should be enough to earn yourselves an alliance with us."

"We don't have that kind of time, Turrell! The Bishops aren't the only gang we need to get on board."

"Fine. Four months. No less," Turrell stood up and offered his hand.

Lazarus took Turrell's hand, sealing the deal.

"From now on, y'all will be a part of Ezra's crew. That don't mean y'all are Bishops, but regardless, you will do everything he tells you. You want us to help you against the Lyones, then you prove that you can work with us and do what we need y'all to do. In four months, we'll reconvene and see where we at, a'ight?"

"Sure, man." Lazarus sighed.

"Good. Now, relax. Enjoy yourselves! We celebratin' right now!" he raised the liquor bottle up high before taking a sip.

Everyone followed suit as they all raised their glasses and drank, and casual conversations started up once again. Seraph remained quiet as his eyes met with Lazarus and fruitlessly attempted to force a smile. He wanted nothing more than to bring down the Lyone family and get his best friend back but wondered how much more blood needed to be spilled before that could be achieved. *Does this make me a murderer?* he wondered. Never did he think he would have to kill anyone.

"Here, lil' homie. Smoke this," DeAndre held out a thinly rolled blunt of scratch in front of his face.

"What?" Seraph came back to reality.

"It'll help, dawg. Trust me," he took a drag and held the smoke in his lungs for a few seconds before exhaling a cloud of thick smoke.

Seraph narrowed his eyes at the blunt and ran his fingers through his hair. "Give it here," he took it and drew from it, causing the end to glow. The smoke burned the back of his throat instantly, more so than cigarettes ever had, which caused him to cough and hack while DeAndre stood there laughing.

Lazarus looked at his friend with concern as Seraph instantly seemed to mellow out. "You alright, bro?"

Time seemed to slow down for Seraph as he looked from left to right and then at Lazarus. "Yeah . . ." His voice seemed to echo and then transform into a dull ringing as darkness consumed his vision and he slowly faded out of consciousness.

"Is he okay?" Zero stood up in alarm.

"He's alright, man. It's gotta be his first time. Scratch usually makes people pass out their first time," Lazarus explained, still watching his friend, who was now lying back against the sofa, eyes closed and mouth slightly ajar.

"After tonight, it'll probably do him some good," DeAndre took the blunt from between Seraph's fingers and offered it to Lazarus.

"I'm good, man. Thanks."

DeAndre shrugged and took another hit before blowing another cloud into the air above him. "You sure? Tonight was just the beginning . . ."

CHAPTER SIX

"Yo, tighten up. Here they come." Edge nudged Seraph's elbow as he narrowed his eyes in the direction of Pawn Road and watched as Andron, the Disciple who brought the Bishops' cut each week, approached the intersection at Bishop Street.

The four Switchblades remained silent, staring Andron down as he made his way over to them. They had nearly reached the four-month mark of working for the Bishops and their duties had been relatively easy in contrast to their initial task. Collecting taxes from the Disciples was by far the easiest. A certain numbness had grown over Seraph's heart, like a suit of armor to protect his conscience from the actions in which he now partook regularly. He often ignored his inner voice during these times, keeping the end goal of saving Lance and the city at the forefront of his mind.

"Whatchu got for us this week?" Lazarus asked as the Disciple stood in front of the four Switchblades and reached into his back pocket, retrieving an envelope and holding it out to the Switchblade leader.

Lazarus took the envelope and pressed it tightly between his thumb and index finger. "This seems kinda thin."

"What?" Andron blinked, craning his head forward. "That's the Bishops' percentage, man!"

"I'm just messin'." Lazarus cracked a grin and then nodded toward Pawn Road. "You're good, man. I'll see you next week."

Zero and Edge chuckled at Lazarus's little prank. Seraph pressed his lips together and rolled his eyes.

Andron scoffed and shook his head as he made his way back to Pawn.

"We gotta keep those suckers in check. Can't have them getting too familiar with us, ya know?" Lazarus waved the envelope at each of the members of his gang before storing it in his back pocket and then squinted at Seraph. "What's your problem?"

Seraph raised an eyebrow and shook his head. "Nothing, man. Just trying to stay focused."

"*Focused?* Man, I'm focused on this paper that we're about to get when we deliver this to Ezra tonight. It's payday!"

"And we got that party tonight," Zero reminded them. "Don't forget. Actually, I gotta head out a little early. I promised Keyshay I'd help him set up his equipment for the music."

"I said I'd help, too, so I'll go with you," Edge started to stand.

"A'ight, but just be careful with what you lift. You're still healing, bro," Lazarus admonished.

Edge smirked and placed his hand on his ribs "I should be fully healed up by now. Those Royal Priests took good care of me thanks to Seraph."

"Thank Ezra, man. If it wasn't for him, I don't know what I would have done."

"I'm just glad you're all right." Zero smiled and placed a hand on his friend's shoulder.

"Okay, okay. Chill out with all that. You guys sound soft," Edge teased and pretended like he would burn Zero with the lit end of his cigarette, causing him to jump back.

Lazarus chuckled and shook his head. "A'ight, kids. We'll catch you later!"

"For sure!" Zero grinned.

"Peace!" Edge held up two fingers as he and Zero started back toward the Bishop projects.

Seraph and Lazarus quietly watched their two friends disappear down one of the nearby streets. "Looks like it's just you and me," Seraph lit up a cigarette of his own.

"Yep. Whatchu wanna do, man?"

"I actually was hoping to talk to you one on one if that's cool."

"Yeah? That's fine, man," Lazarus looked down at his gold-plated watch that he'd picked up from the Diamond Cutters. "We have a few hours before the party tonight. Wanna hit up TNT's for old time's sake?"

Seraph nodded. "Sounds good, brother. My treat!"

"Ha, we'll see about that!" Lazarus shook his head as the two got into Lazarus's cobalt-colored SUV, another of the many new toys he had purchased with his earnings from working for the Bishops.

Seraph joined Lazarus on the back porch of TNT's with two cold bottles of Schmigg's beer and handed Lazarus one before they clinked their bottles together and took a long sip. "Ahh . . ." Seraph sighed in satisfaction as he could hear one of the bands inside the main bar setting up for their performance for that night.

"You said it, brother. So, uh, what did you want to talk about?"

"Well . . ." Seraph wasn't sure where or how to begin. "I'm a little concerned about our direction, if I'm being honest."

"*Direction?* What do you mean?"

Seraph looked at Lazarus's watch and raised his chin. "The watch. The car. The crowns . . . I thought our mission was to take down the Lyones."

Lazarus looked down at the watch for a second before flashing a smirk at his friend. "This is just a bonus to what we're doing, man. I mean, yeah, our priority is liberating this city, no doubt. But you gotta live a little, right? Who wants a life that's all work and no play?"

"Under normal circumstances, I would totally agree, but man, haven't you asked yourself what we're really doing? I mean, we're selling drugs for the Bishops! What's the difference between what you were doing before you started the Switchblades and what you're doing now?"

A sour look spread across Lazarus's face. "Dude, how can you be judging me when you are doing the exact same thing? This wasn't a problem for you when you decided to change up your wardrobe," he said, pointing at Seraph's fresh clothes. He now dressed more like the Bishops, in typical Amakoran fashion, with dark baggy jeans and button-up shirts. He also wore name-brand shoes—the first pair he had ever owned.

"Look, I'm not saying I'm innocent, okay? I'm just worried that we're not only losing focus, but also losing ourselves."

Lazarus sighed and looked away. "I hear ya, man, I do. The four months are almost up. What if we mention it to Turrell tonight—if he seems like he's in good spirits?"

"Sure, but what if he doesn't give us a straight answer or seems like he's just stringing us along?"

"I don't know, man. That's a bridge we'll have to cross when we get to it."

"And if they *do* agree, where do we go from here? I almost feel like I'm a part of the Bishop Brotherhood for as much time as we spent with them." Seraph chuckled and shook his head.

"I feel you there. We've really formed some bonds with some of those dudes. Shoot, if it weren't for Ezra, I doubt we'd even have a chance at getting Bishop on board."

"Ezra's solid, man. Maybe we should mention it to him before going straight to Turrell."

Lazarus stared at Seraph with a preoccupied look. "What?"

"You know, sometimes I wonder if you would make a better leader."

"*Leader?* Are you high, man?"

"I'm serious, bro! The plans and ideas you come up with? The way you always take initiative, even sometimes to your own misfortune. You've got a natural inclination for it."

Seraph had never pictured himself as a leader. What did that mean anyway? Like a gang leader or a general like Ezra or O'Connor? From childhood, he had been taught by the Royal Priests to hold fast to his values, no matter what the circumstances, and to always act courageously in light of them. Being a leader was not an idea that Seraph was comfortable with in the least. "You're crazy."

"Thanks, Seraph."

"Huh? For what?"

"I was losing myself. I honestly forgot about the mission entirely. I mean, even when Kendyl broke up with me, sure I told her that this was for the bigger picture, but truthfully, I was too focused on the money. It's hard for people like us, Seraph—street kids, I mean—who grew up without anything. Yeah, Amakorans got it kinda rough, but it's like us orphans are just one step lower than them. At least they stick together and earn for themselves. Us? We just scrape by with whatever we can. Shoot, most street kids end up as junkies if they don't join a gang or find some other way. This city, the way things were before the Lyone family took over—it wasn't no paradise, that's for sure, but people were working together. Sartovans, Amakorans, Sengoans, L'Orandans. Biker gangs, street gangs . . . sure, they had their beefs, but there wasn't this—this hate. I guess that's just the way things are, right?"

"Wrong. Things don't have to be that way. We will make a difference."

Lazarus stared at Seraph again before a smile

appeared. "You're right. Tonight, we'll talk to Ezra and begin planning our next course . . . no matter what happens."

"Now you're talkin'!" Seraph turned toward Mongrel, whom he noticed at the periphery of his vision.

"Hey there, fellas. Been a long time."

"A long time, indeed," Lazarus took a swig from his beer.

"How's the new project going?" Seraph lifted his chin in Mongrel's direction.

Mongrel's demeanor shifted slightly as he looked over his shoulder and then back at Seraph. "Going good, bro. What about you guys? Making progress?"

"It's hard to say, man," Lazarus sighed.

"Yeah, it's definitely been eventful," Seraph agrred and rubbed his forehead.

"That's for sure," Lazarus set the bottle down and began fiddling around in his pants pocket. "Where's Ram at?"

"Uh, Ram's a little tied up lately. I actually came by because I heard you all stopped by."

Seraph and Lazarus exchanged glances before leaning forward to hear what Mongrel had to say.

"I'll make this quick. Whether we're ready or not, things are gonna start happening. It's no secret that the Lyones are becoming more hostile. No one really knows what's going on, but that son of Lucien's seems to be leading the vanguard on this."

"We're aware of that, but what does that have to do with you?" Lazarus's eyebrows pressed together as he retrieved his electronic cigarette from his pocket and took a deep drag.

Mongrel checked over his shoulder once more. "That project that we mentioned before. Let's just say we've been working on reviving Ram's crew. We're done sitting by and watching these jerks ruin our town."

Lazarus's eyes widened in shock. "Are you sure this

is such a good idea? I mean, I get that Ram wants revenge after what they did to the Jackals, but imagine what would happen this time if the Lyones caught wind of this?"

"I get it, little brother. Trust me. I'm not necessarily saying we're going to try to initiate anything…" Mongrel paused for a moment. "Anyway, listen- word around town is that Black Lotus just scored a big contract, and once it's completed, they will more than likely have enough to bail out Blackjack."

The two Switchblades exchanged perplexed looks, before Lazarus took another drag. "Is there something we're missing here? What does that have to do with the Lyones? And what do you mean by 'we're not trying to initiate anything'?"

"There's not a whole lot that I can say at the moment, but I can assure you that everything is connected. More so than you could ever imagine."

With furrowed eyebrows, Seraph looked off to the side, wondering what exactly was going on and trying to draw a connection between what was happening with the Lyones and what Mongrel was saying about Black Lotus bailing out Blackjack.

"Like I said, I can't say much more at the moment. I mainly came here to tell you one thing—and this comes from Ram himself: no matter what, we're on the same side."

"I would have never thought otherwise, bro."

"Good. You boys be safe. You need anything, just swing by. We got you," Mongrel assured them before exiting through the main bar.

Seraph looked back at Lazarus in bewilderment. "What in the world?"

Lazarus shook his head. "I have no clue, brother," he then looked down at his watch. "We better head back to Bishop. We still gotta get to Ezra before they start cracking bottles open."

Once the two Switchblades arrived back at Bishop,

they made their way to Ezra and DeAndre's apartment. DeAndre answered the door, barely acknowledging the boys as he left the door open and shouted out to his brother, "Yo, Ezra! Yo' white boys is here!"

Lazarus and Seraph entered the small apartment and closed the door behind them as they stood in the living room, awkwardly waiting for the Bishop general.

Ezra stepped out from the bathroom, wearing purple basketball shorts and a white sleeveless shirt. He had a small hand towel that he was using to wipe off excess shaving cream from his neck as he approached them with a large smile on his face. "What's up, Laz? Seraph?"

"Yo, man! Got yer package right here." Lazarus retrieved the sealed envelope from his back pocket and held it out to him. "I may have broken Andron's balls a little bit over this."

"Good! Keep those punks on they toes!"

"Damn straight. We, uh, were hoping we could talk to you for a few before we head over to Turrell's."

Ezra gave Lazarus a puzzled look. "Sure, homie. Whatchu got fo' me?" he took a seat on the sofa, holding out a hand and inviting them to sit.

"We wanted to mention that we are kinda getting close to that four-month mark that we—"

"Say no more, dawg. Honestly, I was planning on mentioning something to the big man soon anyway. Y'all boys have really worked to prove y'selves. I can say I'm pleasantly surprised."

DeAndre scoffed. "Man, y'all jus' lucky that my bro vouched for you. E'rybody know that he went easy on you 'cause he got a soft spot for Sars."

"You wildin', bro," Ezra shook his head. "Don't pay him no attention. Y'all did good. I didn't know Sartovans could have so much heart. Y'all Switchblades know how to get down."

"Much appreciated, man. Ezra, I can't thank you enough for endorsing us."

"Y'all earned this endorsement, cuz."

Seraph cleared his throat. "What do you think our chances are with the rest of the generals?"

"Don't worry about DeAndre. He might be sour, but he'll back me up," Ezra reassured them. "Ain't that right, lil' brotha?"

"Yeah, sure, whatev'a. This a stupid-ass idea though, fo' sho. We all gon' end up dead over these white boys."

"Chill out with all that, bruh. Damn!" Ezra shot his brother a dirty look.

Lazarus and Seraph sat uncomfortably, choosing to remain silent.

"Yo, let's bounce. I tol' Charita we'd get some mo' drinks for the party," Ezra stood up and walked toward his bedroom to finish getting dressed.

DeAndre stood in the archway of the kitchen and stared at Seraph and Lazarus.

"We'll wait outside," Lazarus fidgeted nervously for a moment before also standing. "See ya at the party."

"Whatev'a," DeAndre scowled before going back into the kitchen.

"Man, what's his *problem*?" Seraph questioned Lazarus once they had closed the front door behind them.

Lazarus sighed. "Try to be a bit more understanding, brother. For years, these dudes had one focus, and that's making money. To gangs like the Bishops, they don't really have anything else to look forward to."

"Makes sense, I guess," Seraph shrugged.

"Yeah, so when some random Sartovans come to them saying that they're going to do something as big as what we're trying to accomplish, it's no wonder there would be so much skepticism. It's up to us to help them see the forest through the trees, ya know?"

"You're right, man. I was just caught off guard by how aggressive he seems toward us."

At that moment, the door opened, and Ezra

stepped out, now fully dressed. "That's just De, man. Don't worry about him."

"No worries," Lazarus laughed uneasily and pressed the button on his key-fob to unlock the SUV. "Ready to roll?"

"Yeah, let's get movin'. Hit up Bishop Convenience first," Ezra directed.

"What about DeAndre? He's comin', right?"

"Oh yeah, he'll be there. He's got somethin' he gotta take care of first," Ezra put some Amakoran hip-hop on the radio.

Seraph, Lazarus, and Ezra were greeted by Zero, Edge, and Mercedes as soon as they arrived at Turrell's house. There were so many cars that it looked like they went all the way up and down the street. The driveway was so full that Seraph wondered to himself how anyone could leave if they wanted to. The smell of barbecued meats welcomed them. The glass panes from the windows vibrated to the bass from the loud hip-hop music, and they quickly realized that the party had started earlier than intended. Ezra offered to take the liquor inside, while Seraph and Lazarus got caught up with the other Switchblades.

"Long time no see, Mercedes." Seraph smiled and gave her a quick hug.

"Hey, Seraph, nice clothes," Mercedes giggled, giving him a once-over.

"Ha, thanks." Seraph blushed and cleared his throat.

"How ya doin', Laz?" Mercedes asked as they embraced.

"Oh, you know, as good as can be." Lazarus forced a smile. "How's, uh, Kendyl doing?"

Mercedes pursed her lips and shook her head. "She's hangin' in there. It sucks that things couldn't work out between you two."

"Hey, not everyone can be a *ride-or-die* chick like

you, babe," Edge teased and then socked Lazarus's arm. "Cheer up, boss! It's a celebration!"

"Yeah, yeah. I'm gonna go find the bathroom," Mercedes smirked and planted a kiss on Edge's lips before heading towards the hallway.

"Back door on the right!" Edge called after her.

Lazarus smiled before looking back at the others. "So, do you all know what we're celebrating anyway?"

Just as Mercedes left, Turrell approached the group, bottle in hand, and placed a hand on Lazarus's shoulder. "I'm gonna be a father, dawg!"

"Dude! Congratulations!" Lazarus gave him a tight hug.

"Thanks, homie!" Turrell stumbled a little. "I'ma give him a name like you, man. Call his ass 'Turrazzus' or somethin'."

"So, it's a boy then?" Lazarus prodded as he tried to help stabilize the Bishop leader.

"That's what the Priests said."

"Congrats, T," Seraph grinned.

"Thanks, bro."

"Hey! There he is!" Ezra approached and put an arm around Turrell.

"Ezra! My top general! What's good, dawg?"

"On the real, I was hopin' you and me could chat business tonight about our Sartovan friends here?"

"Oh, f'sho, man, f'sho! Once things start to calm down, you and I can dip out for a few and talk bui'ness."

The party grew, as more and more people arrived. After catching up with each other, the Switchblades helped themselves to hamburgers, hotdogs, and refreshments as they branched outside of their own group to socialize with some of the Bishops with whom they had become more familiar over the past few months. Although there were those like DeAndre who showed resentment toward the Switchblades, there were others that Lazarus and company had formed significant bonds with, even some of the high-ranking generals who originally seemed skeptical of them.

Things started to quiet down after a few hours, and most of the patrons seemed exhausted from dancing or too drunk to continue with the festivities. At this point, Lazarus, Seraph, and Zero sat around Turrell's well-furnished living room and chatted with Ezra and a small group of Bishops.

"—and Keyshay was like 'oh, that's yo' girl?' and I tol' him, 'Yo, back up, cuz' and then '*boom!*' I stuck that fool right in the chin!" Antoine, one of the Bishop generals said, as everyone laughed.

"Man, y'all boys out here actin' crazy!" Ezra shook his head and chuckled.

There was a moment of silence before Lazarus spoke. "Not to get too sentimental or anything, but this, right here, us just chillin', havin' a good time? This is my dream for Royalty."

"Whatchu mean, lil' homie?" Ezra lifted a brow.

"I mean, just the way we're all united. Different gangs. Different races, cultures . . . I heard that this is how things used to be."

"You say that like you was there. Shoot, I was hardly even there," Ezra smiled. "But from what I know, yeah, things used to be a lot more chill back then between the gangs."

"Do you think it changed when the Lyones came to power?" Seraph received a few surprised looks from those gathered around.

Ezra pondered this and then shook his head. "Nah. It started befo' that, actually. I mean, yeah, things definitely got worse when the Lyones took over, no doubt, but they weren't the catalyst."

The Switchblades, along with the Bishops that were listening, all leaned forward intently in anticipation of what else Ezra had to say about the history of Royalty.

"Yeah?" Seraph's eyes widened.

"Ha, y'all really gon' make me teach a history

lesson, ain't you? A'ight, check it. I know since you boys been rollin' with us that you heard that we the oldest gang in the city. After the Sartovan Civil War, Royalty was left without much of a government. Things seemed to function as normal, but there wasn't a whole lot of structure, so everyone just kinda did they own thing. Lotta violence in them days. So, Arkell Bishop and his homies started this lil' neighborhood protection thing. That was before Bishop Street was called 'Bishop'. Back then, it was like 'Rainbow Street' or some shit."

Ezra had everyone's full attention.

"And that's about the time flare hit the streets. No one knows where it came from originally, but when it hit, it hit. People was runnin' around out here thinkin' they was gods or superheroes or somethin'. Originally, Arkell was opposed to gettin' involved with the junk, but his homies didn't share the same sentiment. That's what caused Bishop to split and the first war. Reshard Campbell and almost half the Bishops at that time moved north and became what's known as the Pawn Road Disciples. Yeah, that's how that began. But war costs resources, and resources costs crowns. So, what did Arkell and his generals decide to do?" Ezra paused for effect, then continued, "They sold flare to fund the war with the Disciples. One of Arkell's top dawgs and a handful of other Bishops were given the option to leave Bishop peacefully, as they were still against the dope. That's the Soldiers, and that's most likely why you don't see them in the dope game to this day, although I heard they got they fingers in the gun trade."

"Dude, that's crazy!" Zero was in awe.

"So much history . . ." Seraph shook his head.

"Well, what happened next?" Lazarus spoke up, eager to hear more.

"Yeah, profess'a Ez!" Marcus, another Bishop general teased.

Ezra grinned and touched his beard. "A'ight, here's some facts: did y'all know that Royalty wasn't always called

'Royalty'?"

"*Maaaan*, now I know you flodgin'!" Antoine shot a dismissive gesture toward Ezra.

"No, I think he right, dawg," Marcus said with serious expression.

"I *am* right, sucka! Anyways, Royalty used to be called 'Harmony.' Facts."

"*Harmony*?" Seraph furrowed his eyebrows.

"Yeah! Y'all ain't ever heard of the Kings, have ya?"

The Switchblades all looked at one another and then at the other Bishops, who all looked equally perplexed.

"Long story short: after the flare wars started bleeding out into the rest of the city, this group called the Kings came up for the same reason Bishop originally did. They was just tryin' to protect they neighborhoods. Sartovans didn't really understand us Ama's too good back then. Anyway, the Kings was a lil' mo' ambitious than the Bishops, the Disciples, and the Soldiers, 'cause they started expandin', even to the point where they was pushin' in on our territory. They was aggressive too," Ezra downed the rest of his drink.

"Man, I gotta be honest. Even with all the time I spent around here before our current situation, there's still so much I don't understand about the history of this city and how much Amakoran people played a role in it."

"Yeah," Seraph touched his chin. "I knew plenty of Amakoran kids at the orphanage, but they were probably just as ignorant about your culture and history as anybody else. The Priests taught us a little bit, and a lot of what you're saying sounds familiar, but it definitely wasn't a priority. I'm sure you know their focus is God." He laughed uncomfortably.

Ezra nodded and stroked his beard. "Well, look, the history of this city ain't all just about Amakorans. I mean, look at the city now. We're a blend, dawg. Everyone has played their part. It's easy for an Amakoran man to point to the Sartovan and blame them for our mess. You know what

I learned, dawg? —And this ain't just the liquor talkin—havin' y'all boys roll with us has really opened up my eyes. If even half these dudes out here had the hearts that y'all have, then maybe there could be some change . . . no—*progress.*"

"That's real, Ezra," Lazarus's eyes started to cloud up. "We're just trying to look at the bigger picture, you know? There's more to people than race or skin color. How will we ever thrive if we find any excuse we can to be at each other's throats?"

"Word," Ezra nodded. "Now, where was I?"

"The Kings were expanding . . ." Seraph reminded him.

"Ah, yeah. So, not only was the three Ama-gangs beefin' against each other, but now they fightin' against the Kings. Thems was bloody times, f'sho. That's when gangs started poppin' up all ov'a Royalty. No one felt safe, so people started comin' together to protect theyselves and they neighborhoods. The White Crows, the Shadows—they sprung up around that time, and then of course started beefin' each other over turf. From what I understand, the city was a cluster-mess."

"So, what happened to the Kings?" Zero scratched his head.

"Well, because so many gangs started poppin' up and fightin' against the Kings, their territory became smaller and smaller and mo' divided. What really ended them, though, was the internal conflict they had. Three of the leaders started disagreeing and arguing over territory. You know who they were?"

Everyone except for Lazarus shook their heads.

"The Vallarios, the Mazzarellis, and, of course, the Lyones."

"Dawg, when you become a historian, though?" Antoine said.

"I ain't no historian. I just read. You should learn how sometime," Ezra quipped, and everyone burst into laughter, including Turrell, who had just joined them. "Hey, boss man!"

"What up, cuz? Where yo' brotha at, man? I ain't seen him all night," Turrell asked with a concerned look.

"Shoot, I don't know. Said he had somethin' t'take care of. I didn't think it would take this long."

"Well, never mind, then. I wanted to talk to both of y'all togetha, but I guess I'll just have to fill him in." Turrell looked over at Lazarus. "You ready to have that talk, dawg?"

Lazarus's nodded.

"Good, let's head to the ba—" Turrell was cut off by the loud rattle of gunfire and shattering glass as a hail of bullets entered the house from every window.

CHAPTER SEVEN

"Get down!" Ezra shouted as everyone hit the floor and drew their weapons.

Seraph happened to be on the ground right next to Ezra and noticed that his upper arm had been grazed, which in turn caused him to check whether he had been hit. The bullets almost endlessly continued flying overhead as what sounded like a thousand firearms were going off at once out front of Turrell's home. Charita, Turrell's wife, could be heard shrieking from the kitchen, screaming, "My baby! My baby!" which reminded Seraph of the reason for the party to begin with—to celebrate Charita's pregnancy.

As soon as the gunfire died down a little, Ezra got to a crouching position and cocked his pistol. "Let's hit 'em back!" he made his way to one of the broken windows and started busting shots off.

Lazarus crawled over to Seraph. "Are you alright, bro?"

"Yeah," Seraph gave Lazarus a once-over. "You?"

"Yeah, man . . ." Lazarus hesitated and motioned toward a lifeless body that lay about ten feet away from them. "But we got a serious problem."

Seraph recognized the body as Turrell, the small

form riddled with bullet wounds from head to toe. "No . . ." he said under his breath.

The rest of the Bishops, including Edge and Zero had joined Ezra near the windows and helped return fire blindly. Before long a different group, who they recognized to also be Bishops came from the back of the house with their guns all pointed at Ezra and the others who had been returning fire. "That's enough!" one of the shooters called out to Ezra, who turned around in confusion.

"Whatchu doin', Varus?" Ezra recognized his fellow general and started to lower his pistol.

Seraph and Lazarus looked at each other in panic as one of the enemy Bishops took their weapons from them and herded them over toward Ezra and the others.

"Toss your guns over, homie. We havin' an intervention," Varus pointed the barrel of his shotgun toward Ezra.

Ezra glanced at Marcus and Antoine, who were equally distraught, but the three of them complied, tossed their pistols toward Varus's feet, and sat there helplessly. "I don't know what this is about, but y'all way outta line!"

At that moment, the front door opened as everyone turned to see DeAndre, followed by his crew and a small group of Amakorans wearing red.

Ezra looked at his brother in bewilderment. "DeAndre?!" he uttered in disbelief.

DeAndre shook his head. "I'ma explain in a minute, big bro," he then nodded toward Varus. "Go on."

Varus and his men cocked their guns and aimed them at Marcus and Antoine, who were separated from the rest of the group, and pulled the trigger.

"DeAndre!" Ezra shouted, standing up in outrage as the enemy Bishops turned their guns on him, causing him to freeze. "What the hell is you doin', man? You workin' fo' the Disciples now?"

DeAndre shook his head. "Naw, bruh. I'm workin' *with* some of the Disciples, who are likeminded and care about the future of Amakorans in this city, unlike some of these suckas," he nodded toward Turrell's lifeless body.

Ezra looked over at his leader as tears formed in his eyes. "You killed him . . ."

"Turrell? *Turrell!*" came Charita's voice from the kitchen as the newly pregnant, now newly widowed woman stepped out and ran over to Turrell's body, wrapping her arms around him and sobbing into his chest. "No! Turrell! Baby! Please! They killed my baby!"

DeAndre looked at Varus. "Take care of her."

"No!" Ezra stepped forward despite the various guns that were trained on him. "She's pregnant . . ."

DeAndre frowned at his brother, then looked at the poor woman and then back to Varus. "Just get her out of here!"

Varus nodded and took Charita by the arm, dragging her toward one of the back rooms as she struggled the entire way, wailing about the atrocity that had just taken place in her living room.

"Why?" Ezra stared in despair.

"Look, bruh, this is much bigger than Bishops n' Disciples. If it makes you feel any betta, that fool Letrelle is lyin' face down in his living room too," DeAndre hoped this news would help ease some of his worry. "Listen, man. Turrell was gonna get us killed messin' around with these Sartovan boys." He sighed and pointed his gun toward Lazarus. "I'd kill all fo' of them right now if Vince didn't want them alive."

"Vince?"

"Vincent Lyone," Deandre grinned.

"You workin' for the damn Lyones?" Ezra bellowed.

Seraph noticed Lazarus subtly fiddling with his cell phone while DeAndre turned back toward his brother.

"You got it twisted, bro. The Lyones is the ones tryin' to *protect* this city. They the ones tryin' to unite everyone. It's these cats who want things to continue going downhill for everyone. They're jus' opportunists. Another war is only gonna result in mo' people dyin'. More of *our* people."

"You fool! You jus' killed *our* people!" Ezra pointed to the two former generals, who lay dead on the ground.

"A necessary sacrifice. They was Turrell's boys, n' we both know that Turrell woulda been dumb enough to follow along wit' these Sar-suckas."

The sound of roaring motorcycle engines caught everyone off guard as the sound grew increasingly louder, until it could be heard right in front of Turrell's home. DeAndre and everyone else inside the house grew silent and listened as they heard one of DeAndre's people out front say "*Whatchu want?*" before a chain of gunfire went off once again. Everyone hit the floor, except for Ezra, who took this opportunity to lunge at his brother and disarm him, taking his pistol and holding it to his head.

Lazarus pulled Seraph down next to him.

Seraph looked back at his leader, perplexed, wondering if Lazarus had sent out some sort of distress call to someone.

"Yo, what the hell *was* that?" Ezra looked over his shoulder.

"If I had to guess, I'd say it was the Cut-Throats," Lazarus carefully stood up once the gunshots ceased.

"Cut-Throats? Are they your other allies that y'all were talkin' about?" Ezra questioned the young Switchblade leader.

Lazarus shook his head. "Not quite."

"Man, y'all gon' mess this whole thing up!" DeAndre struggled before Ezra raised the pistol and struck the hard metal handle against the side of his head.

"Shut up!" Ezra growled through clenched teeth as he and the other Bishops stood up, now with DeAndre's men at gun point. "Waste 'em," he ordered as the other Bishops complied and killed everyone that had been working with DeAndre, except for DeAndre himself, whom

Ezra dragged toward the front door, which was riddled with bullet holes of various sizes. "Ay, yo! We comin' out!"

Lazarus raised his hand in an attempt to get Ezra to reconsider before the mutinous Bishops were all executed in front of him, but to no avail, as Ezra then led his men slowly outside with the Switchblades following. Twenty or so Disciples' bodies littered the street, which was lined with a neat row of fully armed Cut-Throat soldiers mounted on their motorcycles. Seraph felt his stomach twist in knots from the gruesome sight as he swallowed and tried his best not to focus on the horrific scene.

"What's this all about?" Ezra's eyes scanned the massacre before him.

Judge, the leader of the Cut-Throats smirked. "Heard you were in a bind. Thought we might come and help relieve some of the pressure."

Ezra gave Lazarus a perplexed look.

"As much as we'd love to stay and cherish this moment of unity, we really oughta be going," Judge revved his engine. He nodded to his men, and the convoy of motorcycles took off down the road, back toward Kings Avenue.

The Bishops stood silent. Not in a million years would they ever think a Sartovan, no less a Cut-Throat, would come to rescue them in a time of desperation. In truth, they didn't know how to feel. Ezra felt a mixture of gratitude and shame well up in him while staring at the leader of the Switchblades.

"I sent out a call for help, and the Cut-Throats came. I don't know what else to tell you," Lazarus's attention was redirected toward an approaching black SUV with a chrome sword with wings emblem fixed atop the hood.

The vehicle pulled up and came to a halt on the sidewalk, and the engine turned off. The driver's door swung open and out stepped the same man that Edge recognized as Ghost, who months ago had saved him from the Hustlers. He sported the same navy-blue trench coat with the same emblem as the one on his SUV. His expression was serious as he approached the Bishops and Switchblades, looking directly at Lazarus. "We need to get out of here, *now*."

Seraph squinted at Ghost and then at Lazarus. *Has this been Lazarus's contact all along?*

"Hold up," Ezra took a step toward Lazarus, and pointed to Ghost. "The Arch Angels is your guys' allies?"

Lazarus smiled. "I figured it was best to keep this from you until the right time, given their bad reputation."

"I can assure you that now is not the right time either," Ghost reached out for Lazarus, but Ezra stepped between them.

"Oh no, y'all ain't leavin' until I get some answers. Half my gang dead in there, man. I need to know what's going on *right now*!" the Bishop general demanded.

Ghost shot a fearsome glance at Ezra as the sound of approaching vehicles caused everyone to look away.

Six silver vehicles of different makes and models pulled up, some of them boxing in Ghost's SUV as they all seemed to turn off in unison. All the doors opened and out came a large force of Lyone soldiers led by Vincent Lyone, who was accompanied by a tall man who was distinctly more well-dressed than the others, wearing an all-white suit that encompassed his wide body-builder frame. He had a dark-brown pompadour hairstyle and held a fat cigar between his front teeth. Seraph also noticed Lance, who walked closely behind Vincent as they moved toward the Bishops and Switchblades.

"Drop your weapons immediately," Vincent called out in a stern manner that seemed relaxed at the same time.

Ghost nodded to Lazarus, who tossed his pistol, and the rest of the Switchblades and Bishops followed his lead. Ghost turned to face the Lyones and slowly walked toward them but was seized, frisked, disarmed, and detained.

"Woah, easy there, Vincent. I'm an envoy," Ghost reminded the young Lyone captain "I know that your father is strict about immunity for diplomats."

Vincent totally ignored Ghost, as he seemed focused on the Switchblades, more specifically, on Seraph. His eyes narrowed as he stared with disdain at Seraph, questions circulating in his mind as he tried to comprehend what he was doing with the Bishop Brotherhood. The young Lyone swallowed and then looked at Lance, whose gaze was fixed on his childhood friend. "What is *he* doing here?"

Lance's thoughts raced as he looked at his leader and shook his head. "I don't know, Vince. I'm just as confused as you are."

Vincent locked eyes with his subordinate, seemingly unconvinced, as he lifted his chin toward Lazarus. "DeAndre told me about this one's little plan to bring together some of the gangs to overthrow the Lyone family," Vincent informed Lance, who stared with confusion at his leader. "Tell me the truth. Do you have anything to do with this?" he rested his hand on his side arm, while two other Lyones came from behind Lance and removed the pistol that was strapped to his leg.

Ghost and Lazarus held eye contact, as if they were communicating telepathically about the chaos that was beginning to unfold in front of them.

Seraph stepped forward with his hands up. "Hey, Lance doesn't have anything to do with this."

"You shut up!" Vincent pulled his gun, aiming it at the young Switchblade, who shrunk and winced at this threat.

"Vincent . . ." Ghost said pleadingly to the Lyone lieutenant.

"And you too!" Vincent shouted as one of the Lyone soldiers brought his knee sharply against the Arch Angel's diaphragm, knocking the wind out of him.

Ghost's eyes watered as he looked up toward the

familiar face of one of the Lyone generals approaching after getting out from one of the sedans. "Maurice . . . please . . ."

The man, now addressed as Maurice, made a mocking sad face at Ghost and simply shrugged as if he were powerless to do anything.

Vincent cleared his throat and ran his fingers through his hair before looking from Seraph to Lance. "If you're not working with him, then kill him," he held the pistol out for Lance to take.

"What?" Lance's eyes grew wide. "You want me to *kill* him?"

"Are you deaf? Yes, I want you to kill him! Didn't you hear me? He and his little buddies have been trying to stage a coup against my father!"

Lance stared back at Seraph, a look of shock on both of their faces.

"Lance, did you hear what I just said? *Kill him*!" Vincent ordered and pressed the gun against Lance's chest.

Lance stood frozen as his eyes trailed from Seraph to Vincent. "I can't . . ."

"Useless!" Vincent spat in disgust and then nodded to the other two Lyones, who had previously disarmed Lance. The two grabbed Lance by his arms and forced him to his knees. Vince raised the gun back at Seraph and cocked back the hammer.

"No!" Lance cried and broke free from the grips of the Lyones and charged Vincent, tackling him to the ground. "Run Seraph! Run!"

Seraph shook violently as he looked at Ghost and Lazarus, who shook their heads and signaled with their eyes that many of the other Lyones had their guns trained on all of them. There was no escape. Seraph stood helplessly and watched as his childhood best friend was apprehended by a few of the Lyone soldiers and forced to his knees once more.

Vincent got back to his feet and dusted himself off

as one of his subordinates brought the cocked pistol back to him. He held the barrel against the side of Lance's head.

"I'm sorry, Seraph," Lance met eyes with Seraph one last time before his brain matter painted the sidewalk and his lifeless body fell over.

"Lance! No!" Seraph instantly became sick as he collapsed to the ground and emptied his stomach all over the grass in front of him.

Vincent then redirected the muzzle of the gun at Seraph, his eyes burning with hatred.

"That's enough!" shouted a powerful, unfamiliar voice. "Stand down! All of you!"

"Father?" Vincent lowered his weapon and turned to face Lucien Lyone, head of the Lyone family.

The rest of the Lyones obeyed immediately, lowering their weapons and stepping back. At this opportunity, Seraph ran over to Lance's body, buried his face against his chest, and sobbed after he saw the small burning hole in his friend's temple. Lucien Lyone was average height, with light-brown hair that was slicked back and a neat goatee. He wore a gray suit with a blue vest and matching blue tie, which had a small lion head pinned on it near the top. He also wore a short gray trench coat that had another lion design across the shoulders. On his right knee was a leg brace, and he leaned against a simple walking stick with a silver handle as he slowly approached the group of Lyones.

Lucien's eyes then darted to Maurice. "I want an explanation. *Immediately.*"

Maurice pointed a fat finger toward Lazarus and spoke, his voice deep and gruff. "Apparently, this one and his little group were trying to get the Bishops and some other gangs to join together and go to war against our family. I came to keep an eye on Vincent once he told me that one of the Bishops approached him about the matter."

"Ah, and you decided to do this without informing me first. Why?" Lucien narrowed his eyes and held up a dismissive hand before Maurice could answer. "We will talk about this later. In the meantime, take my son and the rest of our men back to the compound."

"Yes, sir."

"Father, please—"

"We will discuss this later. For now, you are stripped of your rank and are to wait in your room until I return home. Do not make me come looking for you."

"Yes, Father," Vincent obeyed, getting into his vehicle with his men and leaving the area. Only Lucien's personal guards remained.

Ghost slowly approached the Lyone leader with his hands up before Lucien beckoned him over.

"What do you have to do with all this?" Lucien raised his eyebrows at the Arch Angel envoy.

"The kid's a friend of mine. Said he got himself into some trouble, so I came to make sure he was alright. That's all," Ghost turned as another black vehicle with the Arch Angels' insignia stamped on the grill pulled up. The back door of the sedan opened, and a L'Orandan man, short in stature, wearing a fine black suit and a black and red tie approached. His hair was short and black, and he sported a van dyke style goatee.

Lucien directed his attention toward the man and offered a polite yet brief smile. "Mr. Martinelli. What brings you here?" he looked from him to Ghost and then to Lazarus, who remained next to Edge and Zero.

"Lucien, it's been a while," Armand Martinelli firmly shook hands with the Lyone leader before continuing. "I heard there was a possible mix-up between your men and Ghost, so I decided to come and make sure all was well," he maintained a smile until he started noticing all the dead bodies that littered the ground. "What in the hell happened?" he gave Ghost a confused, disturbed look.

"It seems that there was a shootout between the Bishops and the Disciples. I passed some Cut-Throats on the way here as well—not sure what that's about."

Lucien narrowed his eyes suspiciously, then pointed to Lazarus and the other two and beckoned for them to come over. "You too," he lifted his chin in Ezra's direction. Once the four all stood in front of the Lyone leader, he studied each one, then spoke. "What is this business about you all wanting to start a war with my family?"

Lazarus cleared his throat and spoke through the shakiness in his voice. "Because the Lyones extort the gangs and the people of Royalty. I know how you came to power—by killing people, wiping out entire gangs, just to show force. You're a murderer who only cares about power. We wanted to change that and help bring back the times where people were united and equal."

Lucien listened carefully, a frown plastered on his face. "I think you have greatly misunderstood me and my intentions. There was never a point where the gangs were united and equal. There was always tension, always war. I did what I did to put an end to that. Our goals are not so different, um . . .?"

The Switchblade leader looked down and quietly uttered his name. "Lazarus."

"Ah, Lazarus. Thank you," Lucien continued. "In regards to taxes, not that I think you'll fully understand that anyway, but what would taxes have to do with you? I don't recall you ever having to pay any."

"Honestly, that part is irrelevant when it comes to how this affects me personally." Lazarus looked back at Edge and Zero and then back at Lucien. "We're orphans. All of us. All as a result of what you did almost twenty years ago. You even kill your own people."

Lucien squinted in Seraph's direction at Lance's body, instantly recognizing him as his son's right-hand man. "Who killed him?"

"Your boy!" Edge barked.

The Lyone leader's frown drooped even further. He carefully used his walking stick to make his way over to

Seraph, who was grieving over the loss of his oldest friend. Lucien slowly knelt down next to the young man and placed his hand on his back.

Seraph pushed Lucien's hand away and dove at him, taking the esteemed leader to the ground and placing his hands around his throat in an attempt to throttle him. "I'm gonna kill you! And then I'm gonna kill your son! I'll bring down the Lyone family!" Seraph swore as Lucien's watery eyes bulged and looked helplessly up at the angry Switchblade.

Lyone's guards dashed to Seraph and ripped him off their leader, pinning him to the ground while another helped Lucien to his feet and handed him his walking stick.

Lucien scowled at Seraph. "Take him to the Dragon's Lair! He needs time to cool off and think about his actions," he pointed toward his car. He pulled out his phone and began making a phone call. "Hello, Segundo. … Yes. … Don't keep me waiting," he ended the call before walking back toward the Arch Angels, the Switchblades, and the Bishop general.

Seraph fought and struggled the whole way as Lucien's guards dragged him to the car in which Lucien had arrived. The young Switchblade was pressed against the car, handcuffed, and a black sack was placed over his head and fastened around his neck before he was thrown into the back. The Lyone guards got into the car and drove away toward the Dragon's Lair.

At that moment, DeAndre approached Lucien. "Yo, uh, Mr. Lyone. It was me who tol' your son about what these fools was up to."

Lucien turned to face DeAndre and raised a single eyebrow. "Is that so?"

"Yeah . . . I didn't know things was gonna get so crazy. Vince said that this was the best way to handle it."

"First of all, I don't want to hear any more about this *plan* to go to war with my family. I will deal with my son and my general. I can promise you that. In the meantime, if you have issues, be it with taxes, social justices, or what have you, then you come to me directly, and I will be happy to address whatever concerns you have. Is that understood?" He looked directly at Lazarus this time.

"Yeah," Lazarus glanced up at Ghost, who ever-so-slightly narrowed his eyes at him. "Yes *sir*, I mean."

Lucien then turned back to DeAndre. "If you want to know how to really handle these issues, then you are welcome to join my family." He invited the young Bishop and then looked around at the rest of the surviving Bishops and projected his voice. "That goes for all of you here! I imagine that Turrell is dead, as he is not here now. If that is the case, then who do you owe allegiance to? Are you tired of paying taxes? Join me and collect taxes. Anyone here who leaves this ghetto behind and joins the Lyone family today will receive a sign-up bonus of one thousand crowns, and together you can help me bring order to the remaining chaos of this city!"

The Switchblades all looked at one another before silently looking down as it seemed like all of the Bishops, aside from Ezra, came forward and accepted this invitation.

"And *you*?" Lucien turned to Ezra, who screwed his face and shook his head. "No matter." The Lyone shrugged and then smiled at his new batch of recruits.

"Anything else I can do for you, Lucien?" Armand cleared his throat.

Lucien thought for a moment and then smiled. "Yes, actually. Step aside here with me, Armand. You too, Ghost," the three walked the two Arch Angels over to their vehicles. Once they were away from the others, Lucien spoke again. "These boys are all troubled, but it seems that they look up to you. Do me this favor, and just keep an eye on them, okay? Especially that kid that I had taken away. When he's released, he's going to need some guidance. We wouldn't want him doing something that might get him killed, right?"

Armand looked at Ghost and shrugged before

looking back at Lucien. "I don't see why not. We'll watch the kids. Have no fear."

"I never do," Lucien winked at the Arch Angel leader before heading over to his new recruits and instructing them to wait for their escort to the compound so that they could begin their training.

Ezra angrily retreated back into Turrell's house to check on Charita.

Before long, everyone—Arch Angels, Lyones, and Bishops—was gone, leaving Lazarus, Edge, and Zero standing in the middle of the bloodbath that they had just been a part of and listening to the approaching sirens of the Royal Priests. Zero faced his leader with a sorrowful look and said, "What do we do now?"

Lazarus's shaky hands pulled his electronic cigarette from his pocket, and he brought it to his lips and inhaled deeply with his eyes closed before releasing a large cloud of smoke and shaking his head. "I don't know . . ." his eyes wasted away with grief.

CHAPTER EIGHT

"Father, you have to understand that I was doing this for the good of the family!" Vincent spoke in his attempt to defend his actions.

Lucien sat behind his desk, stone-faced, "What you did was reckless. We don't have to handle things like that anymore. It was necessary at first so that they would fear us, but don't you see how quickly that fear turned into respect? If we continue to mistreat them, there will never be any peace, which, I should remind you, *is* our goal."

"But the Bishop Brotherhood is one of the most violent gangs. I saw an opportunity to take care of them when DeAndre told me about their plan to come after our family. That's why I got Maurice involved. This isn't just some trivial matter!"

Segundo, Lucien's second-in-command, raised his eyebrows at Vincent. "That's not for you to decide. Your father managed to recruit the remainder of the Bishops and Disciples aside from a few individuals, by simply offering them a position in our ranks."

"Yeah, because they all practically killed each other off. They joined us because I helped reduce them down to almost nothing!"

Lucien let out a heavy sigh. "I'm sure you meant well, but you must learn that we can no longer do things like this. You will remain demoted until you can prove to me that you have enough self-control to continue our efforts in a restrained manner."

"Father, *please*—"

"I won't hear any more of it! You are dismissed. I want you to think about how you could better serve this family."

Vincent's head hung low as he stood up and exited Lucien's office, cursing under his breath as he slammed the door on his way out.

Lucien opened a desk drawer, and pulled out a long silver case with the Lyone crest on it. "Cigar?" he said as he opened the case and held it out toward Segundo.

"No thanks, boss." He rested his hands behind his back. "Just give the kid time; he'll learn. I'm sure he'll grow into a fine man."

"That son of mine can be a real monster." Lucien took out a cigar for himself and placed it between his teeth. He then lit a match and slowly brought the flame to the end of his cigar, puffing hard until it burned a soft orange and a cloud of smoke rose from it. "You know what I saw him doing when he was just five years old? He was torturing a bug . . . a praying mantis or grasshopper or something. He ripped the poor thing's legs off and just watched it roll around helplessly. I made him step on it to put it out of its misery. I think he was disappointed because he couldn't watch it suffer any longer."

Segundo shook his head as he walked over to the minibar, poured himself a glass of scotch, and took a long sip from the crystal glass. "Well, what about Dante? He's almost to the age where we should be able to steer him in the right direction."

Lucien rolled his eyes. "In that case, I may as well entrust the future of the family to my daughter."

"What do you plan to do about Maurice?"

"I don't see any other option but to demote him."

Segundo sipped his scotch and nodded. "An example has to be made. That's for sure."

"Yeah. I can't have my own generals doing things behind my back—I mean, did he not realize how serious something like that was and how severe the consequences could and very well be as a result?"

"I can't say, Boss . . ." Segundo narrowed his eyes as he stepped over to the window and looked out at the courtyard below, "but I know that if we let this slide, then it'll condone similar actions in the future."

"Exactly. Have everyone meet at the compound in a half hour. The sooner this gets dealt with, the better."

"I'll start making calls now," Segundo retrieved his cell phone from inside his suit jacket. "Anything else?"

Lucien began to say something but hesitated and then shook his head. "Thank you, Segundo."

"Of course, sir."

Dante felt his heart tie into a knot when he heard his father insinuate that he would never be capable of leading the family, as he listened from outside of his office. The young Lyone had just turned thirteen years old that month. He had medium-length black hair that he wore combed over to one side and that almost completely covered his right eye. He knew that he was not favored in his father's eyes, and this hurt him deeply, but he also did not envy his older brother Vincent, who seemed to always be disappointing their father in one way or another. Ever since he could remember, Vincent strove to earn their father's approval, which to Dante felt next to impossible. Although he knew that his father did love him and took good care of him, there was a distance, a mild neglect that he could not seem to shake. Perhaps because, rather than torturing bugs, he preferred to study them. Dante was never much of a fighter, unlike his older brother. Instead, he had a high capacity for learning and retaining knowledge, often studying works of literature or science. In terms of maturity, he was well beyond his age and often preferred to keep the company of his father's advisers like Segundo, or his older sister, Sophia. The young Lyone frowned as he continued down the hallway and halted in front of his sister's room. The door was already ajar, but he knocked anyway with one knuckle. "Come in!"

Dante gently pushed the door open to find Sophia sitting in front of her vanity, braiding her hair. Her smile greeted him from her reflection in the mirror. "Hello," he spoke softly.

Sophia turned around in her chair to face her little brother, who was only three years younger. "What is it, baby brother?" Her heart felt heavy, knowing that there was something troubling him.

"Why is Father so cruel, Sophie?" Dante addressed his big sister by her nickname, which only family members used.

"Oh Dante, Father isn't cruel!" Sophia paused. "Okay, he is a little hard on us, but you know why, right?"

Dante nodded sheepishly. "Because he wants us to *always do our best*."

"That's right," Sophia walked toward her younger brother and placed an arm around his shoulders as he rested his head against her.

"Father said that he was going to entrust the future of the business over to you someday."

Sophia giggled and shook her head. "He only said that because he is frustrated with Vincent. What did he do this time anyway?"

"It sounds like he got a lot of people killed today." It hurt him to say this. He knew that death was not good, especially murder. He didn't want to see his big brother as a murderer, but the word wouldn't leave his mind.

"Oh no . . ." she played with Dante's hair, her heart breaking. She wondered what must be going through Vincent's mind after causing such an atrocity. "I know it's hard, little brother, but this is just the way things are. At least for now. Hey, I'll tell you what! If we do our best and strive to make Father proud and do well in the family, perhaps someday we can make Royalty a better place. What do you think?"

Dante's face lit up. "I think that's a good plan!"

The Lyone generals assembled in the meeting room on the second floor of the main building of the Lyone compound. Lucien sat at the head of a large mahogany table with Segundo at his right. On his left was Lucien's older brother, Giovanni, who oversaw the training of new recruits. Next to him was Maurice Passamonte, who oversaw the west side of the city, and across the table from him was Alvaro Rossi, who oversaw the east. Everyone sat in silence, waiting for Lucien to speak, as he sat leaned forward, elbows resting on the table, with his fingers laced and covering his mouth, his eyes focused on Maurice, who looked away uncomfortably. Segundo quietly cleared his throat, stealing Lucien's attention for a brief moment as he gave his leader a single nod.

"I'm sure everyone knows why I called this meeting?" Lucien lowered his hands from in front of his face and placed them palms down on the table.

"Boss," Maurice started, "I'm s—"

"Sorry? I'm sure you are," Lucien's face was expressionless. "Do you all know who runs this family?"

"You do, Boss!" Maurice exclaimed, with Giovanni and Alvaro nodding in agreement.

"Wrong. *We* run this family. This council. If I ran this family by myself, then I wouldn't bother having you all as generals, now would I?"

Everyone shook their heads in silence.

"So, when one of you decides to go off on his own and make major decisions that needlessly cost a large chunk of our citizens their lives, he not only disrespects me, but all of you. Am I making sense?" Lucien looked around the table as the other generals nodded, except for Maurice, who looked down and folded his hands in front of him. "This thing that we have here—it cannot continue to properly function unless the people at the top are working together. In harmony. That would be us. If we want to keep what we have and continue improving this city, then anytime one of you gets a bright idea—which, let me clarify, was not Maurice's but my twenty-three-year-old son's—then you are to bring that to me or Segundo, so that we can conduct a meeting and decide as a team if that idea is in the best interest of the family and ultimately Royalty. Do I make myself clear?"

"Yes, sir," they all spoke in unison.

"Good. Maurice, you've been demoted to captain for the foreseeable future. You will work under Giovanni, supervising and training new recruits. Understood?"

Maurice opened his mouth as if to contest, but after a sharp look from Segundo, he only let out a sigh and nodded his head in defeat.

"Excellent. In his place, I want to nominate Jalen Elders to take over as general of the west and to be a part of this council. Any objections?" Lucien looked at each of his generals, all of whom remained silent. "Very good. Segundo, please inform Jalen of our decision as soon as the meeting concludes. Also, I know you had some things you wanted to mention while everyone was present. I will allow you to stay until the end of the meeting, as some of this information is relevant to you."

"You got it. Alright, guys, here's the deal. From what we understand, there is a group of four kids calling themselves the Switchblades who apparently had some sort of plan to get Bishop and whoever else to declare war on our family to free the people of Royalty from our tyrannical rule or something to that effect." Segundo paused to give everyone a chance to laugh at his melodrama. "Our newest recruit, DeAndre, who was a Bishop general, confirmed this information. Apparently, these boys nearly had Turrell convinced before he met his demise. These boys also seem to be working either for or with another group, potentially the Cut-Throats, who showed up and gunned down the men who were working with DeAndre. One of these boys was taken to the Dragon's Lair after he made threats to Mr. Lyone because Vincent killed his friend, who Vincent claims was working with the Switchblades. Frankly, we don't know too much about this whole situation at the moment. Mr. Lyone spoke with a boy named Lazarus briefly, and we are hoping that this was just a delusional kid's misunderstanding; however, we must exercise caution and not give anyone, civilian or gang, a reason to want to 'overthrow' what we have created together."

"We don't know how serious this really is and even so I'm certain that none of the gangs really pose a threat to us, but that's not the point. We want our people to love us, not hate us. I want you to all make sure that the captains under you are not abusing their authority. If our people are mistreating the people of Royalty, then it's no wonder that young men like this Lazarus want to come at us. We must be wise *and* benevolent."

"Exactly," Segundo began. "On another note"—he removed a fat envelope from inside of his suit jacket and tossed it toward the center of the large table—"Rin Yamato handed this to me just this morning. I'm sure you all know why."

"Blackjack's bail . . ." Giovanni said in a near whisper.

Segundo nodded. "That is correct. Ten million crowns. This has taken her nearly twenty years to obtain. We knew it was a stretch when we set the bail so high, but finally, it has been paid off, and we can have the Golden Dragons release him to her when we're ready."

"She's gonna kill him right then and there," predicted Alvaro Rossi, the youngest of the generals.

"I told Rin that she is free to do what she likes with him on her own property, so there will be no bloodshed in the streets. We have to at least appear like we're keeping the peace. We're not entirely sure what implications, if any, this may have. We know that the Arch Angels have distanced themselves from Blackjack since the incident with their former leader, but we still don't know if the man has any connections outside the Arch Angels. Therefore, we need to keep an eye on the situation—not up close and personal, but at a distance. It's important that we stay informed about this whole situation."

"Very good," Lucien rose from his seat. "Thank you for coming on such short notice, and do keep in mind what I said at the beginning of this meeting."

As the generals started leaving, Maurice approached Lucien with a large frown plastered on his face.

Lucien guffawed and shook his head, holding out his arms and embracing Maurice, giving him a quick kiss on the cheek. "You disappointed me, Maurice. You remember this, and don't ever let me down like this again."

"I won't fail you again, Mr. Lyone," Maurice said, exiting the room behind Alvaro and Giovanni.

Segundo shut the door behind Maurice and approached Lucien. "Well, it seems that we accomplished a lot with that meeting."

Lucien sighed and shook his head. "Unfortunately, it's the only way to keep things in order."

Segundo nodded solemnly.

"Listen, that kid—Seraph? I want you to go down to Dragon's Lair after you inform Elders of his promotion and give him his orders. Go and see the kid, and see if he's all right. Vincent did a terrible thing today. I spoke with Armand Martinelli and he said he would keep an eye on this Seraph kid once I give the Dragons the go ahead to release him."

"Listen, I know my father made you the leader of my crew, but if you do as I say, I can guarantee that once I make it to the top, you will be right there next to me,"

Vincent explained to DeAndre, who was now decked out in full Lyone officer attire.

DeAndre looked down at his new threads with a smirk. "Is that so? Way I see it, your daddy ain't too happy about how you handled things."

Vincent narrowed his eyes at DeAndre as he stepped closer to him, their faces inches apart. "Who do you think's going to run this family when my father's gone? Sure, you could do exactly as he tells you while he is alive and well. That will keep you in his good graces. But when someone else takes over the family? When *I* take over this family—then what?"

"I don't know, man. There's that uncle of yours," DeAndre's gaze met Vincent's.

"Fine. I'm sure you'll do a bang-up job. Just like you did for me."

"That wasn't my fault! That was them Sartovan boys. Lazarus n'dem."

"Yeah? So what? You couldn't handle a few *no-names* to accomplish the mission that we'd been planning for months? Shows how competent you are . . ."

"You know them boys was planning on trying to get the Bishops to go to war with your family? Well, they had Turrell convinced. Even my brother! They sneaky, man. They got other people workin' with them too. Lazarus is smart—I'll give him that. But the plans? I don't think they were his."

"Oh, really?" Vincent's tone changed. "You see? This is why we need to continue working together, DeAndre. We see who the real enemy is. You made a good choice in accepting my father's offer. The gangs are parasites. But why stop there? If there really is some grand master plot to remove my family from control, then the only hope for this city is to stop them. Right?"

DeAndre touched his chin where his goatee used to be. "I mean, you right. I blame them for everything that happened. Things didn't have to get crazy like they did, and

I *know* that it was Lazarus that had the Cut-Throats come and shoot everybody up! That means they in on it too."

"And this brings us back to square one. All I am asking is that you do a little . . . investigative work for me. While I'm suspended from my duties, I need you to be my eyes and ears on the streets. I heard that Seraph kid got locked up, but if I know my father, he won't be locked up for long. Once he's out, you have to keep an eye on him—the other ones too."

"Yeah, okay. And when we get some dirt on them, then what?"

"I'll handle that. But this is what will prove my innocence before my father and get me that much closer to becoming the head of the family. And I won't forget your efforts. Trust me."

DeAndre nodded and went back to admiring his new clothes.

"Just report back to me when you get any information. I'll decide what to do from there."

Seraph's eyes shot open to nothing but total darkness. His breath was heavy, and his body was drenched in sweat. After a moment of feeling around, he realized that he was lying on what seemed to be a small uncomfortable cot in what looked like a large walk-in closet. It was cold and musty. He slowly sat up, leaning back against the wall, and hugged his knees.

"Lance . . ." he whispered as tears rushed down his cheeks in two hot streams. *Take him to the Dragon's Lair. He looks like he needs some time to think things over before he makes a big mistake*, came the faint echo of Lucien Lyone's voice inside his head. "No!" Seraph shouted in anguish as he banged his fist against the concrete wall to the left of him. "No, no, no, no!" He choked as a mixture of mucus and saliva came out in gobs and dripped from his chin. Blood ran down his hands from his knuckles scraping against the coarse wall. He would have continued to bang his hand against it but lacked the will to even speak anymore. Instead, he curled into a ball and allowed the tears to keep flowing, sniffing between sobs.

"Why are you crying?" came an unknown voice from the other side of the wall.

Seraph stopped crying, trying to stifle his sniveling. *Who was that? Probably another Lyone.* He pressed his lips together, not wanting to give them the satisfaction of hearing him cry. *How did this happen?* He carefully recounted the events that had transpired in the short span of time. *How could I have allowed my friendship with Lance to be ruined?* He choked back a sob. *We were going to be friends forever. We were going to make it out of the orphanage. We were going to start our own business and do our own thing, apart from the gangs.* The word very word now angered him. *Gang. What does that even mean? What a joke.* Seraph ran his fingers through his oily hair and grabbed a handful, tightly pulling it in deep frustration. He wondered what would have happened if he had just ignored Lazarus's warnings. It wasn't his business to begin with. *Why did he feel the need to warn me? We didn't know each other. He didn't care about me. So, what was it?*

Father, Seraph recited as he defaulted to what he had been taught by the Royal Priests, *I don't know what to do. I don't even know where I am.* He looked around the room, his eyes not yet fully adjusted to the utter darkness. He knew that he was at the Golden Dragon's private prison but never would have guessed that it was such a dark, solitary place. *Please Father,* he prayed. *Please make what happened to Lance right. Please bring justice,* he pleaded, not caring that he wanted the Lyones to pay for everything that they had done—not just to Lance, but to Ram and O'Connor and everyone who suffered losses at the hands of the Lyone family.

A noise nearby of what sounded like a small slot opening and closing startled Seraph. He used what little strength he had to push himself up to a sitting position and listened carefully as he heard the voice of the same person who spoke to him earlier softly say, "Thank you." This perplexed him.

He flinched again when he heard the sound of an opening slot coming from the door of his cell. A bright light flashed and then disappeared instantly after a small tray with bread and water was slid through. "Wait!" he shouted, but no answer came, just fading footsteps.

Seraph slowly slid off his bed and onto the floor and proceeded to crawl on his hands and knees to where he saw the food had been pushed. He groped the air in front of him until his hand touched the edge of the tray and he pulled it forward, causing the glass to spill some of the water out onto the tray. Ignoring this, he picked up a small bread roll but then hesitated. *Maybe it's poisoned. Maybe this is their way of making an example of me so that people will continue to stay out of the Lyones' way.*

"The food's okay to eat," came a slightly amused-sounding voice from the other side of the wall once again. "I should know . . ."

Seraph wiped away the tears on his cheeks with the back of his hand. He brought the small roll to his mouth and took a bite. It wasn't terrible. Just bland. "Thanks."

"Not a problem," said the voice. "Your life isn't over yet."

Seraph laughed bitterly. *Who knows if I'll ever get out of here.*

"You must have done something pretty bad, huh?"

"I guess so. I tried to kill Lucien Lyone after . . ." Seraph felt his chest become immensely heavy. It hurt him to think about his best friend. He took another bite of bread, then took a deep breath and continued, ". . . after his son killed my best friend."

The voice remained silent for a moment. "I'm very sorry to hear that. What would you do if you got out?"

Without hesitating, Seraph said, "I would use every resource I have"—he thought of Lazarus and the Switchblades, Ram and Mongrel, O'Connor and the McDroogins, and Ezra—"to bring down the Lyones once and for all and end this hellish system they've created."

"That's admirable, but if they *did* let you out, don't you think they would be watching you carefully to make sure you didn't try anything after what you did? I admire your heart, but if you're not careful, you'll only end up dead, and all of this passion will have been in vain."

Seraph groaned. *I'll probably just end up rotting in here anyway . . .*

CHAPTER NINE

Ezra tilted his glass upward as he drank down a shot of whiskey, followed by a glass of beer. "Gimme anotha', Juice," he said to the short, young dark-haired beauty who was bartending at the Wild West.

"Sure thing, honey. Just don't overdo it, okay?"

Ezra shrugged and pulled out a menthol cigarette. He didn't usually smoke, but he was so distraught with sorrow and hatred that he no longer cared. Neither about his sobriety, nor his health. Charita shrieked and sobbed uncontrollably when Ezra went to check on her after the Lyone family had left. The look of hysteria haunted his mind. His face contorted in disgust, he lit the cigarette and inhaled deeply, instantly coughing out the smoke that briefly filled his lungs. He took another drag. Juice placed another shot and a beer in front of him and gave him a weak, sympathetic smile.

"You're in my seat, boy," came a gruff voice from an older Sartovan biker who wore a vest similar to the ones that the Cut-Throats wore, except the back of his read 'Devil's Sons'. With him were four other bikers, each more intimidating than the next.

Ezra scoffed and took the shot of whiskey after

removing the burning cigarette from his lips. He exhaled the smoke through his nostrils once he had swallowed the liquor.

"Hey!" the biker put his hand on Ezra's shoulder as he attempted to force him to turn around and face him.

Ezra grabbed the biker's hand tightly and turned around, pushing the man back into his friend. "Take that stuff someplace else, skim milk," he said as he dragged so hard from the cigarette that it burned down to the filter and then blew the thick cloud of smoke in the bikers' direction before snubbing the butt out in the ashtray behind him.

"You're in the wrong bar, powder burn," the biker said as he and the others approached Ezra.

"A'ight then." Ezra downed his beer, which leaked out from both corners of his mouth, wiped the condensation from his beard, and put his fists up, spreading his feet into a sturdy stance.

The ringleader lunged at Ezra, who slammed his fist into the biker's face, sending him staggering to the ground.

All at once, the four other bikers came at Ezra. They struggled to get hold of him, but Ezra shook them off, hammering his fist into one of their chests, knocking the wind out of him. Another came up and threw a few jabs, which he carefully weaved. He then cocked back his fist to put the biker down but felt an arm around his bicep pull him back. Before he realized it, one of the larger bikers had him in a full nelson. Ezra shifted from left to right, trying to shake the biker off his back, but the other began throwing his knee into Ezra's gut.

"ARRRRGHH!" Ezra growled.

At that moment, Judge, followed by two other Cut-Throats, entered the bar and stood in the doorway as they watched Ezra take on the bikers. All the patrons at the bar moved out of the way to give them room and avoid getting hit themselves. Juice looked pleadingly over at the sergeant-at-arms of the Cut-Throats.

Terrace grabbed a pool cue from the wall to the left of him and started forward, but Judge placed a hand on his shoulder. "Hold on. Let's see what happens."

Ezra's eyes met with Judge's for a brief moment as a loud roar escaped him. The powerful Amakoran shifted his weight forward before slamming his head back into the center of the biker's face. He then put his fists back up before sending his left elbow into a different biker's jaw. Another caught his fist twice in the eye. He then faced the last standing biker, covered in sweat and blood, most of which wasn't his. Breathing heavily, he closed the gap between them.

"Wait—now, hold on . . . y-you win, big fella," the defeated biker held up his hands in surrender.

Ezra smirked and shook his head before lunging at the frightened biker, grabbing him by his vest, spinning him around, and pinning him to the bar, where he began to beat him out of consciousness, pummeling the biker's face with his fist.

"Alright, alright! It's over!" came Judge's voice.

Ezra released the biker, who slid off the bar and then hit the floor with a loud *thud*. He kept his hands up, ready for round two as he turned and faced the other biker gang.

"Easy. We got no beef with you," Judge narrowed his eyes at the Bishop.

"You had no problem wastin' half my brothas n' all them Disciples back at Turrell's house."

"What? We saved your ass, kid! You should be thanking me, if anything!"

"*Thanking you?* Boy, you out your damn mind. I didn't ask for your help." Ezra lit another cigarette and leaned against the bar.

Juice quietly attempted to clean up what she could of the broken glass on the floor.

"Well, *someone* did and we answered. The way I see it—you owe us."

"Owe you? Man, get on outta here with all that." Ezra turned his back on the Cut-Throats and took a long sip from his drink.

"You ain't got nothin' to lose. Or I guess you could just sit here and drown yourself in liquor. Either way, it doesn't look like you got anything going on."

"Oh, I got somethin' planned. I'm gonna finish drinkin', n'then I'ma head ova' to the Lion's Den, and I'm gonna kill all of 'em. Every last one a'them murderers!"

"You'll die before you even get through the front gate," Judge cautioned. "Listen, I know how you feel—"

"No! No, you don't know nothin', dawg! They killed my fourteen-year-ol' lil' cousin! Then almost half of my people! They wasted our leader and then bribed the rest of my peoples to join them. You gon' tell me you know how that feels?"

The president of the Cut-Throats removed his glasses and cleaned them with his shirt. "Not exactly, but to say we haven't suffered similar losses from the Lyones isn't true. And trust me when I say that we do plan on getting our revenge, but if we do this without careful planning, then it'll be in vain because we'll all end up like those who we want to avenge."

Ezra slowly shook his head, puffed his cigarette again, and laughed dryly. "So what? You want me to join your little butt-boy biker gang and help y'all take out the Lyones? Y'all out'cho simple minds."

"Woah, I didn't ask anyone to join the Cut-Throats, first of all. All I'm sayin' is that there's strength in numbers, and since you don't have any"—he paused to let it sink in—"you can roll with us until all of this is over. Then you can go back to whatever corner you were standing on before all of this went down," he put his glasses back on and folded his arms over his chest.

After taking a moment to consider his options, Ezra nodded slowly, "A'ight, I'll roll witchu for now, and when I handle my business, we'll go our separate ways."

"This is going to set our efforts back even further," Armand watched the vibrating glass of two-way mirror that looked out onto the dance floor. The weekend had started, and La Noche was filled with the usual patrons: businessmen and women, gangsters, and young bachelors mobbed the largest nightclub in Royalty. The leader of the Arch Angels and his right-hand man Ghost sat in his office and discussed recent events.

"It wasn't anybody's fault, honestly. Things got out of hand because of the Lyone boy," Ghost mused. "Lazarus had just reported that things were going well with the Bishops."

Armand rubbed his temples with the tips of his fingers and closed his eyes briefly before standing up from his chair and pushing it against his desk. He then walked over to the two-way mirror to look out at the patrons. "And what should we do about Lazarus and his crew now?"

"They're distraught. They weren't expecting things to play out so gruesomely. I didn't either," he joined Armand at the mirror.

"None of us did. Maybe it wasn't the best idea to get a bunch of kids involved in this."

"I know what you mean, boss. Reminds me of my own meager beginnings. I was an orphan off on my own, just like they were, before I joined. I hate that we got them involved in this situation, but they're a key piece on the board. It's their lack of affiliation that helped them establish such a strong bond with the Bishops." He paused and then smiled. "Lazarus has a lot of heart. He genuinely believes that we can restore this city to what it once was."

"Do you still think we can?"

"I definitely think it's possible. We just have to be all the more careful. If the Switchblades are still up to it, I think we can pull this off."

"What about the new kid that was with him? Any idea what's gonna happen to him?"

"That's a whole 'nother story. He watched his best friend die at the hands of Vincent Lyone. He's going to be pretty messed up for a while, I imagine."

"I want you to find out when they're going to let him out. Let me know right away."

Lazarus, Zero, and Edge sat at a table toward the back of the Asylum, accompanied by Damien, leader of the Immortals with his generals Shade, Heavy, and Blitz. A round of drinks had just been brought to them.

"Thank you again for meeting with us on such short notice," Lazarus forced a smile.

"What a nightmare," Damien rested his head in his hands.

Lazarus stared off into space as he tried to figure out the present situation. *What can I even do to fix this? I can't raise the dead, that's for sure. And what can I do about Seraph? The poor guy had to watch his best friend die, and now he's been locked away in the Dragon's Lair for the past two weeks. Are we just supposed to demand that they release him? Yeah, right. That would just land us in prison with him, and then we'd be useless.*

"Ghost and you seemed to be well acquainted. Is he the one that you've been answering to this whole time?" Edge squinted in Lazarus's direction.

"He's the whole reason I started the Switchblades in the first place. Just two years prior, I sat at TNT's with Ram and Mongrel, enjoying an evening of blues-rap and booze. Ram was recounting some old war stories from back in the day when he used to run the Jackals. I remember it like it was yesterday. This particular story involved them running away from a much bigger force after they had bitten off more than they could chew. No one died, of course . . ."

"Man, those were the days!" Mongrel sighed as he folded his arms behind his head and leaned back in his chair.

"Yeah, we had such a good thing going . . ." Ram exhaled a cloud of smoke.

"Until the Lyones ruined it," Lazarus slurred his words somewhat.

Ram gritted his teeth. "We'll make a comeback someday."

"Did you ever go after them?"

"Ha—funny kid." Mongrel shook his head.

"And do what? It was just me." Ram's eyes welled up. "I'm the only one . . ." He shook his head and stared at the table.

Lazarus felt for him but couldn't help but become frustrated. "If it were my friends, I would have at least tried."

Ram slammed his fist against the table, causing drinks to topple over and roll over the edge of the table, glass shards exploding onto the back porch of TNT's. "Oh, yeah? And what would you have done? Besides get yourself *killed*. It's not that simple!"

Lazarus raised his hands. "Woah, I'm sorry, man. I just . . . you know what? I'll just shut up." The young man stood up and pushed his chair in. There was an uncomfortable silence as Ram breathed heavily while he and Mongrel watched Lazarus. "I'll go grab a broom."

Lazarus headed inside through the back door and asked the bartender for a broom and dustpan.

"Ram getting wild back there again?" He went to the closet behind him to retrieve the broom.

"You know, it's not completely futile," came a voice from a man who looked about ten years older than Lazarus. He had long white dyed hair that hung in front of his face and round tinted sunglasses over his eyes. He wore a navy-blue trench coat with a small silver sword with wings emblem pinned to the front of it.

Lazarus turned and smirked, not recognizing the man's voice. "I'm sure he's got a broom back there somewhere."

"I meant about taking down the Lyones."

"I'm listening."

"That was the beginning of my relationship with Ghost and the Arch Angels. Ghost taught me the history of the Lyones—about how they were inadvertently responsible for the death of the Arch Angels' original leader and founder, Jin. He explained that Jin had already been planning to unite the other gangs to bring down the Lyone family before they became too powerful, but before any moves could be made, he was suddenly killed by his most trusted general, Blackjack. The Arch Angels never forgot this and since then have been working in secret to remove the Lyones from power and get justice for the death of their fallen leader," Lazarus continued his story.

"So, are you asking me to join the Arch Angels and work with you guys?" Lazarus asked Ghost as they sat in the parking lot across from TNT's.

"Not exactly. I want you to start your own gang. Keep it under wraps though. Only recruit orphans. This will ensure that they have no ties to any other gangs. You will be the first neutral gang to exist in a very long time. This will make it easier for the others that you will be visiting to trust you and agree to work alongside you."

"No offense or anything, man, but why don't you guys just do this yourselves?"

"Let's just put it this way: we don't have the best reputation among the other gangs—not like we used to. When Jin died, so did our rep. The other gangs knew that if anyone had the power to go head-to-head with the Lyone family, it was us. Only, at the time, well . . . we chose not to."

"Why not?"

"When Jin was murdered, so was the heart of the gang. Especially since it was his most trusted friend that did it. Everyone looked up to Blackjack and would never have thought he could do something so evil. After Armand had Blackjack locked up, he became the new leader by default because of his status and willingness to step up. It took a while for the gang to heal, but eventually we did, and now we're ready to try again."

They remained silent for a while, then Lazarus nodded, and his eyes met with Ghost's. "I'll do it."

Lazarus sat quietly after finishing his story as everyone processed everything that they had just learned.

"Don't give up so easily, Laz," Damien said. "For what it's worth, the Immortals got your back. It's about time things changed around here."

Lazarus gave him a weak smile, "Thanks, man. All of you."

"I say while we wait to hear from Ghost, what's to stop us from continuing to make moves?" Zero suggested.

"That's probably not a bad idea," Edge ashed his cigarette, "Maybe we could split up this time; that way we can cover more ground."

The last thing Lazarus wanted was to be separated from his friends. He needed them now, more than ever, and the thought of continuing the work on his own made his heart fill with anxiety. "I'm not so sure, bro . . ."

Edge shook his head. "It won't be forever, and we can keep in touch regularly to check in. I just think that this will help pull things back together. We lost a great ally. We need a few more to make up for that loss."

"He's right," Zero said, looking at the Immortals, who nodded in approval.

Lazarus nodded solemnly. "Edge, I want you to make contact with the Cut-Throats. From what I understand, they've been on board all along, but we need to make sure that relationship is solid." He paused for a moment and then continued, "If any of you see Seraph, let me know. Keep an eye out for him. He's going to need us now more than ever."

"Right. I'll go wherever I'm needed." Zero volunteered.

"Honestly, I hadn't really thought much past the

Cut-Throats," Lazarus contemplated. "We lost a lot of time while working with the Bishops, so it only makes sense that we split up and try to reach out to some of the different gangs and see what we can do to get them on board."

"What about the Shadows?" Damien chimed in. "I'm sure if you could help end the war between them and the White Crows, they would be willing to work with you all."

Lazarus looked at Zero. "Maybe we could go to them together, ya know? Just in case."

"Yeah, not a bad idea."

"Better yet, what if one of you approached the Shadows and the other the Crows and work internally with each gang to bring them into the plan?" Damien suggested. "Two for the price of one."

"Now there's an idea!" a grin formed on Lazarus's face.

"What do we have to lose?" Zero's eyes lit up.

"So, what did you do?" Seraph sat on the small cot, alone in the dark cell with his back against the wall that separated him from the stranger.

"You mean professionally?" came the voice with an amused tone.

Seraph chuckled and shook his head, although no one could see him. "No, I mean, like, to land in here. I take it we're both in solitary confinement, right?"

"That would be a correct assumption. You want to know what I did to end up in here? It should suffice to say that I engaged in a lifetime of evil. Everyone pays for their sins—one way or another, in this life or the next."

"Yeah . . ." Seraph recalled the teaching of the Royal Priests about the final judgment of mankind.

"Have you changed your mind about getting revenge?"

"I-I don't know . . ." Seraph thought long and hard about the question. Having been locked away for at least two weeks, he'd had time to process things a bit. The sadistic look on Vincent's face would not leave his mind, and it caused his blood to boil—but did he really want to kill him? "I wish that none of this had happened. I wish I didn't have to decide whether to take someone's life."

"Taking another man's life is a hard decision to make, but I do agree that being in the position to have to make that decision in the first place is an unfavorable one. What about forgiveness?"

Again, the man reminded him of the ones who raised him. "You're not a Royal Priest, are you?"

The man let out a deep, hearty laugh at this question. "Now, *that's* a good one!"

Seraph smiled and shook his head once more. "Yeah, the thought's crossed my mind. I just dunno if I can do it. You should have seen the look in his eyes . . ."

"An eye for an eye only leads to more violence . . ."

"Huh?"

"It's from a poem I heard a long time ago."

"I see. You know, I've been locked up in here for . . . well—for a while now, anyway, but I realized that I never did ask you what your name was. I'm Seraph."

"It is a pleasure to be formally acquainted with you, Seraph. I—" the stranger began, but was cut off by the sound of a pounding on Seraph's cell door.

"Boy! You have a visitor! Stand up and walk over to door now!" came a thick Sengoan accent from the other side of the door.

Seraph sat up and cleared his throat. He wondered if he was in danger or not, but what could he do? He decided to obey the voice and stand, slowly walking over to the door as it opened from the other side.

The light from the hallway seemed blinding as he was taken by both arms by two Sengoan men, who roughly dragged him down the corridor. Seraph struggled slightly to try to prevent them from causing him further discomfort, but this only caused them to grip harder while they neared the end of the hall to a door that had a single glass pane. One of the men opened the door, and the other pushed Seraph into what seemed like a small interrogation room with a L'Orandan man sitting behind a metal table with an empty chair in front of it. In the middle of the table was what looked like a tea pot and two empty Sengoan-style tea cups.

"You must be Seraph. I am Segundo, second-in-command of the Lyone family and personal adviser to Mr. Lyone. Please have a seat."

Seraph did not protest. He made his way over to the other side of the table and sat down.

Segundo poured two cups of tea, passing one over to the young Switchblade, and produced a pack of cigarettes from the inside of his coat pocket. "Smoke?"

Seraph studied the pack of cigarettes. "No, thank you."

"Not a smoker, huh? I try not to indulge as much as I can help it." Segundo chuckled, set the full pack on the table next to the ashtray, and placed a disposable lighter on top of the package. "I'll put them here in case you change your mind. So, you've been locked up here for going on three weeks now, yes?" he asked and lifted his cup of tea to his lips and blew on it before taking a small sip.

"What do you want?" Seraph asked coldly as he lifted the cup and contemplated throwing it in the Lyone's face.

"I heard about your encounter with Mr. Lyone—the day your friend was killed."

"So, what? I don't care anymore," Seraph swirled the cup around for a moment before setting it back down and pushing it away. "One way or another, I am going to make him pay for what he did to my friend," his eyes met Segundo's. "I promise you that."

Segundo nodded slowly and set the cup of tea down in front of him. "You know that I can't allow that. Lucien is a good friend of mine, and his family is precious to me. I've been with him since the beginning. Does that mean that I agree wholeheartedly with his methods? Not entirely. Especially not the way things were handled the day you were locked up in here. Of course, that was not Lucien's doing, but his son's, who has been dealt with most severely."

"*Severely?* What—did you send him to bed without dessert?" Seraph scoffed and folded his arms over his chest.

"Had your friend been a regular civilian, Vincent may have faced a steeper penalty; however, this was considered an *internal* matter. It's still tragic, nonetheless, and should never have happened. I am sincerely sorry for your loss."

Seraph closed his eyes and sat silently before eventually speaking. "How could you support someone like him? He's hurt—no, *killed* so many people. How can you live with yourself?"

Segundo shifted in his seat and lifted the cup to his lips once again, not blowing on it this time, allowing the hot liquid to burn his tongue slightly. "I'm going to have you released after this meeting. I need you to assure me that you've let go of whatever grudge you held against the Lyone family so that we can all move forward from this horrific situation."

Seraph's eyes widened in confusion. "Why would you release me?"

"Because you're a victim in this whole situation. Mr. Lyone sees that. He didn't want to have you arrested in the first place, but he thought it might be good to give you some time to think about what you are going to do from here on out. There is no reason to pursue vengeance of any kind, as it will only result in the loss of your life. Mr. Lyone would rather you see this as a second chance. That is why, once you are released from here, you will have a ride waiting for you. You're going to take that ride, and those people are going to help give you some direction so that you can get past this and try to lead a normal life."

"Normal life? I don't know what *normal* is." Seraph

shook his head. "And I'm just supposed to trust that whoever you have waiting for me down there isn't just going to kill me and make it look like an accident?"

Segundo smiled. "If we intended for you to die, we would have done it already, and I would not be wasting my time with you here. Like I said—this is a second chance. I suggest you take it." He paused, allowing what he had said to sink in. "You're free to go," he said and held out his hand, beckoning Seraph to stand.

Seraph stood, slowly pushed in his chair, and walked toward the doorway before halting. "I don't believe that you are so completely numb to what the Lyones have done. Even if you truly believe that the Lyones have made Royalty a better place. Even if what Lucien Lyone is responsible for works in the long run—will you be able to face God on judgment day with a clear conscience?" Without waiting for a response, he stepped out and headed back down the corridor toward the exit.

At the end of the hallway, Seraph saw two members of the Golden Dragons waiting for him by the door. As he approached, one of them held out his hand for him to halt while the other pressed a button on a small metal pad beside the door and said some words in Sengoan. After a moment, following a faint buzzing noise, the Golden Dragon pushed the door open, and the other allowed Seraph to pass through. They escorted him out into what appeared to be a lobby that was beautifully furnished with Sengoan-style furniture and paintings. They directed Seraph over to the booking desk, and a document was slid over to him by an attractive young Sengoan woman. "Sign here, please," she said, pointing to the signature line with the tip of her pen, then placing it on the sheet of paper.

Seraph signed the document without reading it and passed both the pen and paper back over to her before looking at the two Golden Dragons. "Is that it?" he asked.

They motioned toward the front door and walked Seraph out to a paved area with a tall chain-linked fence topped with barbed wire that surrounded the entire premises. His two escorts closed the door behind him as he exited the building. Seraph hesitated momentarily before taking a few steps toward the large gate that was straight ahead of him, where two Golden Dragons armed with automatic rifles stood and impatiently motioned for him to come toward them. On the other side of the gate was a glossy black sedan with tinted windows.

The armed Golden Dragons looked Seraph up and down before they opened the gate and allowed him to exit the prison. He glanced at the car again and then looked from left to right. *This must be Noble Road*, he thought.

Before he could take another step forward, the back door of the black sedan opened, and Ghost stepped out, a smirk on his face, as Seraph squinted in his direction, frozen in place. "Glad to see that you're alright."

"Alright seems to be as good as it gets lately."

Ghost's smile faded. "Why don't you come with me? I've got someone who would like to talk to you," he motioned toward the car.

Seraph looked at the car as a small sigh escaped from his mouth, "Alright . . ." he gave a single nod and climbed into the back seat. Ghost shut the door behind him and got into the driver's seat and shifted the car into drive.

Seraph instantly noticed that he and Ghost were not the only ones in the vehicle. A L'Orandan man who appeared to be in his late thirties, who Seraph recognized to be Armand Martinelli, leader of the Arch Angels, sat across from him. "Hello, Seraph."

The young Switchblade felt small in Armand's presence as he bowed his head slightly in respect. "Hello, sir."

"Please"—Armand raised both of his hands—"call me Armand."

"Yes, si—*Armand*," Seraph corrected himself. "I'm sorry if I caused you guys any trouble. Lance is—was . . ." he paused and tucked his lips in and bit down on them gently to restrain himself from becoming outwardly emotional.

"What happened to your friend is inexcusable. You didn't cause *any* trouble for us. Things certainly went further than we would have preferred, but what's done is done. It is I who is sincerely sorry for your loss."

Seraph nodded back and looked down, his teeth still pressed against his lips.

"We have an offer for you, Seraph," Ghost looked back at him through the rearview mirror.

Seraph looked up at and met eyes with Ghost, then looked back at Armand.

"We want you to come and work for us directly," Armand offered.

"You're asking me to join the Arch Angels? I . . . I don't know. What about Lazarus? I'm still technically a Switchblade, aren't I?"

"And the Switchblades are technically a branch of the Arch Angels. Ghost has been keeping an eye on your friends, by the way. They're all doing just fine."

Seraph heaved a small sigh of relief.

"I was actually the one who created the Switchblades," Ghost smirked. "The idea was for the Switchblades to act as a secretive branch of the Arch Angels, working on the street level to help bring the gangs together to help further our cause."

Seraph remembered the night when he heard O'Connor's story. *Did that oath even mean anything?*

"Yes. Ghost is the brains behind this whole operation. The most loyal and most trusted member of the Arch Angels."

Ghost smirked and shook his head slowly as he continued to drive.

"So, what exactly is your *cause?*" Seraph wondered aloud.

"Our agenda is the same as yours: to bring down the Lyone family and restore balance and stability to

Royalty," Armand's eyes met the young man's.

"What do I have to do?"

"We've made an arrangement with the Lyones whereby we take you under our wing—just to make it look like we're keeping you from causing them any trouble," Ghost informed him. "You would start off just like any other new member," he started but then paused for a moment. "It's been a while since we've had a new member . . ." his voice faded as he looked back at the road in front of him nearing La Noche.

"Why don't we put him with Ardent?" Armand recommended. "He can show Seraph the ropes—maybe give him a better idea of what we're all about."

"I just . . . I just want to make sure that I'm not going to be wasting any time," his eyes still locked with Armand's. "When are we actually going to take the fight to the Lyones?"

"One thing at a time, Seraph," Ghost reproved. "We have to wait for things to calm down before we make any decisive moves against them. Like we said, Laz and the others are still working on getting the other gangs on board. It's going to take time, but it *is* going to happen. Sooner than you would expect."

Seraph looked out the window at La Noche as Ghost parked the car beside the building. "Alright." Accepting the offer would at the very least give Seraph more time to process everything that had just happened. Everything still felt so fresh to him. He knew that there was a time for everything, just as the Royal Priests had taught him. He could hear the voice of Brother Luther echo in his mind: "There is a time for everything under the sun—a time to kill and a time to heal."

Ghost turned around to face Seraph as he and Armand both looked at the broken young man. "What do you say? Are you with us?" Armand placed his hand on Seraph's shoulder.

"I'm with you."

CHAPTER TEN

Once they passed through the entrance of La Noche, Armand pulled Ghost close to him and whispered something in his ear. After a brief moment, Ghost nodded, and Armand directed his attention back to Seraph. "Ghost will get you set up with Ardent. He'll be your crew captain, so if you have any concerns, you can take them to him . . . and me, of course. I like to think I have an open-door policy anyway," he patted Ghost on the back. "Take good care of him." Armand walked ahead of them to what looked like an elevator door at the back of the club.

"Right this way," Ghost beckoned Seraph to follow him as he led him up a spiral staircase to the second floor. "This is the VIP lounge."

Seraph scanned the lounge. The bar was more elegant than the one downstairs. A few men dressed in Arch Angel attire sat at the bar, as well as others whom Seraph assumed must be high-ranking members of different gangs and their bodyguards.

Ghost led Seraph toward a door behind the bar that led to a hallway. It reminded Seraph of the dorm hall back at the orphanage, which slightly resembled a hotel. "These rooms are for our members who either choose to live here or don't have their own residence. Ardent will show you to your room once you two get acquainted."

"Sounds good," Seraph swallowed as they came close to the middle of the hallway where there was a large open room with two large, flatscreen television sets, a billiard table, a few computer terminals against the wall, and some black leather sofas that were spread out across the room. There was L'Orandan hip-hop playing from the various speakers that surrounded the room and about five Arch Angels standing in a circle talking and laughing with one another. The group quieted down and acknowledged Ghost as soon as he came into their view. "Yo, Ghost is here! Straighten up, fellas!"

"Ardent, I want you to meet Seraph. He's your newest member—just joined today," Ghost put his hand on Seraph's shoulder.

Ardent was a tall, stalky man with a short beard and light-brown hair. He wore square-framed glasses and, rather than a full black suit like most of the other Arch Angel leaders, he wore neither a jacket nor a tie and left the top button of his dress shirt unbuttoned with a pistol fastened securely in a shoulder holster. "Yo, I'm Ardent. Welcome to the Arch Angels, my brother." He grinned and clasped hands with Seraph, bringing him in for a hug and giving him a tight squeeze.

"Thanks!" Seraph choked and cleared his throat.

"You're in good hands, Seraph." Ghost smiled and patted his shoulder before reaching into his own coat and pulling out a black business card with the Arch Angels logo on it. "If you ever wanna talk, just shoot me a text."

Seraph took the card and quickly inspected it before pocketing it. "Thanks," he said as Ghost nodded and exited the room, holding up the 'peace' sign as he walked away.

"Good to have you on board, brother," Ardent clasped hands with Seraph and introduced him to each member of his crew.

"Nice to meet you all," Seraph struggled not to show how overwhelmed he was felt.

"You too, bro. We gon' put in work together," Sly, one of the members smirked.

"That's right," Ardent nodded. "We were actually just chilling for a little bit before going out on patrol."

"Patrol?" Seraph's eyebrows rose.

"Oh, man. Ghost didn't tell you anything about us, did he? Yeah, we patrol our turf, making sure the neighboring homes and businesses are kept safe. Keeping some of the . . . less sophisticated gangs out so they don't cause any problems for our people."

Seraph listened and nodded slowly, thinking that the Arch Angels seemed to be a bit more chivalrous than he would have thought. This was a side of the Arch Angels that Seraph realized wasn't emphasized when outsiders spoke of them. "Interesting . . ."

"Of course, we do collect a little protection money for this, but trust me, we make it worth their while. This neighborhood was a dump before we took over."

Seraph couldn't remember a time when the Arch Angels didn't control Kings Avenue from Bishop to Sunrise. "What was that like?"

"Story time!" a heavy-set member named Mallow cried out in excitement.

Ardent looked at Mallow and smirked before looking back at Seraph. "Later. We got stuff to do and Seraph ain't even dressed yet," he beckoned at Seraph to follow him out of what seemed to be a recreation room. "I'll show you your room and give you some time to wash up and put on your new duds before we head out."

"Okay," Seraph followed Ardent back into the hallway where he led the new Arch Angel a few doors down, unlocked the door, opened it, and held out a hand, inviting Seraph to enter first.

"Here's your new home!" Ardent grinned as Seraph entered.

Seraph had to blink a few times as his eyes scanned the room. Right away, he thought about how much nicer this room was compared to any room he had ever stayed in before. There was a small kitchenette with a half-sized refrigerator, a stove with a microwave above it, and a sink. In the right corner of the room was a twin bed and a night stand with a lamp on it. There was also a small hallway toward the back of the room, with a door on either side.

Ardent pointed toward the small hallway. "The door on the left is your closet. There should be plenty of clothes in there for you. The choice is gonna be a little . . . bland, but don't worry; I'm not as strict about dress code as some of the other captains are." Ardent chuckled and then nodded back toward the small hallway. "The door on the right is your bathroom. Your shower's in there. There should also be clean towels under the sink. When you need your clothes washed, just put them in one of the laundry bags under the sink, and just leave it outside your door. It's best to write your name on the bag so you get *your* own stuff back. Any questions?"

Seraph continued to blink as he tried to take everything in that had just been said to him. "This is *my* room?"

"Yeah," Ardent brushed off Seraph's surprised demeanor. "We're Arch Angels. We take care of our people. You need something, you let us know and we provide. The gang comes first. Everything else is secondary."

"Right. I guess I'll go ahead and get ready then."

"Great, but don't be too long. We gotta move," Ardent told Seraph as he held out the key toward him.

Seraph took the key and clutched it tightly once Ardent let go of it. "I'll be quick," he promised as Ardent left the room, closing the door behind him. Seraph then took a step back toward the door, looked at the push-button lock that was on the handle, and slowly pressed the button. *Privacy*, he thought to himself and then walked over to his kitchenette, set the key on the counter, and began emptying his pockets and setting all of his possessions next to the key before getting undressed and tossing his clothes into a pile on the floor.

Seraph made his way to the bathroom and stood there in silence, staring at how simple and clean everything was. The room was devoid of color. Everything in the bathroom was either black, white, or gray, which reflected the Arch Angels' color theme. Seraph took one of the towels that was neatly folded on the vanity and placed it onto the closed toilet lid before getting into the shower and setting the dial between hot and warm.

The water burned a little as it ran over his head and cascaded down the rest of his body. Seraph heaved a long sigh, the water having a soothing effect as he felt the pain of loss and regret washing away. He closed his eyes and tilted his head upward so that the water ran over his face, slightly impairing his ability to breathe, yet not entirely, so that he could stay there and feel his sins being temporarily washed away.

After washing his hair and body, Seraph stepped onto the bathmat and thoroughly dried himself. He took a few steps toward the mirror that was still slightly fogged up and used a corner of his towel to wipe a spot in the middle clear so that he could look at himself. Seraph's eyes met with his reflection's as a mixture of loathing, disgust, and pity filled his heart. He shook his head and started brushing his teeth, combing his hair back, and shaving his face, leaving just a small, thin patch of hair on his chin.

As he finished up, there came a sudden knock on the door. "You ready yet?" came Sly's voice.

"Uh, yeah," Seraph scrambled to grab his effects and pocket them before coming to the door. "All ready," he said, now face to face with one of his new comrades.

"Didn't mean to rush you, bro. Ardent's not always the most patient though."

"No worries," Seraph followed Sly outside the club, where Ardent and the rest of the crew stood waiting.

"It's about time! Let's get moving," Ardent chided playfully as he led the group of Arch Angels down Knights Way in the direction of the Lion's Den.

The others made conversation along the way, but Seraph remained silent as he attempted to mask the feeling of discomfort as they approached whom he deemed to be his mortal enemies. As they passed civilians on the street, he became instantly aware of the burning looks that he and his crew were receiving from them. Seraph briefly met eyes with a middle-aged woman who was exiting one of the Quick Markets across the street. A look of intimidation and disdain pierced through him before she looked away and carried on in the opposite direction. Ardent's crew halted as they got to the intersection at Noble, right across the street from the Lyone compound.

Ardent looked at Double and Midnight and gave a single nod. "You two know the mission. Be quick. We'll regroup behind the Shamrocke," he ordered as they nodded back and crossed the street. Ardent then turned and looked at the rest of his crew. "Let's move. We're gonna stop and check in with the Wisemen." He led the crew down Noble toward Golden Road.

Seraph had known of the Wisemen for years, although only came across them in passing.

The group of Arch Angels turned down a small street that led toward the back of the Shamrocke, where an elderly bearded man sat in a wheelchair. He wore an old gray coat and camouflaged pants, with combat boots resting on the ground. He sat parked in an empty parking space, with two other elderly men sitting on either side of him who stood up once Ardent and company approached.

Ardent grinned and extended his hand toward both men as they got up to greet him. "Good to see you, Zee. Blyer." He smiled and shook both of their hands. "Nyx," Ardent said, addressing the man in the chair and giving him a friendly nod.

Nyx sat in his wheelchair, slightly hunched forward

as he stroked his long beard and smiled kindly. "Ardent," came a voice like sandpaper. "Good to see you, son. Come here and let me see your face."

Ardent swallowed as he looked back at his crew quietly. Sly and Mallow looked away quickly. Seraph cleared his throat and tried his best not to stare at Nyx and the other Wisemen.

"Don't be afraid now," Nyx croaked. "Come here and say hello to a crippled old man."

Ardent adjusted his coat and took a few steps forward and held his hand out toward Nyx, who, rather than gripping Ardent's hand, gripped his forearm and squeezed it tightly. "Now that's how warriors shake hands."

"Yeah . . ." Ardent struggled to keep eye contact with Nyx.

Nyx grunted and nodded in Seraph's direction. "New recruit?"

Seraph met eyes with Ardent, who looked back at him after Nyx released his arm. "Uh—y-yes, sir. I'm Seraph," he took a step forward.

"I know who you are." Nyx narrowed his eyes. "Come here and shake my hand."

Seraph swallowed and looked at his companions before approaching Nyx and gripping his hand.

Nyx snarled and gripped Seraph tightly by his forearm and bolted up from his wheelchair, pulling Seraph close to his face. "A warrior *always* grabs the forearm!" he shouted and pushed Seraph back a few steps before howling with laughter.

Seraph stumbled backward, almost completely losing balance before straightening up and staring back at Nyx wide-eyed.

"You thought I was some feeble old man, didn't ya? Serves you right, kid! Appearances are *always* deceiving!" Nyx continued to roar with laughter as he plopped back down on his seat.

One of the other Wisemen, a tall, elderly man who

wore matching blue sweats and a straw sun hat with a gray ponytail sticking out the back shook his head at Nyx and scoffed. "Sorry about that, kid. Nyx is a little rough around the edges."

The remaining Wiseman smirked and stepped forward. He was short and bald and sported a thin goatee. "Nah dude, he's gotta be tough if he wants to hang. That's the problem these days. These kids ain't got no respect. No clue how the world works," he said dismissively to the taller fellow and then addressed Seraph directly. "You're aw'right, kid. The next time you shake one of our hands, you give 'em a warrior's handshake, and you don't let *nobody* push you around or try t'punk you—not even Nyx. You understand me?"

"I-I think so." Seraph blinked and scratched his elbow.

"Good! You listen to the Wisemen, and you'll do well for yourself."

"Come here," Nyx ordered, beckoning Seraph over once more. The Wiseman stroked his beard slowly as he stared at Seraph's face. "You've seen some things, kid."

Seraph swallowed and nodded. "Rough city . . ."

"'That's not what I meant," Nyx replied with a slight shake of his head. "You still have a lot of growing to do."

Seraph tried to give a half smile but ended up just nodding, trying to maintain eye contact with Nyx.

Nyx extended his hand a second time toward Seraph, who this time gripped his forearm tightly and braced himself. With a quick, effortless jerk, Nyx pulled Seraph close to himself and said hoarsely next to his ear, "Always be wary of those around you," then released the young man and lounged back in his chair, nodding slowly and stroking his beard.

Seraph knitted his eyebrows, looking at the Wiseman. Ardent tapped his arm and chuckled. "Don't let these old timers rattle you too much." Seraph remained silent but nodded as he turned to face Ardent, spotting two of his crew members approaching from the distance.

"Heya cap', we took care of that thing," one said.

"Good . . ." Ardent said, distracted by his phone for the moment. "We're needed back at La Noche."

"Well, that was short lived," the other remarked as the group said goodbye to the Wisemen and started walking down Golden Road toward Kings Avenue, passing by the front of the Shamrocke as they neared the intersection.

"What's a matter—?" A familiar voice called out from the porch of the Kaelish pub. "Can't stop and have a pint with an old friend?"

Ardent looked back and smirked. "Sorry, O'Connor, we're just taking care of some Arch Angel business. Maybe next time?"

O'Connor stepped through the iron gate that led to the sidewalk, approached Ardent and his crew, and lowered his voice. "How's things going on your end?"

"Makin' moves, my man. Always makin' moves. What about you?" Ardent shifted his eyes.

"Tryin' my damndest. Timing is going to be key in my particular situation," O'Connor lit up a smoke. "I won't hold ya up any longer. Just wanted to check in," he started to turn, but then froze as he recognized Seraph and a grin spread across his face. "Hey, I know you! Yer the lad that was runnin' with Lazarus there for a bit, huh?"

Before Seraph could answer, Ardent spoke up. "Seraph here is moving up in the world. That's all."

"Right," O'Connor said in a flat tone, his eyes still fixed on Seraph. "You take care of yerself, lad. Come by and have a pint some time—on the house."

"Thanks," Seraph nodded before following Ardent and the others back to La Noche.

Ardent and his crew stepped through the double doors of the club and halted once everyone was inside. He then turned, locked the entrance doors behind him, and cleared his throat.

Seraph raised an eyebrow at his captain, who didn't acknowledge him. He then turned and looked at his comrades, who likewise seemed to be alert and focused. *It's still pretty early. Why's he locking the doors already?*" Seraph wondered, looking at all of the civilians still dancing and drinking at the bar, unaware that Ardent had locked the main entrance.

Double, one of Ardent's crew, nodded over toward the bar to a man who was dressed in a fine business suit with a glass full of strong liquor in front of him. "This guy's been coming in here and causing trouble all week. He's already been asked not to come back," he explained under his breath to Seraph.

"Mallow, you and Sly watch the door. The rest of you—with me," Ardent ordered and led Seraph, Double and another called 'Midnight' to the bar. The bartender, a pretty young woman with strawberry blonde hair and bright red lipstick, stood silent as she made eye contact with Ardent and gave him a single nod.

"Excuse me," Ardent addressed the patron.

"Excuse yourself," the man waved his hand at Ardent as if to *shoo* him away.

Ardent's pupils turned into flames as he clenched his teeth. "*What?*"

"What? You hard of hearing? I'm trying to enjoy my drink," the man lifted the glass and brought it to his lips.

Ardent turned and looked at the rest of his crew and then placed a hand on the man's shoulder, forcefully turning him around so that they were now face to face.

The man stood up and pushed Ardent away from him. "That tough guy *gang* crap won't work with me, buddy. I work for the Lyones. You better think twice before messing with me. One quick phone call and I'll have an army here that will turn this place upside down."

Ardent stood there, taken aback by these words, but his surprised look instantly turned into one of caution as he watched Armand and Ghost approach the man from the other side.

"Is there a problem?" Armand stood there expressionless.

"That's up to you, pal. Call your goons off and leave me alone." The man turned his nose up at Armand and attempted to bring the glass to his lips once more.

"He's not your *pal*," Ghost's gaze piercing through the man. "Howard, is it?"

The man closed his eyes and set the glass back down. "How do you know my name?" he attempted to reach into his coat pocket.

Ghost held out his hand, motioning for Howard to stop what he was doing. "Keep your hands where I can see them."

Howard let out an arrogant chuckle, pulled out a cell phone, and began going through his contacts.

Like a bolt of lightning striking the ground, Ghost snatched the phone from him and turned the power off before pocketing it.

"Hey!" Howard lunged at Ghost, but was met with a swift knee to the gut from Armand, who up until that point had stood perfectly still.

Howard clutched his midsection and dropped to the ground and groaned.

Armand gave a hard kick to Howard's leg and flared his nostril, narrowing his eyes at him. He leaned in toward Ghost and whispered something before turning and walking toward the elevator in the back of the building.

Seraph stood watching silently, wincing both times Howard was kicked. His mind raced as he felt his senses becoming dull.

Ghost met eyes with Ardent. "Take care of this," he ordered and promptly followed behind Armand.

Howard lay on the floor, swearing and groaning pathetically as the other patrons now noticed what was happening and watched quietly.

Midnight did not hesitate as he bent down, grabbed

Howard by his suit jacket, and began dragging him toward the back of the bar with Double helping. "Let's go!" Ardent barked at Seraph, who snapped out of his stupor and followed suit.

Howard was dragged through the back door into a small dark alley behind the club. "What're you doing? Get *off* me!"

Midnight sneered at Howard as he tossed him into the adjacent wall and shrugged. "No problem."

Howard groaned as he hit the wall, head first, and then melted to the floor. "Please . . . stop."

Seraph stood frozen, his senses once again becoming dull as he felt his heart beating in his ears.

Howard quickly scrambled to his feet in an attempt to get away. "Seraph!" Ardent shouted.

Seraph reactively extended his arm and clothes-lined Howard, his forearm connecting with the man's throat, sending him straight back, his head smacking the pavement.

"Nice job!" Ardent smirked.

"Did you see how his head bounced?" Midnight cried in excitement and nudged Double with his elbow.

Seraph looked down at Howard and instinctively kicked him square in the face as he made an attempt to sit up.

"*Oh!*" Midnight cheered as if Seraph had just scored a goal.

"So," Seraph said through clenched teeth, "you work for the Lyone's huh?" He knelt down, lifted Howard's head off the ground by his suit collar, and punched him in the eye.

"Ugh . . ." Howard groaned in pain. "Just office work, I swear! I don't even own a weapon!"

Seraph struck Howard again, unsatisfied by the man's answer. "Yeah, but you were quick to threaten to call in the cavalry, right? To come turn La Noche upside down, *right?*"

"Please!" Howard begged and held up his hands.

"Alright, Seraph. That's enough. Get him to his feet," Ardent said and lit a cigarette.

Double helped Seraph lift Howard by his arms, propping him up against the wall. "Oh, thank you!"

Ardent took a deep drag from his cigarette and exhaled the fumes in Howard's face. "For what?" he pulled out his handgun from his shoulder holster and pressed the barrel underneath Howard's chin.

"No! Wait!" were Howard's last words as Ardent pulled the trigger, painting an abstract design of pink and red on the brick wall behind him before his body dropped to the side and slumped over.

Seraph stepped back. His heart fluttered with shock as he watched Howard's life taken from him.

"You three, get this cleaned up," Ardent ordered, taking another deep drag from his cigarette.

"The usual spot, boss?" Double asked for clarification.

"No. Somewhere different," Ardent lifted his chin in Seraph's direction. "You alright, bro?"

Seraph, still shaken, nodded. "Uh—yeah. Yes." He choked and rubbed his sweating palms against the back of his slacks.

"Alright. Get moving," he rubbed the half-smoked cigarette against the wall next to Howard's brain matter, and walked back inside La Noche, leaving a trail of smoke behind him as the rhythm of the L'Orandan music leaked out for a brief moment until the door shut again.

Seraph looked at his two counterparts before bracing himself against the building and vomiting.

Midnight rolled his eyes. "I'll get the car."

"We didn't expect you to get sick, man. This must've been your first, huh?" Double patted Seraph on the shoulder as Midnight drove them toward the outskirts of town on the other side of Sunrise Road while Howard's body lay tucked in the trunk, wrapped in a blue tarp that was duct taped securely around him.

Seraph swallowed and winced at the mental image of his vomit splattering on the pavement behind La Noche still playing vividly in his mind. "Not exactly . . ." he replied, recalling his time in the Bishop projects while they warred with the Pawn Road Disciples.

"Well, either way, you better toughen up," Midnight said. "It's not like we go around killin' people for fun, but it happens, ya know? This job ain't for the faint-hearted."

Job? This is supposed to be my shot at bringing down the Lyone family, not some career path.

"It's rough out there and we have a reputation to keep. We let jerks like that guy in the trunk come to *our* establishment and threaten us, next thing you know, the whole city will come and start flexin' on us like we're some chumps," Double explained.

Seraph pressed his lips together and closed his eyes for a moment. "I get it… It just caught me off guard is all."

"We're here," Midnight spoke quietly as he pulled the vehicle onto a dirt road that led into a wooded area. It was approaching dusk when they arrived at a gravel road under a thick canopy of tall trees that blocked out the moonlight. Midnight drove until he reached a spot near a small bog and pulled the car over. "This should be good," his eyes darted back and forth around the site.

Double nodded to Seraph, and the three exited the sedan and walked around to the trunk. Midnight used the key-fob to pop it open and then reached in and retrieved two spades, which he handed to Seraph and Double.

"You two dig," Midnight lit up a black colored cigarette.

Seraph looked at Double, who shrugged and said, "Seniority."

Seraph nodded but rolled his eyes after Double had turned away from him.

Double picked a spot away from the trees and they started digging. After about a half hour or so, they had managed to dig a sufficiently large hole for Howard, and together, they all carried the body from the trunk and lowered him into the crude grave. Double and Seraph filled the hole, then placed sticks, rocks, and leaves over it.

"You done yet?" Midnight, who had been chain smoking next to his car the entire time, called out, "I'm startin' to get hungry!"

"Just a sec!" Double looked at Seraph and then down at the grave. "I'm not really religious or anything, but did you wanna say some words? I know you're from St. Titus and all."

Seraph swallowed as the Royal Priests came to mind. "Uh . . . sure." He closed his eyes and slightly bowed his head, folding his hands in front of him. "Father . . . no one in this world is perfect. We, uh—all make mistakes. Please . . ." He paused with self-loathing. "Please receive his soul. Amen."

"Yeah, amen. That was nice, man."

"Yeah . . . let's not keep Midnight waiting."

"Yo!" Ardent greeted Seraph, Midnight, and Double as they returned to the Arch Angel recreation room. "Everything go smoothly?"

"Yep. These two did a fine job." Midnight grinned with satisfaction.

Ardent beamed at Seraph. "Good job, man," he touched fists with him. "By the way, Ghost wants to see you in the VIP lounge. Why don't you go get cleaned up, and I'll let him know you'll be about . . . thirty minutes?"

"Cool," Seraph nodded. *Two showers in one day? The life of luxury at its finest.* He put on fresh clothes after a quick rinse, this time choosing a red shirt, leaving the top two buttons undone, and decided to go without a jacket. He grabbed his personal effects and walked down the hall to the VIP lounge, mentally preparing himself for whatever it was that Ghost wanted to see him about.

Ghost sat at the bar, apart from everyone else, sipping from a short glass filled with some clear liquor and ice and was garnished with a slice of lime. Seraph approached and took a seat next to him.

"Thanks for joining me," Ghost offered the young recruit a seat next to him. "What do you drink?"

The same pretty bartender from before slinked over toward them from the other side of the bar and smiled.

"Um . . ." Seraph thought for a moment, not actually in the mood to drink. He glanced at Ghost's glass and raised his chin toward it. "I'll have what he's having."

"Gin n' tonic? No problem, sweetie." Her smile grew even bigger as she reached for a bottle on the counter.

"Cherrie, this is Seraph. I'm sure you recognize him from that little incident earlier," Ghost took a small sip from the glass. "He's our newest recruit. Gonna be running with Ardent's crew."

"Pleased to meet you, Seraph." Cherrie finished fixing the drink, placed it in front of Seraph, and offered a dainty hand to him from across the bar.

Seraph took her soft hand in his and gave it a firm yet gentle shake. "You too, Cherrie," his cheeks slightly burned as he picked up the glass and took a long sip. Instantly, his face contorted and he coughed a little before regaining composure.

Ghost and Cherrie chuckled. Ghost patted Seraph's back. "You alright?"

"I wasn't expecting it to taste like a pine tree," Seraph confessed, taking another much smaller sip.

"It's an acquired taste." Ghost shrugged and then looked back at Cherrie. "That's all for now. I'll flag you down if we need anything."

"Sure thing, Hon." Cherrie gave them a bright smile and went down to the other end of the bar to check on one of the patrons.

"So," Ghost started. "How did things go tonight from your point of view?"

"It's not what I expected. That's for sure." Seraph let out a heavy sigh. "I didn't expect to be a part of murder tonight."

Ghost nodded.

"Look, I want to be honest with you," Seraph began, swallowing hard as his eyes connected with Ghost's. "I only agreed to join because I want to help take down the Lyones. I wasted enough time getting my hands dirty for the Bishops, and I don't plan on doing the same for you."

"I know, Seraph. Your intentions are no mystery to me. Yeah, you ran into an unfortunate situation today, but that's business. Given the nature of what we are trying to accomplish, discretion is our number-one priority."

"I get that. I just want to make sure I'm not being jerked around. The Lyone family has been in power for too long, and now's the time for us to do something about it."

"Why do you think Ardent had Midnight and Double break away from the group near the Lion's Den earlier?"

Seraph thought for a moment, then shrugged.

"I can't go into detail here, but I assure you that they were working on advancing our goals," Ghost looked over his shoulder.

"Alright."

"A lot of changes are coming, Seraph. Even when it's for the better, change can be uncomfortable. You rolling with the Arch Angels is your chance to recreate yourself. You don't have to live with pain from the past. You can let that go now and make your own way for yourself. We do some tough things for the gang sometimes, but that's the life. Is the new Seraph going to learn to accept this, or will you let it continue to destroy you?"

These words sank into Seraph's mind as he sat there silently, staring at the drink in front of him. *My chance to recreate myself?*

"The best part is . . . you don't have to do this alone. The Arch Angels are your family now. We're more than a gang. We're a brotherhood. We got your back, yeah, but we are here for you when you are going through tough times as well."

A genuine smile escaped from Seraph as he turned his head to look at Ghost. "I appreciate that," he said, lifting his glass to his lips.

Ghost returned the smile. "It's only a matter of time before things are in place and we can finally put an end to the Lyones. Lazarus and the guys are doing their part as well. We just have to be patient until everything comes together."

"How *are* Lazarus and the others?"

"Doing just fine. They're on the right course. I would tell you to go and see for yourself, but given their current operation, we can't risk you being seen with them . . ." Ghost's expression twisted slightly. "That's a big part of the reason why we have you here with us."

Everything finally came together for Seraph. "I see."

"I know . . ." A look of guilt played across Ghost's face. "We probably should have mentioned that right off the bat. That's on me."

"No. I understand. This is war, and we all have to make wise decisions."

"Believe me—if we can do this without anyone having to die, that would be ideal."

"Not for me." Seraph's expression darkened.

Ghost's eyebrows raised. "You want revenge, huh?" He pulled out a metal cigarette case with the Arch Angel emblem on the front of it and popped it open, took out a cigarette, and lit it up before offering one to Seraph, who took one and leaned forward as Ghost lit it up for him. "You ever hear of a man named Blackjack?"

"I've heard about him before. He killed our original leader, right?"

"Heh, that's putting it lightly . . ." Ghost sneered. "It goes a little deeper than that with Blackjack and me."

Seraph finished his drink and set it on the counter as he stared quietly at Ghost.

Ghost shook his head. "What? You're gonna make me teach a history class?" he sighed before getting Cherrie's attention. "We're gonna need another round over here."

Cherrie smiled and winked at Seraph as she fixed two more drinks.

"Thanks, Cherrie," Seraph said warmly, before focusing his attention back on Ghost. "Well?"

"Yeah, yeah." Ghost puffed the cigarette and took a sip of the fresh cocktail. "A long time ago, when Jin originally founded the Arch Angels, we were more like an anti-gang than an actual gang. Rather than just looking out for our own interests, Jin wanted to look out for smaller gangs and civilians as well."

"If that's the case, how did we earn such a bad rep?"

"Blackjack, who was also an Arch Angel at the time, murdered Jin right before the Lyone family came to power. This was sort of a wake-up call for us. Armand took over as chairman and quickly appointed me as his right hand and head of intelligence to ensure that there were no other traitors associated with Jin's murder. Surprise, surprise . . . Blackjack acted alone."

"Wow . . . but that doesn't explain—"

"I'm getting to that. At the time, we decided that it wasn't in the Arch Angel's best interest to try and take the Lyone's on directly. Jin's murder really lowered everyone's morale. It was almost as if we all believed he was invincible. Like his good heart would protect him from death. Maybe if I wasn't so devastated at the time, I would have tried to convince Armand then and there to unite the gangs and take on the Lyone family. That and Blackjack . . ."

"You knew him personally, didn't you?"

"*Ha.*" Ghost rolled his eyes. "I *thought* I knew him."

"Why do you think he killed Jin?"

"Blackjack and I aren't from Royalty originally. We

were refugees from the Wastelands. Boy soldiers. Trained to assassinate public officials. I was fourteen when we escaped together and made it to Royalty." He took a long drag from his cigarette and exhaled through his nostrils. "I think we both suffered some post-traumatic stress from the stuff that we went through over there. I just didn't realize how much it twisted Blackjack's mind."

Seraph curled his lips inwardly and shook his head. "I didn't know . . . I'm sorry."

"He'll get what's coming to him someday. I'm sure of it," Ghost stared straight ahead.

"I appreciate you sharing that with me. It puts a lot of things into perspective."

"That's hardly even half of it. The part that makes it so terrible is that Jin and the Arch Angels took us in. We were just two street urchins with a dark past, and Jin took us in and redeemed us. He gave us a new purpose. One that served a greater good. I truly thought Blackjack had changed. I know I did."

"To answer your question, I simply do not know why Blackjack would have killed the only person who gave us a chance in this life. Greed? Power? Who knows? Regardless, look where he ended up. Serves the bastard right."

CHAPTER ELEVEN

"I don't know, brother. This seems too risky," Zero began feeling doubtful as he sat with Lazarus on the back porch of TNT's and discussed their plan.

"I know, man, but after losing the Bishops, we have to get everyone that we can to help us. The Shadows and the White Crows combined will almost help us make up for that loss."

"I get it. There are so many things that could go wrong, though. What if we end up killing each other by mistake or something crazy like that?"

"We'll just have to be extra careful. We don't have a whole lot of options. What we need to do is find the most level-headed, high-ranking member of each crew and coordinate with them once we gain their trust."

"That could take years, man."

"It would be worth it. Someone has to try. This is what the Switchblades are all about."

Zero grew silent, then asked, "When were you gonna tell us that we were actually working for the Arch Angels this whole time?"

"I'm sorry . . . I swore to Ghost that I wouldn't say anything until he gave me the okay—to protect the mission."

"I understand, man. I grew up always thinking that

the Arch Angels shouldn't be trusted. Now I find out that I pretty much am one." He laughed dryly.

"They are better than you think. Trust me."

"I do . . . more than anyone."

Lazarus put his hand on Zero's shoulder and gave him a brotherly squeeze. "Come on, bro. We got work to do. Give it some time before we get in touch with each other. We'll give them time to trust us. Be smart. We got this!"

Zero smiled and gave a solid nod before standing up, clasping hands with Lazarus, and bringing him in close for a hug. "I'll be in touch."

The streets were silent as Zero entered White Crow territory, located in a small section of Royalty, in a neighborhood called Ivory. A slight chill in the air caused Zero to cross his arms over his chest as he scanned the area, looking for the White Crow's hideout, commonly referred to as The Crow's Nest. He had never been to this particular part of town before, which made him feel even more uncomfortable about the current situation.

"CAAAAAAAAAAAAAAAW! CAAAAAAAAAAAAAW!" came the loud sound of a bird nearby, which caused Zero to jump.

"Hello?" Zero turned around to try to spot where the noise was coming from.

When he turned, he was surprised to see that there was no sign of life behind him where he had heard the bird call come from.

"AHH!" Zero shouted as he turned back around only to be face to face with a tall figure wearing all white with a black bird beak-shaped theater mask poking out from under a white hood. The figure wore a long white trench coat, with black baggy jeans and carried a lead pipe, which he had propped over his right shoulder.

"You are trespassing," came a masculine voice from beneath the figure's mask.

Zero swallowed. "I was actually hoping to speak to

one of your leaders about possibly joining you all," he said.

"Join us? The White Crows?" the figure laughed as he swiftly used the pipe as a bar against Zero's throat and placed a leg behind Zero's legs, pushing him backward and onto the ground. "Who sent you?!" the White Crow demanded.

Zero hit the ground hard and raised one of his hands as he braced himself with the other. "No one sent me! I just lost my crew and was looking for a new one to join. You guys seemed pretty cool, and I think I may be able to help you against the Shadows."

"Help us against the Shadows? Do you think we need anyone's *help*?"

"Yes. I do. It's no secret that you guys have been losing this war. Maybe I can help even the playing field," Zero carefully started getting back on his feet.

A few more White Crows revealed themselves, surrounding Zero as he stood up. "We will bring you to our leader, and she will decide what to do with you," said the one with the pipe, then beckoned Zero to follow him.

Two streets over, Lazarus faced similar circumstances as he lay in the middle of the street, taking various kicks and punches from a small group of people dressed in black who wore masks that covered all of their faces except for their eyes. Thankfully, they were not using the straight-edged swords strapped to each of their backs. Lazarus hadn't even had a chance to speak before being ambushed and beaten to the ground. This was a much less cordial treatment than he was used to and why he had always avoided the Shadows in the first place.

"Most everyone knows that the Shadows don't take kindly to unannounced strangers trespassing in Ebony," one of them said as the beating was put on pause.

Lazarus panted, trying to regain his breath. His entire face felt swollen, and his back and ribs ached tremendously. His elbows were scraped, and his jeans had fresh holes where his knees were. "I... wanted to see about joining..." Lazarus choked out and closed his eyes tightly in pain, as it hurt him to speak.

The Shadows burst into laughter at Lazarus's request, and one of them ran up and kicked him once more in the stomach. "Well," he said, "you're halfway into becoming a member as far as your 'blood in' initiation goes. Now there's only one more thing that we need from you," he said.

"Whazzat?" Lazarus groaned as he struggled to get on all fours.

"A White Crow mask. You bring us one of their masks for our collection, and you can join the Shadows. It shouldn't be too tough. They're a weak crew as it is. We just need to make sure that you're down."

"And if you can't get one of their masks, don't bother coming back," another warned.

"Yeah! You might as well try to join them if you can't get one," said a third as the others laughed.

Lazarus made it back to his feet and wobbled back and forth. "I'll be back soon." He flashed a bloody grin before turning and walking toward the way he had come. *That was a close one. How am I going to get a White Crow mask? I could try to catch one out by himself, knock him out, and grab his mask,* he thought, but he knew the chances of a White Crow actually being alone were slim. *Or I could try and sneak into the Crow's Nest and nab one,* he thought, but he wasn't sure where exactly their hideout was or how heavily fortified it would be. *I could reach out to Zero . . . but that could potentially cost him his life.* Lazarus took a seat on a bench in front of an old, rundown storefront that was located on the corner of Diamond Road and Ivory Street. He reached into his pocket, retrieved his electronic cigarette, and puffed on it as he weighed his options.

The Crow's Nest was deep within the center of an old apartment building off Ivory Street. It had a single room, which looked to be a living room originally but now served as a common room for the White Crows. There was a round table in the middle of the room and various sofas, a kitchenette, and several black banners with the White Crow symbol on them hanging on the walls. Surrounding the room were other apartments that appeared to serve as housing for the gang members. Guards were posted in front of certain doors, including the main room where Zero now sat among the White Crow leadership.

"So, you just show up out of nowhere, without anyone knowing who you are or having ever heard of you and then you tell us that want to join and that you think you can help us win our war against the Shadows?" Talon, the leader of the White Crows, asked Zero. Talon concealed her face with the same crow mask that the rest of the White Crows wore.

"Like I told him"—Zero pointed to Toki, the White Crow who originally approached him—"I lost my crew. I was rolling with the Bishops before they got wiped out. I've heard about you guys. Heard that you're a solid crew but need help fighting the Shadows," he explained as he sat across the table from Talon with his hands folded on the table in front of him.

"You look a little pale to have been a member of the Bishops," one of the Crows remarked.

"And since we are losing so bad against the Shadows, why not join the winning side?" Talon inquired.

"The Shadows have a reputation for not being so welcoming to strangers. Let's just say I'm inclined to fight for the underdog," Zero explained.

"I see . . ." Talon considered what he said. "How will you prove your loyalty to us . . . *Zero*, was it?"

"I could go and kill one of the Shadows right now, but that will only stir things up for you. How do you usually test the loyalty of new recruits?"

"All of us come from this neighborhood. We have never taken in an outsider," Toki informed him.

"Therefore, you will have to do *something* to earn our trust," Talon said. "We will give you some time to come up with a plan. In the meantime, you may stay here at the Crow's Nest. Once you have something good, come and talk to me, and we will see if it is sufficient."

"That sounds fair. I will have something for you as soon as possible."

Brutus tossed a leather vest at Ezra that had *PROSPECT* patched on as a bottom rocker. "Put that on," he ordered the lone Bishop.

Ezra inspected the vest. "I told y'all, I ain't interested in joining," he reminded the aging vice president of the Cut-Throats.

"I don't care what you told me. Put it on. If you ride with us, you wear our colors, and in order to wear our colors, you need to prospect."

Ezra's expression changed as he raised his eyebrows back at Brutus, who was practically a complete stranger to him, giving him orders. Ezra smirked and licked his lips. "I'll tell you what, grampa. I'll put that stupid vest on if you can throw hands with me and win."

Brutus instantly stood up from the stool that he was sitting on at the bar inside the Cut-Throats' clubhouse. He began removing the heavy stainless-steel rings from each finger and setting them on the surface of the counter that was next to him. He then cracked his knuckles and began moving some chairs and tables to clear a space in the middle of the room.

"This is why I think you would have made a better sergeant-at-arms." Terrace chuckled and shook his head as he and the other Cut-Throats took a seat to watch the fight.

Ezra finished the beer in his hand and set the empty bottle and the prospect vest down on a table. "You sure about this, ol' man?" he smirked arrogantly as he approached the veteran biker in the center of the room.

"Just shut up and show me what you got, kid,"

Brutus raised his massive fists.

Ezra didn't hesitate to put up his fists and swung a few times at the old biker, who seemed to block each attack with ease.

"That *it?*" Brutus chuckled and then faked two jabs to Ezra's face before coming with a right hook to his ribs.

Ezra pushed Brutus back when he felt the sharp sting of the blow. "ARGHH!" he growled as he came back at Brutus with greater speed and fury.

Brutus managed to block a couple of the punches until Ezra landed a hit on the side of his head. Brutus got his balance back, the side of his head throbbing from the blow, then lunged at Ezra, gripping him in a tight bear hug, and squeezed him violently. This sent Ezra into a rage as he struggled with all of his might to get his left hand free and began to pummel Brutus's face. This caused Brutus to release his grip, and instead he charged him with both hands extended, grabbing Ezra by the throat and dragging him to the ground. He held him down with one hand and used his other to pound Ezra's face, which seemed to swell and cut with each punch.

Ezra cried out in pain, which started off as a yell but quickly turned into a moan of defeat.

Terrace and the others ran over and restrained Brutus. "Alright! That's enough, big guy!" Terrace told him as he, Wolf, and another member pried him off of Ezra.

Brutus stumbled over to the table that Ezra was sitting at before the fight, where he had set down the prospect vest and picked it up. He tossed the vest at Ezra, who was now being helped up by Wolf and the other Cut-Throat. "Put it on!" he barked as he turned back toward the restroom to go clean himself up.

Ezra groaned as the vest hit his chest. Because of the swelling around his eyes, he struggled to look down at the vest and watched small droplets of blood from his face stain the white leather.

At that moment, the front door to the clubhouse

opened, and everyone turned to see Edge, the young Switchblade, walk through the entrance. Terrace and Brutus, who had just stepped out of the restroom, looked at each other until Judge, president of the Cut-Throats, entered from the meeting room at the back of the clubhouse.

Judge's gaze went from Ezra, who sat on the floor, bloody and bruised with the prospect vest in his hands, to Edge, whom he didn't recognize at all. "What do you want?" he asked Edge, crossing his arms over his chest.

Edge looked at Ezra, felt a shiver run down his spine, "Are you accepting new members?"

"I don't know," he looked at the Cut-Throats, continued, "did you two just decide on your own that the Cut-Throats accept blacks and children?"

"Should we call a vote?" Brutus slumped down on one of the stools at the bar and slipped his large rings back onto his thick, bloody fingers.

Judge sighed and looked at Wolf and Ice, who shrugged at him. "Fine. To the meeting room!" he shouted at the members of his gang before looking at Ezra and Edge once again. "You two sit tight!"

Lazarus sat crouched between some tall bushes in front of a decrepit apartment building as he tried to spot a member of the White Crows to jump, then steal their mask. It was now dusk, and he felt relatively undetectable; however, he thought about how convenient it would have been to have one of the uniforms that the Shadows wore. A glint of white in the distance caught his eye as he saw a figure turn down one of the corners into an alley across the street from where he had been crouched. "Perfect!" Lazarus thought as he stood up to pursue the figure.

"THWACK!"

Lazarus dropped to the ground, unconscious.

"Two in one day?" Toki mused as he stood holding the lead pipe that he used to knock Lazarus out. "I'm going to figure out what exactly is going on here," he said as more

White Crows approached, tied the young Switchblade up, and carried him away to the Crow's Nest.

I gotta get creative here . . . Zero thought. A light knock on the door startled him, so he rose to his feet and walked over to it. When he opened the door, he was greeted by Talon, Toki, and two other White Crows with whom he was not yet acquainted, all standing in the hall in front of the room.

"We think we may have found a way that you can prove your loyalty to us," a smile appeared from under the long beak of the mask. "Come with us," she beckoned as she and the others turned and started down the hall.

Excellent! Zero thought to himself, relieved that he didn't have to come up with something on his own and decided that whatever task that they gave him, he would be able to figure out a way to get it done.

Zero was led down the hallway and up a flight of blue carpeted stairs that led to an upper hall, where he was taken to one of the middle rooms. The White Crows who escorted him remained silent as they lined up to the side of the door, facing Zero, while Talon unlocked and opened it, motioning for him to walk through.

Zero felt sweat collecting on the palms of his hands as he glanced at each of the Crows before entering the room. He gasped when he noticed Lazarus suspended off the ground by ropes tied to his wrists. "What is this?" Zero looked back at Talon, who entered behind him with the other White Crows.

"We found him sneaking around the neighborhood," Toki told Zero. "Do you know him?" his head slightly cocking to the side.

Zero pushed his eyebrows together before turning to Lazarus and squinting in his direction as he hung there and stared at the floor. "Haven't I seen you at TNT's before?" Zero slowly approached his leader, realizing that he couldn't conceal the fact that he knew him.

Lazarus looked up weakly with a small glint in his eyes. "Probably," he groaned as the movement caused a strain on his underarms that were being stretched uncomfortably.

The White Crows in the room looked at each other, and then Talon nodded as she stepped forward. "What were you doing sneaking around our neighborhood?"

"I came to get one of your masks," he stared at the White Crow leader.

A couple of the Crows gasped at the audacity of Lazarus's statement. Zero's eyes widened as he stood there, frozen—fearing for Lazarus's life.

Talon stood still and stared at Lazarus. "I see . . ." she began as she reached behind her back and produced a large jagged-edge dagger that had been concealed under her waistband against. "Then why don't you try and take one?!" she screeched as she lunged at him with the dagger aimed at Lazarus's throat.

"Laz!" Zero stepped forward, causing Talon to halt and turn toward him.

Talon slowly walked up to Zero, placed the jagged blade against his throat, and pressed in just enough so that he could feel the bite of the sharp teeth of the blade as little droplets of blood began to run down his neck. "Your next words will determine how much longer I decide to let you live."

"I don't know him!" Lazarus shouted, but was swiftly silenced as a nearby Crow walked over to him and gave him a hard punch to the gut.

Sweat collected all over Zero's body as he sat there helplessly with the knife against his throat. He swallowed before answering. "We're trying to remove the Lyones from power."

Talon looked back at the other White Crows and then pushed the dagger even deeper against his skin. "What does that have to do with the White Crows?!"

"I wasn't lying when I told you that I was a part of

the Bishops. Well, not officially, but we were working with them to help form an alliance substantial enough to go against the Lyone family."

"And you thought that you could gain us as allies by lying to us?" Talon squinted at him with deep anger from under her mask.

"Once the Bishops were wiped out and the remainder were absorbed by the Lyones, we didn't have anywhere else to turn. We need as many allies as possible if we're going to beat them."

"And your plan included the Shadows as well?" Talon removed the blade from Zero's throat, placed the tip of the knife against his forehead, and slowly began scratching a line down the surface of his face.

Zero shuddered in pain. "Please!" he struggled to pull his face away from the knife.

"Stop!" Lazarus shouted. "It was *my* plan!"

The White Crow punched Lazarus again but was told to stop by Talon, who sauntered over to Lazarus, knife still in hand. "Go on."

Lazarus took a deep breath. "Just hear me out. My name is Lazarus. This is Zero. We are both orphans as a result of the Lyone's genocide before they came to power. I've been trying to win over the Shadows, while Zero was trying to work with you. There are two more that are a part of our crew, which we call the Switchblades. One of them is currently working with the Cut-Throats. The other is locked up in the Dragon's Lair for threatening to kill Lucien Lyone after his son Vincent killed his best friend." Lazarus paused briefly as he felt the weight of grief that had not quite left his heart. "We have been networking with as many gangs as possible to form a super alliance, strong enough to crush the Lyones and remove Lucien from power. No more taxes. No more oppression. And most importantly, no more war," his eyes locked with Talon's, whose face remained unchanged.

Talon slipped the dagger back into its sheath and

looked at the other White Crows in the room once again. "And what about the Shadows?" she looked from Zero to Lazarus.

"The plan was to negotiate a ceasefire until we sort out the Lyones and then work toward final peace terms between you two once everything is resolved," Lazarus exhaled.

"The White Crows and the Shadows will *never* be at peace," Talon said matter-of-factly before turning to her men and nodding. "We have some things to discuss," she and the rest of the Crows exited the room, leaving Lazarus and Zero still restrained, facing one another, and locked them inside the room.

"At least we're still alive." Lazarus smirked, trying to make the best of their uncomfortable situation.

Zero sighed. "For now, anyway."

"This is harder than I thought," Lazarus admitted as he watched his shadow swaying slowly back and forth on the ground.

"The right thing usually is," he smiled, and continued, "but it's always worth it. You taught me that, boss."

Tears formed in Lazarus's eyes as he bit his lower lip slightly to hold back. "You're right," his voice was shaky. "Even if we die here and now, it will be worth it because we did the right thing."

"You're right," A small smile began to form on Zero's face.

The sound of the door being unlocked caught both boys' attention. As the door flung open, Talon and her entourage hastily entered the room and walked right up to Lazarus. "You led an *entire* squad of Shadows to our doorstep?!"

"*What?* No! My initiation was to just bring them a Crow mask. I'm not even a member!" Lazarus felt his heart sink as he realized that the Shadows had played him.

"You idiot! They used you as bait to find our

hideout!" Toki berated.

"I should kill you both right now!" Talon growled, reaching for her dagger once more.

"Wait! Let us try and help!" Zero pleaded. "If you guys are willing to cooperate, we can try for that ceasefire right now, but you gotta give us a chance to explain things to the Shadows!"

"I might even be able to reach out to my contact in the Cut-Throats to help mediate," Lazarus interjected.

"The Cut-Throats helping some kids mediate peace between the White Crows and the Shadows? You're insane!" Talon shrieked.

"What choice do you have?" Lazarus challenged. "Either use your brain and do the best thing for this city *and* your gang or die with your pride!"

Talon shook her head as she looked to the other Crows for guidance. Toki was silent this time and simply shrugged. Talon sighed and shook her head once more. "If this doesn't look like it will end well, I will make sure that both of you die instantly."

"That's fair. Untie us so we can get in touch with the Cut-Throats," Lazarus requested.

Talon gave the other Crows a nod to release him and Zero.

"If we can get the Shadows to back off, you have to agree to help us against the Lyones," Lazarus propositioned.

Talon responded with harsh laughter. "You'll be lucky if I allow you to live after this is over," she spoke coldly as Lazarus was lowered to his feet and freed.

Zero cringed at this statement but did his best to remain strong as he was also untied and stood up. "Thank you."

Talon licked her teeth and nodded impatiently. "Let's go!" she directed them while Lazarus got on his phone and began sending a text message to Edge.

"It's good to see you again, bro. How did you end up here?" Edge asked Ezra, who was holding a damp washcloth against a scrape on his forehead.

Ezra shook his head. "I dunno, man. They showed up while some other white boys were givin' me a hard time and offered to help me get back at the Lyones. I told 'em I didn't want to join," he looked down at the prospect vest which he now wore. "Look how far that got me." He chuckled bitterly. "What about you? Where Laz and them other dudes at?"

Edge smiled when Ezra mentioned the rest of his friends. "I'm hoping to be wearing one of those soon myself," he motioned toward Ezra's cut. "Lazarus and Zero went to do the same thing that I came to do here: getting the other gangs on board to help. The Bishops were our biggest ally and with you guys gone"—Edge paused and frowned—"we have to work twice as hard to get more groups to join us. As for Seraph, he made some threats to Lucien Lyone and is currently locked up over at the Dragon's Lair."

Ezra swore and shook his head. "Man, everything went to hell. I wish we woulda taken y'all more seriously when you first came to us. I'm partly to blame for that."

"I get it, man. How seriously could you have taken four kids with such a huge goal? I'm just sorry for how things turned out. It just goes to show how much the Lyones really need to be removed from power."

The door to the Cut-Throats' meeting room swung open, and Judge and the rest of his officers came out. "We've come to a decision regarding your membership."

Edge felt his phone buzzing in his pocket and decided to check it. Judge and the rest of the Cut-Throats stared at him in a mixture of anger and disbelief as Edge opened up a message from Lazarus.

"Something you want to share with us, kid?" Terrace squinted at Edge.

"Lazarus and Zero are in trouble. We gotta help

them," Edge calmly stared back at Terrace.

Terrace and Judge glanced at each other. "I told you this was gonna get us involved in a big mess," Judge shook his head.

"We've already come this far . . ." Terrace shrugged and looked at Edge. "What's going on?"

"The White Crows are on board, but the Shadows are attacking them now in full force. Laz is asking us to come mediate to negotiate a ceasefire and get the Shadows on our side as well."

Judge smirked. "That's not *so* bad, I suppose. Both are small-time hood gangs. Surprised you all even bothered."

"We need everyone that we can get at this point. Otherwise, we will never be rid of the Lyones. We only have one shot to do this," Edge's eyes beamed with urgency.

"Right." Judge's expression became more serious as he nodded to Brutus. "Let's mount up and head on over to Ivory," he said as they headed toward the door. "You two, come with us. You'll have to ride with Wolf and Iceman."

Terrace waited at the door for Edge and handed him a black leather "prospect" vest that matched Ezra's. "From now on, you wear this cut until I tell you otherwise. Understand?"

"Got it."

"Let's move it!" Judge roared over the loud engine of his motorcycle.

Only the moon was lighting up the neighborhood of Ivory. The White Crows stayed barricaded in the disheveled apartment building they called the Crow's Nest while the Shadows surrounded them in full force. Lazarus and Zero had been led near the entrance by Talon and the rest of the White Crow leadership.

"Well?" Talon spat at Lazarus as they peered out the window at the Shadows, who outnumbered them at least two to one.

Lazarus swallowed hard. "I'll go out and try to explain the situation. The Cut-Throats should be here any minute . . . hopefully."

"*Hopefully*?" Talon glared at Lazarus from behind her crow mask.

Lazarus ignored her as he slowly unlocked the entrance door before opening it and stepping through with his hands up. The Shadows were not known for using firearms, so Lazarus wasn't too afraid, though he had heard rumors that they sometimes used throwing stars or Sengoan throwing knives called *kunai*. The door was shut and locked behind him immediately after he stepped through. The small wave of about forty or so Shadows seemed to move in unison closer toward the building as three individuals approached Lazarus.

"What's going on, initiate?" asked the same Shadow who seemed to do the majority of the talking on behalf of the rest of the Shadows.

"Obviously, I have some explaining to do," Lazarus smiled uncomfortably.

"I would say so. We came here to save you after my man Ketsujo here saw you get nabbed by the Crows. Now it seems like you are in cahoots with them," the Shadow observed, as Ketsujo, who was next to him, chuckled.

"Not exactly," Lazarus attempted to clarify as he lowered his hands to his side. "Myself and a few others are a part of a secret alliance that is working to remove the Lyone family from power. We were working with the Bishops, but as you know, we were massacred by the Lyones and the Pawn Road Disciples. At this point, we are trying to get everyone that we can together to help us, or else our plan will never work."

The three Shadows all laughed at Lazarus. "So, you attempted to infiltrate us to try and sway us to help in this cause that we honestly couldn't care less about? I would have killed you on the spot," the one who did the talking said sternly, and in one swift motion pulled his straight-edged sword from the sheath that hung from his back and placed the sharp edge of the blade against Lazarus's neck.

"Easy, Rafa." The one named Ketsujo put a hand on his arm. "Maybe the boss would want to hear this."

"*Hmph.*" Rafa scoffed and sheathed his blade in another smooth motion.

Lazarus let out a deep breath that he was holding back while the blade was against his neck. "Yes, please, have your boss come and we can sit down with the White Crows and figure this all out," he suggested as he felt sweat run down the right side of his face.

"A sit down with the Crows?" came a deep voice from above Lazarus, who instantly looked up to see a figure clothed in the Shadow's uniform perched on top of the overhang that was over the entrance of the Crow's Nest. The Shadow leaped down in front of him and said, "If Talon is brave enough to come out and face us, then sure, we'll talk." He chuckled harshly and continued, "But we will only accept peace terms if the Crows give up Ivory." The other Shadows nodded in agreement.

At this, the door to the Crow's Nest flung open as Talon, Toki, and Zero all stepped onto the front porch to face the leader of the Shadows.

Talon made her way right up to him, and instantly the size difference between the two became apparent to everyone, as Talon was small in stature, even for a female, and she had to look up to make eye contact with the Shadow who towered over her. "I'm not afraid of you, Kai," she glared, "and I will *never* surrender Ivory to you!"

"Why is control of Ivory so important to you two?" Lazarus butted in, taking a step toward the rival leaders.

Kai glanced at Lazarus. "We don't have time to give history lessons, kid."

"Listen. Both of you! The future of this city is so much bigger than your stupid turf war. You have to step out of Ebony and Ivory and look at the bigger picture. Do you guys *really* want to continue spending the next few generations still fighting over which gang Ivory belongs to?" Lazarus reasoned.

Talon frowned and looked at Lazarus, letting her guard down for just a moment before looking back at Kai, who had swiftly grabbed the handle of his *ninjatō* and attempted to strike her neck as the blade of the sword seemed to glow in the moonlight. Talon gasped as she became paralyzed in shock.

"No!" Zero shouted and dove at the leader of the Shadows as his blade started to come down, and dragged him to the ground, the sword flying from his grasp and clattering down on the concrete porch next to him.

Instantly, every Shadow advanced on them. Rafa pulled Zero off of Kai while Ketsujo and the other Shadows with him approached Lazarus, Talon, and Toki and warned them not to interfere. The windows of the Crow's Nest began opening as White Crows began jumping from them to come to their leader's aid. Everyone but Lazarus had their weapons drawn.

Kai grabbed his blade and jumped to his feet. "Time to end this!" he growled through clenched teeth as he walked toward Talon.

"That's enough, Kai!" shouted Judge as he and the Cut-Throats pulled up on their motorcycles behind the cluster of Shadows. Everyone was so caught up in the commotion that no one noticed the sound of the Cut-Throats arriving.

Kai and some of the other Shadows turned to face the Cut-Throats. "This doesn't concern you, Judge!" Kai shouted back as the motorcycle gang dismounted and drew their guns.

"Actually, it does!" Judge grinned as he fingered the trigger of his black combat shotgun. "We didn't come here to cause trouble. We're here to mediate a ceasefire until we can get this all sorted out."

"We're not interested in going to war with the Lyones!" Kai looked back at Talon, desperately wanting to separate her head from her body and claim Ivory for the Shadows.

"That's not what we're asking!" Judge clarified.

"Yeah, now, unless you want us to turn this place into a bloodbath, I suggest you lower your weapons and hear what we got to say!" Brutus roared and cocked his large hand cannon.

Kai swore under his breath and hesitated before nodding, and he and his men all sheathed their swords. Zero was released and made his way back over to Talon's side.

Judge and the other Cut-Throats briefly glared at Brutus for being so direct before they slowly made their way through the sea of Shadows and approached the two leaders. "Do you have a place where we can discuss terms?" Judge smirked arrogantly.

CHAPTER TWELVE

"Bring him in," Segundo said to two Golden Dragons, who nodded at him and exited the small interrogation room where he had previously spoken with Seraph. They approached the only occupied cell in the solitary confinement area of their prison and unlocked the door. The door creaked loudly as one of them gripped the handle and pulled the door open, and the smell of must instantly hit their noses. The cell had a small uncomfortable-looking cot against the left wall and a small desk with some paper, writing utensils and a short stack of books neatly placed on it. There was a single cordless lamp on the desk that just barely lit the room and showed the faint cracks on the blank gray walls.

"Is it time for my execution already?" came a smooth, masculine voice from the right corner of the cell. The man sat with his legs crossed and his back leaning against the wall. He was skinny and covered himself with a tan-colored blanket that was draped over his shoulders. Long black hair hung in front of his eyes and a matching beard from his face. His eyes were light blue and seemed to illuminate his face, which was gaunt from malnutrition.

The Golden Dragons looked at one another. "Please come with me, Blackjack. Segundo is here to see you," one said. Blackjack rose to his feet, the blanket still draped over his shoulders like a cape as they slowly approached him.

Blackjack held out his wrists for them to cuff him, but the two looked at each other and then shook their heads. "Aren't you worried that I will try to escape?" he smirked.

One of the Golden Dragons shook his head. "No. You are being released today," he paused for a moment. "But before that, Segundo requests a word with you. Would you prefer to bathe and put on a fresh change of clothes first? We held onto your belongings from when you were originally booked."

"A shower *would* be nice . . ." Blackjack admitted. It had been almost a week since he had last been permitted to shower.

Blackjack dried himself off with a towel that had been left for him. He then wrapped it around his waist and noticed a pile of his old clothes neatly folded, resting on a chair in the center of the washroom. On top of the clothing was a slim black watch, an outdated flip phone, a money clip with some crown bills in it, a black 9 mm pistol, and a shoulder strap with two holsters, one on either side.

Blackjack put on his briefs and dress socks, followed by a dark-gray turtleneck with long sleeves, which he tucked into a pair of black slacks. He then tightened his watch onto his left wrist, pocketed the flip phone and money clip, strapped the gun holster over his shoulders, and holstered the pistol. Finally, he slipped the dark trench coat on, which now felt a little big on him. Blackjack walked over to a mirror, chuckling at his reflection. 'Homeless' was the word that came to mind.

By the faucet there was a basic shaving kit. Before he was incarcerated, Blackjack had been clean shaven;

however, he decided that he liked the bearded look. Even his long hair seemed like it could work for him. Rather than slicing it all off, Blackjack used the scissors to shape and trim his beard to make it look less scraggly. He also trimmed the dead ends from his hair, but it still hung at shoulder length, which he decided he might tie back into a ponytail once he got out.

Once Blackjack was fully ready, one of the Golden Dragons, known as Tuan, politely asked Blackjack to come with him. Tuan was short, even for a Sengoan man. He had a round face with spiky black hair and was well dressed, much like the other Golden Dragons.

"After you," Blackjack spoke with a charming tone, holding out his hand in front of him.

Tuan led him down the corridor to the room where Segundo waited for him. Tuan halted at the entrance and this time invited Blackjack to enter the room with the same hand gesture.

"It's been a little while, Mr. Blackjack," Segundo smiled as he poured a cup of green tea for both of them.

"It certainly has been. I wondered how long it would be before we met again." Blackjack returned the smile and took a seat in the chair across from Segundo. "No chess this time?"

Segundo smirked and shook his head before taking a sip of his tea. "Unfortunately, we have run out of time together. I'm sure that you have heard by now that you are being released today," he motioned for Blackjack to drink his own tea.

Blackjack took the cup and indulged in a long sip. He licked his lips and then looked into Segundo's dark-brown eyes. "Who?" his demeanor became more serious.

"The Black Lotus," Segundo responded and pulled out his cigarette case and matching silver Lyone flip-top lighter. "Take one," he offered as he took one for himself and lit it up.

Blackjack studied the cigarettes and lighter for a

brief moment before taking one and lighting it up, inhaling the smoke deeply before exhaling a thick cloud from his nostrils. "Rin . . ."

"So, what's the plan?" Segundo took a puff from his own cigarette before taking another sip of hot tea.

"I could try to get in touch with Ghost. That might be my only option."

Segundo nodded slowly and pulled out his phone. He found Ghost in his contact list and pressed *Call*. Segundo pushed the phone over to Blackjack as it started ringing.

"*How can I help you, Mr. Castraco?*" came Ghost's voice.

"Hello, Ghost," Blackjack said softly.

There was a long pause before Ghost said anything. Finally, he managed to utter his name. "*Blackjack?*"

"That's right," Blackjack answered calmly. "Listen, there isn't much time. Rin has paid for my release, which means that as soon as they let me out of here, I'm dead. That is, unless the Arch Angels intervene."

"*You have the nerve to call and ask for our help after what you did? Rin has every right to kill you. You murdered her brother!*" Ghost snarled, tempted to hang up.

"I have valuable information about Jin's death that you and Armand will want to hear. I know I am asking a lot right now, but if you would just trust me, I will tell you what I need to tell you, and then you can do whatever you like with me."

There was another pause. "*I'll call you right back.*"

Blackjack set the phone down on the table between him and Segundo and took a final drag from the cigarette before snubbing it out in the ashtray.

"What do you think?" Segundo did the same with his own cigarette.

Blackjack sighed. "My only other option would be to try and reason with Rin, which I don't see going very far."

The phone rang. Ghost's name flashed on the

screen. Segundo motioned for Blackjack to answer.

"Well?" Blackjack's eyes locked with Segundo's.

"*Be ready to leave in ten minutes. Your escort will be out front by then,*" Ghost said abruptly and disconnected the call.

Blackjack sighed with relief. "That was a close one."

Segundo smirked with pleasure. "Excellent! Now don't forget our deal. As soon as you gain their trust, get in touch with me. Or if anything else happens for that matter."

Blackjack chuckled. "Forget? It's practically my plan!" He grinned and then straightened up. "I won't forget your kindness. Together, we will finish what we started."

"You are certainly right about that. Be cautious and don't reveal too much."

"Not a problem."

"I'll see you on the other side." Segundo grinned as the two firmly shook hands.

Tuan and the other Golden Dragon were still waiting next to the doorway when Blackjack exited the interrogation room. They escorted him through the prison down what seemed to be at least four agonizingly long corridors before they ended up in the booking area of the facility. The receptionist, a small, young Sengoan woman, watched in silence as a buzzer sounded and Blackjack was led through the secured double doors. She would have only been a toddler when Blackjack was first locked away. The woman had a mild hint of fear on her face as the two Golden Dragons led Blackjack right in front of her desk.

"Fae," Tuan addressed the young receptionist, who pushed a lock of dark-brown hair back behind her ear and smiled nervously. "Process the release form for . . ." He looked at Blackjack. "Just Blackjack?"

Blackjack smiled. "Just Blackjack."

"Blackjack," Tuan said to Fae, who nodded and bowed her head twice politely before turning in her office chair and rummaging through a metal filing cabinet.

Blackjack looked around and studied the reception area. It had changed quite a lot since he last saw it, as he was being dragged into the prison by those whom he once called 'brother'. There was now a gorgeous fountain shaped like a pagoda in the center of the room that flowed into a koi pond filled with a dozen or so koi of various sizes and colors. There was a Sengoan pattern that bordered the walls in gold and various pieces of art on the walls. Blackjack's eyes fixated on the entrance door before the sound of the filing cabinet door closing caught his attention.

"Here we go," Fae began to thumb through the back pages of the stack of paperwork and wrote a tiny x next to several lines. "Please sign next to each x," she instructed as she handed Blackjack the papers and a gold-plated pen that was engraved with the Golden Dragons' insignia—two gold dragons entwined within a red circle.

Blackjack signed next to each x and handed the papers and pen back to Fae. "There you are," he bowed his head politely.

This caused Fae to blush as she quickly took the papers and pen and set them in front of her before taking a stamp from the drawer to her left and then stamped the word 'RELEASED' on the top sheet of the stack of papers.

"He's all set," she made brief eye contact with Blackjack before immediately looking away.

Tuan turned to Blackjack. "Are you ready?"

Blackjack touched his underarm where his pistol rested securely. "I'll have to be at this point," he stared at the door once more.

Tuan looked at the other Golden Dragon and nodded, after which they led Blackjack past the fountain. Another buzzer went off as Tuan pushed the door open and invited Blackjack to walk through. As Blackjack passed by Tuan, he saw him mouth the words "They're waiting for you." This caused Blackjack to hesitate at the threshold for a few seconds and swallow. He smiled weakly at Tuan as if to say "Thank you" and passed into the gated and heavily fortified entrance of the Dragon's Lair. There were watch towers on either side of the prison yard, with guards posted up in both of them. There was also a small guard booth at the gate.

Blackjack quickly closed his eyes after fully stepping outside. The rays from the sun were too intense for him to handle. He then raised his hand over his eyes to provide some shade so that he could see and continued walking down the walkway toward the front gate. As he neared, he saw those who had paid his ransom: the Black Lotus Syndicate. They stood all lined up in perfect uniform next to their black sports bikes. Their leader, Rin, stood in front, her eyes blazing with hatred as she watched her mortal enemy approach. Rin, like the other members of the Black Lotus Syndicate, wore a formfitting leather bodysuit and had a pair of machine pistols strapped to each of her thighs. Her hair was auburn and styled in an angled bob. She had many Sengoan features, such as small pouty lips and high cheek bones. She was average height and looked physically fit.

Blackjack halted at the gate, hand still shielding his eyes as the buzzer sounded a final time and the gate slid open to one side. *This is it* . . . he thought to himself.

Once the gate was fully opened, Rin and four other Black Lotus members stepped forward, but paused as a small convoy of black and yellow jeeps with two matching sports bikes riding behind the caravan pulled up in front of the prison and a force comparable in size to that of the Black Lotus filed out of the vehicles all armed with a mixture of rifles, submachine guns, and combat shotguns. They each wore a similar uniform of black with yellow accents, most notably each one wore a hood that covered their head with a gas mask peeking out, which completely covered their faces.

"What are the Yellow Jackets doing here?" one of the Black Lotus asked Rin.

Rin's eyes widened with fury as she stared at the Yellow Jackets, who seemed to also be at the Dragon's Lair for Blackjack.

Blackjack's expression changed to a smirk as he watched the Yellow Jackets approach the scene.

"What are you *doing* here, Ginzo?" Rin asked as she and her men approached the Yellow Jacket's leader, who was distinguished by the shape of his gas mask, which had three different filters.

"We're on contract to take Blackjack," Ginzo buzzed, his voice slightly muffled due to the mask.

"*Contract?*" Rin fumed. "Wh-who?!"

"I cannot disclose that information to you, Rin. I'm sorry . . . but business is business."

Rin gripped the automatic pistol holstered on her right thigh. This caused all parties to react, as everyone, both Black Lotus and Yellow Jackets raised their weapons. "Ginzo . . ."

At that moment, a green dot appeared at the center of Rin's chest. "We do not have to go down this road, Rin."

Rin looked down at her chest and then at Ginzo's chest. She gestured to him to look down at his own.

Ginzo looked down to see a red dot on his own chest and looked upwards to see if he could figure out where it was coming from before he looked back at Rin. "It's not personal. We're on contract. No need for anyone to die over this."

"Not *personal?*" Rin stared at Ginzo and shook her head as she removed her hand from the gun. With this, everyone else eased up as well, and the dots disappeared from both of their chests. Rin looked back at her men and mouthed the words 'Tail them' as the Yellow Jackets approached Blackjack, patted him down, removed his pistol, and led him into the back seat of a jeep.

"Well, it was quite thoughtful of you to get me out of there. Things could have gotten ugly for me real fast!" Blackjack broke the silence as he sat tightly between two Yellow Jackets in the back seat of one of the black and yellow jeeps.

They both silently stared at Blackjack for a moment as another Yellow Jacket, who was driving, glanced in his rearview mirror and watched the small wave of Black Lotus on their sports bikes following closely behind them.

The convoy turned onto Kings and headed toward La Noche. As the caravan of Yellow Jackets, followed by the Black Lotus Syndicate, approached the night club, they were greeted by a large assembly of Arch Angels, all heavily armed, with gunmen on the rooftop and the second floor.

Before the Yellow Jackets got out of their vehicles, Rin and the rest of the Black Lotus were already walking right up to Armand, Ghost, and their entourage. "What's going on here, Armand?" Rin quickly removed her helmet as she glared at them.

Armand raised his eyebrows and looked at Ghost, who answered for him, "Blackjack has valuable information that we need. Once we get what we need from him, I will contact you personally and let you know what we decide to do with him," he said, pressing his lips together tightly.

"Is that so?" Rin reached for the pistol strapped to her right thigh.

One of the nearby Arch Angels dove at her without hesitation and restrained her, keeping her from reaching her gun. The rest of the Arch Angels advanced aggressively with guns raised to show the Black Lotus that they were more than prepared for a confrontation. This caused the Black Lotus to back off; however, Rin continued to flail violently as she was lifted off the ground and brought over to her motorcycle. The Yellow Jackets quickly escorted Blackjack into La Noche during the commotion.

Seraph was outside with Ardent and the rest of his squad, watching everything from a short distance. This was the Seraph's first time seeing Blackjack despite having heard so much about him.

Armand looked at the various captains, including Ardent. "Guard the perimeter. No one comes or goes until I say otherwise," he directed before he, Ghost, and the rest of the Inner Circle entered La Noche behind Blackjack and the Yellow Jackets who escorted him in.

Rin shrieked curses at Armand before getting back on her bike and shouting, "This isn't over!"

Seraph stared blankly and watched as the vengeful Rin and her band of contract killers peeled off down Knights Way.

"I'm sure you're wondering what that was all about," Ardent chuckled, placing a hand on Seraph's shoulder.

"That woman? Was that Rin Yamato?" Seraph raised a brow towards his captain.

Ardent nodded. "That's right. Our founder's sister. She's been plotting to get to Blackjack ever since Jin was murdered. She's the one who paid for his release, actually."

Seraph knitted his eyebrows. "She paid for his release so she could kill him herself?" he asked as another thought entered his mind. "Then why do *we* have him?"

"That right there! That's why I like you!" Ardent chuckled once more. "Always asking the important questions. Screw the little details! You're a big-picture guy. I love that." Ardent cleared his throat. "I don't know for sure, but from what I heard, Blackjack offered some important information in exchange for our protection."

"What do *you* think of all this? Do you think Blackjack really deserves to go free after what he did?"

"It's hard to say, Seraph. On the one hand, no, because he murdered our leader in cold blood, but on the other hand, if the information is enough to help us in our efforts, then that might warrant a pardon. It all depends."

Blackjack was led to the elevator at the back of the club, where two Arch Angels stood guard, armed with submachine guns. Armand thanked Ginzo and handed him a thick yellow envelope.

"Much obliged." Ginzo let out a sharp whistle before exiting La Noche with the other Yellow Jackets.

Armand nodded to Ghost, and he and the rest of the Inner Circle guided Blackjack into the elevator and pressed the number '3' button once everyone was in.

Blackjack looked at each of his former comrades. "Well . . . it's certainly nice to see all of you. I see there are some new faces as well. Pleased to make your acquaintances," his tone was pleasant which caused Armand to shift uncomfortably before clearing his throat.

The elevator dinged and halted on the third floor. The door opened, and the group of Arch Angel leaders led Blackjack down a hallway and into a dimly lit room. At its center, there was a wooden armchair with straps on the arms and legs bolted to the floor.

"This is a new addition." Blackjack smiled and looked at each of the others. "Shall I take a seat?"

Ghost rolled his eyes and violently grabbed Blackjack under his arm and forced him into the chair, while the other leaders began strapping him into it securely.

Blackjack chuckled and shook his head before looking down and fixing his gaze on the floor in front of him.

Armand cleared his throat once more. "Ghost tells me that you have some valuable information regarding Jin's death."

Blackjack looked up and locked eyes with Armand for a brief moment before his lips curled into a smile. "That's right, but more importantly, I have information that will help you all end Lucien's tyrannical reign in Royalty. I couldn't say as much considering whose phone I was using to make the call; however, that is the main reason why I wanted to get in touch with you."

"You're full of it!" Ghost spat. "You got in touch with us just so you could save your own ass!"

Blackjack chuckled again with a few nods. "Well, that too, I suppose."

"Start with Jin's death," Armand raised his eyebrows.

"There are only two things that I can tell you regarding the death of our beloved founder. The first is that *I* did not kill him." The room went deathly silent. The Inner Circle members stared in disbelief. "The second is that Lucien Lyone knows who did."

"And that helps us how?" asked one of the Arch Angel generals.

"Because . . . I have contacts within the Lyone family who are ready to aid us against Lucien. Not only can we remove him from power, but doing so will also give us the ability to find out who actually murdered Jin." Again, silence infiltrated the room. Everyone continued to stare at Blackjack as he just smiled back at them, confident that he had them right where he wanted them.

"So, we are just supposed to trust you all of a sudden?" Armand narrowed his eyes at Blackjack. "What's in it for you?"

"It's simple enough. I want my name cleared from the murder of Jin Yamato."

Ghost clenched his teeth. "Armand and the others caught you at the scene of the murder holding your pistol— the one you used to shoot him."

Blackjack looked down at the floor again. "Not everything is as it seems."

"Is that so, Blackjack? Then how do you explain having such loyal contacts within the Lyones? I suppose they just felt pity on you and offered to help, right?" Armand folded his arms over his chest.

Blackjack remained silent for a moment before speaking again. "Get as many of the gangs as you can to aid us against Lucien. Once we are ready, I will get in touch with my contacts and coordinate a plan. There are some conditions, of course. Immunity for the Lyones who help us remove Lucien from power, including Lucien's family. Also, freedom for the Lyone family to continue working as an independent entity under Royalty's new leadership. That is their stipulation. You know mine. You have until the end of the night to decide."

Armand raised his eyebrows in Ghost's direction. "We will discuss your . . . *proposition.*"

"Excellent!" Blackjack grinned, his demeanor changing drastically. "I trust that you will make the right choice."

Ghost lunged at Blackjack, grabbing him by his coat lapels and pulling him so close that their faces were only a couple inches apart, "Believe me—we will!" he spat before releasing him by pushing him back into the chair roughly.

"In the meantime, you will remain locked up in this room. We will decide what to do with you once we've made our decision," Armand informed him.

Blackjack sat there smiling at Armand, yet remained silent.

Armand and Ghost glanced at each other once more before they and the rest of the Inner Circle exited the room, locking the door behind them.

"He's out of his mind," Ghost followed Armand across the hallway into the council chamber.

"Clearly. I think I have a solution to figure out if he's sincere or not. We could threaten to execute him unless he gives up his contact within the Lyones," Armand suggested.

"Nah, that won't work." Ghost shook his head. "He doesn't have anything to lose."

"His life? I'm sure he isn't ready to meet his end, even after almost two decades. The real question is, what does he have to gain from this? Do you really think that he just wants his name cleared? There has to be something more," Armand took his seat at the head of a large black glass-top table surrounded by leather office chairs.

Each of the seven Inner Circle members took a seat. Some lit up cigarettes or began puffing on electronic cigarettes. Each member was assigned to a different sect of the gang.

"There has to be," said one of the Arch Angel generals.

"I mean, he murdered Jin in order to take his seat as Warlord, right?" asked another. "What if he's trying to do the same, except with the Lyones this time? We would be better off killing him either way."

"I second that," another said, raising his right hand slightly.

"But if Blackjack is our only connection to the Lyones on the inside, then killing him will eliminate that as an advantage toward our overall goal."

"I think we should—" another started but was interrupted by a pounding on the door.

The generals all drew their pistols, got up from their seats, and walked over to the door. "I got it," said one as he felt a cold surge in his diaphragm and slowly unlocked the door and turned the handle.

One of the Arch Angels came through with a panic-stricken look on his face. "He's gone!" the Arch Angel shouted.

CHAPTER THIRTEEN

Seraph was becoming uncomfortable standing still so long with his fellow Arch Angels guarding the entrance of La Noche. Most of them stood quietly and watched vigilantly as if expecting an attack from the Black Lotus Syndicate at any moment, or perhaps another group that might want Blackjack's head. Seraph wondered if Armand would just decide to have Blackjack killed after everything that he had done. *They wouldn't be wrong to kill him*, Seraph thought.

Just then, the entrance of La Noche opened and the Arch Angel leadership, led by Armand and Ghost, filed out and called each crew leader over to them. One by one, the crew leaders were informed that Blackjack had escaped and Armand directed each one to take their respective crew to patrol a different part of the city.

Ardent returned to Seraph and the rest of his crew with a look of urgency. "Alright, boys. Looks like Blackjack managed to get away. The boss is sending us down Knights Way. Why don't we split up and each take a different road?" he suggested as Seraph and the others nodded in agreement and started down Knights Way.

"What do we do if we spot him?" one of Ardent's crew members asked.

"Do not engage. Blackjack is extremely dangerous. Call one of us right away and keep him at gunpoint until we can get over to you. Is that clear?" Ardent looked at each of his members gravely.

As they continued on the path, Ardent ordered one of the four down an alley that led to Noble Road, then directed another to go down the other side of Noble going east. "Seraph, you take Rooke. I'll head up to Diamond, 'cause it's a little dangerous there. Mallow, you head up to Pawn," Ardent directed as the three split off, Seraph turning down Rooke Avenue, which happened to be the road upon which both the St. Titus Orphanage and the Lion's Den were located.

Seraph kept his cell phone out as he looked back and forth down the empty street past the Lion's Den. The sun had already gone down at this point, which caused Seraph to take his time scanning the street. At the end of the perimeter of the Lyone compound was an alley that he decided to check. He quickly turned the corner and slammed straight into someone, causing his phone to fly from his hand and onto the street, while he landed hard, face forward, breaking the fall with the palms of his hands.

"Crap! Sorry about that," Seraph apologized as he started to stand and met eyes with a familiar face.

"Seraph? Once again, you are in the wrong neighborhood, my man," came the voice of DeAndre, who Seraph was surprised to see decked out in full Lyone attire.

"DeAndre?" Seraph scanned his former comrade's getup in confusion. "You're a Lyone now?"

"That's right, playa. I look fresh, right?" DeAndre smirked. His hair was now short, almost to his scalp, and he sported a neatly trimmed goatee. "You lookin' pretty sharp y'self!"

Seraph was at a loss for words. He had heard that the Bishops and the Pawn Road Disciples were forced to disband, but would have never imagined that DeAndre of all people would join the Lyone family.

"Seriously, bruh, you can't be around the Den at this time of night. Don't worry, though; we'll escort you safely off the premises." DeAndre flashed his pearly white teeth at Seraph.

"Uh, sure . . ." Seraph cleared his throat and started at his phone, which was still lying in the middle of the street. "Let me just grab—"

"Don't worry about that," DeAndre nodded to one of the Lyones who was with him. The Lyone quickly picked up Seraph's phone off the ground and put it in his pocket.

Seraph paused and stared at DeAndre for a moment. "You can give that back to me now."

"You'll get it back when I'm ready to give it back to you." DeAndre gestured for Seraph to start walking.

"I'm not going to say it again, DeAndre." He took a step back and took a fighting stance.

DeAndre raised his eyebrows as Seraph challenged him. He sighed and looked back at the Lyone, who had picked up Seraph's phone and nodded. The Lyone walked up to Seraph and reached into his pocket, but instead of pulling out Seraph's phone, he produced a long-handled pocket knife and flicked the blade out.

Seraph stepped back, reached for the pistol tucked in his waistband against his back, and pulled it out, aiming it at the Lyone who had drawn the knife. "Drop it!"

"That's enough! All of you!" came a familiar voice.

"Segundo?" Seraph lowered his gun slightly.

"Yo, Segundo! We caught this fool lurking around a little too close to the compound. We was only tryin' to escort him away, but he was tryna act hard and wouldn't listen," DeAndre quickly said in his defense as the Lyones with him nodded in agreement.

Segundo stepped forward and narrowed his eyes at Seraph. "Is that so?"

"I just wanted my phone back," Seraph motioned to the Lyone who still had his phone.

Segundo frowned and looked at the younger Lyone.

"What's wrong with you? Give the kid his phone back!"

The Lyone put away the knife, retrieved Seraph's phone from his pocket, and held it out toward Seraph with a look of embarrassment on his face.

Seraph gave the Lyone a dirty look before snatching his phone back from him. "*Thanks*," his eyes met with Segundo's once more.

Segundo smirked and looked at DeAndre. "Take your men back inside. I'll deal with *him*." DeAndre and the other Lyones obeyed and walked back toward the Lion's Den. Segundo then turned back to Seraph. "What exactly *were* you doing around here at this time of night?"

"I . . ." Seraph hesitated, trying to be careful not to say too much. "I was just walking by."

"Just walking by? Doing what? Were you going somewhere?"

"I was on my way to meet a friend, okay?"

Segundo eyed him suspiciously.

"I honestly didn't even know that I was trespassing."

"You weren't necessarily trespassing. Naturally, we grow concerned with people lurking around our compound at night. You *do* remember the conversation that we had back at the Dragon's Lair, right?" Segundo's eyes narrowed at Seraph.

Seraph swallowed and nodded. "I'm with the Arch Angels now." He motioned to the silver insignia of the sword with wings pinned to the front of his coat. "I'm not looking to cause any trouble."

"Right. Why don't you head to wherever it is you were planning to meet your friend. Hopefully not anywhere near the Lion's Den. I cannot guarantee that I will be able to protect you next time," Segundo motioned with his head for Seraph and to leave.

Seraph felt like there were a million different things that he wanted to say to Segundo, but he decided to go with his better judgment and get far away from the Lyones and their compound.

As Seraph approached Knights Way, a familiar SUV pulled up next to him. Instinctively he started to reach for his pistol, but before he drew it realized that it belonged to Lazarus.

"Yo, Seraph! Get in, man!" he shouted through the opened passenger's side window.

Seraph didn't hesitate as he opened the car door and crawled into the vehicle.

"I thought that was you back there talking to the Lyones. What was that all about, bro?" Lazarus asked Seraph, looking surprised to see him after everything that had happened, not least as an active member of the Arch Angels.

Seraph half-ignored the question as he produced his phone and began to call Ardent. "I'll give you the lowdown in a sec," he said hastily to Lazarus as they turned right onto Knights Way back toward La Noche. "Ardent! ... No, I ran into some Lyones instead. ... No. Almost, but Segundo intervened. ... Yeah, I got someone with me now too. ... A friend. ... We're heading there now. ... See ya."

"You're really with the Arch Angels now?" Lazarus was still perplexed. "When did you get out? What all have I missed?"

"Haha, easy brother! I'll fill you in. Let's just get somewhere secure first. I'm sure Ghost will wanna see you as well." Seraph grinned and patted Lazarus on the back.

"So, Armand bailed you out?" Lazarus asked after Seraph had filled him in on everything that had happened. The two now sat at the VIP bar on the second story of La Noche.

"Well, I'm not entirely sure, but he and Ghost were there when I was released. They told me about you and the Switchblades and the plan. I figured that I pretty much was already an Arch Angel anyway, so I've been rolling with Ardent's crew ever since," Seraph explained as he finished the last bit of his rum and soda.

Cherrie took Seraph's glass and smiled. "You want another, sweetie?"

Seraph returned the smile. "No thanks, Cherrie. Maybe just a water."

"Sure thing, Hon."

Seraph focused his attention back on Lazarus. "So, anyway, the Yellow Jackets got Blackjack here, and within twenty minutes they say he just vanished. That's how I ran into you. We were spread out trying to find him."

Lazarus took a deep drag from his e-cig and exhaled the smoke through his nostrils. "Wow . . . this just keeps getting more and more crazy. I wonder why they didn't just kill the bastard when they had the chance."

"All I know is that Ardent said Blackjack may have some information that could help us take down the Lyones." Seraph shrugged and took a sip from the glass of water that Cherrie had just placed in front of him.

"It's a little more complicated than that," came Ghost's voice from behind them as they turned around to face him.

"Ghost! Long time no see!" Lazarus grinned and embraced Ghost tightly after clasping hands with him.

"It's good to see you too," he said before his expression became more solemn as he turned toward Seraph. "We didn't have any luck finding Blackjack. At this point, there's not a whole lot that we can do. I've got my eyes and ears all over the city, so we'll just have to wait until we get a lead. In the meantime, just keep your eyes peeled, and notify me if you hear anything at all."

"You got it," Seraph nodded in unison with Lazarus.

"Ghost, I've got some things to fill you in on," Lazarus blurted out with a grin.

"Oh?" Ghost raised an eyebrow.

"The Switchblades have been busy. At this point and time, you can rest assured knowing that the Shadows and the White Crows have set aside their differences for the time being and have agreed to join the cause."

Ghost's eyes widened. "*What?* That's incredible! How did you—?" he started to ask but then shook his head. "Never mind. Lazarus, you've done a fine job," Ghost placed a hand on his young protege's shoulder.

"All in service to Royalty and her people," Lazarus replied with a mock salute. "Edge is currently prospecting for the Cut-Throats, who actually helped mediate between the Shadows and the Crows."

"And what about Zero?" Seraph wondered.

"He pretty much saved Talon's life and was offered a position as her bodyguard within the White Crows. It also appears that the two may be . . . *smitten* with one another." He grinned sheepishly.

"Wow . . ." Ghost shook his head. "So, I guess that just leaves you and Seraph, huh? You might as well become an active member now that everything is starting to come together."

Lazarus's grin grew wider. "For sure, man. You're the boss. I still have some loose ends to tie up with the McDroogins in the meantime. Was there anyone else that you need me to reach out to?"

Ghost touched his chin in silence for a moment. "So, we've got the Cut-Throats, the Shadows, the White Crows, the McDroogins possibly . . ."

"The Immortals said that they are down as well," Lazarus added.

"Alright. I'll go over all of this with Armand in a minute. He's going to be very pleased. Once I get word from him, I'll call you with further instructions. In the meantime"—Ghost turned toward Seraph—"you are relieved from Ardent's crew. I want you to take some time to work with Laz as he finishes solidifying the last of our allies. Stay away from the Lyones, and if you see or hear anything about Blackjack, contact me immediately."

"Done and done."

"Excellent. You two go and do what you do best," Ghost started back toward the elevator.

"He's a good guy," Lazarus watched Ghost get into the elevator.

Seraph nodded. "So, where to now?"

Lazarus looked at his phone. "Well, the Shamrocke's still open for another two hours. I'll give O'Connor a call and see if we can set up a meeting."

Seraph and Lazarus decided to walk to the Shamrocke. The Kaelish fiddle music could be heard from almost a block away. They made their way past the thick clouds of smoke that covered the front patio, the smell of liquor and tobacco drowning out their senses. When they got inside, they were greeted by O'Connor, McGregor, and Malone.

"Close 'er down!" O'Connor shouted as the bartender nodded and began closing out the tabs of each of the patrons that sat at the bar. "Come wit' me," O'Connor said as he and the other two McDroogin officers led Seraph and Lazarus toward the back of the bar.

It didn't take long for the pub to empty out, and then they turned the porch lights off and locked the front doors, keeping a single McDroogin posted up to stand guard. A bear of a man stepped out of the back office, wearing a light-green polo shirt and a golf cap. He was heavyset and had a dark-gray goatee. The man approached Seraph and Lazarus and shook both their hands.

"Padraeg McDroogin, owner of the Shamrocke and head of the McDroogin clan."

"Seraph."

"Good to see you again, Mr. McDroogin," Lazarus grinned.

"Aww, cut the pleasantry shite!" Padraeg chuckled heartily. "What can I do ya for, lads?"

O'Connor cleared his throat. "They're here to propose an alliance to remove the Lyone family from power."

Padraeg's eyes grew wide as he stood frozen in silence. "No way. Too dangerous."

"Wait!" Lazarus held up his hand. "We already have a handful of gangs on board who've agreed to fight."

"Oh, yeah? Like who?"

"Well, the Cut-Throats for one. The Immortals. The Shadows. The White Crows . . ."

Padraeg closed his eyes tightly when Lazarus mentioned the Cut-Throats, but then chuckled as he heard the rest. "So, a handful of unorganized streets urchins and a motorcycle gang is all ya got?"

"The Arch Angels," Seraph spoke up uncomfortably.

The smirk faded from Padraeg's face. "Oh, so *now* the Arch Angels wanna step up to the plate?" he asked as his temper started to fray. "And where were the Arch Angels twenty years ago when the Lyones took over, when that bastard killed my—" He stopped himself.

"Pat . . ." O'Connor laid his hand on his leader's back.

Padraeg snarled and shook O'Connor's hand off him. "The answer is no," he tried to regain his composure. "Now, go on home. You boys would be smart to stay away from these ridiculous fantasies of taking out the Lyones," he turned his back to the two boys and walked back toward his office.

"And you're alright with your daughter's murderer just getting off the hook with no consequences?" Seraph shouted.

Lazarus's eyes widened in fear as he placed his hand on Seraph's shoulder as if to hold him back.

Padraeg froze. His breathing intensified; however, instead of reacting, he entered his office and slammed the door behind him.

Seraph, Lazarus, and the McDroogins sat there in silence, everyone unsure of what to do.

"I'm sorry, boys," McGregor frowned.

"Oh no, we're not giving up that easily!" O'Connor looked at Seraph, and gave him a solid nod. "You—come with me!"

Seraph looked at Lazarus in confusion and shrugged as they both stood up and followed O'Connor back into Padraeg's office.

O'Connor closed the door behind them and walked over next to Padraeg, who sat at his desk with his hat in his hands, staring at the mahogany surface of his desk. "I won't change my mind."

"Look at the boy!" O'Connor ordered Padraeg, who looked back at him in confusion.

"Who? *Seraph*?" Padraeg grabbed a nearby napkin and used it to wipe the tears from his eyes.

"Aye. Take a good look at him."

Padraeg stared at Seraph, who was just as perplexed as he was, and then looked back at O'Connor. "So bloody what? What am I s'pose to be lookin' at?"

Seraph also looked up at O'Connor, "What's going on, man?"

O'Connor ignored Seraph and continued to address Padraeg. "Does he look familiar? Perhaps bear any striking resemblance?"

Padraeg squinted in Seraph's direction once again and shrugged. "What the devil are ya getting at, O'Connor? Spit it out already!"

O'Connor lowered himself next to Padraeg, who was still sitting and pointed at Seraph. "That boy right there . . . is your *grandson*."

Padraeg squinted once more and then looked back at O'Connor as he felt his blood beginning to boil. "I am in no mood for your games, O'Connor! You know damn well I don't have any grandkids!"

"Aye, but you do. The Cut-Throats boy and Rayn married in secret. That part you found out. But the union wasn't the only thing they were planning to announce that night," O'Connor told him as tears formed in his own eyes. "I didn't know it at first, until I met the lad not too long ago when Lazarus and his crew brought him over. I got to thinkin' and did a little background check, and sure enough, he's the one."

"But she died, O'Connor! How could she have had a baby?" Padraeg tears formed in his eyes and came down in thick streams down his cheeks.

O'Connor stood up tall and walked over to Seraph, who looked just as pale with shock. "The Priests performed an emergency C-section to save the lad's life," O'Connor looked back at Padraeg and then at Seraph. "The most premature baby born in Royalty ever to survive. You're a miracle child, m'boy," O'Connor said, placing a firm hand on Seraph's shoulder as tears ran down his cheeks.

Seraph's mouth hung slightly ajar while tears formed in his eyes. Words failed him as he stood there and stared at Padraeg McDroogin before looking back at O'Connor and then at Lazarus. *What does this even mean?* he wondered, lost in confusion.

Padraeg stood up slowly. He walked over to Seraph and placed Seraph's head between his massive hands as he looked down at him. "My grandson . . ." he sniffled a bit to keep his nose from running. "He has her eyes . . ." He turned toward O'Connor and then back to Seraph. "You have her eyes."

Seraph sat there frozen. "I . . ."

O'Connor stepped closer, placed his hand on Padraeg's back, and chuckled through his tears. "Easy boss, or you'll scare the poor kid," he said as Padraeg released Seraph's head.

"R-right, sorry," he took a step back.

"I'm sorry to have to drop such a bombshell on you three, but you needed to know," O'Connor looked around the room at the other three. "This is all too important to keep it hidden any longer. We need this reminder"—he placed a hand on Seraph's shoulder and gave it a squeeze—

"so that we can get focused and mend everything the Lyone family broke."

Padraeg frowned and looked away, remaining silent.

Seraph wiped the tears from his cheeks.

Lazarus slowly raised his hand and spoke up. "So, would you reconsider helping us?"

Padraeg frowned and continued staring at Seraph. "I-I don't know . . ." his voice was shaky. "I just found out I have a grandson, and if we fight, there's a chance I could lose him too."

Seraph wiped his eyes. "I'm not afraid to die. I would rather die to prevent anyone else in this city from losing their loved ones than to continue to live with the injustice of the Lyones."

Padraeg silently looked at his grandchild and then back at O'Connor.

"It's about time, Pat. Time to exact justice on these bastards that took Rayn from us," O'Connor's heart began racing.

"Right!" Padraeg stood tall, opened the door to the office, and beckoned for the others to follow him.

They all exited the office and joined the rest of the McDroogins in the back of the bar, who sat around, all stone-faced as they waited to hear from their leader.

"Alright, boys. I've decided that the McDroogins will help in the fight against the Lyones," Padraeg announced to his men.

The McDroogins all cheered loudly and raised their glasses. O'Connor, Seraph, and Lazarus all looked at one another and grinned in satisfaction.

"With that said," Padraeg continued. "I would like to introduce you all to my grandson." He smiled proudly and brought Seraph, who felt uncomfortable, next to himself and put his arm around him. All of the McDroogins looked confused to one degree or another but cheered nonetheless. "I'll explain that later." He chuckled as his face turned red.

"I say this calls for a celebration!" O'Connor looked at Seraph.

Seraph blinked and looked away nervously. Everything felt surreal to him, as if he were in a dream. "I . . . um—"

"I'm sorry, but we still have another stop make," Lazarus took the cue from Seraph. "Once the Lyones are done with and stability is restored, we should celebrate with all the gangs!"

The McDroogins loved any excuse to have a celebration, and all their faces lit up at the sound of this. "Aye, that's probably best." O'Connor smiled and placed a hand on Seraph's shoulder. "Be well, lad. Make all of us proud."

Seraph and Lazarus exited the Shamrocke and started down toward Bishop Avenue to meet up with Edge and the Cut-Throats. It had been months since Seraph had last seen Edge or Zero. Although he had taken to Lazarus more, he still felt close to the other Switchblades, especially after everything they had all been through together.

The street was quiet, and there was a slight chill in the air. Seraph shivered and buttoned up his blazer. "Fall must be coming early this year."

"Yeah . . ." Lazarus said as they neared the intersection of Kings and Bishop. "That was quite a load that O'Connor dropped on you just now, huh?"

Seraph halted and stood there silently. A cool breeze brushed against his face as he felt the short hairs on his chin sway. "I don't know *what* to think, bro."

Lazarus stopped as well and turned to his friend. "It's a lot to take in. But it's good that you know now. Most importantly, you know what they stood for."

"But that's the problem, Laz! My goal was never to save the city! I just want wanted to save Lance and now that he's gone"—Seraph's eyes welled up with tears again—"I just don't know anymore!"

Lazarus quickly wrapped his arms around Seraph, embraced him tightly, and let him cry on his shoulder. "It's okay, bro. It's alright. Saving Royalty wasn't even my plan, man, but I joined in, just like you. We both had our own reasons. Everyone does, but that doesn't make you selfish, brother. Saving Lance was a noble cause. The man was your best friend!" Lazarus rubbed Seraph's back as he tried to console him.

"And then I just let him die. Some best friend I was," Seraph wiped his nose.

"There was nothing you could have done, man. You tried to talk him out of it. But you know what? In the end, Lance made the right choice. He did the right thing. He died a good man, with his morals still intact."

"Man, I just . . . is this what I really wanna do? Or am I just going along for the ride?"

"This is how I see it, Seraph. You're in it, one way or another. What you decide to do or how you decide to handle this is entirely up to you. No one can make you feel what you don't want you to feel. Saving Royalty is either something you are passionate about or not. Like I said, everyone has their own reasons. The question is whether or not you decide to use your reason to kindle a passion to reclaim this city."

Seraph nodded as he considered what Lazarus had said.

"There's no rush, bro. Take some time to think it over," Lazarus gave Seraph a pat on the shoulder.

"I will . . ." Seraph used the sleeve of his coat to wipe his eyes.

"Good. Now let's go see how Edge is doing." They crossed Bishop and approached the Wild West. They passed all of the motorcycles that were out front and entered the main bar area where many of the Cut-Throats turned toward them to see who they were.

"Laz! Seraph!" came Edge's voice as he hopped off his bar stool and ran over to his friends.

"Hey, bro!" Lazarus grinned and clasped hands with Edge.

"Seraph! How are you, man?!" Edge shouted as he grabbed Seraph and pulled him into a tight embrace.

"I'm good!" Seraph choked out as Edge squeezed him in a bear hug.

"You look *good*, brother! Are you rocking Arch Angels colors now? Sharp!"

"It's official now."

Judge and all four of his officers approached the reunion. "Good to see you, Lazarus."

"You too, Judge. Thanks for taking the time. Sorry we're late."

"No problem. We got something we gotta take care of first anyway," Judge said and then turned his head to where a strong Amakoran man was sitting by himself. "Hey, Prospect! Get over here!"

"Ezra!" Seraph stood up and walked over to them.

Ezra clasped hands with Seraph. "Glad to see you a'ight, brotha."

"You too, bro."

Judge looked at Ezra, shook his head, and then looked over at Edge. "You two!" he said in his normal gruff voice.

"What's up, boss man?" Edge grinned. He had grown used to being barked at by the various members of the Cut-Throats.

"Take off your cuts."

"What?"

Ezra stared blankly at Judge but said nothing.

Terrace stepped forward and pointed to the leather vest that Edge was wearing. "Take it off!"

Lazarus and Seraph gave each other an uneasy look.

Ezra slipped his cut off and held it out before Terrace snatched it out of his hand.

Edge's face fell. His heart sank as a deep hurt settled within him. He swallowed hard, removed the leather vest, and reluctantly handed it to Terrace.

"We talked it over," Judge looked at both of them. "You two aren't fit to prospect for the Cut-Throats."

Edge felt his eyes beginning to water as he looked down at the floor and hung his head. Ezra just stood there and smirked, showing that he couldn't care less.

At that moment, Wolf and Iceman stepped forward with brand-new, fully patched cuts and presented them to Edge and Ezra.

Judge's expression changed to a grin. "Instead, we think you two have earned the right to be full members."

Edge's face lit up as he grabbed the cut and quickly put it on. "Oh, man! Oh, man! This is awesome!"

Judge stepped forward, embraced Edge tightly, and kissed his cheek. "Welcome to the Cut-Throats, brother!"

One by one, the officers hugged Edge and welcomed him among their ranks as an official member of their motorcycle brotherhood.

Ezra took the cut that was for him and studied it quietly.

"What's a matter, bro? Put it on!" Brutus slapped Ezra's arm.

Ezra smiled weakly and shook his head, handing the vest out to Brutus. "Look, man, I appreciate this—I really do. But this . . ." Ezra looked around at the Cut-Throats, "it's not me. When I fight against the Lyones, I'ma die a Bishop or live and restore the Bishop Brotherhood. I love y'all, and I don't think I will ever be able to repay y'all for takin' me in, but I can't be a Cut-Throat."

Judge stepped forward and placed his hands on Ezra's shoulders. "I respect that, Ez. You're a standup guy. As much as I want to have you in our ranks, I respect your decision. You can continue to roll with us for as long as you need to or until this all gets sorted out."

"I appreciate that, Judge."

Judge pulled Ezra in and gave him a tight hug. "And once you do reestablish the Bishops, I swear we'll never have another beef with you all ever again."

"For sure. Same goes for us. You white boys is alright!"

Just then, two Cut-Throats came from behind the bar with a large bucket filled with beer and dumped it over Edge's head.

"Now let's celebrate our new brother and our new ally!" Judge shouted at the top of his lungs as everyone in the bar cheered loudly, and the festivities began.

CHAPTER FOURTEEN

"What? How could you put me in check so early in the game?" Dante Lyone, Lucien's youngest son, complained as he and Segundo sat in a pavilion within the Lyone Manor grounds playing their weekly game of chess.

"It's as I always tell you," Segundo instructed, "you have to watch the whole board. How will you ever help lead the family if you aren't constantly looking at all the pieces on the board?"

Dante thought about what Segundo had said. "But life isn't chess, Segundo. And people aren't pieces on a board."

"In many ways, you are right, Dante. But in another sense, you are wrong. Life is much like chess. Think about it like this. If you do something in life without thinking it through and looking ahead to anticipate what the consequences could be, then you risk losing something, right?"

"And just like in chess, sometimes losing one piece could cost you the whole game, right?"

Segundo's grinned. "Exactly! You got it!"

"What about when you are the one responsible for taking another person's pieces?"

"What do you mean?"

"Like Vincent. He wiped out the Bishops and the Pawn Road Disciples. Was it right for him to do that?" Dante's eyes met with Segundo's.

Segundo frowned and looked down at the board. "It's hard to say, Dante. It's a complicated situation. I don't believe his motivation to do that was purely malevolent."

"So, as long as his heart was in the right place, it doesn't make it wrong?"

"Not necessarily." Segundo looked down the walkway toward the house, where he saw Lucien approaching them.

"Well, good day, gentlemen!" Lucien greeted them.

"Hey, boss." Segundo stood up to shake hands with him.

"Hello, Father." Dante produced a weak smile as he looked up.

Lucien looked at the table and studied the chessboard with a smirk. "How are your studies going this afternoon, son?"

"They're going well. Segundo was teaching me about how chess is like life."

Lucien smiled and looked at Segundo. "Is that so?"

Segundo chuckled. "Yes, sir. This one is very bright."

"I know," Lucien beamed proudly at his son.

Segundo knelt down next to Dante. "Alright, young man. I've got some business to discuss with your father. We will have to continue our game another time," he gave Dante a gentle pat on the shoulder.

"Pfft. You're just scared because you know that I would have turned this game around!"

"Guilty as charged!" Segundo jested and stood back up.

Dante stood up from his chair and gave his father a quick hug before running off toward their home.

"I'm telling you, Lucien. He is *sharp*!"

"He comes from good stock." Lucien chuckled and gave Segundo a playful punch on the arm. "Come, let's take a walk."

Segundo nodded and followed his leader as they began to walk around the courtyard of the Lyone Manor. The pathway was elegantly paved with pebbles. The grass was emerald green, and there were tall hedges on either side of the walkway. In the middle of the courtyard was a large fountain of a lion that shot water from its mouth. The house was two stories tall and sat on four acres of land. The exterior was bright white with light-gray plantation shutters covering the windows. There were ten bedrooms where Lucien's family and his top generals lived. Each room had its own full bathroom and kitchenette.

"What's on your mind, boss?" Segundo asked as they passed the lion fountain.

"I'm sure you know that the Arch Angels now have Blackjack?"

"Yes, although I haven't quite figured out why they would want to keep him alive."

"That's what's bothering me. Armand should want to kill Blackjack himself, but it doesn't appear that he has killed him yet."

"I agree that this is concerning."

"Why could they possibly want to keep him alive? It makes me wonder if there is something more going on here that we don't realize."

Segundo's eyes widened for a moment. "I guess I would be lying if I didn't say I felt the same, but what could they possibly be up to?"

"I don't know. But then the Arch Angels go and take that Seraph kid in. What's that all about? I know I asked Armand to keep an eye on him, but I didn't expect him to recruit him."

Segundo cleared his throat and lightly shrugged. "Maybe they felt sorry for the poor kid after what happened to his friend?"

"How was he when you went to see him?"

"Well, he was definitely still grieving. I let him know that it would be in his best interest to forget everything that happened and continue on with his life. I believe we understood each other clearly."

Lucien shook his head, dissatisfied with this answer. "I don't know what exactly, but the Arch Angels are definitely up to *something*."

"What would you like to do, boss?" Segundo asked as they stopped walking.

"I want both of them brought to the compound. Blackjack and Seraph. Once we have them, make a call to Rin and tell her that Lucien Lyone personally invites her to come to the Lion's Den, where she may execute Blackjack."

"What about the kid?"

"Recruit him. Offer him everything he could ever want. Rank, status, money, clothes—I don't care. Whatever the kid wants. I want to keep him close. The closer he is, the less I will have to worry about him feeling like maybe he has to prove some sort of point."

Segundo frowned and cleared his throat. "Boss, I have to be honest—this doesn't sound like a good idea. First, getting involved in the personal business of other gangs could create a lot of bad blood between us and them. Secondly, based on my meeting with the kid, I don't believe he would ever join the family, no matter what we offered him. He may not try to get revenge for the death of his friend, but he most certainly will not join us."

Lucien sighed. "Well, in that case, we may have to have him killed too." He looked up at the clouds. "I don't know what it is, but there is something about him. I'm going to put Elders and Ward on finding out everything they can about this kid. Once I see him face to face, I'll know what to do with him."

"Lucien . . ." A look of concern came over Segundo's face. "I thought that we were doing things differently now?"

Lucien placed a hand on Segundo's shoulder and gave it a squeeze. "Don't worry, Segundo. I haven't lost my way, but I *have* been thinking lately . . ."

"What's that, boss?"

"What if the answer isn't keeping the gangs under control? What if the answer is no gangs at all? Maybe we've been going about this the wrong way completely."

Segundo rubbed his chin. "You may not be wrong, Lucien. But even if that is the answer, just like in chess, we have to play our pieces the right way. Just as I taught your son earlier, if you do not look at the whole board and anticipate all the potential moves from both sides, then one mistake could cost us the whole game."

"Always my voice of wisdom and clarity," Lucien said and started walking again. "Take care of this Blackjack and Seraph thing for me."

How could he have gotten away? Ghost thought as he gripped the steering wheel of his glossy black sedan. He and a small group of Arch Angels conducted a thorough search of the room in which Blackjack had been detained before taking to the streets. There was no sign or trace indicating how he escaped or where he had gotten out. The Arch Angel who had been guarding the door was thoroughly questioned and was currently being detained until Blackjack was caught once again. *Think! Think!* Ghost tried to retrace the events that led up to Blackjack being in their custody. *The last people before us that he was in contact with were the Yellow Jackets*, he thought to himself, deciding that it wouldn't be a bad idea to stop by the Hive and do a little investigating. Ghost's phone began to buzz as he turned onto Diamond Road.

"Hello?" Ghost answered the call as it transferred to the overhead intercom.

"*Ghost*," came Armand's voice. "*Anything?*"

"Not quite. I'm heading over to the Hive to do a little poking around since they were the last ones before us that had any contact with him.

"That's a good idea. Come by La Noche and take some men with you. I'd like to join you too."

"Sounds good, boss. I'll be right there," Ghost ended the call before turning the car around and heading back onto Knights Way toward La Noche.

It would be even better if we knew where to find the Black Lotus Syndicate, Ghost thought to himself, believing that it was more than likely them who had somehow gotten a hold of Blackjack considering how badly Rin wanted to kill him.

As Ghost neared La Noche, he heard four sharp sounds, struggled to keep the steering wheel straight, and quickly lost control as he realized that his tires had been blown out. The car swerved into a lamp post that towered over the parking lot of La Noche. A loud crashing noise filled the air as Ghost was jerked forward, then back, his airbags deployed, smashing against his face, which caused his sunglasses to snap in half at the nose.

Four motorcycles pulled up next to his car, all of the figures dressed completely in black with their faces mostly concealed, each armed with a pistol strapped to their upper right thigh. One of the figures approached the driver's side door and opened it, peering at Ghost, who lay against the steering wheel. The black-clad figure placed a hand on Ghost's shoulder and attempted to pull him back against the driver's seat.

Ghost's eyes shot open as he pulled his hand from the inside of his coat, drew his machine pistol, and unloaded a few shots into the torso of the figure. He then swiftly undid his seatbelt and exited the car, pointing his pistol in the direction of the other three as more motorcycles of similar style pulled up to reinforce the original group that had shot out Ghost's tires. Ghost used his other hand to pull his cell phone out of his pocket, pressed the *Emergency* button, and placed the phone to his left ear. "Yep! Bring them all out!" he shouted as he slowly backed up toward the building.

Rin, leader of the Black Lotus Syndicate, stepped forward, her pistol still strapped to her thigh as she glared in Ghost's direction. The rest of the Black Lotus had their guns aimed at Ghost as she continued walking forward. "Hand Blackjack over now, or we will kill you!" she demanded.

The entrance to La Noche swung open, and an army of Arch Angels led by Armand poured out, all heavily armed, and aimed their weapons at the Black Lotus members. Ghost continued backing up until he was surrounded by his comrades. Other Arch Angels appeared from the neighboring streets and surrounded Rin and her people completely.

"You can't survive this; take your people and leave immediately," Armand threatened Rin, gripping his small submachine gun.

"I'll say it one more time. Hand Blackjack over now!" Rin repeated unwavering.

"We already told you, he will be dealt with accordingly—all in due time. But for the moment, he is of some use to us, and if we kill him, then he loses his usefulness. As soon as we are done with him, you can have him. You have my word!" Armand shouted back at her.

Rin shook her head and walked toward Armand, who was standing in front of the entrance of La Noche. "Step aside, or you will be shot."

"Enough of this, Rin! If you kill Armand, then we will kill you and the rest of the Black Lotus, and neither side will benefit!" Ghost shouted at her as he started toward her.

Rin flung her head back and cackled loudly before meeting eyes with Ghost. "I swear to you that I have a lot less to lose," she said, her eyes wildly ablaze.

At that moment, three silver sedans pulled up between the squad of Black Lotus Syndicate members and the small army of Arch Angels. Segundo, accompanied by eleven other Lyone soldiers, stepped out from the three cars and walked toward Rin and Armand.

"Everyone put your weapons away." Segundo projected his voice calmly as he neared the two leaders.

Rin's eyes narrowed at Segundo as she swore under her breath. "I'm not leaving until I get Blackjack."

Segundo smirked. "I know. That's why I came here. Lucien wants to make good on his word."

Armand gave Segundo a puzzled look.

"I've come to collect both Blackjack *and* Seraph," Segundo told him as Armand's eyes widened with shock. "I'm sorry, but Mr. Lyone will not compromise."

Rin stepped forward toward Segundo and met eyes with him. "As long as I am the one who gets to kill Blackjack."

"That is the plan," Segundo assured her. "In the meantime, I need you to stand down and leave. Await further instruction once we have Blackjack, and we will make everything right."

Rin stared at Segundo. "Alright," she said and looked back at her men, giving them a nod as they all lowered their weapons. Rin and her men walked back over to their motorcycles, mounted them, and peeled off down Knights Way as one.

Once the Black Lotus Syndicate was far away from La Noche, Armand approached Segundo. "What is this all about?"

Segundo loosely took Armand by the arm and guided him away from earshot. "Like I said, Lucien won't compromise on this."

Armand shook his head and peered over Segundo's shoulders at both of their men. "Well, that's going to be a problem because Blackjack is gone."

Segundo's eyes widened. "*Gone?* What do you mean?"

"We had him in our holding room and left for maybe ten minutes, and he just disappeared."

"Didn't you have anyone guarding him?"

"We had one of our men watching the door. He's

the one who reported that Blackjack was missing. We've got him in holding now and have been questioning him thoroughly."

Segundo sighed and touched his forehead. "This is *not* good, Armand."

"You don't think I know that? We've been searching for him since last night," Armand said under his breath as Ghost approached them with a concerned look on his face.

Segundo briefly acknowledged Ghost with a nod before turning back to Armand. "Well, what about Seraph? I have to bring *someone* back to Lucien."

"He should be at the Wild West with some friends. That was the last place they were heading when they left last night," Ghost said, careful not to give too much information.

Segundo scratched the short black hairs on his chin. "Okay. Why don't you go and retrieve him? Bring him to the Lion's Den, and give me a call when you're out front."

Ghost looked at Armand for approval. He only shrugged and nodded to him.

"Alright," Ghost started on foot toward Bishop.

Segundo returned to his convoy and then looked back at Armand. "I'll be in touch."

Seraph and Lazarus sat out front of the Wild West chatting while the majority of the Cut-Throats were still asleep or treating their hangovers inside. It was late afternoon, and the sun warmed their faces as they each sipped on warm beers from the night before. Edge stepped out to join them. His medium-length hair stuck up in the back where he had a cowlick, and his white T-shirt had a yellowish tint to it due to the beer that had been dumped over his head the night before.

"Morning fellas." Edge yawned as he closed the door behind him and leaned against the exterior brick wall.

"Morning, brother," Lazarus scratched his belly.

"Morning, man." Seraph smiled and took another gulp from the bottle in his hand.

"Did you guys even sleep last night?" Edge cocked an eyebrow.

"Nah, we've just been out here chatting. There's something that we wanted to tell you, but figured it could wait until the party was over," Lazarus looked to Seraph.

"Oh? What's going on?"

Seraph cleared his throat. "I, uh . . . I found out who my parents were."

"Oh yeah? Good for you, man!"

"Remember that story O'Connor told us about the Cut-Throat that was in love with Padraeg McDroogin's daughter?" Lazarus asked him.

"You're *kidding* . . ." Edge furrowed his eyebrows at Seraph.

Seraph shook his head and looked away nervously.

"The news is, uh . . . still settling in," Lazarus patted his friend on the back.

A young man and woman approached them from North Bishop. Edge squinted in their direction and then grinned broadly. "Zero!"

Zero returned the grin, took the young woman by the hand, and walked briskly toward his friends. "Hey guys!" The woman with him looked uncomfortable as he pulled her along.

Edge and Zero embraced each other tightly, then Lazarus grabbed his friend and pulled him in for a hug as well. Zero turned to Seraph with eyes wide. "Seraph! You made it out!" he practically tackled Seraph, embracing him tighter than either Edge or Lazarus.

"Haha—hey, Zero!" Seraph chuckled.

"I'm so glad you're okay, bro. We were so worried about you!" Zero admitted.

"Here I am."

Edge then pointed to the girl who was with Zero and asked, "Who's your friend?"

The girl's face flushed a deep red as she looked at Zero and then at the sidewalk under their feet.

Zero's cheeks turned red, and he cleared his throat. "This is Talon."

Lazarus's eyes grew wide in astonishment. Seraph's eyebrows came together in confusion.

"Like the leader of the White Crows, Talon?" Edge blurted out as he carefully studied the girl's face. Talon was short in stature and had pale skin. Her pretty, dark hair stopped right below her ears. She had chocolate-brown eyes and a small mouth with cupid's bow lips.

Zero nodded as Edge extended his hand toward her.

Talon gripped Edge's hand tightly, giving it an uncomfortable squeeze.

"Ow!" Edge cried out in pain as his knees bent slightly.

Seraph burst into full laughter, and Lazarus and Zero joined in. Talon's stern expression also changed into a look of amusement as she and even Edge joined in on the laughter. Seraph politely offered his hand. "I'm Seraph."

"Nice to meet you," Talon looked away shyly.

"Zero! I gotta introduce you to the guys! C'mon!" Edge insisted as he grabbed Zero under his arm and pulled him and Talon toward the entrance of the Wild West.

"Okay, okay! We're coming!" Zero followed his friend into the Cut-Throat's bar.

Seraph and Lazarus looked at each other and laughed again.

"Seraph, I need you to come with me," came the voice of Ghost, who seemed to appear out of nowhere from the south side of Bishop.

"What's going on?" Seraph asked.

"I'll explain on the way. I just need you to come with me now," Ghost said with a sense of urgency.

Lazarus nodded at Seraph. "Come on, man. Let's go."

Ghost shook his head and held out his hand toward Lazarus. "No. Just Seraph. I'll fill you in later."

"Can you just—" Seraph started as another figure approached from the corner of Kings and Bishop armed with a pistol that was pointed at Ghost.

"Why don't you tell him why you want him to come with you," Blackjack suddenly appeared from the alley beside the Wild West, a black pistol pointed at Ghost.

Ghost's eyes widened as he started to reach into his coat. "Put the gun down, Blackjack!"

Blackjack took an aggressive step forward. "Keep your hands where I can see them!"

Seraph looked from Blackjack to Ghost and then said, "What the hell is going on, Ghost?"

Ghost rolled his eyes. "We don't have *time* for this. I just need you to trust me!"

Blackjack stepped forward again, this time grabbing Seraph and pulling him close as he placed the barrel of his gun to Seraph's head and walked backward. "Back up! Both of you! Or I'll kill the kid!"

"Okay, man! Chill! Don't hurt him!" Lazarus pleaded, raising hands and stepping backward toward the entrance of the Wild West.

"Easy Blackjack . . ." Ghost followed suit.

Seraph struggled a little as Blackjack dragged him backward to the small street that was next to the Wild West. A white van pulled up, and the side door slid open. Blackjack turned and pushed Seraph into the van just as Ghost and Lazarus came around the corner. Blackjack fired off a few rounds in their general direction to keep them at bay, leaped into the van, and slammed the door shut as the vehicle took off down the side street.

Ghost and Lazarus ducked back around the corner of the building as the shots fired. "Damn!" he cursed and then looked at Lazarus. "You alright?"

Lazarus looked down and patted his body down. "Yeah, I think I'm good," his breath was shaky from the adrenaline rush. "What's going on, man?"

"I can't say too much, but Seraph's danger."

"Danger? How? Why?"

"The Lyones . . ."

"So, then what did Blackjack want with him?"

Ghost loaded a fresh magazine into his machine pistol. "I don't know, but he seems to know a lot more than he should . . ."

Just then, Edge, Zero, Talon, and the rest of the Cut-Throats filed out of the Wild West, all armed.

"What happened?" Terrace asked Ghost.

"I was coming to get Seraph when Blackjack came out of nowhere and kidnapped him. He fired some shots off at us to get away, and I fired back at a white van that they got into," Ghost said, putting his pistol back inside of his navy-blue coat.

"Crap! I guess that means Blackjack escaped, huh?" Judge said under his breath. "A white van, you said? I can have my guys go after them."

"No, that's alright. The Arch Angels will take care of it. Thank you, though," Ghost didn't want to involve the Cut-Throats any further. He then turned to Lazarus. "Let's go!"

"Alright," he said reluctantly, still not entirely sure what was going on.

The two quickly walked south on Bishop toward Kings. Ghost pulled out his phone and called Armand. "Hey. ... No. ... Blackjack showed up and took him. There was nothing I could do. ... Yeah, I'm on my way with Lazarus now."

"What's going on, Ghost?"

"I'll explain everything back at La Noche."

"Let me go! Pull over and let me out right now!" Seraph yelled as Blackjack, accompanied by a few other men who Seraph thought looked homeless.

"Relax, Seraph! No one is going to hurt you,"

Blackjack said as he tried to hold Seraph back and keep him from struggling.

"What do you want from me?" Seraph asked, shaking free from Blackjack's grasp and leaning his hand against the interior of the van. "If no one is going to hurt me, then what's all this about?" He panted, trying to catch his breath.

Blackjack cleared his throat and relaxed a bit. "Listen, I'm sorry for how that just went down, but I didn't have any other option to get you out of there."

"Get me *out* of there?"

"Ghost was going to hand you over to the Lyones."

Seraph chuckled dryly. "Sure, he was. And how would you know that, anyway?"

"I can assure you that I have reliable sources."

"Uh huh . . ." Seraph rolled his eyes. "And what did *rescuing* me from Ghost have to do with you?"

Blackjack shook his head and chuckled.

"You can trust him, Seraph," came a familiar voice from the driver's seat.

"*Ram?*" Seraph directed his gaze to the front of the van.

Mongrel, who was in the passenger's seat, turned around and smiled back at Seraph. "You're safe with us, man."

Two sharp sounds went off as the van began to swerve to the left and then to the right. Motorcycles could be heard on either side of the vehicle.

"It's the Black Lotus!" Mongrel shouted as he looked at Ram, panic stricken.

"Don't worry! Just remember the plan!" Blackjack shouted and then looked at Seraph. "Hold on!"

Ram slammed on the breaks as everyone in the van shot forward. Every door of the van opened, and everyone scattered out. Blackjack gripped Seraph tightly under his arm and pulled him along closely as he started running in the opposite direction to Ram and the others. Shots were fired in all directions. Seraph felt a bullet whiz past him and hit a nearby wall. He kept up as best he could, and the two turned a corner crossed the street. Seraph looked up. The sign read *Diamond Road*.

Blackjack and Seraph approached a back alley near the Lion's Den and ducked behind a large green dumpster. Blackjack gripped his side, leaned back against the wall of the building, and slid down onto the ground.

"You're hit!" Seraph exclaimed with dismay as he crouched down next to Blackjack.

"Just need to rest for a minute," Blackjack's breathed heavily as he removed a bloody hand from the wound, which began to soak his shirt.

"We gotta get you some help, man. That doesn't look good at all!" Seraph looked over his shoulder to make sure that they hadn't been followed. "We're not far from St. Titus. I could take you to the Royal Priests!"

Blackjack grinned through the pain and shook his head. "I doubt they would risk getting caught up in all of this."

"No. They'll help."

CHAPTER FIFTEEN

"And they just drove away?" Armand asked Ghost and Lazarus after they finished briefing him on what had transpired.

Ghost looked down without saying a word.

"There wasn't a whole lot that could have been done! Blackjack busted off a few shots as soon as we tried to turn the corner," Lazarus said in their defense.

Armand pressed his lips together tightly and closed his eyes. "I suppose we must assume that Blackjack is dangerous enough to kill any one of us if provoked," he mused and reached into the right drawer of his desk, producing a thick cigar and a small metallic flip lighter with the Arch Angels insignia on it. "Here's what we'll tell the Lyones:"—he placed the cigar between his front teeth and brought a flame to the end, puffing hard until it began to glow a bright orange—"that as you were on your way to get Seraph, a white van pulled up and snatched him. We can tell them that we suspect it was Blackjack but we aren't positive."

"Yeah, that could work," Ghost watched the smoke

rise up from the end of the cigar and dissipate. "One thing that we need to consider is that Blackjack has a small group working with him. There was definitely more than one person in that van."

Lazarus nodded in confirmation.

"It never ends . . ." Armand rubbed his temples.

"Hello?" Ghost answered his phone and listened. "Okay, get back to La Noche immediately. Let the other captains know that, as of right now, we are on full lockdown. I want everyone armed and ready. I'll be down shortly."

"What now?" Armand ashed the cigar.

"That was Ardent. His crew just took fire from the Black Lotus. One of his men is down."

Armand took a long drag from the cigar before setting it down in the ashtray. "Rin's out for blood. It's good that you ordered a lockdown. We need to play it safe for a while."

Lazarus touched the back of his waistband, where his pistol was tucked. "Should I head downstairs for now?"

"Yeah, go ahead, Laz. Make sure Magnum and the others are fully aware of what's going on."

"On it," Lazarus replied before exiting Armand's office.

Once the door was closed, Armand stood and walked over to Ghost. "I guess it's better to let Segundo know what's going on before he finds out otherwise."

"I'll call him now," Ghost searched for Segundo's number in his contacts and called him.

Armand walked over to the one-way window that overlooked the dance floor to see his army of Arch Angels preparing to defend La Noche. He watched the members of the Inner Circle spread out and give orders to the various captains, and the captains then relay orders to their crew members. A light knock came on the door, and Armand walked over, slowly taking out his own pistol from his suit jacket as he approached and turned the knob to see Lazarus standing there.

"Back so soon?"

Lazarus smiled back nervously. "Uh, yeah. I told Stephen Magnum about the lockdown. He said he would take care of it. I, uh . . . was hoping I could talk to you for a moment."

"Of course," Armand welcomed the young man back into his office as his eyes shifted over to Ghost, who was still on the phone with Segundo.

"This whole thing with Blackjack and Seraph . . . what can we do?" Lazarus expressed a look of concern.

"Blackjack is extremely dangerous and even more deceptive. He will tell Seraph anything to make him believe him and trust him. Blackjack is a snake and a murderer and at this point cannot be reasoned with. If we come into contact again, we must execute him on sight, especially if he still has Seraph alive. I only worry about what lies he is feeding the poor kid."

"I'll do whatever I can to help rescue him. Just tell me what I can do!"

"It's not safe to go out and do anything right now," Armand said and then walked back over behind his desk, where the cigar still sat smoldering away in the ashtray. He opened a drawer and retrieved a chrome pistol. He then beckoned for Lazarus to come forward.

Lazarus swallowed and walked over to the desk as Armand held the pistol out toward him, motioning for him to take it. "What's this for?" Lazarus awas sure that Armand knew that he was already armed.

"This was the gun that Blackjack used to kill our founder, Jin. I kept it so that if the opportunity ever arose for the Arch Angels to avenge our original leader, it could be done with the same murder weapon that Blackjack used to kill him. When the time is right, I want you to use this gun to put a bullet in Blackjack's head, just like he did to Jin."

Lazarus took the pistol and studied it before

meeting eyes with Armand. "I . . . I don't know what to say . . ."

Armand smiled and placed his hand on Lazarus's shoulder. "You are an official member of the Arch Angels now, Lazarus. I have always seen great potential in you. Someday, you'll make a fine leader."

"Thank you, sir."

"Why don't you head to the armory, grab yourself a uniform, and then head downstairs to join the others? Ghost and I will be down shortly."

Lazarus gave a firm nod before tucking the pistol into the front waistband of his pants and walking down the short hallway to the elevator. Armand closed the door behind him and then turned toward Ghost, who was just finishing his phone call with Segundo.

"Well?" Armand asked with a cocked eyebrow.

Ghost pressed his lips together tightly and nodded. "He's on his way."

Seraph stared at Ghost's name on the contact list of his phone. He sat next to Blackjack, who was lying in bed after getting patched up by the Royal Priests' doctors. Seraph debated calling Ghost and letting him know that Blackjack was vulnerable. He then remembered Ram saying that Blackjack could be trusted. But Seraph didn't know who he could trust. He wondered how Ghost could so easily be willing to betray him by handing him over to the Lyones. *I can't completely trust anybody until I find out the whole truth about the situation.*

The door to their hidden hospital room opened, and Welch, Grand Master of the Royal Priests and two other Masters who Seraph recognized as Brother Calvin and Brother Knox entered the room and closed the door securely behind them.

Seraph looked up with excitement at Welch, but his expression quickly faded to one of shame as he realized that Welch would most likely be disappointed in him because of the decisions that he had made since leaving the orphanage.

Welch approached Seraph and placed a hand on his shoulder. "What have you gotten yourself into, Seraph?" he asked sullenly.

Seraph took a deep breath before explaining everything he'd been through since he and Lance had left St. Titus. He recounted everything until tears ran down his face and then sat there, a mixture of hurt and confusion flooding his senses.

Welch frowned and gave Seraph's shoulder an affectionate squeeze. "I heard about Lance. I am sorry, Seraph," he said, remembering how Seraph and Lance would run around and play together at the orphanage when they were little boys.

Seraph wiped his eyes, looked back up at Welch, and folded his fingers together. "Welch . . ." he said weakly and cleared his throat. "Did you know who my parents were this whole time?"

"I did."

"Why didn't you ever tell me who they were?"

"To protect you. Lucien Lyone was doing such irrational things in those days when he first came to power. We wouldn't have put it past him to murder the baby of the man who had completely destroyed his leg. We figured that if no one ever knew of your existence, you would be safe. Of course, there was one other who knew that you lived, which I assume is the one who told you?"

Seraph nodded, as hot tears trailed down his cheeks. "I'm sorry . . ." his eyes locked with Welch's. Seraph felt even more ashamed for thinking that Welch or the Priests would have lied to him to hurt him.

Welch smiled at the young man and knelt down in front of him. "As you know, I do not believe in coincidence. Everything that happens is governed by the sovereignty of the Almighty. If I understand correctly, based on what you just told me, it does not seem that your path is so different from that of your mother's and father's. In my experience, I am a firm believer that the Lord has a way of bringing redemption in these kinds of ways, and I know for sure that He always ensures justice is upheld."

Seraph smiled at Welch, as his words gave him solace.

Blackjack groaned a little, stirred in the bed, and tugged on the sheets.

Welch and Seraph looked over at Blackjack. "And him?" Welch raised an eyebrow.

Seraph shrugged. "I'm not sure, honestly. But I think he may have saved my life."

Welch looked back at Blackjack and smiled warmly. "He couldn't have been any more than fourteen years old when I offered him a home at St. Titus."

"You knew Blackjack when he was younger?"

"Oh, yes." Welch chuckled. "Blackjack drifted over from the Wastelands when he was barely just a teenager. He didn't even have a shirt to cover his back. He respectfully declined my offer and instead took to the streets. Shortly after, he ended up joining the Arch Angels, who were a newly formed gang at the time. They were just a pack of misfits when they first started. Two years later, Blackjack was taken to the Dragon's Lair for the murder of the Arch Angels' leader."

Seraph looked over at Blackjack, studying his face, which seemed to be getting some of its color back.

The door to the small hidden room opened, and a different Royal Priest hastily walked through and approached Welch closely, whispering in his ear before Welch nodded and told him to "take care of it."

"Everything alright?" Seraph became tense.

Welch nodded. "Nothing to fear. The Black Lotus Syndicate is here and wants to search the premises. Not to worry; this room is well hidden, and we will keep both of you safe. However, I would suggest making arrangements to leave as soon as possible. Unfortunately, you both are putting the orphans and our patients at risk by being here."

"You're right . . ." Seraph tried to decide where he and Blackjack could go.

Blackjack stirred a little more, and his hand peeked out from under the sheets, holding his cell phone out toward Seraph. "Jackals . . ."

Seraph took the phone and scrolled through Blackjack's contacts until he came across the name *Ram* and hit the call button.

"Got it," Edge ended his phone call with Lazarus. The Cut-Throats, along with Zero and Talon, were still at the Wild West discussing what had just happened in front of the bar and what they should do about it.

"What's going on?" Judge lit up a cigarette.

"So, now it looks like the Black Lotus are in full offense mode toward the Angels. They apparently think that Armand is secretly holding Blackjack and have refused to stop attacking until Rin gets him," Edge explained. "Right now, the Arch Angels are holed up at La Noche, preparing for an attack."

"Maybe we should go and reinforce them," Iceman suggested.

"Yeah, we can get the rest of the Crows too," Talon offered and looked at Zero.

Zero shook his head. "I don't think that would be a good idea. It would give away our alliance, for sure."

"True," Edge nodded. "Plus, Lazarus said that we should just be on standby and that he would keep me posted. For now, we should probably just chill until we hear otherwise."

Terrace nodded to Judge. "That sounds like the best plan of action for now, Prez."

"Okay, fine," Judge resolved. "Just be ready to roll in case anything goes down."

"Zero and I will head back to Ivory in the meantime and get our people ready as well," Talon stood up.

"Good. I'll hit you up if anything pops off," Edge

told Zero.

Zero gave Edge a tight hug before he and Talon exited the Wild West.

"Be safe," Edge watched the door swing shut behind them.

Segundo stepped past the front entrance of La Noche, after which the two Arch Angels standing guard quickly locked the doors. The dance floor was crawling with Arch Angel soldiers, all armed and ready to defend their compound to the death.

Armand and Ghost walked across the crowded dance floor and greeted Segundo. "Welcome back," Armand said to Segundo as he extended his right hand toward him.

Segundo sighed heavily and took Armand's hand in his own, giving it a quick yet firm shake. "Armand. Ghost," he said, simply acknowledging Ghost with a nod.

"Right this way," Armand beckoned Segundo to follow him and Ghost up the small flight of spiral stairs that led up to the second floor of La Noche. They made their way up to the bar, where Cherrie began pouring a glass of water for each of them. "Did you come alone? I half expected to see Lucien Lyone himself," Armand remarked as he took one of the glasses of water that was set in front of them and took a small sip.

Segundo shook his head. "It wouldn't have been safe for Mr. Lyone to come here. I haven't told him yet."

"No? Why the delay?"

Segundo's eyes widened as he looked at Armand condescendingly. "I know about your plan."

Armand and Ghost looked at each other and then back at Segundo. "Our plan?"

"Yes. Your plan to remove the Lyone family from power," Segundo said, his gaze locking with Armand's, whose face began to perspire.

Armand and Ghost both contemplated killing

Segundo right where he stood, but curiosity got the better of them, as they assumed there was more to the situation.

"I'm not entirely opposed to that idea," Segundo said, which came as a simultaneous shock and relief to Armand and Ghost. "Under the right circumstances, I may even help you."

Armand swallowed. "And what circumstances would those be?"

"You must agree not to harm Lucien Lyone or his family. Instead, have him locked away in the Dragon's Lair indefinitely. As for the Lyone family, I will assume control and maintain peace between the family and the other gangs while we work out our differences."

"And how exactly do you expect to make this work?"

"If the Arch Angels and the other gangs assault the Lion's Den, I can take some of my trusted soldiers and seize Lucien before things get too far out of control. I have a contact within the Golden Dragons who will coordinate with us, and once I give the word, take Lucien into custody and have him locked up. Once he is removed from power, we will call a ceasefire and work toward settling things."

"That all sounds good, but we won't be able to assault anything with the current threats from the Black Lotus we're facing," Ghost chimed in.

Segundo gave a light shrug. "You are going to have to figure that one out for yourself. There is not a whole lot more that I can do for you in that regard, especially since you were unable to deliver Blackjack or Seraph. Why not find a way to keep the Black Lotus on the defensive? That could give you a chance to make moves without having to worry about their interference."

"Not a bad idea," Ghost nodded.

"Once you feel like you are ready to set things in motion, you know how to reach me, but time is of the essence. We don't have long at all, and once Lucien realizes that you won't be handing Blackjack or Seraph over, he will take things into his own hands," Segundo warned as he took his leave.

"Maybe I should take some guys and hit the streets to see if we can keep BLS back," Ghost proposed.

"No." Armand shook his head. "Call each leader from the allied gangs. It's time."

"Are you sure you don't wanna come with us, Seraph?" Ram asked as he and Mongrel helped Blackjack into the back of their van, where a couple more Jackals were waiting inside.

Seraph looked back at Welch for a moment. They all stood behind St. Titus as the sun was just beginning to rise. "I definitely appreciate the offer, but I do still have some friends I can trust that I'm gonna try and coordinate with."

Ram closed the back door of the van behind Blackjack and walked up to Seraph, offering him a folded piece of paper. "Well, here's my number if you change your mind."

"Thanks, Ram. Be safe out there."

"Likewise, little brother." Ram got into the driver's seat and started up the van, while Mongrel waved at Seraph before getting into the passenger's seat and leaving with the rest of the Jackals.

Welch stepped forward and placed his hand on Seraph's shoulder. "Will you be alright, Seraph?"

"You know, I think I will actually."

"Come back and visit us when this is all over."

"Will do," Seraph started down the back road toward Vespula Way and the Shamrocke.

A silver sedan seemed to come out of nowhere once Seraph turned the corner onto Vespula, and the car came to a screeching halt on the sidewalk just a couple feet away from him. All four doors opened as the same group of Lyone's who had confronted Seraph two days prior, led by DeAndre, approached him. Seraph reached for his pistol, but DeAndre was faster, smacked the gun out of Seraph's hand, and grabbed him by his jacket.

Without hesitation, Seraph brought his right elbow up and across DeAndre's cheek and kicked him in his shin as he felt DeAndre's grip loosen from his jacket. One of the Lyones with him grabbed Seraph from behind, putting him into a secure reverse chokehold. Seraph violently resisted, using all of his strength to try to break free as DeAndre regained his balance and planted a deep uppercut into Seraph's diaphragm. The sharpness of the blow caused all of the breath in Seraph's lungs to deplete as he leaned forward and groaned. The other two Lyones joined DeAndre as the three of them took turns hitting Seraph as hard as they could in his face and body. Seraph gasped desperately to try to regain his breath, his energy quickly draining. DeAndre and the other two then stepped back as the one that held Seraph released his neck and instead gripped him around his waist, lifting him up as high as he could before slamming him down onto the pavement.

This is it . . . They're going to kill me right here. He felt the four Lyones continue to kick and stomp his body as he lay slumped down on the ground.

Seraph felt himself fading out of consciousness as the Lyones seemed to take a break from stomping him. He wondered if perhaps someone had come to his rescue as he struggled to open his eyes. Just then, the sound of automatic gunfire rang out for what seemed like an entire minute. A mixture of fear and relief began to settle within Seraph as he hoped that the gunfire had come from an ally.

"Grab him and let's go!" came a familiar voice as Seraph was able to open up his eye just a sliver to see Rin Yamato, leader of the Black Lotus Syndicate, standing near the four dead bodies of the Lyones who had just assaulted him.

A small group of Black Lotuses quickly ran over to Seraph, bound him tightly with black cords, duct taped his mouth shut, placed a black sack over his head, and tied it securely around his neck. Seraph then heard another vehicle pull up as he was dragged for a moment and then tossed into what he assumed was a van before the door was closed immediately after, and the vehicle sped away.

Rin glanced down at Seraph's phone and gun, which lay in the middle of the sidewalk near the bodies of the four dead Lyones before getting back onto her motorcycle and tearing down the road.

CHAPTER SIXTEEN

The meeting room across the hallway from Armand's office had been prepared for the different gang leaders beforehand by some of the lower-ranking Arch Angels while the main force still occupied the first level defensively. Armand, Ghost, and Lazarus were the only Arch Angels who were to meet with the other leaders. In the center of the room was a long, dark wooden table surrounded by comfortable black office chairs. Armand sat at the head of the table toward the back wall. Ghost and Lazarus stood on either side of him. One by one, each of the liaisons from the different gangs arrived, escorted in by fledgling Arch Angels.

The first ones to arrive were Judge, Brutus, and Edge of the Cut-Throats, and shortly after came Padraeg and O'Connor from the McDroogin family. Next to arrive were Talon, Toki, and Zero, who represented the White Crows with their former nemeses, the Shadows, following behind, represented by Kai and Ketsujo. The last to show up were Damien and Shady, representing the Immortals. Armand formally greeted each guest as they showed up and invited them to take a seat at the table.

Ghost looked next to him at Lazarus, noticing a troubled look on his face. "You alright?" he asked.

Lazarus's bit down on his lip and slowly shook his head. "I'm worried about Seraph."

"It'll all get sorted out," Ghost said, trying to reassure him.

"I hope so . . ." Lazarus said as Armand stood up to address everyone.

"I want to thank everyone for joining us tonight on such short notice." Armand cleared his throat. "As much as I would have liked to take more time to prepare, it appears that we have run out of time and must move much faster than we had anticipated. As I am sure most of you have heard, we recently took Blackjack into custody after he was released from the Dragon's Lair. Unsurprisingly, this did not sit well with the Black Lotus Syndicate, who have now taken a fully offensive stance against the Arch Angels. They believe that we still have Blackjack, which we no longer do." The room became deathly silent. "Somehow, Blackjack managed to escape, and at this moment, no one knows where he is. Unfortunately, this does not eliminate our problem with the Black Lotus—nor the Lyones. Just a couple days ago, Lucien Lyone demanded that we hand over both Blackjack and Seraph to them-which, of course we would have never done, but now, both of them are missing, which is going to cause even greater trouble with the Lyone family, and that is why we must act much sooner than later."

When the news about Blackjack and Seraph was brought up, a light murmur began to trickle throughout the meeting room.

"Where is my grandson?!" Padraeg shouted in worry and anger.

Armand's eyebrows furrowed, and he leaned his head forward in Padraeg's direction. The gang leaders looked at one another, unaware that Padraeg even had a grandson.

"He means Seraph," O'Connor said.

"Seraph is your *grandson*?" Armand asked in deep confusion.

"Yeah! What of it?" Padraeg growled back as he felt his face become hot. "Where is he?"

Armand blinked a few times before shaking his head. "Once Blackjack escaped, Seraph somehow ended up with him, and the two have disappeared. Blackjack is immensely deceptive and full of lies. I fear that he may be poisoning the kid's mind against us."

Judge's eyes widened. "What do you mean?"

"Listen—at the moment, Blackjack and Seraph are out of our hands," Armand said. "We need to stay focused on what we will be facing here very soon. Once the Lyones are dealt with, we will worry about those two. Besides, there is speculation that Blackjack is working for the Lyone family as it is. Personally, I believe that's why they demanded him from us- to protect him. He had no problem murdering our leader for them years ago." The other leaders nodded in agreement. "There is some good news that I did want to present to you all, however. We currently have some high-ranking Lyones secretly working with us to remove Lucien from power. I can't say too much at the moment, but I did want you all to know that we have a major advantage now," Armand said, which seemed to bring a measure of relief to the room.

Suddenly, the door to the Inner Circle chambers flung open, and Ram, accompanied by seven or so Jackals all armed with shotguns, entered the room with Blackjack at the center of the group. One of the Jackals in the back closed the door behind them and stood guard as Blackjack and the other Jackals made their way to the end of the table opposite Armand. Blackjack proceeded to take a seat with the armed Jackals fanned out behind him. "Were my ears just itching a moment ago? I could have sworn somebody was talking about me," came Blackjack's smooth voice as a smirk spread across his face.

Everyone besides Blackjack and the Jackals looked at each other in confusion and horror, trying to figure out how to handle the situation. Lazarus stared questioningly at

Ram, who tightly gripped a double-barreled shotgun across his large belly.

"What are you doing? How did you get in here?" Armand asked Blackjack in deep frustration.

Blackjack met Armand's eyes and simply chuckled.

"I don't recall inviting any murderers to my table this evening," Armand said.

"We came to offer our assistance against the Lyone family," Blackjack said.

It was now Armand's turn to laugh. "Offer us assistance, huh? We will *never* trust you, Blackjack. Why would we allow you to be a part of our plan?" he asked, then looked up at Ram. "You should be wary as well. You, of all people, should know that type of person Blackjack is. He will turn on you as soon as he gets the chance."

Ram looked down at Blackjack and shook his head. "Blackjack has convinced me otherwise."

Lazarus's face twisted in turmoil as he stared at Ram, wondering how someone who seemed to hate Blackjack almost as much as he hated Lucien Lyone would now display the utmost allegiance to him. *Could Blackjack really be that crafty?*

Padraeg now stood up and placed both of his palms on the table and looked at Blackjack intensely. "Where is Seraph?" he demanded.

Blackjack stood up and slowly lifted his shirt.

Everyone in the room but the Jackals immediately became on edge and reached for their weapons, but stopped as Blackjack brought his shirt up just above his abdomen, revealing a blood-stained bandage.

"Not long after I came in contact with Seraph, we were attacked by the Black Lotus Syndicate. We both got away together, and he was safe when I left him."

Everyone in the room seemed to relax a little.

"We're just supposed to trust that you want to help us?" Judge asked. "How do we know that you aren't working for the Lyone family? I mean, that's probably who put you up to killing Jin back then anyway, right?"

"That's if you're assuming that I was the one who killed Jin—which I'm not. Do you really think that if I had been working for the Lyone family this whole time, they would have just kept me locked away in the Dragon's Lair for all these years in solitary confinement and then released me to the Black Lotus Syndicate as soon as they were able to pay the ransom? Don't you think they would have kept me protected if I was one of theirs?"

"Well, when you called me," Ghost said, "it was from a Lyone's cell phone, so obviously you were in some sort of contact with them. Why would a Lyone care whether or not you make it out alive and give you a chance to call us to come and rescue you?"

"Because he wants the same thing that everyone here wants. Liberation from the Lyone family. That's why he was willing to work with me, so that together we could try and make an impact. The only way that we will overcome them is if everyone who loves this town works together to restore it. Believe it or not—not all of the Lyones are out for blood. There are some who want peace and stability."

"Why did you kidnap Seraph?" Lazarus asked. "You can't deny it—I was right there! I watched you put a gun to his head and run off with him. What was that about?"

Blackjack shook his head. "The same contact I have within the Lyone family mentioned that they were after the kid. Apparently, he felt bad for him and asked me to get the kid out of there before Ghost handed him over to Lucien."

Lazarus looked back at Ghost in disbelief.

"I wasn't going to turn Seraph in. I was trying to get him somewhere safe where the Lyones couldn't get to him."

Armand now stood up and cleared his throat loudly. "As I have said before, we will worry about Blackjack and Seraph once matters are dealt with. Now is not the time for this."

Blackjack looked at Armand with a devilish smirk. "So, what's the plan?"

"Plan? Wasn't there some *special* contact within the Lyones that you were working with who is supposed to give us the person that *allegedly* murdered Jin?" Ghost narrowed his eyes at Blackjack.

"That option is still on the table. I already told you what you need to do. Launch an attack on the Lyones. Once my contact gets things under control on their end, we will take Lucien and his top generals alive. The Lyones that help us are granted full immunity."

Armand laughed and shook his head. "And we're just supposed to trust you?"

"If I was working for the Lyones, don't you think I would have had Ram's men take you all out as soon as we entered the room? What purpose would it serve for me to sit down and waste my breath? I've got you all dead to rights," Blackjack said taking a moment to look around the table at each individual.

Armand narrowed his eyes at Blackjack briefly before also looking around the table at everyone else who all seemed resigned to what Blackjack had said. Armand sighed and cleared his throat. "Tomorrow the majority of us will march on the Lion's Den and assault their compound head on. The Cut-Throats could do a sweep through the city before meeting up with us to take out any Lyones that might be outside the Lion's Den. The Shadows can go to the Lyone Manor, secure Lucien's wife and children, and take out any Lyones who may be posted there. Once we have secured their compound, we will make contact with our Lyone contacts who will bring Lucien to us, and we will deal with him immediately."

"Sounds good enough to me," Judge said as Brutus and Edge nodded. The rest of the room also seemed to be in agreement.

"Very good. In that case, tomorrow, we will contact you in the afternoon to make sure all of you and your people are ready to move out, and then coordinate from there. Until then, meeting adjourned."

Ghost swiftly drew his pistol and aimed it at Blackjack, who simply reclined in his chair. In response, the Jackals pointed their shotguns at the gangs' leaders.

Blackjack smirked. "If you kill me, every leader here will die, and the Lyones will come out all the stronger."

Ghost gritted his teeth. "You're full of shit! What are you really after?"

"You wouldn't believe me if I told you . . ." his smirk faded as he stood up, pushed his chair in, and walked toward the exit—the Jackals still aiming their shotguns at the leaders as they backed away towards the door.

The room sat in silence as Blackjack left. Ghost cursed under his breath. Once Blackjack and the Jackals were gone, Armand spoke once more. "Before all of this is over, Blackjack *must* die," he said sternly as his eyes met with each other leader's. "I don't believe a single word that maniac said—and neither should any of you!"

The room remained silent as the various leaders looked around at each other in confusion.

Ghost set his pistol on the large table and sighed. "He's had a lot of time to work on his alibi, but we all have to remember what he did. Armand *literally* caught him in the act, pistol in hand!"

"That's right," Armand said. "Don't let him try and twist your minds. We need to take any opportunity that we get to kill him. He's too shifty. If you get him in your sights, you take him out. Remember, if it weren't for Blackjack, then we wouldn't even be in this predicament with the Lyones. He murdered Jin *and* our chance to strike early and prevent them from ever taking over Royalty."

Lazarus swallowed and nodded slowly.

"And then you took over and then decided that Jin's plan was no longer any good?" Judge spoke up with raised eyebrows.

Armand shook his head. "It was obvious that after

they used Blackjack to kill Jin that they were already aware of our plan. On top of that, the rest of the Arch Angels were devastated after his death. The opportune timing had unfortunately passed."

"Don't worry, boss. We'll get him," Ghost reassured Armand, placing a hand on his shoulder.

"I know . . ." Armand swore and closed his eyes.

"I get your point," Judge stroked his beard and leaned back in his chair.

"Look, let's not waste any more time. Head back to your territories, put your affairs in order and start preparing for war. We'll see you all tomorrow when we're in the thick of it," Ghost said solemnly as the various gang leaders stood and each exited the Inner Circle meeting room to ready their men for the anticipated battle.

"Alright, until then," Segundo said as he finished his phone call. The sun had already gone down, and he had just finished a meeting with Tuan of the Golden Dragons. He was now on his way to the Lyone Manor to meet with Lucien. As he neared Diamond Road, Segundo could see from the brightness of the headlights what looked to be a few dead bodies lying on the ground near St. Titus Hospital. He pulled his car over next to the sidewalk and immediately drew his pistol before stepping out to investigate.

As he got closer, Segundo recognized DeAndre and his crew who all lay dead in their own blood, their bodies riddled with bullet holes. As Segundo got closer to examine his fallen comrades, he noticed a cell phone and a pistol, different from the one that Lyone soldiers carried. He picked up the phone to see if he could determine who might have killed them. Just as his finger touched the *Contacts* button, the phone started ringing and the name *Laz* appeared on the screen. Segundo then touched the *Answer* button but remained silent.

"*Seraph? Are you okay, man?*" came Lazarus's voice.

"Seraph?" Segundo said into the phone.

"You're not Seraph . . . Who is this?"

"Just a friend," Segundo said as he looked over the dead bodies once more for any other clues before heading back to his car.

"Seraph has been missing for a couple days now. How did you get his phone?"

"I found it next to a group of dead Lyones," Segundo said as he got into the car and pressed the *Start* button as the engine turned on.

"What? Who is this?! Tell me!" Lazarus demanded, but Segundo ended the call and turned the phone off before pocketing it and driving off toward the Lyone Manor.

Seraph awoke, gasping for oxygen. He blinked hard a few times, trying to see where he was, but the room was so dark that his eyes were having a hard time adjusting. He attempted to rub his eyes but quickly realized that both of his wrists and ankles were tightly bound and that he was positioned on some sort of bed or flat surface that was tilted forward. Seraph struggled to get free, but his body was still sore and weak from the beating he had taken just before being abducted by the Black Lotus Syndicate.

"No need to struggle, young Seraph," came the voice of Rin Yamato. "I will let you go the moment you tell me where Blackjack is."

"I don't know . . . I don't even know him!" Seraph said hoarsely.

"Don't lie to me. One of my people told me they saw you with him behind the hospital. Whose van did he get into? Who is helping him?"

"I told you—I don't know! He kidnapped me, and then you all attacked the van that they snatched me up in and then he pulled me with him when everyone ran away. One of your bullets hit him, and I helped him get to get St. Titus so that they could save him!"

Rin's eyes narrowed. "So, you helped that murderer and your kidnapper instead of letting him die like the dog that he is?”

“He told me that he was rescuing me because apparently Ghost was gonna turn me into the Lyones,” Seraph told her.

“Turn you into the Lyones? Why?”

Seraph frowned. “I don’t know. All I know is that Blackjack was there to save me . . .”

“Typical Blackjack. He acts so kind and smooth and convinces you that he is a good and loyal man, but I can assure you that he is a snake and a deceiver. He will stab anyone in the back to get what he wants. A serpent, Seraph. The devil himself,” Rin insisted.

Seraph remained silent for a moment before speaking up. “Are you sure he’s the one who killed your brother?”

Rin’s eyes went ablaze. “Allow me to tell you a story,” she said, regaining her composure.

“Okay . . .”

Rin cleared her throat. “It was about two years before the Lyone family came to power. Jin had just recently formed the Arch Angels in response to a conflict between the Castle Road Soldiers and the Immortals. Jin and Damien were actually pretty close before he formed the Arch Angels. After seeing how the Immortals were harassed for simply passing through Castle Road, Jin decided he would form a gang that would go out of its way to keep the streets of Royalty safe, hence ‘Angel’ in the name; Jin fancied himself the guardian of the city.

“Ghost was one of the original members of the Arch Angels, and he was the one who originally invited Blackjack to join them after they became a little more established. Blackjack was a street kid who came here from the Wastelands and somehow, despite his small build, ended up being one of the best fighters at Damien’s fight club, long before he owned what is now known as the Asylum. It was all history from there. Blackjack ended up becoming the champion of the Arch Angels. Even when I first met him,

I sincerely believed that his ideals were the same as my brother's, but I was wrong . . .

"Fast forward almost two years later, and the Lyones started making moves. It started when they massacred the Jackals, leaving Ram as the only surviving member. I distinctly remember the conversation I had with Jin as I tried desperately to convince him to stay out of the conflict. I knew it would only end in our loved ones getting killed. But Jin was willing to sacrifice his gang and, more importantly, himself, for his cause. When I realized he wouldn't listen to reason, I urged him to at least keep Blackjack close for protection while he prepared a secret meeting between all the leaders of Royalty's gangs to plan their opposition to the Lyone family. I wish he'd never told me about it . . .

"Not even a week later, Blackjack was found in Jin's room, pistol in hand, standing over my brother's dead body. Armand and Ghost, with a small group of Angels, found, apprehended, and dragged him to the Golden Dragons. At that time, the Arch Angels were relatively against murder; otherwise, they would have just killed him themselves. Armand was voted in as the new leader pretty soon after, and instead of opposing the Lyones, he agreed to Lucien's terms and secured peace for the rest of his gang. But Jin remained dead and Blackjack alive, sitting comfortably in the Dragon's Lair, while I formed the Black Lotus Syndicate in order to raise money to pay off the Lyones to release him to me so that I could execute the bastard myself."

Rin's head hung low. "Eighteen years of killing for crowns, and as soon as he was within my grasp, he was taken from me!" Rin growled through clenched teeth. "He trusted him, Seraph!" she shouted, a streak of tears running down her cheeks as she made eye contact with the young Arch Angel. "Jin trusted Blackjack more than anyone in the world, and he murdered him!"

Seraph blinked a few times as he felt his eyes become cloudy. "I'm so sorry . . ."

"Unfortunately, sorry will never bring Jin back, nor justice to his murderer." Rin sniffled and cleared her throat. "It's a terrible world that we live in, Seraph."

"Tell me about it . . ." Seraph sighed. "I just found out that Lucien Lyone murdered my parents before I was even born."

Rin wiped her cheeks and squinted at Seraph. "What do you mean?"

"Well, my mother was pregnant with me when Lucien shot her in the chest." Seraph felt his own chest become tight. "I didn't even know who my parents were, and then I came to find out my mother was Padraeg McDroogin's daughter and a member of the Cut-Throats was my father—and Lucien Lyone killed them. I still don't even know how to process it . . ."

Rin stood up and placed her hand on the straps that were keeping Seraph's arms restrained. "Are you *serious*?"

Seraph's eyes widened. "Yes, at least that's what I was told. O'Connor confirmed it. Apparently, he was close friends with my father."

"I want to show you something." Rin undid the straps that kept Seraph restrained and helped him sit up. "Can you walk?"

Seraph groaned as he extended his legs. "I guess we'll find out." He slid off the table and onto his feet.

"There you go. Here—" Rin offered her arm as she led him through the door. "Come with me."

Rin led Seraph through a small room that was dimly lit where a few other members of the Black Lotus Syndicate were training. She took him through a small door that led outside. The sun was just starting to peek over the horizon, and the smell of freshly bloomed flowers penetrated Seraph's nostrils. The fragrance was sweet and soothing. Rin carefully guided him to what he recognized as the Harmony Gardens, which he had only seen in passing.

"*This* is the Black Lotus Syndicate's secret hideout?" Seraph said as his eyes scanned the lovely gardens, taking in all the different colors and shapes of magnificent flowers.

"If you tell a soul, I'll kill you myself." Rin squeezed Seraph's arm roughly and continued to lead him toward the center of the gardens where there were two plain gravestones right next to each other. "Look," Rin said, pointing to the graves.

Seraph read the gravestones: *Ash of the Cut-Throats* on one and *Rayn McDroogin* on the other. "Oh—" he gasped.

Rin then brought her hand from Seraph's arm to his shoulder and gave it a sympathetic squeeze. "I thought you deserved to see this . . . I had no idea."

Tears formed in Seraph's eyes as he looked from one stone to the other, seeing that both graves had been regularly maintained and both had fresh flowers lying in front of them.

"O'Connor comes once a week to pay his respects."

Seraph forced a smile.

One of Rin's men came to her through the back door and quietly said something to her before she nodded and dismissed him.

"Everything alright?" Seraph asked.

"It seems like the gangs are preparing to mobilize against the Lyones."

"How did you—?"

"I try to keep tabs on everything that goes on here. I just can't seem to be able to follow the person that I want the most."

"If I see him—is there a way that I can contact you?"

"You would help me get him?" Rin asked, caught off guard. The Black Lotus leader sighed and shook her head. "Listen, from what you told me, you have just as much reason to kill him as I do. If you get the chance, do us all a favor, and do it yourself."

Seraph's eyes widened before blinking a few times, but he remained silent.

"Blackjack killed Jin before that meeting could even

take place. Maybe they would have stopped Lucien before he could kill your parents if Jin had lived." Rin took him by his arm again. "You should go join up with the Arch Angels. Come on, I'll walk you out," she said as she guided him through the Black Lotus hideout and through the front door, which was disguised as a flower shop.

Seraph stopped in front of the entrance of the shop with a concerned look on his face. "I don't know if it's such a good idea for me to go back to the Arch Angels if Ghost was really gonna turn me in to the Lyones."

"Look, if the only reason you have to believe that is something that that bastard, Blackjack said, then I wouldn't hold too fast to it. I know Ghost. He's a good guy. He loved my brother and has always been loyal to the Arch Angels."

Seraph thought about this and nodded slowly and then changed the subject, "I never thanked you for saving me from DeAndre and those other Lyones. I thought I was done for."

"Don't mention it." Rin said as she released Seraph's arm. "Are you going to be able to make it on your own? I could have one of my men escort you."

"I'll be fine."

Rin paused for a moment and then smirked. "All right, kid. Just be careful out there."

Seraph pressed his lips together tightly and nodded once before making his way down the street, back towards La Noche.

While he ventured down towards Rooke Avenue he noticed that the streets were mostly empty. He wondered what had caused the Arch Angels to decide to finally attack the Lyone family. Was it something having to do with him and Ghost not being able to deliver him to the Lyones? Seraph was still unsure who exactly he was supposed to trust.

As soon as he made it to Rooke, two silver sedans pulled up in front of him, blocking his path as two full squads of Lyones got out with guns drawn and surrounded him.

"Hands where I can see 'em!" a large Amakoran man commanded, his gun trained on Rin, who complied.

"What's going on?" Seraph said as another Lyone grabbed him, put him in handcuffs, and shoved him into the back of his car.

"What's happening out there, Segundo?" Lucien asked as his vice commander stepped into his office and closed the door behind him.

Segundo pulled out a cigarette from inside his coat pocket, lit it with his silver-plated flip lighter, and took a deep drag. "A lot, boss," he said and exhaled through the side of his mouth.

"One of our spies tells me that he saw a bunch of the gangs' leaders leave La Noche just a few moments ago," Lucien said. "This is concerning, Segundo. It seems like they are up to something. What do you think?" he asked, lighting a cigar.

Segundo shook his head. "It's hard to tell. I'll tell you one thing, though. They deny having either Blackjack *or* Seraph and claim that the two escaped together before I showed up."

"Well, I've got the Seraph situation under control. I just got a call from Ward that he and Elders have Seraph and are on their way here with him now."

"You should probably see this then." Segundo reached into his pocket, pulled out Seraph's cell phone, and placed it on Lucien's desk. "That's Seraph's phone. I found it lying on the ground next to DeAndre and his crew."

"What? That kid killed DeAndre and his squad?" Lucien asked in disbelief.

"Yes. However, I would like to note that just the other night, I caught DeAndre and his crew sweating Seraph while he was near the compound."

"And what was he doing near the compound?"

"I suspect he was looking for Blackjack. Armand claims that after Blackjack disappeared, he sent out his men all over Royalty to find him."

"Very convenient. I don't like this . . . It all seems strangely connected. I need to know why those other gang leaders met at La Noche so soon after you paid them a visit."

"You think they might be planning on rebelling?"

"That's what I'm afraid of . . . Listen, we can't afford to take any chances. Here's what we're going to do: send out the captains to each of the gangs and inform them that all gangs are currently suspended. It's time we start dismantling this feudal system and finally get this city under control. Tell the captains to take out anyone who resists. Have the rest of our men lock down the compound and remain here to defend it. This ends once and for all."

"Yes, sir. I'll contract the Yellow Jackets to defend the compound while most of our men are out taking care of the gangs."

"Good. Get the Golden Dragons, too. This might just turn into a blood bath, but I'll tell you, Segundo, it has been long overdue!" Lucien spat with malice.

"Excellent idea, sir. Anything else?" Segundo asked before snubbing out his cigarette in Lucien's ashtray.

"Yes," Lucien said with a look of gravity. "Call my son, Vincent. I want him here with me. Have Alvaro and two of his captains guard my family at the manor."

"Right away, boss." Segundo got on his phone and began making calls while he exited the office.

Just as Segundo stepped out, Seraph was brought in by two of Lucien's captains.

"Let me go!" Seraph shook free from them once they were all in Lucien's office.

"We meet again," Lucien said with faux pleasantness. He nodded toward his two captains. "Good work, boys. You're dismissed."

The two captains grinned with satisfaction and took their leave, closing the door behind them.

Lucien inspected Seraph. "You don't look so good. Why don't you take a seat?" he said as he stretched out his hand. "Who did this to you?"

Seraph glared at Lucien. "Your men."

"You mean DeAndre?"

"That's right," Seraph replied, standing firm.

"Is that why you killed him and his men?"

Seraph squinted at Lucien. "I'm not the one who killed them."

"I see . . ." Lucien said and took a puff from his cigar. "Then who?"

"You have a lot of enemies—pick one," Seraph replied with contempt.

Lucien chuckled dryly. "I know all about the little rebellion you're involved in. I'll have you know that I've already brought it to a halt. My men have already been dispatched. The involved organizations are being dismantled as we speak. The only question I have is *why*. What would make all of these different gangs come together in order to depose me?"

"You're a thief, a liar, and a murderer! Who *wouldn't* want to rid this city of you? You had Jin Yamato killed. You massacred the Jackals. *You killed my parents!*" Seraph barked as he took a step toward Lucien's desk, no longer fearing any consequences for his actions.

"Your parents?" Lucien set the burning cigar down in the ashtray and leaned forward.

"Ash and Rayn McDroogin. The young couple you murdered in front of the Shamrocke almost twenty years ago!"

Lucien sat there silently and studied Seraph's face. Through the bruises, cuts, and swollen eye, he saw a boy who was only a few years younger than his oldest son. He saw a boy who had grown up amid struggle, who had suffered tragedy after tragedy, starting with the death of his parents and ending with the death of his best friend at the hand of Lucien's own son. The Lyone leader swallowed and cleared his throat. "I did this to you?" Although it was uttered as a question, it was more of a realization.

"Yes. To me. To Ram. To Rin. To the McDroogins. To the Cut-Throats. Everybody! Everything wrong with this city is *your* fault!" Seraph shouted, taking another step toward him.

"I didn't mean to kill her . . ." Lucien frowned and looked down at his desk.

"What?" Seraph asked as his eyes pierced through the Lyone leader.

Lucien's, "The girl—your mother. She ran in front of McDroogin as I pulled the trigger," he said, staring at the surface of his desk.

Seraph blinked several times. "You didn't kill her on purpose?"

Lucien looked up and locked eyes with Seraph. "I would sooner die myself! My baby girl had just been born—not a month before it happened."

Seraph swallowed and pressed his lips together firmly. "And my father?"

"That's . . . a different story." Lucien placed both of his palms on the surface of his desk to prop himself up and grabbed his cane. He walked around the side of the desk so that Seraph could see his legs and pointed to his brace. "Your father ran his motorcycle into me as I was getting ready to make an example out of the former president of the Cut-Throats. After my men helped me up, I was in a rage, and I unloaded my gun into your father. I acted completely on impulse and would have never harmed your father had he not attacked me. Brutus, on the other hand, was business; however, after I killed your father, I decided that enough blood had been shed. His sacrifice saved Brutus's life."

Seraph stared down at Lucien's leg. "Why were you even there in the first place? From what I've heard, you and your men just started going out and threatening to massacre the gangs unless they paid taxes."

"Is that what they're saying? Maybe they're right, but it was never my intention."

Seraph stood there quietly watching him.

"The war that my family fought against the Vallario and Mazzarelli families was a bloody one. Much worse than street gang-level brawls. My own mother was killed in the crossfire during an assassination attempt on my father's life. Fortunately, my family gained the upper hand, and we were able to not only force a ceasefire, but also vassalize the other two families. Once I took over leadership of the family, I decided to take things further and end gang warfare entirely—not just between my family and other organizations, but between all the factions in this city. I thought that if I could restrict the gangs and take a hefty percentage of their income from less-than-benevolent activities, it would discourage them from continuing operating as they had. Perhaps I was wrong. In fact, I've begun to see that more and more clearly lately—even before this talk of ours . . ."

Seraph weighed everything Lucien had told him in his conscience. What was he supposed to believe? Was Lazarus wrong and manipulated into carrying out someone else's dirty work for a lie? Or was Lucien the one lying to cover himself? These two questions swam around in Seraph's mind as he contemplated the two options. "So, you've just been trying to help the city this entire time?"

Lucien let out a heavy sigh and leaned against his desk. "In short, yes. Seraph, I've done many things that I am not proud of. I have committed atrocities in the name of 'peace'. I have been harsh and have ruled Royalty with an iron fist to do what I thought was best. Although I have acted treacherously, I still wholeheartedly believe that the only way this city will truly know peace and harmony is if the gangs are disbanded and everyone lives as a civilian. I went about it the wrong way before because I feared resistance, but look where that got me."

"You . . . may not be entirely wrong." Seraph never

thought he would ever be able to agree with the man who was responsible for so much death, even the deaths of his own parents.

"It's not too late for us to put aside our differences and work together. You have a special place in all of this, Seraph, and I do not believe it is a coincidence. Together, you and I could turn this city into what it was supposed to be. No more gangs. No more violence. Truth. Honesty. Compassion. These are the principles that will guide us toward a brighter future."

"No more killing?" Seraph lowered his eyebrows.

"No more killing," Lucien replied firmly.

"And if there is resistance?"

"Isn't there already?" Lucien chuckled dryly. "That's where you come in. You have a good rapport with the gangs. Seraph, your story moved my heart and helped me see the error of my ways. I believe that it could do the same for the others."

The door to Lucien's office opened as Vincent entered, closed the door, and locked it behind him. He held a chrome-plated pistol. "So, this is it, Father? You choose *him* over *me?*"

CHAPTER SEVENTEEN

"What did he want?" Armand asked Ghost, who had just finished a phone call with Segundo.

"Lucien has decided to declare all gangs illegal from this point on and is sending a squad to each territory to force them to disband. He also mentioned that they have Seraph." Ghost took a deep breath. "Apparently, Segundo found a group of dead Lyones with Seraph's phone close by. The crew was led by the brother of the Bishop who has been rolling with the Cut-Throats."

"This is not good," Armand said grimly as he plopped down into his chair and placed his head in his hands. "We have officially run out of time. Call each gang and let them know that the time is now. They need to be ready to take on any squad that the Lyones send at them. Once they've dealt with them, we'll all meet up outside the Lion's Den."

"Got it, boss," Ghost said and then walked over to Armand and held out his hand. "We're gonna win this. We're finally going to make him pay."

Armand took Ghost's hand and stood back up, bringing him in for an embrace. "You're right. We just have to be smart and make sure everything goes smoothly," he said. "Do you really think we can trust Segundo?"

Ghost shrugged. "I don't know, man. But he tipped us off about this, so he must be good for something at least. We ought to be cautious with him, though. He could just be using us to gain power for himself."

"That's true . . . We'll cross that bridge when we get there," Armand said, as the two went to inform the others of the situation.

Back at the Wild West, Judge, Brutus, and Terrace approached Ezra, who was sitting at the bar having a beer with Edge and laughing about some of the memories that they shared while working together back in the Bishop projects.

"Wuz goin' on, Judge?" Ezra smiled as he and Judge shook hands tightly.

Judge swallowed and removed the welder's glasses from his face and frowned. "Ezra, we have some bad news, brother . . ." he said as he watched Ezra's smile fade.

"What is it? What happened?" Ezra blinked a few times as he stood up from his stool and braced himself against the bar.

"It looks like your brother and his crew may have gotten into it with Seraph," Terrace said, looking down.

"Did DeAndre hurt my white boy?" Ezra asked as he felt the anger rise up within him and looked at Edge and then back to Terrace.

"Not quite," Brutus said sadly.

"Well, what then?" Ezra asked, cocking his head to the side.

"From what they were able to tell, it looks like Seraph may have killed all four of them and then fled. Seraph's phone was found near their bodies, but Seraph himself is still nowhere to be found."

"What? No! Where? Where he at?" Ezra felt his breath shortening, and he felt his head begin to spin.

"Just outside of St. Titus—on Vespula Way,"

Brutus told him. "Why don't we go together, kid?"

"Nah, man!" Ezra pushed his way through Brutus and the others toward the exit.

"Wait! Ezra!" Edge shouted after Ezra as he caught up to him and grabbed his arm.

Ezra turned and shoved Edge hard to the ground. "It was your friend that murdered him!" he shouted.

"He's your friend too!" Edge shouted back as Terrace and Judge ran to his side and helped him up.

Ezra scoffed and exited the bar in a hurry.

As Ezra neared St. Titus, a squad of five Lyones stopped him on the sidewalk. "Easy there, big guy. We can't let you go any further than this," said the one who appeared to be leading the squad.

Ezra's eyes flared in rage as he got right into the face of the one who spoke. "I don't have time f'this. You best get out my way."

One of the other Lyones stepped up and put a hand on his leader's shoulder. "I think that's DeAndre's brother," he said quietly, giving Ezra a sympathetic look.

The leader of the squad looked back at Ezra, frowned, and stepped aside, allowing him to pass.

Ezra's brisk walk turned into a light jog as he approached the four bodies that were now neatly lined up in a row and mostly zipped up in body bags. There were various members of the Royal Priests, as well as Lyones, in the area asking questions and making preparations for the dead. He pushed aside one of the Priests near the body bags as he recognized his brother's face.

"DeAndre!" Ezra wailed in grief as he flung his arms around his brother's lifeless body and sobbed into his chest. "No . . ."

"There is a time for everything under the sun," came Welch's voice as he placed a comforting hand on Ezra's back.

Ezra swiftly turned around and flailed at Welch in

rage. "Man, getcha hands off of me!" he shouted and attempted to shove Welch back, who casually stepped backward and to the side, letting Ezra fall completely forward.

"*Easy,*" Welch cautioned and offered Ezra a hand.

Ezra smacked Welch's hand away and got up on his own. He ran over to the side of a building and swore loudly before leaving the area, "I'ma kill all of these bastards, D! Every last one of 'em!"

Dante Lyone quietly pushed open the door to his sister Sophia's bedroom and entered slowly. "Sophie?" he said when he saw his sister, sword in hand, practicing as she often did in her spare time.

Sophia had just finished a forward thrust before hearing her brother and turned toward him, lowering her blade. "Hey, Dante!" She smiled and walked over to hug him.

Dante embraced his big sister tightly. "You're pretty good with that thing," he said.

"Aww, that's sweet of you to say," Sophia replied, patting her brother on the head. "It's about time you start learning how to use one."

"I prefer to do battle with my mind," Dante replied, pointing to his head and grinning.

"*Oh?*" Sophia smirked playfully before putting Dante in a headlock and ruffling his hair.

"Sophie! Stop!" Dante shouted and wriggled to get free.

Sophia laughed as she playfully pushed him. "What's a matter? Did I mess up the young lion's mane?" She stuck her tongue out.

Dante scoffed, walked over to her vanity, and looked into the mirror to straighten out his hair. He then cleared his throat and looked back over at his sister, who continued beaming at him. "Sophie, can I ask you something?"

"Of course! What's going on?" She leaned her sword against her nightstand and plopped down on her bed, beckoning for Dante to come sit with her.

"I heard Father's men talk about tightening up security," he said, sitting next to Sophia. "Do you know what's going on out there?"

"Can't keep anything from you, can they?"

"You can thank Segundo for that." Dante smirked. "*Look at the whole board*," he quoted his mentor.

Sophia giggled. "Truth be told, I heard that there's been a lot of tension between the family and the gangs ever since that man called Blackjack was released from the Golden Dragons."

Dante furrowed his eyebrows. "But how could Blackjack being released cause such a big problem for everyone?"

"From what I understand, Blackjack is a very bad man," Sophia said, feeling a cold chill creep down her neck. "A long time ago, right around the time I was born, this Blackjack guy killed his own leader—the leader of the Arch Angels, if I'm not mistaken."

"Why would he kill his *own* leader?"

"I don't know, little brother. Maybe to gain power or respect or something. The gangs are bad. They do crazy things for stupid reasons. That's why Father works so hard to keep them in line. *It's in the best interest of Royalty*," she mimicked her father.

Dante took his sister's sword in his hand and raised it up, making eye contact with her. "I will protect you from the gangs!" he swore to her valiantly.

"I know, dearest," Sophia said as she flung her arms around him and gave him a warm embrace. "I know . . ."

Padraeg stood behind the counter adjacent to the entrance of the Shamrocke. He was just finishing drying off the last glass from the afternoon rush when a group of about six Lyone soldiers walked in and told the couple of patrons who had been sitting at the bar that the Shamrocke was losing early. The guests rummaged through their pockets, put some crowns on the bar, and left in a hurry. Padraeg sighed and shook his head, looking up at the squad of Lyones. "Agrusa! Long time, no see! What can I do fer ya boys?" he asked, struggling to sound even somewhat welcoming.

Agrusa smirked at Padraeg and leaned against the counter as his goons spread out behind him. "We just came to bring you news from the big man himself."

Padraeg continued to dry the glass in his hand. "I'm listening," he said, turning to put the glass back in the cabinet behind him.

Agrusa cleared his throat. "Well, um . . . as of this morning, Mr. Lyone declared all gangs and gang activity illegal. I'm instructed to tell you that from this point forward, the McDroogin family must disband and cease all gatherings, meetings, and activities under that name," he said, his voice slightly shaky as he spoke to the massive Kaelish man.

Padraeg turned and met eyes with the Lyone, making him feel even more uncomfortable. "Is that so?" he asked nonchalantly. Agrusa looked even more confused until four of Padraeg's men popped up from behind the counter, each armed with a shotgun aimed at the squad. Padraeg's lips curled into a smile as he crossed his arms over his chest. "Keep your hands where I can see 'em!"

Agrusa's look of confusion quickly faded as he returned the smile and shook his head. "Easy there, Padraeg. You don't want a repeat of what happened the last time you tried to defy the Lyone family, do you?"

Padraeg roared with laughter as even more McDroogins led by O'Connor came from the back of the Shamrocke, all armed with various types of bludgeoning weapons. The group approached the Lyones and roughly frisked them, removing their weapons and setting them aside, out of their reach.

"So, what? You think you're going to beat us and that will send some kind of message to Lucien that he should think twice before messing with the McDroogins? That it, tough guy?" Agrusa chuckled arrogantly and shook his head. "Let me know how that works out for you, chief," he said and attempted to walk away, but was forcefully grabbed by Malone and shoved into a stool.

Padraeg met O'Connor's gaze, and he nodded once, taking a step back and grabbed a shotgun of his own from under the bar and watched with satisfaction as O'Connor and his men proceeded to bludgeon the squad of Lyones, using the bar as leverage to pin them as they smashed their blunt weapons into them. Within minutes, they'd beat every one of them to death.

Padraeg came around the bar and kicked Agrusa's lifeless face before spitting on his corpse. "I woulda let ya live if you'da just kept yer mouth shut," he said and shook his head. "Get this mess cleaned up and prepare to move out!"

The sun was at its highest point, shining brightly down on Ebony and Ivory as the White Crows and the Shadows, both gangs in full force, stood in the middle of the road facing each other, each member of either gang armed and ready for combat. There was a grave silence in the air as the two menacingly scowled at each other, both gangs prepared to fight to the death without holding back. While the two gangs stood there, ready to face off, a large squad of Lyones approached. They seemed amused at the faceoff between the two rival gangs who had been mortal enemies for so many generations.

"As much as I hate to interrupt," Reese Ward, the leader of one of the Lyone crews said, "I am here to inform you that, from this point on, all gangs are officially banned." As he finished speaking, the Lyones with him each drew their pistols.

Kai and Talon both looked at Ward and then back

at each other. "Whether we can have our gang or not anymore means very little to me," Kai said, cracking his knuckles. "But I have a score to settle with these little birdies, and I intend to handle it right here and now."

The Lyones looked at each other and burst into laughter. "Right here? Right now?" Ward asked with a broad grin.

"With your permission, of course," Kai said.

Ward looked around to determine the consensus. "Okay, fine. Go ahead and *settle your score*," he mocked and crossed his arms over his chest.

Kai and Talon nodded at one another as they tightly gripped their weapons. The Shadows were mostly armed with their straight-edged Sengoan swords and a few sickles with chains attached to them here and there. The White Crows carried a variety of weapons, though the most popular one seemed to be a short iron staff. Talon wielded her twin daggers as she braced herself and then shouted, "Kill them all!"

The Shadows and the White Crows charged at each other, weapons raised, both gangs shouting their battle cries at the top of their lungs as they clashed. The Lyones watched excitedly as some of them even began making bets on which side would win the brawl. Ward squinted as the gangs collided and realized that neither of them were actually attacking each other, and his eyes widened with fear as it occurred to him that both gangs were now charging him and his squad as one combined force.

"It's a trick!" one of the other Lyones cried loudly as the rest of them raised their pistols and fired off as many shots as they could before they were overwhelmed by the large force of Shadows and Crows that seemed to almost engulf them in a wave of black and white, cutting the Lyones down ruthlessly, only suffering a few casualties from the gunfire. The two rival gangs fought their common enemy together as one until every last Lyone there lay dead in the street.

The Cut-Throats rode in synchronized formation down Rooke Avenue, on the hunt for any Lyone squad or stragglers that they might be able to take out before they could join up with their main forces. Judge led the formation as they approached the St. Titus Hospital, where a small group of Lyones was speaking with some of the Royal Priests. Judge looked back and nodded at his men as they all pulled up in front of them and all of the Cut-Throats raised their firearms in the direction of the Lyones and Royal Priests.

"Get inside!" Terrace shouted at the Royal Priests, who stood there frozen, hoping that the Cut-Throat death squad would not gun them down with the Lyones. They quickly ran to the entrance as the Lyones turned and faced the Cut-Throats.

"You're all finished!" one of the Lyones yelled out.

"Oh, yeah?" Judge smirked and looked at his men, giving them another nod and each of them unloaded on the small group of Lyones, dropping them instantly. "Good work!" Judge shouted back at his men, who quickly put their guns away.

Ezra stepped around from the side of the building and approached Judge and the Cut-Throats. "What the hell was all that?" he asked in bewilderment.

"Shoot, I didn't realize you were so close by, Ez. You gotta be careful, brother," Judge said.

"Yeah, man, it's started. Full on war against the Lyones," Terrace told the lone Bishop.

Ezra clenched his teeth together tightly and nodded. "A'ight . . ." he said quietly.

"You ought to ride with us until all this is over. There's safety in numbers," Judge said.

"I appreciate it, but what I gotta do, I gotta do alone," Ezra said. "Y'all be safe out there."

Edge felt his phone vibrating in his pocket, quickly brought it out, and answered it. When the call ended, he looked at Judge and said, "The Arch Angels are moving."

Judge nodded. "Alright, boys, time to move out!" he called and revved up his motorcycle before leading the group down Rooke toward the Lyone compound.

Ezra and Edge made brief eye contact before he followed suit, and the Cut-Throats left to aid the Arch Angels.

Ezra scoffed and shook his head as he looked down at the four Lyone corpses. He took their pistols and extra ammunition, arming himself with everything they had, not leaving a single bullet behind. *This should be enough for now*, he thought to himself as he walked in the same direction that the Cut-Throats had gone.

Things were not looking good for the Immortals. The Lyone squad that showed up to order their disbanding outnumbered Damien and the five other members of his gang. The Lyones ended up being faster than them as well. As soon as they even suspected that the Immortals would resist, the Lyones drew down on them and immediately disarmed them. They proceeded to beat Damien and his men while some of the other Lyones kept their pistols aimed at the Immortals, keeping them at bay.

Damien had just had his head slammed against the countertop near the crown register at the bar and Elders. The Lyone leading the squad had the barrel of his pistol against Damien's throat. "Nice try, Damien. The Immortals are finished!"

At those words, Shady, Damien's second-in-command, broke free from the Lyone that had been restraining him and charged at Elders in an attempt to save Damien, but Elders was too quick. He swiftly moved the barrel of his gun from Damien's throat, pointed it in Shady's direction, and fired off a few rounds as two other Lyones did the same, stopping Shady dead in his tracks as his lifeless body slumped over a display case that contained various different bottles of beer, which all shattered under the force and weight of his body stumbling into them.

"No! Shady!" Damien cried out as hot tears streamed from his eyes. "You bastard!"

Elders stood and backed up as he aimed his gun back at Damien and fingered the trigger with a malicious smirk across his face.

The front door of the Asylum then burst open as Ram stepped through the entrance, shotgun raised and blasted Elders in his midsection, the scattershot almost entirely ripping him in half as he fell to the floor, the life instantly leaving him. More Jackals flooded in from behind Ram and the back entrance. The Lyones who had been terrorizing the Immortals attempted to surrender, but they were shown no quarter. The Jackals massacred them right there in the middle of the Asylum.

Ram lowered his shotgun, offered a hand to Damien, and helped him up. "You alright, brother?" he asked as Damien wiped the thick tears from his face.

Damien looked down at Shady's lifeless body and then back at Ram. "I will be . . . Thank you," he said, holding Ram's forearm in his hand and pulling him in for a tight hug.

Ram wrapped his arm around Damien tightly and kissed the side of his head. "For sure, man," he said firmly. "Why don't you roll with us? We're gonna head over to the Den to reinforce the rest of the allies."

"Yeah, sounds good." Damien nodded as he looked at his four surviving members, who were all bruised and bloody from the severe beating they'd taken from the Lyones.

The Arch Angels, led by Armand and the Cut-Throats, met up at the corner of Knights Way and Noble, just down the street from the Lion's Den. The Cut-Throats dismounted their motorcycles as Judge and Armand approached one another and firmly shook hands.

"Looks like everyone made it in one piece," Judge said as he peered over Armand at his men.

"We didn't even let them through the front doors," Armand said with a wink. "We made short work of them right out front of La Noche. They didn't even know what hit them."

"Very nice," Judge said.

"After we took out the squad they sent over to the Wild West," Terrace said, "we ran into another small group near St. Titus. We also ran into Ezra, who was nearby."

"Ah, the last Bish—"

"Lookit!" Ghost interrupted and pointed toward the front gate of the Lyone compound, where they all watched as the Yellow Jacket convoy in full force were granted access to the Lion's Den.

"I figured as much . . ." Armand shrugged.

"Hey, that reminds me—" Judge said, "what's going on with the Black Lotus Syndicate? You run into them at all?"

Armand and Ghost looked at each other and shook their heads.

"My scouts saw a couple of them leave their posts outside La Noche. We thought it might be a ploy to get us to come out, but after a few tests, it seemed like they really left. Not too sure why though," Ghost told Judge, who stroked his beard and nodded.

"Huh . . ." Brutus said before his eyes darted over to his right for a moment, noticing what seemed to be a large squad of Lyones approaching from a nearby side street off of Noble. "Incoming!" he bellowed as both gangs drew their weapons and turned toward the small Lyone army, which wasted no time busting off shots at the allied gangs.

Ghost came to Armand's side as they ran behind their vehicles to take cover and returned fire.

The Cut-Throats also opened up fire, attempting to circle around the Lyone soldiers.

"There's so many of them!" Iceman shouted as he became separated from his comrades and was gunned down in a barrage of fire.

"What do we do, boss?" Ghost asked as he lifted his machine pistol above his head, blind firing in the Lyones' general direction.

Armand ground his teeth together as he thought for a moment and then came to a decision. "We fight! Head on!" he yelled and fired off a few shots of his own from behind the sedan.

Ghost hollered in pain as a bullet pierced his palm, sending his pistol flying far away from him.

"Darn!" Armand cursed under his breath and quickly took Ghost's arm in his free hand and examined the wound. "It went clean through. Will you be alright?"

Ghost clenched his teeth and gave a solid nod before tearing off a piece of his dress shirt. He used his free hand and teeth to wrap his hand as best as he could and then reached for his back up pistol from inside of his coat with his good hand. "Let's do it," he said as his eyes met with Armand's.

Armand nodded back and shouted at the top of his lungs. "Arch Angels!" he cried out. "Engage these Lyone dogs with everything you've got!"

A loud shout erupted from the mouths of each of the Arch Angels as they came out from behind the vehicles and rushed into the Lyone aggressors without hesitation. The Cut-Throats were inspired by this and joined in the foray, running into the mix of gunfire and brawling as the armies collided.

"That's right, boys!" Judge roared as he used a tire iron to bash in the head of one of the Lyones who got too close to him. This caused other nearby Lyones to turn and unload their magazines into Judge's chest. He lost grip of his weapons and dropped to his knees.

"Judge!" Edge cried out as he, Terrace, and Brutus charged the Lyones who'd shot their president.

"Son, it's not like that . . ." Lucien attempted to reason with Vincent.

"Enough!" Vincent shouted and raised the barrel of his pistol at Seraph. "This little prick has ruined everything for me! He couldn't just leave things alone. Constantly interfering and meddling. Lance was *my* right-hand man, and you made me kill him!"

"Vincent, look at me, son. I was wrong, okay? There is a better way to achieve our dreams. I just couldn't see it before," Lucien said as he stepped toward his son.

The knob of the door jiggled, but it was locked. A knock then came from the other side. *"Boss, everything good in there?"* came Segundo's voice from the other side.

"It's fine, Segundo. I've got everything under control!" Lucien shouted back.

"Yes, you always have full and total control, don't you, Father? You just couldn't control me, could you? Is that why you've always hated me?" Vincent asked through clenched teeth.

"I have always loved you, Vincent. Perhaps I was always a little extra hard on you, but only because I've wanted you to reach your full potential and not to make the same mistakes that I've made."

Tears now ran down Vincent's face as he pulled back the hammer of the pistol. "I have to do this! I have to do this for you to love me!" he wailed.

"NO!" Lucien shouted and dove forward, dropping his cane.

Seraph stood frozen and closed his eyes as the gunshot rang out.

"Lucien!" Segundo's voice yelled from the other side as he began pounding on the door.

"Father! What have you done?" Vincent cried out as Seraph slowly opened his eyes to see Lucien lying on the ground in front of him, doubling over and gripping his chest. Vincent then looked up at Seraph and raised the pistol once more. "You made me to shoot him!"

What felt like a giant ice cube seemed to drop in Seraph's stomach as adrenaline surged through his body.

The young Arch Angel charged at Vincent, grabbing the gun from him as he tackled him to the ground. The two young men struggled, first for the gun, until it slipped from both of their grasps and landed next to them. They rolled around and exchanged blows. Seraph managed to get two solid punches into the bridge of Vincent's nose, causing his right eye to almost immediately swell up. Just as Seraph thought he had the upper hand, Vincent sank his teeth into his forearm, causing him to lose his composure and wail in pain. Vincent then grabbed Seraph by his throat and began to squeeze as hard as he could before Seraph reached the pistol, pushed it into Vincent's stomach, and unloaded the entire magazine.

At that moment, the door burst open and Segundo, accompanied by two Yellow Jackets, grabbed Seraph and pulled him off of Vincent, pinning him to Lucien's desk as the Lyone father and son both lay dead on the floor.

Lazarus had just driven his switchblade into the throat of a Lyone soldier when he noticed some Golden Dragons approaching with several other Lyones in custody. "The Golden Dragons!" Lazarus shouted as loud as he could. The Arch Angels and Cut-Throats simultaneously backed off from the Lyones that they were fighting and stood back.

"Hold your fire!" Armand yelled over the commotion to his comrades.

Shen, the leader of the Golden Dragons, nodded to one of his generals, who shouted something in Sengoan before each of his men raised their firearms and unloaded a barrage of bullets at the Lyones who had previously been engaged in combat with the Arch Angels and the Cut-Throats. All the Lyones were dispatched except for the ones that were in custody. "And as for the prisoners?"

Armand stared silently at the Lyone prisoners for a moment, spotting some notable members of the Lyone family hierarchy. "Keep these ones alive. I'll figure out what to do with them once this is over."

Shen smirked and nodded before ordering his men to round the prisoners up and take them back to Dragon's Den.

Judge's men were all gathered around him as blood seemed to flow endlessly from his mouth with each breath that he took. "Take . . . hand . . ." he said weakly as he raised a shaky right hand toward Terrace.

"Hang in there, brother! Just hang on!" Terrace cried as he and the Cut-Throats became increasingly distraught over their dying president.

"*Y-you . . . lead . . . n-now,*" Judge said sternly, his eyes locked with Terrace's as he lost consciousness.

"I will, Judge! I will make you proud!" Terrace sobbed as he laid his head against Judge's blood-caked beard and cried uncontrollably.

Armand, Ghost, and the surviving member of the Inner Circle looked over at the Cut-Throats with sorrow as the Golden Dragons approached. Shen and Tuan stepped forward to greet the Arch Angel leadership. "Good show, fellas!" Armand said thankfully for their aid against the Golden Dragons' former allies.

Shen and Tuan nodded. "It's about time we change things up in this city," Tuan said.

"How many more do you think are left?" Ghost asked.

"There are still plenty of Lyones guarding the compound. We also saw the Yellow Jackets come through with some serious hardware," Tuan informed them.

The McDroogins came from Knights Way as the Arch Angels and Golden Dragons discussed their next plan of action. "Looks like everyone's still mostly in one piece!" Padraeg exclaimed with a grin.

Armand and Shen approached the McDroogin leader and shook his hand as Armand said quietly, "Most of us . . ." and nodded over toward the Cut-Throats.

Terrace stood up and dusted himself off after

cutting the *President* patch from Judge's leather vest and pocketing it. He then joined the group of leaders and shook hands with Shen and Padraeg, thanking them for coming.

"Sorry fer yer loss, lad," Padraeg said mournfully as he gave Terrace a firm pat on the shoulder.

Terrace wiped his face and nodded.

Soon the White Crows joined the allied gangs, followed by the Jackals and the Immortals as the entire alliance except for the Shadows were assembled across the street from the front gate of the Lion's Den. Lazarus was pleased to see that Edge and Zero were okay and took the pause in violence to catch up with them before the battle continued.

"I'm assuming everyone's efforts were successful then?" Armand asked, looking at each of the gang leaders one by one, all of whom confirmed with a nod. "Excellent."

"What's next, Armand?" Padraeg asked.

Armand flashed a grin and pointed at the Lyone compound. "We storm the castle!"

"Okay, Segundo. You too," Sophia said before ending her call with the vice commander of the Lyone family. She reached into the top drawer of her dresser and retrieved a pistol, which she tucked into her front waistband.

"What is it, Sophie?" Dante asked, sensing that something was wrong.

Sophia took her little brother by his arm and stood up. "We gotta go, Dante. Remember our hiding place from when we were little?" she asked.

Dante nodded. "Are we going to be okay?" he asked his big sister as she began to pull him along out of her room and into the main hallway.

"Yes! Everything's gonna be okay! We need to get mother first, and then we're going to go to our hiding place," Sophia said frantically as Alvaro Rossi stopped them in the hallway.

"Slow down there, Miss Lyone. You need to come

with me," Alvaro said.

Sophia froze and blinked a few times, trying to decide what to do before the window that was to the left of Alvaro shattered completely and caused him to fall over dead with a Sengoan throwing knife lodged deeply into the side of his neck. "NO!" Sophia cried and turned to run as she saw a grappling hook fly through the broken window and hook onto the lower window casing.

"There, there, little Lyone," came the voice of one of the Shadows, accompanied by two others who blocked Sophia and Dante's path.

Sophia reached for her pistol and swiftly pulled it out, but was not quick enough as the Shadow launched a backhand at her wrist, sending the pistol against the wall before stepping forward and restraining her by her wrists.

Dante balled his fists and charged the Shadow who held his sister captive. "Sophie!" he cried out.

"Hey kid!" a different Shadow called out from behind Dante, which caught him off guard, as he turned and received a sharp knee to his diaphragm, stealing the breath from his lungs and knocking him unconscious.

"Dante!" Sophia cried out in desperation as her little brother fell to the ground.

"What do you wanna do with 'em, boss?" Ketsujo asked as he turned to Kai.

"Find their mother and keep them together in one of the bedrooms. The rest of you clear the building and eliminate any Lyone soldier you see. No prisoners," Kai ordered his ninja army.

"Kai . . ." Rafa said in a hoarse voice as he looked at the two Lyone children for a moment and then whispered to his leader, "The mother hanged herself in her bedroom."

Kai looked at the children for a moment and then shrugged at Rafa. "Keep that to yourself for now," he instructed Rafa, who nodded and helped take the two children to one of the nearby rooms.

CHAPTER EIGHTEEN

"Lucien, no!" Segundo cried out as he knelt next to his fallen leader and pushed his hair out of his face. He then looked up at Seraph. "What happened?"

Seraph struggled to catch his breath as he pointed at Vincent's body. "He was gonna shoot me, but Lucien got in the way."

The two Yellow Jackets looked at Seraph and then at each other and nodded as they released their grip on him.

Segundo stood up and approached Seraph. "Are you telling me that Lucien gave his life to save you?"

Seraph's eyes welled up with tears as he looked away. "I don't know, man . . ." he said, losing his composure.

One of the Yellow Jackets reached toward the canister attached to the front of the gas mask that he wore and pulled the mask up and off, causing the hood to fall back as a cascade of raven-black hair fell to his shoulders.

"*Blackjack?*" Seraph said.

He nodded and placed a hand on Seraph's shoulder. "You're alright now."

Segundo looked back down at the bodies and shook his head. "Well, this is certainly going to change things . . ." he remarked and reached into his coat pocket, pulling out a cigarette and lighting it. "We gotta get you outta here in the meantime," he said to Blackjack.

Blackjack looked at the other Yellow Jacket. "Ginzo, can you and your men take care of the rest of the Lyones?"

The Yellow Jacket named Ginzo nodded, gripping his rifle. "We'll take care of it. Let the allies know that we're on their side."

"Will do," Blackjack said before leaving the office.

In the corridor near Lucien Lyone's office, the White Crows led by Talon were engaged in full combat with the Lyone guards. Talon and Zero stayed close together, coordinating their attacks against the multiple enemies they faced. Since Zero had joined the White Crows, he had become accustomed to their smooth style of combat, now being able to carefully dodge, weave, and strike fluidly, all while wearing the slightly encumbering crow mask that every member of the White Crows was required to wear.

One of the Lyones came at Zero with his club, but he was able to sidestep the attack, while Talon turned from behind Zero and planted a firm kick into the Lyone's chest. Two more Lyones approached from behind and attempted to rush them. Talon swiftly grabbed onto Zero's forearm and jumped up, kicking the Lyone who came at them from the right, while Zero swung around using the momentum of her jump kick and brought his iron staff against the other's head. He then ducked as Talon let go of Zero's arm, rolled across his back, and sent a dagger into the throat of the first Lyone she had kicked.

"Nice work, Tal!" Zero exclaimed as he bent over to catch his breath.

"You're getting good at this," Talon said to him. She winked through her mask and then motioned to a door down the hall. "I think that's his office."

Zero raised an eyebrow before her remark registered. "You mean Lucien Lyone's?"

Talon nodded. "I have orders from Armand to find Lucien and kill him."

"Oh," Zero said, "I didn't realize . . ."

"Sorry. I was told not to tell anybody until I got close enough."

"I understand."

As they approached the office, they heard voices coming from inside the room. Talon cursed under her breath as she looked up to see another Lyone running at Zero. She quickly shoved her lover out of the way, stuck the Lyone in the middle of his belly, and tackled him to the ground.

"Tal!" Zero shouted as he was pushed against the wall and raised his staff before realizing that she had taken care of it.

"Bastard!" Talon groaned as she twisted the blade roughly back and forth, causing the Lyone to cry in agony.

Zero came to her side and placed a hand on her shoulder. "Tal, that's enough!" he urged.

Talon looked up, her eyes ablaze with fury. "He almost killed you!" she said in her defense as she violently ripped the jagged dagger from the Lyone's stomach.

Zero brought his iron staff up and then swiftly down against the Lyone's temple to put him out of his misery. "Still . . ." he said, feeling disturbed by what he had witnessed.

Ginzo, followed by Segundo, Blackjack, and Seraph all came out of the office and looked down at the two White Crows.

Segundo raised his hands to show that he meant no harm. "It's okay. We're working with you."

Zero and Talon looked at each other for a moment and lowered their guard slightly. "What's he doing here?" Talon asked, pointing to Blackjack with one of her blades.

"Just doing my part," Blackjack said with a smirk.

Seraph stepped forward, his hands raised as well. "It's okay, guys. They're on our side."

Talon looked back at Zero, who simply shrugged and shook his head. "Where's Lucien?" she asked.

"He's dead . . ." Seraph told them. "His own son killed him."

"Are you okay, bro?" Zero asked Seraph as he stood to face him.

"Zero?" Seraph said as his friend removed his crow mask.

"Ha, yeah, man!" Zero said and embraced Seraph tightly. "I'm glad you're okay."

"Likewise . . ."

"I better get out of here while I have a chance," Blackjack said. "You all should head downstairs and meet up with the others. It looks like everything is coming to an end."

"Yeah, for sure. Be safe, Blackjack," Segundo said to his friend as the two clasped hands and embraced briefly.

Zero looked down at Talon, who nodded and helped her up. She wasn't entirely sure what to make of the whole situation as Blackjack retreated down the hall and disappeared around the corner.

"Yes, keep them secure for now. This is almost over," Armand said into his phone, then hung up. He looked at Ghost as they stood just out front of the Lion's Den after having defeated all the Lyones inside the compound. Ginzo had just led the captured Lyones outside, and the rest of the Yellow Jackets followed behind. "The Shadows have the Lyone Manor secure."

"Nice work, boss," Ghost told Armand, patting his back.

"Their poor mother hanged herself . . ." Armand said regretfully.

"Oh, dear . . ." Ghost said under his breath, feeling pity for the Lyone children. He then looked up to see Segundo, Talon, Zero, and Seraph followed by the rest of the White Crows, exiting the Lyone Manor together. "They made it out!"

Armand smiled, then approached his comrades. "Seraph?" he said, surprised to see him. "We weren't sure what happened to you. I'm glad to see you're okay!"

Seraph looked up at Armand's face but did not make eye contact with him. "Yeah, still in one piece."

Armand pressed his lips together and nodded slowly. "Why don't you and Zero meet up with Lazarus and the others? I'll handle everything else from here."

Seraph and Zero nodded to each other and headed over to where Lazarus and Edge were. Talon and Segundo stayed behind.

"What happened? Where is Lucien?" Armand asked his fellow L'Orandan with narrowed eyes.

"Apparently, his boy killed him. And Seraph killed his boy," Segundo said.

"What? Seraph *killed* Vincent?" Armand asked in disbelief.

"I don't know the details. I just know that they're both dead," Segundo said, his voice full of grief. "Where does that leave us?"

"Well, your end of the deal was to bring us Lucien alive . . ." Armand reminded him as some Golden Dragons approached Segundo from either side.

"Are you serious?" Segundo asked in a flat tone. "You're really going to do this?"

"Oh, yes. You are going to join the other war criminals at the Dragon's Lair until we figure out what to do with you for your crimes against Royalty and her people," Armand informed him with a smirk before nodding to the Golden Dragons, who roughly took Segundo to one of their paddy wagons and locked him in the back.

Armand then looked down at Talon. "Is there anything you'd like to add?"

Talon swallowed as she remembered her brief encounter with Blackjack but decided not to say anything until she could find out more. "Me and Zero came in at the tail end of the conflict. The most we heard was some commotion and gunshots."

"I see . . ." Armand rubbed the small hairs on his chin. "Thank you anyway," he said before she nodded and led her men toward Zero and the others.

As soon as Seraph and Lazarus saw each other, they embraced tightly, causing Seraph to groan in pain from the bruises he had acquired earlier from DeAndre and his men.

"Oof! Sorry, bro! I didn't realize . . ." Lazarus said with a frown as he released his best friend and took a good look at him. "Man, someone really let you have it."

Seraph shook his head. "Dude, I'm just glad everyone's alive."

Edge then stepped forward and patted Seraph gently on the shoulder. "You got that right. Good to see you standing, brother."

"You too, man." Seraph smiled, placing his own hand on Edge's shoulder and giving it a firm squeeze.

As soon as Seraph removed his hand from Edge's shoulder, six gunshots rang out from across the street as Seraph fell to the ground limp.

"Seraph! No!" Lazarus shouted as he ducked down next to him and drew his pistol, looking to see where the shots had come from.

A red sedan across the street peeled off down the road, away from the compound as members from each of the allied gangs came to check on Seraph.

"Someone follow that car and find out who did this!" Armand shouted as he jogged over to Seraph and knelt down next to him. "You're gonna be alright, kid! Ghost, get the Priests here immediately!"

Ghost nodded, called the Royal Priests, and told them to bring an ambulance.

Seraph lay there on the ground, not feeling any pain, but fully aware that he was having a lot of difficulty breathing. He could hear the voices of his friends and loved ones around him but was unable to make out what they were saying. He tried to tell them that he was okay and that he wasn't in pain, but because of his shortness of breath, he couldn't vocalize what he wanted to say. Slowly, black spots began to cloud his vision. He shifted his eyes around, trying to make them go away, but only more appeared, before finally, black entirely suffused his vision—and everything went blank.

"Welcome to a new era for the city of Royalty!" Armand said loudly into the microphone as he faced members from all the allied gangs that crowded the main dance area of La Noche. Everyone cheered and applause filled the air. "From this point on, Royalty will be totally different! Together, we will create a city council made up of leaders from each of the gangs to help govern our city and protect our people! Congratulations to the gangs of Royalty! On this day, you have earned everyone here justice and freedom!" Armand announced as the various members of each gang roared in approval of Armand's plans for the city, hope being restored to a people who had almost completely abandoned the thought of it long ago. "Each and every one of you is invited to join the Arch Angels tonight in celebration of what we have accomplished today. We have all lost men, brothers and sisters, on this day of battle! We are all feeling the sting of loss. But tomorrow is when we will bury our dead. Tonight, we celebrate their lives and our victory!"

Drinks were all served compliments of the Arch Angels. Hors d'oeuvres were set out. Dancing and singing and laughter filled the night club as the loud bass from the sound system blared and the neon lights flashed and spun. Despite the sorrow that each one felt about the losses they had suffered, they were able to set aside their grief for the evening to give their hearts over to the festivities of their achievement. This was the first time in the long history of Royalty that so many different gangs had come together for a common cause and now even shared in celebration together. Ash and Rayn's dream was finally beginning to come true.

"Here's to the new president of the Cut-Throats motorcycle gang!" shouted Brutus, as he stood up on one of the chairs and dumped his mug of beer over Terrace's head.

All the Cut-Throats erupted in a cheer as the other gangs joined in as well.

Terrace laughed hard after whipping his wet hair out of his face in Brutus's direction. "I'll get you for that later!"

"Yeah, yeah! Why don't you get your new sergeant-at-arms to deal with me?" Brutus jested as he patted Edge firmly on the back, who now sported Terrace's old *Sgt. At Arms* patch on his cut.

Edge grinned bashfully and raised his eyebrows at Brutus. "You can count on it!"

Lazarus and Zero joined their old friend, and each gave him a hug, congratulating him for his promotion. "Well, I guess that's it for the Switchblades," Lazarus said, as he was now dressed in the Arch Angel uniform. It was the first time he had ever worn a suit in his life, and he was still adjusting to how tight it felt compared to the baggy clothing that he was used to wearing.

Zero shrugged and smiled back at Lazarus. "To be fair, we accomplished everything that we swore to do," he reminded his former leader. "*I solemnly swear . . . to restore peace to Royalty,*" Zero quoted the oath that he swore when he joined.

Edge looked at Lazarus with satisfaction and nodded. "He's right."

Lazarus's smile faded after a moment as he began to wonder about Seraph.

Zero placed a hand on Lazarus's shoulder and frowned. "Any word about him yet?"

Lazarus swallowed and shook his head, looking

down at the brightly illuminated dance floor under their feet.

"He's going to live, though, right?" Edge asked.

Zero bit his lip. "They said his chances of survival are good at the moment. I've been checking up on him every hour . . ."

Just then, Ghost appeared between Lazarus and Edge. The Arch Angels' right hand placed his hand on Lazarus's shoulder.

"The boss would like to see you," Ghost said proudly to Lazarus.

"Really? Okay," Lazarus said. He cleared his throat and said goodbye to his friends for the time being, then followed Ghost up the spiral staircase to the VIP lounge.

Kai had just finished shaking hands with Armand and thanking him as Ghost and Lazarus approached the Arch Angels' leadership. Armand patted Kai on the shoulder before he walked away and then beamed with delight upon seeing Lazarus. He walked over to greet the young Arch Angel protege, bringing him into a tight embrace and kissing him on the cheek. "You did an *amazing* job, Lazarus! After everything that you went through—leading the Switchblades, making connections with the other gangs. If it weren't for you, we would *never* have come out on top like we did. If anyone is the hero today, it's you!"

Lazarus accepted the embrace and stood still, feeling his face flush. "I'm honored, sir," he said as his heart raced with pride.

"You have earned the rank of captain in the Arch Angels. Once things calm down a little, Ghost will get you set up with your new squad." Armand grinned proudly.

Ghost also grinned at his former apprentice and could no longer resist pulling him into a warm embrace and whispering "Congrats" to him.

Lazarus returned the grin and bowed his head humbly. He then looked up at Armand and cleared his throat. "Armand, I do have to ask"—he took a deep death to keep himself from getting choked up—"what are we going to do about Seraph?"

Armand pressed his lips tightly together with a look of concern and nodded toward Ghost.

Ghost placed his arm around Lazarus's shoulder and spoke. "Once Seraph recovers, we're going to debrief him on everything that's happened the past couple of days. We still need to find out what his encounter with Blackjack was all about and what happened in Lucien Lyone's office. There's rumors that Blackjack was there."

Lazarus furrowed his eyebrows as his eyes met with Ghost's. "What? Seriously?"

Ghost nodded slowly. "Keep that on the down-low. Like I said, we're gonna give him some time to recover first, but this thing with Blackjack is not over—plus, we still haven't found out who tried to assassinate him."

"Good idea . . ." Lazarus said.

"Don't worry, man. Everything's going to be okay now. Seraph is under watch twenty-four-seven. We won't let anything happen to him," Ghost reassured him.

Lazarus sighed with relief. "Okay, I feel better now."

Ghost smiled warmly and gave Lazarus another hug. "Good. Now go and join your friends and enjoy the party!"

O'Connor was waiting at the base of staircase and after he pulled Lazarus into a hug, he quickly whispered into his ear, "We will be searching for whoever tried to have Seraph killed and won't rest until he's found."

"Thank you, O'Connor," Lazarus said and looked over to where Padraeg was standing with his men, who looked back at Lazarus and gave him a single, firm nod. Lazarus returned the nod, patted O'Connor on the back and then made his way back over to Edge and Zero.

Ezra sat on the front porch of Turrell's old house in the center of the Bishop projects, sipping on a half-empty forty-ounce bottle of malt liquor, his pistol lying across his lap as he slowly rocked back and forth and stared forward at the dimly lit street in front of him. A scowl remained on his face as he allowed his hatred to stew and fester within him, using his hatred as fuel for what he would be preparing to do to avenge his fallen leader and his brother.

Charita, Turrell's widow, stepped out onto the porch from the house, gently placed her hand on Ezra's shoulder, and lightly brushed her thumb back and forth against his ebony skin. "You about ready for bed, baby?" she asked quietly.

Ezra blinked twice and placed his free hand over hers and rubbed it affectionately before taking a large swig. "A'ight," he said, matching her tone.

"You gon' be a'ight, Ezra?"

"Yeah . . ." Ezra nodded slowly as he kept his gaze focused on the middle of the dark, empty road. "I'ma bring back the Bishops strong."

"Whatchu gonna do?" Charita asked as she took her hands back and ran her fingers over his hair.

Ezra looked up at her for a moment and shook his head. "I don't know," he said and contorted his face. "Seraph was jus' the beginning. Lucien and Vincent are gone, but the power only shifted to the Arch Angels. Things is only gonna repeat theyselves. It's time for the Amakoran people to take back this city."

"And the Lyones that's locked up?" Charita said. "They had Turrell- everybody that we love murdered. They need t'pay too!"

"They already dead, far as I'm concerned. And the Dragons. And the Angels. All of 'em," Ezra declared and spit through the small gap between his two front teeth and removed the pistol from his lap and tucked it into the front waistband of his pants. "Bishop about to be back on top, baby."

Charita then leaned forward, wrapped her arms around the front of Ezra, and planted a tender kiss on his neck. "Good . . ." she said against his ear as she brought one of her hands back and touched her belly. "We'll make this city fit to raise lil' Darius in."

Ezra turned to face Charita, placed a hand on her belly as well and kissed her on the lips. "The Bishops is back, baby," he said and stood as Charita led him back inside the house by the hand as the door closed behind them.

ABOUT THE AUTHOR

Aaron S. Hager was born in Bradenton, Florida. He has been an avid reader since childhood, and it has been his lifelong dream to be a published author. Aaron is married and is currently expecting a son, Lucius Aurelius, and he will dedicate his life to teaching him to live in a way that glorifies Jesus Christ.